Rhiana Ramsey is a serving police detective who has always had a penchant for the macabre. This, coupled with her policing experience, served to spark her fertile imagination and led to the creation of her debut novel, Sweet Oblivion. Before becoming a police officer, Rhiana worked as a writer for a business magazine. She currently resides in West Sussex with her fiancé and is working on her next novel.

Sweet Oblivion

****

Rhiana Ramsey

Published in the UK by Rhiana Ramsey, 2014
Suite 34, New House, 67-68 Hatton Garden, London,
EC1N 8JY
First printed in 2014

A CIP catalogue record of this book is available from the British Library.

ISBN 978-0-9930214-0-4

Layout and design by Mikaella Bennie

www.sweetoblivion.co.uk

To my beloved fiancé

To Mel,

Hope you enjoy it!

Love

Priram x

Chapter I

It wasn't like he was being unfaithful. Janet would never know. She was far, far away. Besides this woman was hot. He'd seen her in the club, her long, lithe body clad in PVC, her hips gyrating to the beats of the club and sweat making her long, red hair stick seductively to her forehead, small beads glistening like diamonds above her red hot lips. She was dancing oblivious - only focused on the music and her body. Eventually, she'd turned her cool blue eyes on him and tossed her fire-like mane, smoky eyes full of lust and passion examining his face and body. She was stunning and David enjoyed her scrutiny.

As the beat of the music changed, she'd slowly walked over to him, her every move a sexual invitation. The strobe lights strategically placed around the club to provide optimum lighting bounced off her cat suit and flickered in her eyes. Her mouth was slightly parted as she walked up to him and buried her face in his neck, breathing in his smell and tickling his skin with her soft, warm breaths. Then she'd kissed him. He hadn't stood a chance. Almost immediately he had felt himself becoming hard, his penis pressing against the smooth fabric of his own PVC trousers. He was bare-chested and the fire-headed beauty ran her ruby red finger nails across his firm torso, her hand descending seductively towards his penis.

Now as he lay in his dark hotel room, waiting for the woman he knew as Mina to emerge from the bathroom and administer his punishment, he strained against the ropes that bound his ankles and wrists to the bed, enjoying the pain. He was naked, except for a tight, leather collar around his neck, erect and aroused beyond belief.

Janet had never understood this need he had to be dominated - to be totally under the control of another person; to be hurt, to be nursed, to be tormented then satisfied. The orgasms were phenomenal. Janet had tried but told him she hated it, he was disgusting and weird, and she would not do it again. Consequently, David had to seek his satisfaction elsewhere. He didn't often go to clubs and very rarely allowed himself to be led away by a virtual stranger. Mina was something else though - a total goddess that any sub would happily succumb to.

The door to the bathroom opened and he could see the contours of her slender body outlined by the orange bathroom light. He felt his heart rate increase as his mind toyed with what she might do to him. Not knowing was all part of the experience. She walked over to him and he could see that she had changed into a tight, red PVC corset over which her full breasts swelled seductively, and a black rubber skirt. She was also wearing long, black rubber gloves and towering stiletto heels. She smiled at him and he felt his body fill with desire.

She climbed on top of him and straddled his erect penis. He could feel that she wasn't wearing anything under the skirt. Her lips teased him as she rubbed her naked self against him. He groaned and she leaned forward, her breasts dangling inches from

2

his mouth. David groaned and felt his penis straining, he was so aroused.

Suddenly, Mina kissed him violently on the mouth her tongue stabbing at his, all the time continuing to rub herself against him. Then she bit his lip painfully causing him to cry out. David tasted blood as she pulled away. Mina slid down his body, her long nails painfully scoring his flesh, her breasts and hair caressing his penis as she rubbed herself all the way down.

Once she arrived at his feet she stood up on the bed, swaying in her high heels, tall enough now to graze the ceiling with her fingertips, which helped her to maintain her balance. She carefully walked up the bed until she was standing over his head. He could see the dim outline of her femininity between her legs

'Like what you see?' she asked, her voice husky and sensuous.

'Yes mistress,' he answered, the words catching in his throat.

She placed a stilettoed foot onto his chest and dug the heel into his flesh. David winced as the sharp heel pressed into him.

'What should I do with you?' she said, pressing even harder with her foot.

'That is your decision,' David groaned in response.

'Should I hurt you?' She twisted the stiletto into his chest.

'Yes.'

'Should I tease you?'

'Yes.' David closed his eyes and savoured the pain.

'Should I kill you?' she said, bending over,

her face within inches of his.

David's eyes snapped open and he stared into her face. Her eyes had changed. The seductive gaze had been replaced with something evil and malign. She grinned, but this time, far from arousing him, her smile chilled him to the core.

'What?' he breathed.

'I said, should I kill you?' Mina repeated

'I… very funny. Untie me now. This game is over,' David said. He tried to pull away from her but the restraints limited his movement. Mina pressed down again on his chest with her stiletto.

'Naughty thing shouldn't be rude to its mistress. You wanted me and now I'm here. You'll let me have my fun,' Mina barked before spitting in his face.

David flinched as the spit hit his cheek. Despite the fear, he couldn't help but be aroused by this domineering siren. This was a fantasy after all. She probably just said these things to heighten the experience, he mused.

Mina laughed gently as she got off the bed, flashing her most intimate body part as she did so. David exhaled and only then realised that he had been holding his breath. He closed his eyes in relief and his mind briefly returned to Janet. What would she do if she found out? It would break her heart. David quickly pushed the thought away and opened his eyes. The last thing he saw was a sharp metallic object plunging towards his left eye ball. He didn't even have time to scream.

Chapter II

Louise's hand meandered out from beneath the rumpled duvet and smacked at the alarm clock on the bedside table, sending it crashing to the floor but still beeping its strident wakeup call.

'Shut up!' she shouted as she threw off her bed covers and reached down, angrily grabbing the buzzing alarm off the floor. After removing the battery, and exercising some considerable restraint, Louise was able to delicately return the irritating device to the bedside table instead of flinging it at the nearest wall.

Yawning in a most un-ladylike manner, she dragged herself from the bed and padded into the kitchen where she flicked on the kettle and grabbed the phone. Steve should be awake by now.

Steve was her boyfriend of two years, a good, loyal man who was able to tolerate her moods and whims. He was her anchor. He kept her sane. With the phone pressed to her ear, Louise set about preparing her morning coffee and breakfast - last night's half eaten pizza. On the fifth ring Steve picked up. He sounded groggy and tired.

'Hello gorgeous. You sound how I feel,' grunted Louise.

'Hey. You woke me.' Steve's voice was thick with sleep. Louise could picture him cocooned in his duvet, head and phone beneath the covers.

'Just got up myself. How was last night?'

5

Steve had just set up his second restaurant and last night had been the grand opening. The restaurant, Lou's, catered to London's discerning diners, offering a fusion of European and traditional British cuisine.

'It was great Lou. We were fully booked and everyone seemed to leave happy. The staff did really well and even Pierre managed to raise a smile after hearing the compliments about his culinary creations.'

Pierre - the French chef whose mood swings were legendary. When in a rage, which fortunately was not too often, Pierre had been known to throw cutlery and crockery around the kitchen, sometimes narrowly missing the unfortunate sous- and comi-chef that worked alongside him. He did however run a very tight ship, everybody knew their place in the kitchen, what they had to do, the exacting presentation that Pierre demanded and how best to avoid being on the receiving end of a flying ramekin. When not in an overt rage, his temper was usually simmering just below the surface. Louise had never had any problems with Pierre though, maybe because she could at times be equally volatile.

'I'll be checking the reviews today though. Had some pretty tough critics in.'

'Ah Steve, I'm so pleased for you. I'm sorry I missed it. Don't worry about the critics, Pierre is a great chef. I bet Melissa loved it - all that attention.'

'Oh don't start Lou. She's alright. She's just insecure.'

'Yeah well, insecure or not, I hope she's not getting ideas about you. I've seen the way she is around you. She is so hot for you,' growled Louise.

'Yeah well as flattering as that is, I'm hot for

you. She knows that,' Steve said in an attempt to smooth Louise's ruffled feathers.

'Hmm....'

Louise could hear Steve chuckling down the phone at her. This was why she loved him. He was the only man she'd ever met who was able to calm her with a look, appease her with a smile and arouse her with a single touch.

'I love you, you know that?' she murmured.

'I know babe. Look, come to the restaurant tonight and we'll get Pierre to knock us up something special. You're the most important critic to me after all. And besides I haven't seen you in what feels like ages.'

'Sounds good, but don't let him hear you say 'knock up' a dish – it is 'de l'art' Monsieur Marden, you stoopid English peeg,' Louise put on an exaggerated French accent. 'I might not be done until quite late tonight though. The deadline is tomorrow and I need to get the final edition ready to go off to the printer first thing tomorrow morning.'

'I thought that was why you worked late last night and couldn't make the opening?'

'It was. You know what it's like Steve. Things get a bit fraught at the magazine just before the deadline,' said Louise, 'I don't even remember what time I left yesterday. It must have been late though because I feel shit today. Got cotton wool for eyes.'

Steve laughed quietly. 'Ok. Just bell me, yeah?'

'Will do darling. See you later.'

'Bye gorgeous. Have a good day.'

Louise hung up the phone and frowned. She knew she'd worked late, but couldn't quite remember what she'd been working on. All the articles she'd been reviewing merged into one. She needed a break. A holiday would do her good. Besides, she had been neglecting Steve a bit lately. He was such a good man, but he probably sometimes felt like he came second to her career. She should have been there for him yesterday, but he didn't moan, he didn't complain. He was a good, good man. She would make it up to him she decided, show him just how much she needed him and how much she loved him.

As she glanced out the kitchen window of her ground floor flat she noted that it was raining. A queue of people stood at the bus stop across the road, huddled together like sheep in a field. One of the commuters, an old man in stained black jeans and a worn rain coat, looked up suddenly and looked straight at her.

Louise stepped back in surprise. She knew that nobody could see into the flat because her lights weren't on and the thin plain nets over the window prevented any nosey parkers from peering in. But it was weird. The old man just stood staring at her, as if he was looking straight into her eyes. He then raised his right hand and pointed at her. Suddenly the man's face broke into a wide smile displaying jagged teeth. Louise inhaled sharply and closed her eyes. When she opened them again the man was gone. She moved closer to the window and scoured the bus stop. The strange man was no longer there.

'Girl, you really do need a holiday,' she mumbled to herself, trying to shake the sense of unease she felt settling upon her. Despite knowing she was alone Louise had the most overwhelming feeling that she was being watched. It was spooky and caused the hairs on the back of her neck to rise.

After standing at the window for what felt like minutes but could only have been seconds, Louise finally stuffed the last piece of pizza into her mouth and headed into the bathroom to begin her morning ablutions.

****

'Mummy, can I have coco puffs for breakfast?' Charlie's little face was so endearing Janet's heart melted. 'Please mum, please!' His chubby little hands reached towards the kitchen counter where the box of coco puffs stood taunting him. There were also frosted flakes and sugar puffs.

'You're so silly Charlie,' said Megan, Charlie's elder sister. 'Coco puffs are for big children. You're only a baby so you should have flakes.'

'That's rubbish. You only say that cos' you want them,' retorted Charlie, throwing his sister a look.

'Sit down, sweetie,' said Janet. 'I'll bring them over to you.'

'Yeah!' shouted Charlie as he sat his plump bum on the seat next to his sister and blew her a raspberry.

'Ugh! Charlie that's disgusting! You got me with your spit!' cried Megan in horror.

'Charlie don't be rude!' admonished Janet.

Where the hell was David? He'd had a meeting last night and had failed to come home. It wasn't uncommon for David to have meetings that lasted well into the night; he worked in promotions, specializing in night clubs and so often needed to work evenings and sometimes into the night. He nearly always came home though, or if he wasn't able to he would at least call to let her know he was alright and tell her when he'd be back. She presumed the he had missed his last train whilst drunk and hadn't called her because he had assumed she'd be asleep and hadn't wanted to wake her. As if she would rather be fretting about him than woken up by a phone call!

'Mummy, can I have the coco puffs now please?'

Janet poured some cereal into Charlie's bowl and then handed the box to Megan. Megan helped herself to some cereal and then poured milk into her and her brother's bowl.

Janet remembered what her husband had said to her: he was seeing a client for dinner and would probably then have a few drinks. He loved his job and that he got to wine and dine people on expenses; he loved her and the kids; he wasn't sure what time he'd be back but she shouldn't worry; he'd take the kids to school so she could have a little lie in.

So, what had happened? She'd tried to ring his mobile several times that morning but it just kept ringing and ringing before finally going to voicemail. She'd left him two messages. Nothing.

'Meggie, it's mine!'

'No it isn't!'

'Get off me! Give it to me!' shouted Charlie. The children were fighting over the toy in the bottom of the coco puff box.

'Charlie, let go!' screamed Megan as she pulled the toy from Charlie's fat hand, her elbow catching her cereal bowl sending it and its contents all over Charlie.

'Mummy!' cried Charlie, tears starting to form in his little eyes, his blond hair dripping coco puffs and milk. Megan sat wide-eyed, knowing she had done something naughty.

'What are you two doing?' shouted Janet, breaking out of her reverie. 'Megan, apologise to your brother!'

'Sorry Charlie,' mumbled Megan.

'Now go and get dressed for school. Charlie, come with me. We'll get you cleaned up.'

Oh David, where are you? Why aren't you home? Janet briefly considered the possibility that David might be having an affair, but as quickly as the thought entered her mind, it disappeared again. He wouldn't. David loved her and the children too much. He knew she would leave without a second's thought if he was playing away. She decided that he was probably just sleeping off a hang over somewhere. She really didn't want to call his office. What would she say? 'I've lost my husband, any ideas where he might be?'

As Janet showered Charlie, washing cereal and milk from his soft, silky hair, she cursed David under her breath for leaving her in the lurch to deal with the kids, do the school run and try and get herself ready for work at the same time. She hoped he had a bloody good excuse and an excruciating hangover.

Chapter III

As Louise picked her way around the rapidly growing puddles blackening the pavement on her short walk to the London Underground, she thought about the strange man she'd seen at the bus stop earlier. She was sure she hadn't imagined him - he'd looked too real - and yet there was a part of her that doubted his existence. She had been working very hard lately, not really getting enough sleep and maybe indulging in a little too much alcohol. That was bound to lead to some sensory confusion, she mused.

Since being promoted to editor-in-chief for Biz Talk, a magazine aimed at the business community offering advice on everything from start-up to marketing strategies, Louise had found it increasingly difficult to sleep and maintain a work-life balance. She wasn't a natural worrier but she didn't want to let Ben down. He'd taken a chance recruiting her three years ago, and had given her this promotion six months previously over a more experienced but less conscientious sub-editor. Louise was great at her job, but she also knew that her closeness with Ben and rapid promotion had caused more than a few playground-style rumours to be Chinese whispered around the office.

The truth was she and Ben had clicked from the moment they'd met. On the day of her initial interview for the position of sub-editor, they'd both known she was the best candidate for the job, that they could easily and successfully work together. After ten minutes of formality, the remaining forty minutes of the interview had consisted of general chit chat about anything and everything. Louise had not disappointed from the day she started work, dressed in a dark suit that was both sexy and strikingly professional.

Louise had also written a number of articles in her first couple of years but most of her time had been spent editing, signing off initial layout proposals and ensuring deadlines were met. Her firm but fair attitude had earned the reluctant respect of her colleagues. Although this of course also bred jealousy - especially from a certain sub-editor who had been passed over.

Louise entered the tube station and groaned as she noticed the crowded platform. Why the hell was it called rush hour when you could barely move for people? The tube arrived and commuters moved forward as one, each determined that they would make it onto the train even if it meant standing crushed against the person in front of them or with their nose in the armpit of some other poor sod desperately trying to hold onto the overhead handrail. Louise decided to wait for the next train, as did a few other people.

She looked down the platform and yawned, suddenly overcome with weariness. Why the hell was she so tired? She made a mental note to put in an application for some time off as soon as she got into the office.

She looked to her left to read the tube arrival board to see when the next train was due - one minute. Also to her left, stood a man. He was wearing a somber suit and was carrying a slim black briefcase and a red and green golf umbrella. He was holding a novel in his right hand. Quite handsome, probably worked in the City, guessed Louise. As she was examining him, the man looked up and caught her inquisitive gaze. Embarrassed Louise averted her eyes and faced front. She could see in her peripheral vision that the man was smiling at her.

She slowly turned back to look at him and smiled back, a small, flicker of a smile. There was something about this man; he looked familiar somehow. The man turned back to his book. Louise felt the wind that preceded the imminent arrival of a tube train tugging at her suit jacket, lifting her hair with its warm gust.

The train pulled in and book man stopped reading as he moved towards the platform edge. As the tube doors slid open and the inevitable crush began, he turned to Louise and said conspiratorially: 'It's ok. You don't need to worry. Your secret is safe.'

'Excuse me?' asked Louise, confused.

She stood staring at him like an idiot as he got onto the tube, crushing himself in, unsure he had actually been addressing her. The man stood in the train doorway and smiled at her again, a smile that suggested he knew something Louise didn't or knew something she should, leaving her no doubt that the mysterious comment was indeed for her benefit. Beeping, the doors closed and book man was swifted away in an instant. Louise stood open mouthed on the platform, trying to understand what the man was referring to.

This was turning into one fucking weird morning.

****

'Housekeeping!' Greta's voice was chirpy as she announced her presence to the occupier of room 501. The 'Do Not Disturb' sign hung from the door handle but it was coming up for two o'clock and Greta had to get the room ready for the next guest. According to the manager, Mr Thomas, this guest hadn't returned his key card, so there was a chance that there may still be somebody in the room; she hated going into rooms when the guest might still be in there.

Indeed she had seen some sights in her five years as a maid in one of London's most prestigious hotels. If her dear strict Catholic mother in Poland knew some of what she'd seen she would demand her daughter return and ask the church to cleanse her spirit.

Greta had left room 501 to last to give the guest maximum time to leave, which is exactly what she would be doing in about an hour – leaving to meet her friends for a late lunch.

'I come in now so cover up, ok?' Greta chuckled good-humouredly to herself. 'I don't want to see no dangly thing ok?'

Greta opened the door and crinkled her nose. Something smelled strange, bad even. The room was dark.

'Hello? Anybody here?'

She moved gingerly into the room, her eyes not yet adjusted to the dark. She couldn't clearly distinguish all the bedroom furniture but she could make out the contours of the bed and the rumpled duvet on top of it.

'Ok, I need to open curtain. It's dark in here and I can't see good.'

Greta often talked to herself when making her rounds as she found it helped her to remember what she had to do and it alleviated the boredom. There were other maids working in the hotel but as they were each allocated a couple of floors to clean, they didn't often come into contact with each other when they were doing their rounds.

'Man, what you do in here to make it stink so bad? You know it's not nice to be maid. Have to clean up after you dirty Scurva.'

Greta pulled back the curtains and turned towards the bed. What she saw caused her to recoil in horror, a guttural scream lodged somewhere between her stomach and her throat. The thing on the bed was not a rumpled duvet.

The body was naked, tied starfish-style to the bed, limbs rigid and pale. The left eye hung out of its socket, dangling uselessly against the person's cheek, blood and bits of tissue the colour of raisins speckled the pillow. The mouth was agape in a silent scream, tongue swollen and ghastly within.

As Greta looked at the body, her cries still trapped within her, her eyes fell upon the area between the corpse's legs. All that remained was a bloody wound where any evidence of manhood had been hacked away. The sheets around the body were stiff with solidified blood, the corpse's thighs streaked with crimson rivers.

Finally, Greta screamed, a terrified and horrendous noise that caused hotel staff and guests alike to come running.

Chapter IV

'Stop crying you stupid fucking creature!' He was shouting at her again and she didn't know why or what she was supposed to have done. She'd only crawled under her blanket because she was cold. The room had no heating, not because he couldn't afford it, but because he liked the goose flesh it gave her. It made her cling to him for warmth too, her little body shivering on his lap, his big, hairy arms wrapped around her, pulling her face into his naked chest.

'Get out of there and lie back on top of the covers,' he demanded.

She nodded slowly, and rubbed her eyes, wiping the tears away. She did as she was asked.

This was their special room, the place he took her when he wanted her to do things. There was a large bed in the middle of the room, which is where they usually did things to her and made her do things to them; there was a large sofa and a couple of comfy chairs in the one corner of the room and in the other was a play mat on which she was sometimes allowed to play with her dollies and horsies. She'd always loved horses and had seen movies where people actually rode them.

He told her that what she was doing would give her good experience of riding. His friends had laughed at this and seemed to find it very funny. One his fat friends had said: 'You can practice riding on me,' and he'd grabbed her, pulling her onto his lap.

Fat man had really hurt her, but she was used to the pain. It was normal, what all children went through; that's what he'd said in the beginning when he first introduced her to

17

riding. But it was never, never discussed. If it was talked about, Mummy and Daddy would die and then she would die with no one to look after her. She'd die a slow horrible death. She hadn't liked the sound of that and so had agreed that she would never tell.

At the foot of the bed there was a video camera. He said it was there so they could view it later and see how well her riding was coming along. Sometimes, he would make her sit with him when he watched tapes of previous riding lessons, commenting on her performance and rubbing between his legs. He'd touch her too and say: 'See how well you did there? He was really happy with you. That's good isn't it?' She always nodded. She didn't know when she'd ever had a bad lesson, he always seemed pleased.

He only got angry when she cried or didn't do exactly as he said. Sometimes it all hurt too much and made her cry. Then he'd get angry. Then he'd shout. Then he'd hit her and then she'd do what he asked.

There were three men in the room today. She'd met one of them before. He was nice to her, told her she was beautiful and a good little girl. He didn't hurt her as much as some of the others did. Sometimes he just watched her playing with her horsies on the mat. She was always naked, and always cold, but at least she got to play and nothing hurt.

'Sam, you want to go first?' he asked.

'Yeah, what are the rules?'

'You can do what you want, just don't hit her or if you must cos she ain't doing what she's told, at least don't leave any marks. We get to watch. And you pay me first.'

Sam grinned and handed over a wad of cash. 'There you go, five hundred big ones.'

He smiled back at Sam, and said: 'For the next hour she's all yours. Look sweetie, Uncle Sam is going to take you riding today. Be good won't you?'

She didn't reply. Just looked at him, her sad eyes

18

wide and expressionless. She'd already fled to the safe place within her mind. She was nothing more than a shell.

Chapter V

'Come in!' Louise shouted at the rapping on her office door. Ben poked his head around the door frame.

'Have you got a minute Lou?'

'Hey Ben. You alright? Come in. I'm just reviewing the layout. Looks good doesn't it? The graphics for this issue are great. Very modern looking; gives us an edge I think. Much better than…'

Ben smiled at her and raised his hand in a bid to silence her. He was a good looking man with his square jaw, deep brown eyes and athletic physique. More than one woman at the magazine had fantasized about the gorgeous Ben Mathews whilst crying out in ecstasy as her partner brought her to satisfaction.

'What is it?' asked Louise, her expression quizzical, eyebrows knitted into a frown.

Ben sighed and quietly shut the door behind him. He sat down opposite Louise in the large chair she had insisted upon for visitors to her office. 'You've got to make them comfortable,' she had argued, when challenged over the cost of the chair. 'Comfortable people are happy people and happy people are open to suggestion,' she had pointed out. Additionally, the shape of the chair made it difficult for people to comfortably cross their arms across their torso - an essential tool in negotiations, according to body language experts. Open posture, open mind.

'It does look great, think this is one of our best issues actually.'

'Yes it is, but you didn't come in here to discuss the layout did you? What's wrong?'

Ben ran a hand through his dark blond hair and sighed wearily, unsure where to start, deciding that he'd better just get to the point.

'Louise, the magazine's in trouble. We've been in trouble for a while, but now we're talking redundancy and pay cuts and cutting overheads. I've spent all morning with the company's accountants discussing options and alternatives,' he began.

'Shit,' breathed Louise, although she wasn't entirely surprised. The whole country was in a recession - pay cuts and job losses were occurring across the board as companies fought to maintain their existence in an economic environment that was spiraling downwards rapidly.

'This has been in the making for the past six months, but we tried to front it out by increasing advertising in our pages. I approached more companies and tried to negotiate higher advertising deals by playing on the fact we're about to receive that award for being the most comprehensive business publication, which is a great accolade. However, unfortunately, and as you know, when the going gets tough, advertising is one of the first areas that companies cut back on. Our income from advertising has dropped by almost forty percent. We're really struggling and unless I lose twenty staff members at least, and cut overheads by twenty percent this company will not survive another year.'

Louise exhaled a long drawn out breath.

'Ben, have you come in here to sack me?' She couldn't keep the incredulity from her voice. The thought of being made redundant turned her stomach. Foolishly, despite all the media coverage of businesses going under and thousands of workers being made redundant, Louise had never entertained the notion that her own job could be under threat. She looked at him challengingly, daring him to tell her this was the case.

'No, no Louise, that's not it. We need to begin by losing non-essential staff. Writers and editors make this publication, so I don't want to lose more then a couple if any at all. I consider you too valuable to this company, which is why I wanted to ask you for help.'

'Flattered as I am that you consider me valuable Ben, would you please get to the point? Why have you come in here to tell me this?' asked Louise, a flicker of annoyance skipping across her face.

'Ok, sorry. It's not easy for me to talk about this crap. You know I founded this company Louise and I never thought it would come to this. I never thought my company could be on the verge of collapse, that I would be forced to sack people, forced to make such drastic cuts.'

Louise's features mellowed. Ben had set this company up ten years ago at the tender age of 23. An entrepreneur through and through, she knew how devastated he must be by the current state of affaires.

'Ben the whole world is suffering from this recession. It is not a reflection of your abilities or business acumen you know,' she said, hoping to reassure him and encourage him to say whatever was on his mind.

'Thanks,' he smiled. 'The thing is, you are more hands on than me, you know the people that work here, and you are better equipped to decide...'

'No,' said Louise, shaking her head.

'..who we can dispense of. I spend too much of my time out of here, I don't know who is essential and who isn't...'

'Ben, how can you ask me to do this? You're the boss for God's sake, please don't ask me to do this.'

'Louise, please. You know you are the best person to help me decide this. Nobody knows the staff as well as you do, nobody has as much input in this publication as you do. I may have the final say but I am removed from the everyday formalities. That is your role and you do it well. I need your help on this. No one will know that you're helping me. I will do the sacking. I just need you to help me decide who should go,' said Ben. He looked at her pleadingly, his big, brown eyes beseeching.

'Ben, that's not my job. I am really not comfortable with this. Why don't you just look at performance and sack those who are the least productive? I don't see why I have to get involved,' retorted Louise, surprised that Ben would ask her to do his dirty work.

'Ordinarily I would, but time is of the essence. I need to have a list of candidates by the end of the week. It would take me longer than that to go through performance records. And besides records are not a true reflection of ability, you know that. I am sorry to have to ask you to do this Louise, but I really need your help. I wouldn't ask you if I didn't think it necessary.'

Louise looked at him; he looked crushed. She noted the dark circles beneath his eyes, the gaunt, ashen appearance of his usually radiant skin. This was a man who was struggling, a man who was not sleeping or taking care of himself. The gorgeous Ben Mathews looked broken and defeated.

Louise sighed and rubbed her forehead.

'Ok. I'll do this for you but you better promise me that no one will know I am the reason they're getting the boot. This is shit Ben, and you shouldn't be asking me to do this.'

'You're an angel, thank you. I promise no one will find out you're helping me with this.'

Louise snorted derisorily and made a show of shuffling papers on her desk.

'I need to get this sent off to the printer. It's all good to go. Another outstanding edition of Biz Talk to hit the shelves.' She stood up a clear indication that the conversation was over and a display of her disapproval.

'Yes, indeed.' said Ben, the silent message of her actions not lost on him. He also stood.

'Just one more thing Lou, don't forget we have the awards ceremony on Friday. We must continue as normal. Who knows, the ceremony could prove to be propitious,' he said, optimistically.

'Yes, I know. I'll be there. Good job really, given that you want my executioner's list by then. I'll need a good drink by the evening.' She smiled at him, a small melancholy smile that left him in no doubt as to her feelings on the subject.

'Lou, I don't know what I'd do without you. Thank you.' Ben turned and walked out of her office, giving her a final smile as he did so.

As the door shut behind him, Louise sat

back down and swiveled her chair so she was looking out the vast office window. The rain had not relented since the morning and continued to cut a dreary, grey swathe across the city. As Louise looked at the cityscape, the matchbox cars and people milling around on the streets below, she felt a pain beginning to spread behind her eyes. So much for taking a holiday. It hardly seemed right to ask for time off now, she was just grateful to still have a job.

Ben hadn't expounded upon the pay cut issue. She wondered what this would mean for her and those she didn't recommend for the chop. She'd be alright she knew; she lived well within her means and so could take a small pay cut. But what about Abbey, the single mum of two who worked in the human resources department? What about Harry, the son who looked after his ailing mother and paid a small fortune for a private nurse? Everyone had their burdens and obligations and now she had to decide whose lives would be turned upside down.

Wincing against the pain behind her eyes, which was rapidly spreading across her skull, Louise spun her chair back around and grabbed the sheets she'd been reviewing from her desk. Time to give the ok and get this month's edition off to the publisher. Then, she could focus on who to sack.

****

'Fucking hell,' said Detective Inspector Scott. 'Fucking, fucking hell. What the fuck happened here?'

He surveyed the hotel room, his experienced eye taking it all in from the threshold. The scenes of crime officers had arrived a few minutes before him and had set about looking for any forensic opportunities that could ultimately finger a culprit. As they busied themselves with the scene, their white suits a stark contrast to the scarlet blood that drenched the double bed in the centre of the room, DI Robert Scott listened as he was briefed by one of his detectives, DC Peter Jackman.

'The body was found just after two o' clock by one of the cleaners, Greta Poletta. She'd been tasked by the hotel manager, Mr Thomas to get the room ready. They thought the guest had left. Ms Poletta came in, drew the curtains, saw this,' he nodded towards the bed, 'and then ran out the room. She told the manger what she'd seen and then he came up here for a look, although he only got as far as the foot of the bed. The vomit in the corner near the bathroom door is his.'

Robert grimaced, 'Great, so the scene has only been contaminated by two people. Makes a change. Usually the world and his wife have walked through the scene.'

'Well, not quite guv. Ms Poletta's screaming attracted quite a few of the neighbouring guests. At least three others came into the room after she had fled, leaving the door open. The vomit at the foot of the bed is the stomach content of a wealthy Russian businessman called Sergiev Rabinovich. The other two were a young Spanish couple on a romantic city break. The scenes of crime officers have been made aware of this and they'll be obtaining voluntary DNA samples from all five individuals once they've finished in the room.'

'Fabulous,' grumbled DI Scott. 'Where are these people now?'

'They're all in one of the conference suites -

the Windsor suite. There are some uniformed officers with them. They're being made to sit apart to try and minimize further cross-contamination, but to be honest I think that damage has already been done.'

'Hmmm. Let's seize all their clothing anyway; you never know what they may have picked up from the crime scene and dragged out with them on their clothes. I want statements taken from all of them before any of them are released. Start with the maid, then the manager. Then get someone looking into this guest's booking. The voluntary DNA samples can be done by uniform, we don't need the SOCOs to do that. I'll get some more uniformed officers on the way shortly. What do we know about the victim so far?' he asked.

'He's a Mr David Saunders - at least that's the name on the bank cards in his wallet and on his driver's license. We don't know much else at the moment other than he is probably married with kids. He's wearing a wedding ring and there are photos of kids in his wallet, along with five-hundred pounds cash. His mobile was still in his jacket pocket as well.

'So he wasn't robbed.'

'Doesn't look like it, sir.'

'And that is quite a bit of cash. Fucking hell,' Robert said again. 'I presume this hotel has CCTV?'

'Yes down in the security office,' answered Peter.

'Ok good. Let's get cracking on getting that secured and viewed.'

'Yes sir.' Peter hurried away to find the rest of his team of detectives, only too happy to be away from the grisly scene.

Robert beckoned to one of the SOCOs.

27

One of the white suits padded over to him, camera slung around her neck. Robert could only see her eyes, but he knew immediately who it was from their striking blue colour.

'Becca, what can you tell me?' he asked.

'Robert, it's grim. One of the worst I've seen.' Her eyes crinkled at the corners as her expression gave way to disgust.

'This guy has been well and truly fucked. His left eye is hanging out of its socket, looks like a sharp implement of some sort was used, and his penis has been hacked away. It's grim,' she repeated, clearly affected by the macabre tableau.

'Christ,' murmured Robert, 'What else strikes you about the scene? What do you see?' he asked.

'Well, the body is tied to the bed by rope, looks like Japanese love rope, and don't ask me how I know that,' Becca said.

'What you do in your own time...' grinned Robert.

To an outsider the banter may have seemed distasteful, but it was how they coped, how they dealt with the depravities of human nature that they witnessed in their work. They had to joke about the dead or they would go quietly insane. It wasn't that they didn't care or that they were being disrespectful, but humour took the edge off, allowed them to distance themselves, at least for the moment, from the fact that what they were looking at was a fellow human being. It was a survival mechanism.

Becca grinned back.

'It's a soft rope, used by practitioners of bondage. Doesn't hurt so much. He is naked, prone and as I already said his genitals have been hacked off. Penis and balls. It's disgusting Rob. There is also a bottle of champagne by the bed, two glasses, but it's untouched. The shower appears to have been used, as it's wet, but whether that was by our man here or by our killer, who knows? The coroner reckons that the cause of death was the punctured eyeball, so we can only hope that the wounds to his genitals were caused post mortem, although of course this will all have to be verified at his autopsy. Poor sod. Time of death hasn't been officially established, but from the colour of the blood and the general colour and appearance of the body we reckon it could be anywhere between midnight and 05:00hrs. That's just us speculating though. Could be way off the mark.' Becca shook her head in disbelief and glanced back at the room behind her. 'Never seen anything like it. Who does that? Who hacks off a bloke's genitals?'

'Somebody seriously fucked up Becca, that's who. Is his penis still here?'

'We haven't found it yet.'

They stared into the room in silence for a few moments then Robert felt his phone vibrating in his pocket. He looked at the caller ID and groaned.

'Fuck it. Now that's a record even for him. He doesn't usually start pestering me until the body's been taken away to the morgue at least. Must be a slow day in the office.'

Becca shook her head quizzically wondering who Robert was talking about.

'It's the boss.'

'Ah, I'll leave you to it then.' Becca padded back into the room to continue her examination of the scene.

Robert grimaced as he connected to

Superintendent Tim Meadows, mentally preparing himself for the barrage of questions he knew would ensue.

'Guv, it's not a pretty sight...'

Chapter VI

'Right here will do fine thanks.' Louise motioned to the left-hand kerb with her hand. The cab driver pulled over and Louise jumped out, shoving the fare through the cabbie's open window.

'Ta love, have a good night.'

'You too.' She smiled at the driver, and mentally kicked herself for being so silly.

She'd preferred to take a fifteen pound cab ride to the restaurant instead of paying a few quid to take the tube because she was spooked at the thought of public transport and more strange people talking to her in seemingly cryptic code. The truth was the old man with the crooked teeth at the bus stop and the handsome stranger on the platform had plagued her all day. She couldn't explain the vision at the bus stop and she certainly didn't understand what the handsome stranger had meant. 'Your secret's safe' he had said. What the hell did that mean? Was she supposed to know him or something? Had they met somewhere? And if yes, why couldn't she remember him?

She walked briskly up the street towards the restaurant, the tall, proud sign gleaming in the street lights, her name so big and visible for all to see. She was overcome by a feeling of warmth, knowing that Steve had named this place after her. He was such a good man. She reminded herself again that she needed to pay him more attention, maybe just a weekend in Paris or Brussels? There were lots of Eurostar deals they could take advantage of which wouldn't require her to take time off work.

She smiled and pulled her collar up high against the wind and drizzle, and stood looking in the restaurant window. The place was almost full - not bad for a Wednesday, she mused. Through the window she could see Melissa, that bitch, playing hostess, like she owned the place.

Melissa had worked for Steve for just under a year and over that time her attitude and arrogance had grown exponentially. To say that Louise disliked her was an understatement. The feeling was, however, mutual.

Louise pushed open the heavy glass door and walked in, pleased to see the smug, prima donna smile scurry off Melissa's face.

'Evening,' said Louise, the attempt at civility contorting her face, making her look like she was sucking a lemon.

'Louise, how are you?' Melissa asked in a manner that sounded friendly enough to the outside ear but which for Louise was dripping with poison. Melissa had quickly recovered her composure. She cocked her head to one side as she gave Louise a practised smile.

Don't get angry, don't get angry. Oh how I would love to beat the fucking shit out of you...

Louise heard herself politely answering: 'I'm great thank you. Not everyone has a restaurant named after them after all. Gave me quite a buzz seeing my name out the front.' She smiled sweetly back.

Melissa looked at her, the fake smile still plastered across her face. The atmosphere between them was almost palpable and full of disdain. They looked at each other for a few moments.

'Steve is in the kitchen. Do you want me to tell him you're here?' Melissa asked, her tone now bored as if she had much more important things to do than stand there shooting the shit with Louise.

'No thank you, but you can take my coat,' replied Louise, removing the dripping garment and handing it to Melissa, rain water pattering to the floor.

Melissa looked like she was going to refuse, but then she smiled again and replied: 'Of course,' clearly disgruntled at being reminded of her place.

'Thank you.'

Louise turned her back on Melissa and strode off in the direction of the bar, mentally applauding herself. Louise Jackson 1; Melissa Vines 0. Petty as the exchange had been, it had cheered Louise up immensely.

As she approached the bar she saw Steve emerge from the kitchen smiling. He hadn't noticed her yet and she savoured the sight of him, his face beaming with happiness, his dark blond hair falling into his deep brown eyes, and his jaw contoured by a rugged and very sexy five o'clock shadow. He was wearing his favourite 'lucky' jeans with the black Lacoste shirt she had given him a month ago. He looked great and she felt a familiar jump in her stomach at the sight of him.

His eyes scanned the restaurant before landing on her, then his whole face broke into a smile which stretched from his sexy mouth to his gorgeous eyes. He spread his hands out as if to say: 'Look at this. It's a success.'

Louise smiled back and glided over to him.

They kissed, then he held her away from him to look at her.

'Louise, you look beautiful. Have you seen our restaurant? It's buzzing and I am so proud.' His eyes twinkled at her.

'Steve, this is amazing. I am so pleased for you. This restaurant is your baby; any success is down to you. I only lent you my name.'

Steve wrapped his arms around Louise's waist.

'You are my muse, you sexy woman.' He lent into her space and gently kissed her neck. Louise inhaled his smell and enjoyed the proximity.

'You will not believe the day I have had,' Louise said, her hand resting on Steve's cheek for emphasis.

'Grab a stool at the bar baby and I'll join you in just a moment. Then you can tell me all about it. I've got some news for you too as it happens, a bit of a surprise.'

'Ooooh! Sounds intriguing!'

Steve kissed her nose and wandered off towards the back of the restaurant, his hand extended to one of the patrons. Louise looked towards the front door and saw Melissa staring at her, jealousy and anger written all over her features, her arms folded across her chest. She held Louise's gaze for a second before turning to attend to a man and woman who had just blustered into the restaurant, shaking moisture from their umbrella and clothes.

Melissa's affection for Steve was obvious for all to see except, apparently, for Steve himself. For a moment Louise considered whether it was possible that Melissa's affections were not entirely one-sided, she was a good-looking woman after all and she was sure that Steve must be at least a little attracted to her, despite what he said. But after the way he had smiled at her tonight, the look he had given her upon seeing her across the restaurant, Louise decided that her feelings of insecurity were unfounded. She turned to the barman, poised behind her expectantly, and ordered a bottle of Pinot Grigio.

She sat on one of the high stools at the bar and watched Steve meander through the restaurant, chatting to his clientele like some kind of rock star signing autographs. As she sipped the crisp, dry white, she hoped and secretly prayed that he wouldn't end up breaking her heart.

****

This was one hell of an unusual case, mused Robert. It wasn't often you came across such a savage murder. The guy's penis and testicles had been hacked off for Christ's sake. That signified a very disturbed individual, but also a very composed and calculating one, who had obviously planned this murder. It didn't appear to have been frenzied, although Becca had pointed out that the cuts made to remove his appendage had been unpracticed and imprecise. So, not frenzied, but certainly not the work of a practiced hand either.

The victim had been tied to the bed, wrists and ankles, with purple rope, soft and pliable and apparently used by practitioners of bondage. A pair of PVC trousers, presumed to have been the victim's, and seemingly supporting the bondage theory, were found at the foot of the bed. A small holdall, containing a clean shirt and tie was on the chair near the door. A suit was hanging in the wardrobe, probably the clothes the victim had worn that day, the dirty shirt in a bundle on the floor. Also in the bag were a couple of files relating to a PR company simply named PR International Ltd and detailing promotion ideas for a London club. This was the company David Saunders worked for. Robert had tasked a couple of detectives to visit the company in the morning.

All these items had been seized by the scenes of crime officers and were now at the lab to be processed on the hurry up. The SOCOs had also taken the champagne bottle and glasses on the bed side table. Two glasses. The victim either had a guest with him or was expecting company. Was the guest the killer? It seemed likely at this point, but Robert was not one to assume. It was a simple as A, B, C. Assume nothing, believe no one and check everything.

Champagne suggested Mr Saunders had been trying to impress. He made a mental note to find out when the champagne had been ordered, if indeed it was hotel stock. Had he invited a client back to his room? Perhaps the champagne was to celebrate a successful business deal? The room was certainly large enough to host a client without it seeming strange, but if that had been the case, Robert would have expected the files to have been on the large desk instead of stuffed away in the holdall. It would have been unusual to have a meeting in the room, he mused, but not totally unfeasible.

Becca had stated that the rope was Japanese love rope, which suggested that the victim was tied up as part of a sex game. Unlikely to have been a business client then, unless it was a woman, or maybe a man, with whom he was having an affaire. Or maybe he had gone out and met this person somewhere, a bar or a club? Had he brought back an unknown person to his room for sex and got more than he bargained for?

There was a photo of a woman and children in Mr Saunder's wallet so for all intents and purposes he was heterosexual. Although, it wasn't unheard of for married men to engage in homosexual activities, sham marriages were not that uncommon. Robert turned his thoughts to the wife.

Two detectives had gone to the family home to deliver the news of Mr Saunder's death. Mrs Janet Saunders had been distraught by the news and unable to tell the detectives anything other than that her husband had told her he had a business meeting that he anticipated would drag on, but he had intended to come home. Sometimes he did stay in London, but he would usually call her to let her know if this was the case. She'd been trying to ring him all day, but he hadn't replied. She'd been so angry with him and caught up in her own day that she hadn't had time to feel too concerned. And then she had collapsed, unable to talk anymore, and had practically thrown the detectives out of the house.

Robert intended to visit her in the morning. It was important they learnt all they could about the victim and who better to tell him than his wife? They would talk to his immediate family members, friends and co-workers as well.

The hotel had CCTV which covered the lobby and the corridors. They hadn't yet been able to view this as it was a digital system that could only be operated by the hotel's security manager, who just so happened to be on holiday in Scotland.

'We've never needed to access it before,' the hotel manager had said apologetically, his face white and drawn.

Robert felt for the man, and for Greta. He was hardened to death and bodies and blood. They, however, were not. The security manager had promised them he would take a flight back to London in the morning, once he was assured he would get his holiday time back and would be suitably recompensed for the inconvenience.

Robert yawned widely, rubbing his hands over tired eyes. 11 o'clock. Time to go home. He couldn't achieve much more and had scheduled a briefing for 7am. He didn't hold out much hope of sleep, but it was worth a try.

****

Louise giggled as Steve led her out of the restaurant. A few glasses of Pinot too many had made her decidedly tipsy.

'Do you know that I love you?' she slurred, wrapping her arms around Steve's neck and trying to kiss him.

'Yes babe, I do.' Steve gently pushed her aside as he attempted to lock the restaurant door.

'You know what? I think we should christen the restaurant. Take me back inside and shag me rotten!' Louise demanded.

Steve laughed.

'Come on, you know you want to!' she chirped as she pushed her hand down his trousers and rubbed his groin.

'Lou, you're a very bad woman,' he pulled her close to him and kissed her, 'but we need to get you home. Aren't you working in the morning?'

'I am. I am. But given that I have to choose who we're going to fire, I think Ben owes me a lie in. What a rotter, eh? Making me choose who to sack. I am going to be the most hated woman at the magazine,' she sniffed loudly, and propped herself up against the restaurant wall.

'Is this the booze talking or do you really give a shit?' Steve asked holding her face in his hands, the street lights reflecting in her glazed eyes.

'What do you mean? Of course I give a shit! Except about that twat Derek. He's hated me since I arrived. Shame he's quite good at his job, or I could've given him the boot....' She giggled again. 'I might still give him the boot actually.'

Steve had successfully managed to lock the restaurant door and was now holding Louise up with one arm. He raised his other arm to hail a taxi.

'Shame you don't give a shit enough about me to come down to Cornwall this weekend. I thought you'd enjoy the surprise,' he said, accusingly.

He'd told her over their late dinner that he had booked them a cottage for the weekend in a quiet little town in Cornwall and they would need to leave Friday night. He wanted to take her away and make her relax because she'd been so uptight lately. She deserved the break and he wanted to spoil her. Wasn't she happy? She'd then told him about her promise to go to the awards ceremony on Friday and they had argued. It was so obvious she preferred Ben's company, Steve had said. Why was he always so low on her list of priorities, why did he always come after her work? Why couldn't she just allow herself to be taken care of for once? Why did she always have to be so bloody difficult? Why? Why?

Why? By the time dessert had arrived they were talking civilly again, but she could tell Steve was still upset.

Louise stopped wriggling in his arms and looked at his face.

'Steve, how can you even think that? I love you and I would have loved to go to Cornwall with you, but I have got to go to this awards do on Friday. The company is in trouble and this is very important to us. If this company goes under, I lose my job. Why can't you understand that?' she said, feeling herself becoming annoyed. 'Ben needs me there. Didn't you listen to what I said over dinner?' she challenged.

'Yes I did and if Ben needs you then I guess it's alright. Look, I don't want another argument. Let's just go back to yours and talk about it later.'

'Oh I see! You're jealous of Ben! What about that bitch Melissa who makes eyes at you all the time? That's ok, is it? I have to accept that, but you won't accept that I am actually needed by my work and can perhaps help my boss, who, by the way is also a friend of mine. One set of rules for the gorgeous Steve Mardon and another for Louise Jackson!' Louise could feel her temper rising, even though she knew she was being unfair.

'Louise you're drunk and I am not going to talk to you in this mood.' Steve was getting angry and Louise knew it but she couldn't help herself. What was his fucking problem? When did she ever say no to him? How was she to know he'd booked them a weekend away?

A taxi pulled up to the curb and Louise tumbled in.

'Steve, I'm going home without you. You

can be such an arsehole, such an infantile, petulant arsehole! So, thank you for dinner, but now leave me alone.' She slammed the door shut and gave directions to the cab driver, leaving Steve standing shocked and open-mouthed on the pavement. She didn't even bother to turn round as the cab pulled away.

Steve shook his head in amazement and disbelief. Ok, so he liked his women feisty and tempestuous, but sometimes he wished Lou would just fucking chill out. Steve crossed the road and successfully hailed another cab. As the taxi headed off in the opposite direction to Louise, Steve gave the cabbie the address of his intended destination. He didn't want to go home yet, he wanted some consolation and he knew exactly where to get it.

Chapter VII

Gatwick airport was throbbing. Thronging crowds traipsed through the airport, some wheeling cases behind them, others with packs slung on their backs, all wearing the same tired yet excited expression. Queues from the ticket counters already twisted around the terminal like restless serpents' tails, people shuffling slowly forward in their long lines, passports and ticket printouts in hand. It wasn't even yet 8 o'clock but the airport was humming with travellers.

DCs Elizabeth Lane and Gregory Hampton sat in one of the airport cafes. They were sitting departures side simply because there was a greater selection of cafs to choose from and because the 'people watching', as Elizabeth called it, was so much more interesting on this side of the airport.

People in arrivals were either happy to have arrived or disappointed a holiday had come to an end. The people in departures, however, demonstrated a whole gamut of emotions, Elizabeth had said. There was the solitary traveller trying to instigate conversation with strangers, the solitary traveller in his own world, the group of stags or hens heading off for a final weekend of hedonism and debauchery, the young couples who could barely keep their hands off each other, the old married couples who travelled in companionable silence... A few seconds of observation were usually enough to slot each traveller into the relevant pigeon hole, Elizabeth had told Greg, her work partner of over three years.

When they'd first been partnered together Greg had been skeptical. After all, he was 53 years old, had completed his necessary thirty years in the job, had dropped out of school to join the army in his teens and spoke with an East-end accent. Elizabeth was the total opposite; she was 30, had only been in the job for eight years, was pursuing an Open University degree and spoke the Queen's English. Chalk and cheese. Greg had not imagined they could have worked so well together.

Despite these apparent differences, however, they had quickly come to realize that they actually shared the same mind set and values. This combined with their shared love of rock music, socializing and their job meant they had quickly forged a strong friendship; they were no longer just partners, they were now firm friends. Neither officer could imagine being partnered with anyone else and the fact that Greg was considering retirement in six months' time was causing them both considerable consternation.

Now as they sat drinking coffee and hot chocolate, overlooking the departure hall Elizabeth felt a tug of wanderlust.

'Wish I was taking a flight out of here, I can tell you,' mumbled Elizabeth

'Huh?' Greg looked at her, coffee cup poised at his lips.

'I said, I wish I was taking a flight out of here. A nice two-week break diving in the Maldives or trekking through the jungle in some far flung place. I would even settle for a weekend in Benidorm at the moment.' She sighed wistfully, stirring her hot chocolate, head resting in her left hand.

'Jesus, how desperate are you?' asked Greg 'Bloody Benidorm! Have you never seen Brits abroad? You'd last a day max then you'd be dying to come home.'

Elizabeth smiled, 'Ok so maybe not Benidorm.'

'Besides, wouldn't you rather be here working this murder? I've never seen anything like it in all my thirty years,' said Greg.

'Hmm… I would, but it doesn't feel like we are working on this murder. We're baby-sitting the bloody CCTV guy, that's what we're doing.'

'Every cog has its place in the larger investigative wheel, Elizabeth,' Greg said sagely.

She looked at him, eyebrows raised in amusement.

'Where did that little nugget come from? You've changed your tune! You hardly said a word after we were tasked with this. Talk about grumpy!'

'Yes well, that's early mornings for you - not the job at hand. What time is this guy due?'

Elizabeth looked at her watch. 'Just over half an hour. I'll go check the arrivals board, check there are no delays.' She got up and sidled off.

During the briefing that morning, Elizabeth and Greg had been tasked by DI Scott with collecting Keith McFadden from Gatwick and conveying him 'as fast as you fucking can' to the hotel so he could begin downloading the CCTV.

The importance of viewing the CCTV as soon as possible was not lost on either detective, but they had been surprised at being ordered to pick the CCTV manager up from the airport. After all, the

Gatwick Express would have got him into Victoria in 15 minutes and they could just have easily met him there, instead of having to drive all the way to the airport. They hadn't even been allowed to hear the rest of the briefing as they were ordered out of the office to 'get fucking cracking' within minutes of the briefing starting.

Greg suspected they had been sent to the airport in order to limit the damage Mr McFadden could cause if he chose to discuss the murder with his fellow passengers. They couldn't stop him talking on the flight, but they could isolate him once he got off.

'No delays. Our protégée should be here on time,' Elizabeth declared sliding back into her seat and grabbing her mug simultaneously. 'We'll drink these then go up to arrivals, eh Greg?'

'Yeah, ok,' he replied.

'I was just thinking. Soon I won't have to worry about where to go on holiday, or the cost,' Elizabeth said, leaning into Greg conspiratorially.

'Oh yeah, why's that?'

'Cos, when you retire and piss off to Poland, I'll be able to visit you whenever I please. I intend to make the most of that open invitation you gave me.' Elizabeth laughed as Greg's smile froze into a grimace.

Greg's plan upon retirement was to emigrate to Poland with his long-term Polish girlfriend, much to Elizabeth's delight. 'Another country I can add to my list,' she smiled.

'That invitation was extended when I was drunk and beyond rational thought!' Greg countered.

'Yeah, yeah, whatever. You can try and hide behind the booze, but you still said it and I will take advantage of that fact.' Elizabeth smiled sweetly at him.

Greg opened his mouth as if he was going to say something, then downed his coffee and slammed the cup down on the table in mock anger

'Right come on, up to arrivals,' he said, choosing to ignore her.

Elizabeth chuckled and drank the dregs of her hot chocolate.

'Yes sir, Greg Hampton, Sir,' she teased. 'Just so you know though, this conversation isn't over.'

Greg, however, was already on his way out of the café marching in the direction of arrivals. Elizabeth smiled to herself, shook her head and then followed him out the door.

****

Her head was banging. It had been all morning.

Bloody Pinot

Louise hadn't spoken to Steve yet. She was still stewing and still couldn't quite believe the argument had escalated as it had. She was furious that he was jealous of her relationship with Ben and her commitment to her work. She was the one who should be jealous, what with that vulture Melissa circling round him, waiting for an opportunity to his jump his bones, if not pick them clean.

When she had told him to leave her alone and that she didn't want him coming back with her, she hadn't really meant it. She'd expected him to get in a different taxi and turn up on her door step, full of apologies and remorse. He hadn't and that had pissed her off even more. Usually, he was the first to give in and that was the way she liked it. Then they would have great make up sex, tell each other how much they loved each other and all would be forgotten. Maybe she had finally pushed him too far.

Louise had never been good with relationships. She found it so hard to trust; she was always scared that if she let someone in and gave them her heart and soul they would leave her. So, she pushed and pushed so nobody could get too close. By keeping people at arm's length, she could protect herself from the emotional agony of being abandoned, mistreated or cheated on. She'd seen and experienced enough heartache in her life; she'd decided a long time ago that she would never allow herself to suffer in that way again.

Her dad had left when she was a child and her mum had gone into meltdown. Louise had been too young to remember in any detail, but she had been told by her foster family that her mother had been sectioned shortly after her dad's departure, and had then promptly committed suicide at the asylum by hanging herself. Louise didn't remember there ever being a funeral, but then she didn't remember a lot of things from her childhood.

A lot of her adolescence was a blank for her too. She guessed no one had ever been able to track down her father to ask if she could stay with him. Not that he would have said yes anyway, given that he had abandoned them in the first place. Why would it be any different now her mother was dead?

And so it was, the eight year-old Louise had lost both her parents within the space of a month and had ended up living in a nice part of London with a new family.

She remembered that she had an older sister, Michelle, but they'd lost touch once they were taken into foster care; Louise's new family had been unwilling or unable to take both children. She didn't even know if Michelle was still alive. Sometimes she thought about trying to track her down, but she felt something dark lurking deep within her when she considered this, as if something unknown, perhaps her subconscious mind, was dissuading her. She felt a sense of foreboding when she thought about her family and was always surprised at how little she could remember of them all. Louise's foster family had been good to her, but she'd gone 'off the rails' by the time she'd hit her early teens.

In a bid to try and curb her self-destructive behaviour, the family had moved to Hertfordshire, hoping the countryside and slower pace of life would help calm her down. Louise had not enjoyed living there, missing the hustle and bustle that she was used to and when she turned 17, she left home and moved back to London, renting out a poky flat with another girl and a couple of boys and working any job she could find.

She'd had a series of boyfriends and the relationships had always been tumultuous and complicated. Some had hit her, all had cheated on her and none had helped her. It was as if she was broken, and instead of trying to fix her, the men she had mixed with had wanted to destroy her. It had become a familiar pattern, as if she was on a destructive carousel, ever spinning and unrelenting. She couldn't get off and didn't know how else to live her life.

She had finally been rescued from the carousel in her early twenties by a man called

Francis, the first man to look at her like she was a person, the first man to support her and love her. He had picked her up and raised her onto a pedestal from which she could finally see she deserved more, was worth more and could change her life. She only had to believe in herself and with his help and reassurance she finally had.

Nine years on Francis was only a lingering memory but his goodness and kindness were not; they had shaped Louise into the woman she had become. She was now doing a job she loved, had people around her that cared and had enough money to enjoy life. She was now confident, independent and resilient; gone were the days of letting someone else dictate her life, put her down and lay their hands on her. She knew she owed it all to Francis and for that she would be eternally grateful; if he hadn't come into her life like some angel sent to protect her, her life would have undoubtedly continued its downward spiral.

On top of her hangover this morning and her frustration at Steve, Louise had to get the 'list of doom' ready for Ben. So far she'd put two names on the list, agonizing over each name for an hour a piece before reluctantly committing her thoughts to paper. Just another 18 names. Not enough time. Definitely not enough time if she was going to spend the day sitting around musing about the past and ruing her hangover. She sighed and leaned forward over her desk, grabbing a handful of personal files. If she was going to do this, she was going to do it right and consider each person's merits in full. She opened one of the files and began to read.

****

DI Scott closed the file containing the crime scene photographs and returned it to his briefcase. He was travelling to Weybridge in Surrey to visit the victim's widow and the train he was on was virtually empty, allowing him to glance through the photographs and case papers in his possession without fearing someone may catch a glimpse of them over his shoulder.

He'd called Mrs Saunders, Janet, after the briefing that morning; he'd had to repeat himself several times to be sure she understood what he was saying, she sounded so distant. Eventually, she'd understood that he needed to speak to her in person about her husband and she had tearfully acquiesced to his request.

This was not a meeting he was looking forward to. Robert had a wealth of experience in dealing with distraught families, he was used to fielding difficult questions and was a master at relaying tragic news in a euphemistic manner. Today though, he felt nervous and he didn't much care for the feeling.

He looked out the train window and watched the countryside whizz past. The sun was poking its nose through the clouds, the rain drops from the previous day and night sparkling with its touch, rendering the fields verdant and resplendent. As a city dweller, Robert didn't often get to enjoy the country. He was saddened to think that today's trip to the country was due to a gruesome murder. Such an horrific, gruesome murder.

He looked at the seat opposite him. DC Tony Jessop's head was tilted back against the headrest of his seat, his mouth slightly open as he snoozed. Robert wasn't annoyed with him. None of the team had had much sleep and he didn't begrudge the detective a few minutes shut eye. Almost as if he was aware of the scrutiny DC Jessop opened his eyes and shifted in his seat.

'Sorry guv. Nodded off for a second there.'

'It's alright Tony. We'll need to be on our game. We're going to have to ask Mrs Saudners some pretty personal questions. I'd like you to lead this meeting. You're young and less threatening than an old git like me.'

Tony was in his mid-thirties and was known as something of a looker. Female suspects and witnesses alike loved him and he was very good at keeping a situation calm. He was also an excellent detective, which was why Robert had picked him for this job.

'Ok, guv. Not a problem. Do you want to discuss a plan of action? What do you want me to leave out?' Tony asked, not sure if he was happy or alarmed at being given the lead in such an important interview.

'Just go with the flow. Obviously she doesn't need to know about the genital mutilation, but we will need to ask her about the bondage side of it. We'll need to ask her if she knows her husband may well practice bondage, if he's having any affaires that she knows about and also if she knows of any clubs he may frequent.' He sighed. 'Nice bit of light general chit chat, you know?'

Tony breathed in, then exhaled sharply. 'I'll be honest Guv, I'm really not looking forward to this. I mean this murder is something else, isn't it? Genital mutilation? It's like something from a bad slasher movie,' his voice trailed off.

'I agree. Still, nothing's ever easy in our job

is it? You could always go and join traffic?' Robert teased.

Tony smirked at him. 'And you could retire and join the slipper and pipe brigade. Not going to happen is it?'

'Touché. Right come on. Get yourself together. We're here.'

Chapter VIII

She lay on her stomach, staring at the little kitten. It just sat there, meowing, its big green eyes looking at her. She'd never seen anything quite so cute. Its fur was soft and spiky, its body was light brown, its little paws white, like someone had forgotten to colour them in, and its ears chocolate. They looked like funny shaped chocolate buttons, she thought, as if they'd melted and then been moulded into a pointy shape. She plucked the top of the kitten's ears and it rolled over, paws raised in defence, its little legs moving as if it was running. She smiled at the kitten and gently stroked its head.

'Little kitten, you're so cute,' she cooed, 'I wouldn't hurt you.'

The animal continued to play scratch her hands, its paws wrapping around her hands and wrists, its firm, little body wriggling under her hands, teeth gnashing as it tried to nibble her. She giggled then gently scooped the animal up in her arms, carrying it away from the mat to the bed, even though he'd told her not to move the cat. She crawled under the duvet, hugging the creature to her naked body, stroking it softly.

'You're going to be my friend and I shall call you Sunshine. My little sunshine kitty.'

The kitten gently pawed at her under the quilt, and started to purr as it nuzzled into her chest. She felt the warmth of its fur against her skin and was comforted by the contact. Eventually, the pair fell asleep.

Suddenly, she was awake, the kitten was screeching and the covers were wrenched off her. Immediately she started to cry and reached out towards the kitten as the man handled it roughly in his big, rough hands. 'Don't hurt Sunshine! Don't hurt Sunshine!' she wailed, pleadingly. 'No! Give her to me!'

The big, rough hands slapped her hard across the face, raising her whole body off the bed. She saw flashes of white behind her eyes and a blackness swept over her briefly. She could hear Sunshine calling for her and she felt powerless. She started to scream hysterically 'Sunshine, Sunshine!' The hands hit her again, but still she screamed. It was as if she felt no pain. She just wanted to save Sunshine, wanted him to stop hurting the cute little kitten.

She looked up just as the man threw the wretched creature at the wall, its legs moving desperately in the air as it tried to cling onto anything to prevent its flight. The kitten's body connected with the concrete wall, a dull sound like a tennis ball being hit with a rounder's bat, and slid to the floor. Sunshine wasn't making any noise now, she wasn't even moving. The girl cried, floods of tears pouring from her swollen eyes. 'You've hurt Sunshine! You've hurt my kitten!'

'Shut it bitch! Who said you could move that fucking thing from the mat? What were you doing with it in your bed, you stupid fucking creature?' he demanded, his eyes wide and mad.

She was sat up on the bed now, her arms around her legs which were curled up to her chest, rocking gently backwards and forwards.

'Sunshine, Sunshine, Sunshine...' she kept repeating as she rocked.

The man stood looking at her, momentarily confused by her behaviour. Then he climbed onto the bed and pushed himself on top of her.

'No, you've hurt Sunshine!' she screamed at him, throwing herself onto her back and raising her arms and legs as Sunshine had done in defence. She kicked him, she

54

scratched him, she bit him, she punched him.

All she could feel was rage, a feeling she had never felt before. She continued to pummel him with her small fists and feet as he tried to subdue her.

His face was scratched and blood was gently seeping from the wounds. She managed to clamp her teeth around his wrist, again drawing blood. She fought him like an animal. Eventually, he pinned her arms and legs to the bed, astounded at her reaction.

'Oh you're going to regret that you little bitch! You've made me bleed!' He hit her several times in the face with his open hand.

'You're going to wish you'd never been born cunt!' Using one hand he pinned her two hands above her head and with his other he undid his trousers. She knew what was coming next, but she didn't care. She'd made him bleed and that felt good.

Chapter IX

DI Scott and DC Jessop sat on the leather couch opposite Mrs Saunders in the spotless living room, looking at each other over untouched tea, steaming on the table between them. At the train station they'd been met by two uniformed PCs who had kindly offered to take them to the house after DC Jessop had called their police station earlier that morning.

They had driven the detectives for fifteen minutes through beautiful Surrey countryside, passing grand houses partially obscured from the road by leafy trees, imperious gates and high walls. Coffee houses, designer clothing shops and farm shops could be found in small clusters along the route, the clientele of each well-dressed and seemingly refined.

It was a far cry from the scenes both detectives were used to in their neighbourhoods, where the streets were populated by groups of hooded youths, single mothers and unemployed males. This could have been an entirely different country.

The Saunders residence was equally grand to those espied earlier; a red Jaguar and a black BMW gleamed in the gravelled drive way, and a landscaped front garden screamed money. The high, wooden front door had been opened by a tall, thin woman even before the police car had fully come to a stop, the poor cousin next to the two sports cars. Mrs Saunders had stood in the doorway in dark trousers and an emerald green blouse, her eyes downcast, her shoulders slightly hunched, the sign of a woman under strain.

She had a beautiful face, arched eyebrows above impenetrable dark, brown eyes, a perfect bow on her top lip and high cheekbones. Her hair was long, black and glossy and her hands were impeccably manicured. Even the dark circles beneath her swollen, red-rimmed eyes did not detract from her beauty.

She'd ushered the detectives in, the two PCs politely declining her offer for tea and heading back to the station. They would return once the detectives had finished their interview with her.

Sitting opposite Robert and Tony in a plush Chesterfield armchair, she appeared slumped, as if all the life force had been drained out of her. It was obvious she had been hit hard by the news of her husband's murder.

'My brother has taken the children out for a while. I didn't want them here when you arrived. They don't need any more upset to their routine. The school's been very good, as have my staff. I won't need to go back until I feel…' She broke off as a sob caught in her throat.

She raised a hand to her eyes and gently rubbed them, long, slender, bejeweled fingers dabbing at their corners.

'I don't know if I'll ever be ready to go back,' she finished.

Tony shifted forward on the sofa.

'Mrs Saunders, you have had the most awful news. It will take you a long time to adjust and you may never fully get over your loss. However, you must know that we will do everything in our power to find who did this to your husband.' DC Jessop's voice was soft and deep, soothing even to Robert's ear.

She looked at him, a small, pitiful smile tugging at the corners of her mouth.

'I'm sure you will detective.'

'Please, call me Tony.'

'Tony. Do either of you want tea? I made it fresh a few minutes before you arrived.'

Even in light of what had happened her respect for etiquette was forefront in her mind, a sign of remarkable strength and courage, Tony thought.

'Thank you,' they said in unison as she handed them a cup each.

'Mrs Saunders…' Tony began.

'Janet. Mrs Saunders makes me sound so old.'

'Janet, we've come down to see you today as we have a number of questions that we need to ask you. Some of these questions will be of a personal and very private nature. I want to assure you that these questions are not designed to pry but may provide us with important information that will assist this investigation. If at any point you feel uncomfortable with what I'm asking you, just let me know and we'll have a breather, ok?'

She nodded silently, head lowered, looking at the tea in her hands.

'Also, you must be aware that there may be certain things about this enquiry that we are unable to tell you at this time, but it is not because we want to withhold anything from you; it's just that it may hinder the investigation if you know it at this time, does that make sense?' Tony asked, gently. Only a small lie. Really they just didn't want to cause her any more unnecessary upset.

She nodded again.

'I may ask you some questions that were asked of you by the detectives when they visited you previously, and again I want you to understand that this is not designed to upset you, or make you feel that your answers on that occasion were inadequate. It is just to ensure that all bases are covered and we get the best possible information from you that we can.'

'I understand.'

'Janet, let's start with your husband's movements two days ago. Do you know what his plans were?' Tony asked.

'David didn't tell me all his business. We are... we were two busy people with a lot going on in our lives. He said that he had a meeting in the evening with some company or other, I have forgotten the name, and that he wouldn't be back until late, but he did intend to come home. Sometimes he would stay up in London you see, but he'd always call to let me know. He didn't call me the other night though,' she sniffed, reaching out for a tissue from the box on the table beside her chair.

'Did it worry you that he hadn't called?' Tony asked.

'Not really. I was in bed by eleven; it was probably around midnight that I turned out the light. I was a little annoyed I suppose but I just assumed that he didn't want to call in case he woke me. He was considerate like that. I figured that there'd be a text on my phone when I woke up, but there wasn't.'

'Did you try to call him?'

'Yes but his phone went to answer phone.'

'Can you remember what time that was?'

'Probably around ten, ten thirty. And I called him in the morning a couple of times too, but again it rang out to voice mail.'

'Can you remember if he told you anything else about his meeting?' Tony prompted.

'I'm pretty sure it was with an existing client. I wish I could remember the name of the company...' Janet trailed off, searching her memory for the name.

After a little while she continued, still unable to remember.

'He also said that he would take the kids to school in the morning as he wouldn't have to go back into work until the afternoon, if he went in at all. I own a beauty salon so I work my own hours and I had been looking forward to spending the morning with him, but as he wasn't here, I went in to work after I'd dropped the children off.'

Her voice trembled as she fought back another wave of tears.

'How does David normally get to the station? I notice two cars out front,' Tony asked.

'Tim, he's our handyman, chauffeur, gardener... you name it, Tim can do it. Tim takes David to the train station in the Jag and then comes back here, does what he has to do and then picks David up in the evening. When David's late back, either I'll pick him up if I'm home, or he'll get a cab. He would have taken a cab the other night.' That explained why both cars were in the drive, instead of one being parked at the station car park.

'Does he take anything to work with him?'

'His briefcase and usually a gym bag. He uses a gym near his office and also the one in town here. It depends on his mood which one he goes to, or if he goes at all,' she replied, with a small smile.

'Can you remember what he took with him when he left the other morning?'

'No, but neither his briefcase nor gym bag are here, so I'm guessing he took them with him. I haven't checked in the car though. Is that really relevant?'

Tony looked at Robert and Robert nodded almost imperceptibly back at him. 'Your husband wasn't robbed, Janet. The briefcase and the gym bag were still in the hotel room.'

'Why did you ask me the question if you already knew what he had with him?' she asked, perplexed. 'And why can't I have his stuff back?'

'You can have his possessions back as soon as we are one hundred percent sure that they are not of any evidential value,' Tony began. 'The gym bag didn't contain gym gear. It contained some other items, some suggesting that he actually anticipated staying in London that night,' he said, feeling a slight tug in his guts as he knew the difficult part was coming.

'What was in it then?' asked Janet, her voice taking on a slightly hard edge.

'There was a clean shirt and tie, some paper work. There were toiletries in the bathroom too.'

Janet looked at him, her face full of confusion.

'No gym gear? So it was like an overnight bag? Why would he tell me he was coming back if he knew he wasn't?' she asked, her eyes watery, lips apart.

'This is what we need to work out Janet. Is it possible that he didn't use a gym when he worked late in London? Maybe he went somewhere else?' Tony asked gently, trying to tread around the subject.

'Well yes, I guess, but why wouldn't he tell me? And where exactly do you mean he might go... might have gone to?' Janet was getting slightly annoyed now, her grief giving in to pique as she contemplated the prospect that she may have been lied to by her late husband.

'Are you suggesting he was having an affair?' she asked, incredulously.

'Was he?' Tony asked.

'No!' she almost shouted at him. 'My husband is dead and you're accusing him of cheating on me!'

'Janet, I don't mean to upset you, but I need to ask you the question. The circumstances around your husband's death,' he inhaled, 'they suggest he may have been engaging in a sex game when he was murdered,' and exhaled. There, it was out now.

He almost felt relieved until he saw the expression on Janet's face. What little colour had been in her cheeks now drained from her face, making her look ashen. The dark circles suddenly stood out in stark contrast against her pale skin and the wounded look in her eyes made him hate himself and his job.

'What... what do you mean? The detectives that came to see me before didn't tell me this!' she said accusingly.

'You had enough to deal with Janet. And they didn't stay long enough to tell you if you recall,' Tony gently reminded her. She had collapsed shortly after being told the news and demanded the detectives leave.

She nodded, her head downcast, tears running down her cheeks and dripping off her nose.

'They should have tried to tell me. They should have tried.' She began to sob and Tony felt an overwhelming urge to go and sit with her, to stroke her back and tell her everything would be ok. Except it wouldn't be ok. Her husband had been murdered and she had just found out that he had probably been playing a sex game at the time.

'Janet, do you know if David was having an affair?' Tony asked gently.

'Not that I knew of. He's never cheated on me to my knowledge,' she sobbed. 'He loves this family. Fuck it! He loved this family. I can't believe he's gone.'

Tony looked at Robert, beseeching him to take over the questioning, but Robert just sat there, unreadable and silent. Tony was annoyed by his DI's silence. He was the senior officer; Robert should be doing the talking, not him. He turned away from him, shooting him the best evil eye he could muster.

'There's something else I need to ask you Janet. Was David into bondage?'

'Excuse me?' she looked at him, her eyes suddenly steely, her voice hard. 'What has that got to do with anything and how is it any of your business?'

'Your husband was found tied to the hotel bed. There was a pair of men's PVC trousers at the foot of the bed. I need to ask the question as we need to consider if he met his killer by chance, or if he met with someone he knew, another woman,' he paused. Here it was the worst bit to come out of his mouth and he wished he didn't have to say it. 'Or another man…?'

Janet looked at him for a moment, then threw her head back and laughed contemptuously.

'Bondage? Gay bondage! Ha! My husband was not gay detective nor was he into bondage as you call it.'

The use of his title was not lost on Tony. Janet was pulling down the shutters. He'd hit a raw nerve.

'Janet, Mrs Saunders. I am not suggesting your husband was gay, and I am not stating he was definitely into bondage. I'm asking you what you think about this. What can you tell me about your husband's sexual proclivities?' he asked.

She laughed again. 'Proclivities! It gets better.' She kept on laughing and Tony thought she'd gone into hysterics. Just when he thought he was going to have to get up and slap her out of it, she regained control of herself and stared at him, the beautiful eyes filled with so many different and conflicting emotions.

'I'm only going to say this once, detective. My husband does not practise bondage. He is an upstanding, decent man. He is not a pervert. We have a great sex life, we love each other immensely and he would never, never expect me to tie him up, whip him or whatever it is those people do. My husband is also not gay. He has never looked at or been out with another man. He also does not dress up in women's clothing nor does he molest small children, got it?'

She was trembling, and again Tony couldn't tell if this was with grief or anger. She'd obviously lost her composure as she was again referring to Mr Saunders in the present tense and not bothering to correct it.

'Ok Mrs Saunders. Thank you. I'm sorry I upset you. I understand these are difficult and upsetting questions. I do not mean to cause offence,' Tony said humbly, almost instantly calming her down and making her think he thought he had over stepped the mark.

In fact the opposite was true. He was now convinced that not only did her husband practise bondage regularly but that it was an area of contention between them. Her views were very reserved and she seemed to think that those who engaged in bondage sex were 'perverts'. He could just imagine how her husband's unusual sexual activities would grate against her traditional values.

'I'm feeling tired now and my children will be back soon. I'd appreciate it if we could end this conversation here. I have nothing else to tell you. I've lost my husband. I don't want his good name dragged through the mire as you spout your theories,' Janet said quietly, no more fight left in her.

'Mrs Saunders, thank you for your time. Here's my card. If you think of anything at all, no matter how trivial it may seem to you, give me a call, ok?' Robert finally spoke, and held out his business card to her.

She looked at him as if she had forgotten he was there. She accepted the card with a trembling hand and mumbled something about them letting themselves out. Tony followed Robert out of the room. As he looked back he saw Janet draw her legs up under her, making her look small and childlike in the large armchair. He'd never seen anyone look so lost and alone.

Chapter X

Louise cursed as she rapped on the front door with her knuckles, the varnished wood fighting back. She made a mental note to buy Steve a door knocker for Christmas. That would be one hell of a Christmas present, she thought amusedly, really show him how much she loved him.

Darling I love you so much, I really wanted to spoil you this year - look! A fabulous new knocker!

After a day of silence, a day of stewing, Louise had swallowed her pride and decided that she would have to make the first move and apologise if they were going to move on from their row on Wednesday night. She was still annoyed, but had come round to seeing things from his perspective. She knew she had been neglecting their relationship, putting her work first and that perhaps her priorities were sometimes a bit skewed. So now, here she was, rapping on Steve's door, ready to eat humble pie.

The door was promptly answered, jerked open hurriedly in one swift movement. Steve stood silhouetted in the doorway and Louise could hear the distorted guitar riffs of some metal band playing on his iPod docking station in the next room. Steve cocked his head to one side and raised an eyebrow, taking in the bag of clothes on the floor by her feet, without saying a word.

'Steve, I'm really sorry I can't come with you to Cornwall tonight, but I thought I'd come here to get changed for the ceremony,' Louise began. 'Besides, I have something for you,' she grinned, her fingers slowly unbuttoning her overcoat.

She smiled at Steve coquettishly, then in one deft movement dramatically opened the coat, revealing her naked body. She gave Steve a little wiggle, her breasts wobbling playfully.

'Come on, let me in. We can't leave it like this. And as you can see,' she looked down at her nipples, 'I'm getting rather cold.'

Steve smiled, moving towards her, wrapping an arm around her naked waist.

'You are one crazy woman, Miss Louise Jackson,' he said.

He kissed her hard on the mouth, pulling her body against his, and backed through the front door, closing it shut behind them with his foot. They kissed passionately as Steve maneuvered her across the living room and tugged off her coat. She could feel him becoming hard against her naked sex, his penis large and firm straining against his jeans; she was overcome with a desperate need to have him then and now. She couldn't wait.

She unzipped his flies and pulled out his penis, rubbing it, bringing him to full strength. Steve groaned and bent his head to kiss her breasts, his tongue darting over her nipples, before clamping them gently between his teeth. His hand trailed down Louise's stomach and rested between her legs.

She groaned loudly as he inserted his fingers into her, moving her hips in unison with his digital thrusts. Her back was now pressed against the settee, her body arching against it. Steve still fully clothed, his manhood protruding through his open flies, leant into her and kissed her.

Still holding Steve's penis in her hand she raised herself onto her tip toes and placed the end of it against her clitoris, moving it slowly against herself, pleasuring them both. Steve moved his hand away from her crotch as Louise placed the tip of his penis inside her. Steve picked her up and she wrapped her legs around him, panting with pleasure as he entered her fully.

He grunted and began raising her up and down as she gripped him hard with her strong thighs. She was vaguely aware that the music had changed, another rock band with heavy guitar chords and a gravelly voiced-vocalist; she was so consumed in the moment she found the music strangely seductive.

Steve carried her over to the correct side of the sofa and lowered them both down onto it, still inside her. He stopped briefly to pull his trousers completely off and Louise hastily pulled his T-shirt over his head.

Now both fully naked, she clamped her legs around him, crossing her ankles, her nails scoring his flesh, her mouth urgently demanding his. Louise gasped in pleasure as Steve resumed his thrusts inside her. Turning her head to the side, Louise glanced at the living room window.

With a start she noticed a face looking in on them, a young woman with flowing black hair, pale skin and sad blue eyes. Her eyes were vacant, as if she had no soul, her mouth slightly open, her jaw slack. Her face was expressionless as she watched them in their intimate act. For a moment Louise could do nothing but gawp incredulously at the woman, shocked, surprised and disgusted that this woman dare spy on them.

Suddenly, the woman turned her gaze directly onto Louise, her expressionless eyes now filled with hate. As Louise watched, the woman's mouth blinked into a grimace, the corners rapidly upturning. The twisted smile lasted less than a second before the former soulless expression returned and the woman's eyes went dead again.

Louise inhaled sharply, 'Steve! There's someone looking at us!'

Steve looked at her and then around the room.

'What?' he asked, his breath coming in gasps, 'Where?'

'The window, look she's...' Louise's sentence trailed off. There was nobody there. The woman had vanished.

'Where, babe? I don't see anyone,' Steve said, raising himself up on his forearms, preparing to get off the settee.

'I... I must have imagined it,' Louise said confused. What the fuck was that? Her mind was reeling. Had she imagined that too? What was happening to her?

Feeling that Steve was about to withdraw and get up she grabbed his shoulders and said, 'Don't get up. Fuck me.'

Steve looked at her. 'It's ok, honest,' she breathed. 'I thought I saw someone but there's nobody there.'

Steve smiled and then kissed her neck, happily picking up from where they had left off.

Despite her confusion over the mysterious face, she told herself that nothing was amiss, she was not suffering some kind of mental break down. So, she'd had three weird things happen in as many days? Stress was a strange and malignant beast. She mentally shook herself and focused on the sensations Steve was causing to tingle through her body.

He began to bite her, on her lips, her neck, above her collar bone, as he knew she liked, and this sent Louise to the edge. Her legs began to tremble and she felt the familiar warmth spreading through her body. She could tell from Steve's now hurried thrusts that he was also nearing climax. Panting together, their bodies sleek with sweat, they climaxed in unison.

Afterwards, Steve lay on top of her, his warm breath tickling her neck. She wrapped her arms around him and nuzzled him with her face, enjoying the closeness and the feeling of the blood pumping through her veins. They lay that way for a while.

'Am I forgiven?' Louise eventually whispered.

'You know I can never stay mad at you for long. You are difficult and trying at times, but you make me feel alive.' He raised his head and smiled down at her, the smile crinkling the corners of his eyes.

'I know I am horrible to you sometimes. I get so… scared, you know? I get overwhelmed by how I feel for you and then my mind goes nuts, does somersaults and tries to make me fuck this up. I sometimes think I truly am crazy. I sometimes don't know how to feel, or I don't understand why I feel a certain way. Then other times I feel so sure, so confident about us… but usually I just feel afraid. Does that make any sense?'

Steve nodded. 'Yeah, it does gorgeous.' He hugged her into him, a little surprised by her sudden openness about her feelings; usually, she was more expressive about the weather than she was her own sentiments.

'You're scared of commitment. It's no great surprise given…'

'My upbringing? My childhood? I will never let that be an excuse for how I am today,' she replied.

She hadn't had much experience of human bonding. The foster home, whilst a place of warmth and love, had not been her place of warmth and love. She knew she was only there because they were getting paid to look after her. Even though they had really tried and treated her as well as one of their own children, she'd always felt like a stranger. She couldn't remember expressions of love from either of her biological parents prior to her dad running off and her mother going nuts, and she couldn't remember her sister.

She could only remember Francis and the semblance of love that had been played out by her in that relationship; even with him, as good and kind as he was, she had held back and kept her own counsel.

'Well, it's a known fact that the most troubled childhoods result in the most interesting adults,' Steve said, gently stroking her hair. 'Tell you what, when I get back from Cornwall we'll go out and talk about all this ok? Really try and work out what's holding you back.'

'Hmmm. Not sure if that's a good idea. You might realise that I am in fact a psychotic knife-wielding murderer who is simply humouring you in order to get her claws well and truly embedded into your flesh before delivering the mercy stroke and thereby ending your miserable existence,' she joked.

Make a joke, always make a joke when the conversation gets uncomfortable.

'Well you already tried to get your nails into my back just now,' Steve laughed. 'But seriously, when I get back we'll go out to dinner or something and if you feel like talking, then we will, if not I'll bore you with my stories of Cornwall and how I pulled three girls on the beach and had a ménage a quatre,' he laughed as she punched him on the arm.

'Trust you to fantasize about a foursome! You're such a greedy bastard,' she giggled.

'Talking of Cornwall, I'd better get my shit together, and you had better get that gorgeous body of yours dressed for that award thing.'

He kissed her, before pushing himself off the sofa and padding towards the bathroom. Louise smiled to herself as he walked away, his cute, little butt receding from view. A moment of pure carnal desire and passion, a moment of bonding and closeness shattered in an instant. He still had his socks on.

****

Steve drove quickly. Despite the traffic, he was making good time thanks to his knowledge of the less travelled routes. He thought about Louise as he drove. They'd first met two years ago in a coffee shop on Tottenham Court Road. She'd been buying a hot chocolate without cream, he remembered, and he'd ordered an Americano. She'd almost knocked his coffee out of his hand as she'd abruptly turned to leave the store, splashes of the hot liquid spattering his t-shirt.

As she stood there apologising to him,

wiping at him with serviettes, he had been struck by her beauty and overwhelmed by her presence, instantly drawn to her. She was bold and she was beautiful and in response to her profuse apologies he had insisted she drink her hot chocolate with him.

She had eventually acquiesced and their coffee break had turned into a lunch break and then into dinner. Before they knew it they had spent six hours together. As they'd parted that evening Steve had thrust his business card into her hand and she had reciprocated. The rest was history as they said.

Now though, he was confused. Louise was a very special woman, full of fire and energy, but she was also extremely complicated and difficult to get close to. Steve had hoped that with time he would be able to break down the walls she had erected around her heart, but now he wasn't so sure. He didn't feel needed, wanted or important to her; he had no doubt that she could very easily walk away from their relationship without so much as a glance back over her shoulder, and it left him feeling uncertain and insecure.

She was scared to commit, he knew, and he was too to a degree, but he needed to feel that this relationship was not just one sided. He needed some sort of affirmation from her, some sort of guarantee that she wasn't about to up and run away. Was it any wonder he had sought affection elsewhere?

Tonight Louise had opened up to him and he was touched. But at the same time he felt it was too late, he needed more, he'd waited long enough. If only Lou was able to let him in, make him feel like less of a stranger. He had meant it when he said she made him feel alive, but sometimes he just wanted to know that she was really going to be there, to feel that their relationship had some substance. Then he would never have strayed, never have been disloyal. He wanted to feel needed and Lou simply didn't make him feel that way. He felt that she couldn't care less if he was around or not.

Steve pulled the car over as he reached his destination, only five minutes late. He sighed deeply, thoughts of Lou drifting out of his mind and gently hit the horn.

After a few minutes the front door of the apartment block opened and Melissa strolled out, giving him a cheery wave. She was carrying a small holdall and she looked divine in a short red skirt, black skin-tight top and high heels. Steve waved at her as she approached the car.

'Hello gorgeous,' she said as she got into the car, throwing her holdall onto the back seat. She leant over and kissed Steve on the lips.

'Hi.' He smiled at her. 'All set?'

'You bet,' she replied, placing her hand on his thigh.

Steve put the car into gear and drove off. Time to forget Lou and focus on the other woman in his life that made him feel alive.

****

Louise was bored. Whilst she agreed that the ceremony itself had been suitably sycophantic, lots of hand shaking and false smiles, the party itself was rubbish. Now that the awards had been handed out and the speeches given, the hired DJ had resorted to chirpy 80s tunes – Louise was not in a chirpy mood. She stifled a yawn as Ben sidled up to her.

'Keeping you up?' he asked, handing her

another glass of champagne whilst sipping his own.

'No,' she answered curtly. 'But this after party is the dullest I have ever been to. You've got to agree. I could be in Cornwall right now, my knees around my ears, Steve over me, enjoying…'

'Ok, ok! Stop there! Too much detail!' Ben laughed. 'I'm sorry Lou. You could've gone you know. We would have managed.'

'Now you tell me!' she snorted.

'Although, I have to say I am personally very pleased that you're here. Good speech by the way. When did you write it?'

'During the taxi ride over here. It seems I work better under pressure,' she smiled at him. Ben took advantage of the moment to study her.

Louise Jackson was one of those rare women who was totally unaware of her beauty, and in fact tended to believe the opposite was true. She was wearing a dark purple full-length dress that contoured her figure and seductively skimmed her ample bosom, the deep V-line displaying a perfect cleavage, a long sparkling necklace trailing from her neck to her breasts.

Her silver high-heeled shoes lengthened her legs, adding inches to her height, making her only a little shorter than Ben himself at 6 foot two. Her eyes were bright, eye liner contouring them into perfect orbs; her skin glowed, high cheek bones gently blushing, and her lips glistened with gloss. Her dark blonde hair was immaculately brushed, falling across her shoulders like spun silk. She looked fantastic.

'Well I thought it was great. You got the tone just right. Lou, I just want to tell you how much I value you as an employee and as a person. I have no illusions as to how much you have contributed to the magazine's success. You are truly amazing.'

He took her right hand and gently kissed her knuckles.

'Why, Mr Matthews. Are you trying to seduce me?' she laughed, sipping her champagne, pulling her hand away.

'No, Ms Jackson, I'm not. I just want you to know how much you mean to me and to this company. And of course to thank you for getting that list to me today.'

He was referring to the 'list of doom' that Louise had reluctantly left on his desk earlier that day.

'You're welcome, I think. But don't you dare ask me to do anything like that again, will you? I agonised over that list and hate myself for putting those people on it. You shouldn't have asked me to do that. I hope you're suitably remorseful,' she tutted.

'Trust me, it's going to be hell next week sacking these people, but it has to be done. You're pragmatic enough to understand that sometimes sacrifices have to be made for the greater good, so to speak,' he replied.

'Of course I understand. Functionalism. Got to do what's got to be done.'

'I did notice that Derek was on the list. I thought you said he was a good writer?' Ben asked.

'He is quite a good writer, but he's lazy, he needs constant pushing. He's also got a shit attitude and rubs people up the wrong way.'

'Does that include you?'

'Yes it does. But he also upsets visitors, he's so damn arrogant. Of all the writers and editors he has to be the one to go.'

'Nothing to do with your history then?' Ben questioned.

Derek Cooper was the sub-editor that had been overlooked six months ago for the post that Louise now held. He'd always borne a grudge because of it and their relationship had become even more strained as a consequence.

'Nothing to do with that, no. Although, if I'm totally honest, I won't be particularly sorry to see him go.' She crinkled her nose over the top of her champagne flute at him.

'So, what did you think of the ceremony? Obviously, I was the highlight...' she grinned, changing the subject.

'You were the number one speaker, it has to be said. You looked stunning as well. I don't know if you noticed Mr Shaman at the back staring at you. He could hardly keep his tongue in his head! But, you know, he could be a potential investor, so a little schmoozing and ego flattering from you could pay dividends,' Ben said, his tone serious, but his eyes sparkling with mischief.

'My God! You sound like my bloody pimp!'

'Come on, take one for the team!' Ben chuckled.

'You git, you nearly had me there.' She sipped her champagne aware that she was starting to feel a little fuzzy.

'I'm glad I came tonight, despite the boring DJ and the sacrifice of the activities I should be engaged in right now with my beloved. It's good to be surrounded by people and making small talk with you.'

'Oh? Why's that?' Ben asked.

'Oh it's nothing really, I've just been a bit…out of sorts, I guess.'

I've been having weird, mind blowing visions that have totally freaked me out and make me think I'm going nuts.

'Out of sorts? Want to tell me about it?'

Louise looked at him, deciding whether or not she would be safe divulging her fears to him, ultimately deciding she had to tell someone.

'I think I'm just stressed to be honest with you Ben. I don't really know what's going on, but it's like my brain is playing tricks on me. It makes me think that maybe I have some sort of problem, with my body I mean, that my mind is subconsciously trying to get me to pay attention to. You know how some people who have a really serious illness suddenly find their bodies rejecting cigarettes or booze, even though they don't actually consciously know that they're ill at that point? Or, it could just be that I am finally losing it and going insane.' Her tone was light but Ben knew her well enough to know that she was in fact deeply concerned.

'What's been happening to you?' Ben asked.

Louise drained her champagne flute and deposited the empty receptacle on the tray of a passing waiter.

'It started a couple of days ago. The first thing was the morning after the launch of Steve's restaurant. It's silly; it was probably just the after-affects of all the booze I'd drunk.'

'Tell me about it then,' Ben said, curious now.

'Well I was in the kitchen, eating pizza…'

'For breakfast? Jesus!' Ben declared in disgust.

Louise ignored him.

'…and I looked out the window to the bus stop opposite. There was an old man there. At first he looked quite normal, but then he looked at me, it was really disconcerting, like he could really see me, in my flat. I felt that he was looking directly at me, even though that there is no way he could see in. I have nets on the windows and my lights were off. But then he just smiled at me.'

'Err, Lou. That doesn't sound particularly strange.'

'I'm not describing it very well. His smile was odd. He had these weird crooked teeth. When I looked back, he'd gone.'

Ben looked like he was going to say something, but Lou raised a hand to silence him.

'Then as I was coming into work the other morning, this random bloke said to me: "Your secret's safe with me." I have no idea what he was referring to, or who the hell he was.'

She reached out and grabbed another glass of champagne as another waiter walked slowly past. Ben followed her lead and took another glass too.

'I just figured I was stressed out over the deadline of getting to print, or that I was just hung over or whatever and I put it out of my mind. It freaked me out though. Then this evening, I went to see Steve before coming here. We were in the process of… you know… in the living room,' Ben looked slightly uncomfortable at this, 'when I noticed a woman looking in on us. She smiled a fucking freaky smile at me and then just disappeared. By the time I'd told Steve there was a face at the window, she was gone.'

Louise paused and sipped her fresh

champagne. 'I don't know what it means, if I should be concerned, or if it's all just a load of bollocks.'

Ben took his time in replying, mulling over what she had said.

Eventually he asked: 'So they're like hallucinations?'

'Not sure. I don't know if they're 'out there' in the real world so to speak, or simply in my mind.'

'Lou, it's probably nothing to worry about. As you say, it's probably just stress. The deadline, and the list I asked you to do. I'm sorry if I have in anyway caused this.'

He looked genuinely upset and Lou was touched.

'Hey Ben, that's business, eh?'

'Well yes and no. I don't want you making yourself ill with worry. Do me a favour and go to the doctor on Monday, ok? Just make sure you're ok and everything is in tip top working order. I'm sure it's nothing but there's no harm in mentioning it to a professional right?'

'Not unless they think I need to be locked up! I hate doctors. They're all so supercilious and patronizing,' Louise began.

'No excuses Lou. I want you to promise me you'll go. Just tell them what you told me. I'm sure they'll be able to allay your fears and reassure you that it's just a phase or something.'

'Alright. I'll call the surgery first thing Monday morning. Happy now?' she asked moodily.

'Yes… if you go. I know what a pain in the arse you are,' he smiled.

'Oh cheers! After everything I do for you!'

'Right come on. I'm going to introduce you to Mr Shaman. He keeps looking over this way and

I'm pretty sure it's not to catch my eye.'

Ben put his hand on Louise's elbow, masterfully steering her through the crowd of people to the back of the room where Mr Shaman stood smiling.

'Don't you dare leave me with him on my own!' she growled at Ben.

'I promise,' he replied. 'Time to plaster on our best smiles. I want him to agree to invest with us before the night is through.'

'A tenner says I win him over before you do,' Louise challenged.

'You're on! Let the games commence,' he whispered to her as they approached.

She smiled at Ben and tried to mentally prepare herself for a winning pitch. However, she was confused and concerned by what had been happening to her and found that she couldn't keep her mind focussed on the present; it kept wondering off of its own accord, like a naughty child that wouldn't stay in bed after lights out.

She couldn't stop thinking about the face she'd seen at the window. Who was this woman? What did it mean? She really didn't want to go to the doctor. What if they thought she was mad? After all, look what had happened to her mother. She'd been sectioned and then topped herself. What if it ran in the family? Was she a nutter too?

Swallowing some more champagne she forced her professional head on and pushed down her negative thoughts and concerns. She'd have plenty of time to try and figure it all out over the weekend.

Now to business.

Chapter XI

DC Elizabeth Lane felt melancholy; she wasn't sure why. Maybe it was the lack of sleep since the murder investigation had begun. Maybe it was because they were no further forward. Maybe it was because she'd had nothing positive to say to DI Scott that morning.

The CCTV had been a total wash out. The cameras had only recorded a fraction of the evening and the footage they had recorded was white snow.

'We've never had to look at the cameras before,' McFadden, the hotel CCTV guy had said, as if this was suitable justification for the hotel's piss poor security.

Greg had just shrugged. C'est la vie - shit happens. The lack of CCTV was, however, a disaster. They were no further forward and as far as Elizabeth could tell, they had no other leads.

She sighed forlornly just as Greg sat down beside her in the briefing room. They were waiting for DI Scott, who had promised them he'd be ready in five minutes, fifteen minutes ago.

'Morning you. What's up?' Greg was holding a double Espresso, his latest addiction.

'Nothing, just tired,' Elizabeth replied, eyeing his cup suspiciously. 'Is that what I think it is?'

Greg raised the coffee cup with a wink and downed it in one large gulp. He grimaced as the bitter coffee slid across his taste buds: 'Yup.'

'Oh God help us all. You're such a pain in the ass after you've had a shot.'

Greg laughed. 'Got to have something to keep my eyes open. This enquiry is keeping us all up at night, judging by the look of everyone else in here.'

Elizabeth looked around the room and had to agree. Every officer there had the same weary look, the same air of fatigue. Rarely were so many paper coffee cups to be seen outside a coffee house, as the officers resorted to caffeine to keep their synapses firing.

'Meadows is in the building by the way,' Greg said to Elizabeth. She rolled her eyes and huffed. 'Well he would have to come and put his oar in at some point wouldn't he? Oversee this investigation, you know, tell us all what to do when we've all already been tasked anyway.'

Superintendent Timothy Meadows was not liked. He had risen through the ranks impressively quickly due to his academic ability but had spent very little time actually on the ground running and leading investigations. Consequently, whilst his legal knowledge was encyclopedic, his policing skills were somewhat lacking. He had failed to garner any respect from the detectives that worked under him due to his lack of policing experience and sometimes irrational and unnecessary orders, which he was only too happy to bark out from beneath the comparative safety of the crown on his epaulettes. He had upset nearly everyone in the briefing room at some point in his career and unlike the detectives who were expected to forgive and forget, Tim Meadows harboured grudges that lasted years. When someone was in his sights, he would make their life very uncomfortable.

'Thought that little missive would cheer you up. He's with the DI.'

As if on cue the superintendent and DI Scott walked into the briefing room. Meadows strode to a seat at the front of the room, his substantial bulk looming large in a room made small by the volume of officers present. DI Scott stood at the front of the room facing them.

'Morning,' he said.

Murmured greetings echoed round the room in response. Robert cast his eyes around the office, his gaze flitting from weary officer to weary officer. It was only four days since David Saunders had been murdered, but it already felt like this investigation had been running for weeks. They'd all been working flat out, desperately scrabbling for clues.

So far, they had absolutely nothing. He'd already been told by DC Lane that the CCTV, which could have provided them with a picture of the killer, was useless. Nothing of any use had come back from the lab either.

Of the samples taken that had been sufficient to provide a DNA profile, not one of them matched any of those stored on the database, and the samples could relate to any number of guests or staff members who had been in the room, so they were as good as useless on their own. Eventually though, the samples could be used for comparison against the suspect, if they ever apprehended the killer, to show that they had been in that hotel room, but they were useless in assisting in identification.

From David Saunder's employer they had discovered that he was well liked, respected, good at his job and had numerous clients on his books. However, on the night in question, his diary did not indicate any appointment in the evening. Wherever he had been and whatever he had been doing, it had not been business related, despite the papers found in his bag in the hotel room.

Mrs Saunders had not been particularly forthcoming either with regards to her husbands sexual preferences. He had wanted her to say: 'Yes, he's into bondage and frequents all sorts of clubs!' But of course, she hadn't.

Where he had met the killer was still unknown. What he had been doing prior to meeting the killer was still unknown. Whether the killer was a man or a woman was still unknown. They still knew absolutely fuck all.

As DI Scott set about tasking his detectives with their enquiries for the day under the watchful eye of Superintendent Meadows, he couldn't help but feel that the whole exercise was a waste of time, they were clutching at straws; they had no investigative leads whatsoever and were just going through the motions.

He felt that the killer was mocking them. The lack of clues in this case was in itself a clue; this killer was not likely to get caught unless he, or she, fucked up. They were too methodical, careful and clean. The Golden Hour in which most leads and clues came to light was long gone, all trails were now cold. It wasn't looking good.

Robert managed to muster up just enough enthusiasm to sound convincing as he reeled off actions to the team, giving them enquiries to undertake so that they could say they'd been done, not really because he thought anything would actually come of them. As the last detectives filed out the office door, he looked across at Meadows. Surprisingly, the smug git actually looked impressed.

****

Louise sang along to the tunes bellowing out of her car stereo as she hammered down the M4. She had decided late the night before, after the awards do, that she would drive down to surprise Steve first thing Saturday morning. When he'd told her at the restaurant that he had booked a cottage, he had given her the name of the place. After a quick internet search, she had quickly obtained the full address and postcode.

With said postcode now tapped into her satnav she was an hour into her journey. Four and a half hours to go, Tim the Tom Tom estimated; but Tim the Tom Tom was a law abiding citizen who did not operate above the speed limit and could not account for Louise's penchant for speed.

Last night at the awards do, she'd told Ben about the weird visions she'd been having and this morning she somehow felt lighter. It was as if she had shed an invisible burden, as if telling someone - without them judging her as insane - had banished her own fears regarding her sanity. She was her mother's daughter, but that didn't mean that she was also a nut, did it? Although the visions were still somewhat worrying to say the least, this morning, as she drove down towards Cornwall and her beloved, she felt on top of the world.

It was a beautiful sunny day, and Louise revelled in the warmth against her skin. She drove with the car windows open, long hair flying around her head like octopus tentacles, sun glasses perched on her nose and a strapless maxi dress bunched up over her knees. She'd already had the thumbs up from one lorry driver, his raised driving position offering him a perfect view of her long, athletic legs. She'd smiled sweetly at him and hit the accelerator, speeding away from him with glee.

God she felt good. She wished she could feel like this every day, bottle up the feeling and let out little whiffs of elation every time she felt blue. Thinking about it now, as she sped along, she decided she had been a little out of sorts lately, even before her first vision, if that was the best way to describe it and she still wasn't sure it was; a kind of melancholy had settled over her.

She presumed it was due to over work, the stresses of her promotion and the lack of time off, which was no one's fault but her own. Ben offered her the time off, she just failed to take it, always finding an excuse to stay at work. There was always this deadline, or that deadline, or this article to edit, that person to chase up.

In some ways her attitude was slightly megalomaniacal, she mused. What did she think would happen if she took some time off? The magazine would suddenly crumble and fade into nothing? She knew she was important to the company, but at the same time she also knew that it would survive quite well without her. The thought displeased Louise. She liked to feel valuable.

Maybe her ambition was half the problem, she thought. Striving for perfection was wearing her out. Who was perfect? Could anyone ever be perfect? Wouldn't perfection be boring, and who decided what perfection was?

'Deep Lou. Very deep,' she said aloud to herself, with a smile.

She had opened up to Steve a little on Friday night, and it had felt quite good, but also scary. She loved him, but she was also afraid of him, afraid of the potential pain he could cause her. She sighed and pulled the car into the slow lane so she could light a cigarette. She considered herself a non-smoker, but occasionally she felt the urge. Today was one of those days.

As she reflected, she inhaled deeply, the end of the cigarette glowing brightly, the wind from the open car windows causing the tobacco to burn faster. Someone had once told her that if you lived in fear of what could happen, you wouldn't be living at all, as you would never do anything. Words of wisdom which she was trying hard to apply to her life. And why she was allowing Steve snippets of her heart and soul.

Her mind wandered to Ben Matthews. She was still angry at him for making her draft the 'list of doom.' As of Monday morning, 20 people's lives would be turned upside down. One of those people was Derek Cooper, the only member of the editorial team to feature on the list, because she had wanted to try to balance the losses across the departments. Derek was the sub-editor who had been vying for her position 6 months earlier. Her promotion over him had always irked him. Louise just hoped that Ben was true to his word and no one discovered she had drafted the list, otherwise Derek would assume he was on it just because Louise didn't like him. The feeling was mutual, she knew, and although one small part of her was relieved that he would be gone as of Monday, she mostly felt guilty that it was because of her that this was the case.

She threw her cigarette butt out the window after checking her side mirrors for motorcyclists. She didn't want to be responsible for a fag butt flying into a biker's jacket and causing who knew what sort of damage. Manoeuvring back into the fast lane, Louise put her foot down, the speedometer needle creeping up towards ninety. She glanced at the Tomtom. Four hours to go. She smiled to herself visualising Steve's face when he saw her at the front door. He was certainly going to be surprised. What Louise didn't know as she happily drove down the M4, was that so was she.

Chapter XII

The phone was ringing but of course when Mark Faversham went to answer it, it wasn't in the cradle on the hallway table. He stood looking at the cradle for a second; ringing phone, whereabouts unknown.

'Where's the bloody phone Peter?' Mark shouted, as he overturned cushions on the sofa looking for the ringing device. He moved to the living room table, lifting various papers and magazines, getting more and more frustrated. After receiving no reply from Peter, he shouted again: 'Peter! Where is it? You were on the phone earlier. Where've you put it, you twat?'

Moving into the kitchen he finally located it underneath a dish cloth.

'Idiot!' he shouted for Peter's benefit, as he pressed the answer button and placed the phone against his ear.

Mark Faversham and Peter Reiley were best friends. They'd grown up together, gone to university together and were now sharing a flat in the suburbs of London. They were more like brothers than friends. They were both high flyers; Mark worked in the City as an investment banker and Peter was a corporate lawyer. Together they rented a plush residence in Richmond and although they each earnt enough money to live alone, they enjoyed sharing, still clinging on to the vestiges of the bachelor lifestyles they had enjoyed at university.

'Hello?' Mark said into the handset, opening the fridge and extracting a large carton of orange juice as he listened to the voice on the other end of the phone. He opened the container with one hand and took a large gulp straight from the carton. He only did it because he knew it annoyed Peter.

'I don't know where you got this number from, but I suggest you remove it from any list you have. I don't need insurance and I don't need you calling me on a Saturday morning, got it?' he said moodily, hanging up the phone as Peter padded into the kitchen, naked but for a towel wrapped around his waist, small beads of water dripping off his torso, black hair slicked back.

'Did you shout something earlier?' he asked, 'I was in the shower.' He picked up the juice carton and poured himself a large glass.

'Yeah, I was looking for the phone. Fucking telesales. They really piss me off. You spend ages looking for the phone because you're bloody flat mate doesn't put it back where it belongs and when you do finally find it, it's some bloody tart trying to sell insurance.'

Peter just smirked at him, dripping beads of water onto the linoleum floor.

'By the way, I'm off to that club I told you about tonight for some fun and games,' Mark said.

'Oh, one of those nights, eh?' Peter looked amused. He leaned against the kitchen work top and grinned.

'Yes one of those nights. You should come; it's a lot of fun.' Mark grabbed the carton and took another large swig.

'Pleb,' said Peter with disdain, wrinkling his

nose for emphasis.

'Prude,' replied Mark, with a wink.

'I'm not a prude, I just don't see the attraction in dressing up like a rubber, whipping some randoms and being called 'Master.' Besides, Melanie is more than enough woman for me.'

Melanie, Peter's long term girlfriend, was a sweet woman, but bloody boring as far as Mark was concerned. She was also another reason Mark and Peter shared the flat. If they weren't living together, Melanie would want Peter to move in with her and he just wasn't quite ready.

Mark laughed. 'You have no idea and you really shouldn't judge until you've tried it. Talking about Melanie, aren't you going to see her this weekend?'

'Yep. Be out of here in a bit so you'll have the place to yourself. I'm going to go to work from hers on Monday so I won't be back here until Monday evening.'

'Ok, so Monday, squash?'

'If you're still up for it after your weekend of hedonism!' answered Peter.

'I'll be up for it. I don't know what you think I get up to, but I am sure the version in your head is far more depraved and sordid than my reality. You really should come one night,' Mark suggested.

'The less I know the better, as far as I'm concerned. Keeping your dirty little secret is hard enough without knowing all the details!'

'Fine, up to you. Have fun this weekend won't you. I know I will!' Mark returned the drink's carton to the fridge. 'Right, got a few things to do…' He strolled out of the kitchen.

'Off to polish your PVC? Oil your chains?'
Peter called after him.

'Ha ha, very funny, you twat,' came the
fading reply as Mark retreated to his room, closing
the door behind him.

****

Janet sat on the large bed in the master
bedroom, which until recently had been her and
David's favourite place to spend their time when the
house was empty. Now as she sat there looking at
the vast wardrobe which housed David's suits and
shirts, she felt nothing but emptiness. She couldn't
believe that he was gone. It was now just her and the
kids.

Part of her was so angry; how could he go
off and get himself killed? The rest of her was just
immensely sad. She would never again see his smile,
touch his face or smell his scent. Never again feel his
loving touch, argue with him over trivial nonsense or
laugh with him over even more nonsense.

She let the tears fall freely from her eyes;
there was no need to hide them now that she was
alone. Charlie and Megan were still in bed; it was if
their bodies were coping with the grief through
sleep. They'd never slept so long and this morning
Janet was grateful. She needed a little time on her
own to grieve. She hadn't cried properly since she'd
been told the news. She had to be strong for the
children. She'd lost her husband but they'd lost their
father and nothing could replace a father.

The tears flowed thick and fast, her eyes
were sore, her cheeks were burning. His clothes
hung there, mocking her. Suddenly she rose and

walked over to the wardrobe. Maybe his scent still lingered on some of the suits? Maybe she would be able to smell him?

She delicately touched the arm of one of his suits, her hand running over the fabric, tugging gently at the sleeve. He was gone, gone forever. She began to sob, the tears choking her, sticking in her throat. She pressed her face against the fabric, her arms grabbing hold of his clothing, as if the contact would bring him back to her.

'David, oh David,' she murmured.

She fell into the closet, pulling the rail down with her, her late husband's suits and shirts covering her. She sat there, in a crumpled, sobbing heap as Megan opened the bedroom door.

'Mummy? Are you ok?' Megan ran over to the wardrobe and threw herself into her mother's arms.

'It's ok Mummy. We'll take care of you now daddy's gone,' Megan said, her childish voice and sentiment breaking Janet's heart.

She wrapped her arms around Megan and pulled her close, kissing her forehead. As she placed her arms around her daughter, gathering Megan and clothes in her embrace she felt something inside one of David's jacket pockets. With Megan's face buried in her bosom she gently extracted the item. Suddenly the tears stopped. She felt nothing but astonishment and confusion that her husband, who she loved, whose memory she cherished and who she trusted implicitly, had been keeping secrets from her.

****

The last stretch of the journey to the cottage felt like it had taken forever. The closer she got to Steve the more excited Louise had become and the longer the minutes had felt. Now, she had arrived.

Steve's car was parked in front of the cottage, gleaming in the sunlight. She reversed her own car into a space next to it, wound up the windows and stepped out, bare legs, long and lithe, briefly exposed before the fabric of her long dress fell and covered them. Her hair sparkled in the warm sun as she ran her hands through it before stretching languorously.

The cottage was one of four in a small cul-de-sac, close enough together to know you had neighbours, but far enough apart for privacy. She noticed an elderly couple sitting outside the front of the neighbouring cottage to the left, separated from the one Steve had rented by a patch of grass and flowers. She gave them a cheery wave and was pleased when they waved back with big beaming smiles.

How nice.

She skipped up the steps to the front door of Steve's cottage and remarked that it was all closed up, the curtains drawn and no evidence of life on the inside that she could discern. She guessed that Steve was probably on the beach, surfing. He'd probably gone out early and not bothered to draw back the curtains. Such a blokey thing to do, she mused.

She knocked on the front door, not expecting a response. After waiting a suitable amount of time to allow Steve to come to the door if he was inside, she tried the handle on the off chance the door was open. To her surprise, it was. She went in.

The interior of the cottage was dark, but she

could see enough to tell it was large, spacious and well kept. The living room was well furnished, a plush sofa and two equally plush arm chairs positioned around a large oak coffee table. No TV. She wondered what Steve had made of that.

At the back of the living room were two full-length patio doors, long curtains pulled almost shut but between which she could see a wood-decked terrace. Bet that's romantic of an evening, she thought, noting that it was West-facing and as such would catch the evening sun. She was touched that Steve had wanted to bring her to such a romantic place.

Louise called out for Steve as she continued her progression through the cottage. Into the kitchen now, round dining table, modern appliances and two used wine glasses on the draining board. She felt suspicion creeping up on her like icy fingers wrapping themselves around her neck, constricting her breathing. Did he have company? Had he brought someone else here?

'Steve!' she shouted, louder this time. 'You in here?'

She heard movement down the corridor, someone walking towards her from where she presumed the bedroom to be.

'Lou? What are you doing here?' Steve came into the kitchen, his hair ruffled, his eyes sleepy, wearing a pair of shorts and a rumpled T-shirt obviously pulled on in a hurry.

He smiled at her but she detected what she thought was a hint of nervousness, like a child caught with his hand in the biscuit jar after his mother had told him not to spoil his appetite.

'Who have you got here?' she demanded,

her face stern, anger bringing red spots to her cheeks.

'Oh nice to see you too. You've just got here and already you're accusing me of something!' Steve replied curtly.

'Two wine glasses, Steve,' she said accusingly, pointing toward the kitchen sink.

'Yeah, one was chipped so I used another one.'

She grabbed the glass and inspected it furious. There was indeed a small chip on the rim. She suddenly felt foolish and guilty for having such a suspicious mind. Why did she always jump to negative conclusions?

'Steve... I...' she began.

'You know what Lou? Don't even say you're sorry. I'm getting so sick of your accusations,' Steve said moodily.

'I am sorry. I drove down here today because I felt bad about having turned you down. I wanted to make it up to you by surprising you, and I've already messed it up. I get so wound up. I truly am sorry.' She moved towards him and stroked his cheek.

Steve pulled away from her and moved towards the corridor, blocking her exit from the kitchen. Again, she felt suspicion creeping up on her.

'It is good to see you Lou. I am surprised you're here, but it's a nice surprise. I just wish you weren't so quick to judge me. And I wish you'd told me you were coming. I would have made myself more presentable,' he joked, his tone softening.

Louise smiled at him and moved in for a hug. He wrapped his arms around her and kissed her hair.

'So, what's your explanation for being half-dressed in the middle of the day? Were you napping like an old man?'

'Yeah, I just came over really tired. Think fatigue has just caught up with me a bit. The bottle of wine I drank last night probably didn't help either,' he replied, holding her to his chest.

'Hmmm. Probably,' she mused.

Louise pulled away slightly from Steve's chest and looked up at him, her eyes searching; she couldn't shake the feeling that he was lying to her and she had learnt long ago to always trust her instincts.

'The cottage seems lovely. You going to show me the rest of it?' she asked.

The question was innocent enough but she saw something in his eyes when she asked it, a flicker of apprehension, of guilt.

'Yes of course. First though come to the terrace, I want to show you the view,' he stuttered.

'No, I'd like to see the bedroom actually.'

She pushed past him into the corridor.

'You still don't believe me? I'm here alone!' he called after her.

She heard him mumble 'shit' under his breath as she continued towards the bedroom; she knew then, without a doubt, that there was another woman in the cottage.

'Lou! Don't, please don't!'

She opened the bedroom door with a hard shove and stormed in. The room was dark as the curtains were drawn but her eyes immediately spotted the outline of a naked female form lying in the bed on her back, bare breasts and stomach on display. The form moved and sat up, shoulder length brown hair falling across her face.

As her eyes adjusted to the dark and she began to recognize the features of the female's face, her stomach knotting with the realization. Louise felt her legs go weak and she put a hand onto the wall to steady herself.

Melissa, looked at her, no expression of guilt, surprise or remorse on her face. Just that same smile, that fucking smile she turned on for customers at the restaurant, that supercilious 'I-know-something-you-don't know smile.'

Louise was aware that Steve was standing behind her as she felt her anger mounting like a torrent of hot lava bubbling through her veins. She suddenly felt removed from herself and heard herself say in a voice she barely recognised as her own: 'Get up and put some fucking clothes on.'

Melissa just looked at her and made no attempt to move.

'Melissa, if you don't put some clothes on right now, I am going to throw you out of here naked,' Louise repeated, her voice calm and contained, her rage simmering just below eruption levels.

'Lou...' Steve began. Louise turned around and shot him a venomous look.

'Don't say a word Steve!'

Melissa lay back on the bed, placing an arm beneath her head in an arrogant, mocking posture.

'I'm not going anywhere, I'm an invited guest,' she sneered back at Louise.

'You fucking bitch.' She turned her back on Melissa and confronted Steve.

He looked scared, she could see him swallowing hard. That he was scared pleased her.

'To think I trusted you and you made me feel guilty for thinking ill of you. No wonder you're knackered, sleeping with me, sleeping with her! The lies come so easily to you, don't they? You're all the same. Lying, cheating bastards! No one woman's ever enough, is she?'

'I think actually, it's just that you're not enough Louise,' mocked Melissa from the bed.

Louise spun on her heel and ran over to the bed, anger sweeping over her in a maddening tsunami-type wave.

'Still haven't put your clothes on, no? Well now it's too fucking late!' she screamed at Melissa, noting with satisfaction that the smug expression had dropped from her face and had been replaced with one of fear.

Louise grabbed Melissa by the hair and dragged her from the bed, naked legs flailing, breasts jiggling, looking totally undignified. Melissa screamed in pain, her hands grabbing at Louise's wrists in an effort to wrench herself free from her tight grasp.

'Louise, for God's sake!' shouted Steve.

Louise was enraged, she couldn't stop herself. She'd never felt so much anger, she couldn't see properly, she couldn't think straight. All she knew was she had to get rid of this woman, humiliate her and hurt her. She wanted Melissa to feel a fraction of the pain she was feeling at that moment.

She pulled on Melissa's hair, dragging her forcefully down the corridor on all fours. She could hear Steve shouting at her to stop, his hands on her shoulders to try and control her. She shrugged him off easily and continued to drag Melissa through the cottage by her hair. She was so angry, so pumped, that dragging Melissa seemed effortless.

'Louise, let go, please! You're really hurting me!' Melissa wailed.

'Good! How could you Steve? With her! And you Melissa, don't you care at all that he's with me? Feel good does it taking someone else's man?' Louise's voice was hard.

She continued to drag Melissa down the corridor, not caring that Melissa's dignity was on display or that she was in agony.

'Louise, please, please…' she pleaded.

'Quit whining you pathetic creature!'

They'd reached the front door now and Louise wrenched it open with her left hand, the right still wrapped in Melissa's hair. She pulled Melissa to her feet, body bent over, breasts dangling. With a hard shove, she pushed Melissa through the door, satisfied, as Melissa fell onto the steps, naked and sniveling.

She noticed the old couple had stood up to watch the scene. She slammed the door shut and turned her attention on Steve. He stood behind her, his hands raised, palms open in submission. Melissa started to bang on the front door.

'Let me in! I'm naked!' she begged.

Louise ignored her and just stood looking at Steve, her eyes cold and hard, her chest heaving from exertion. She felt hatred and anger and pain; she wanted to hurt him, she wanted to hear him cry out in agony.

'Lou… I'm sorry. I didn't want to come down here alone. She means nothing to me…' Steve began.

'How long?' Louise panted.

'What? Why does that matter? She means nothing, you have to believe me!' Steve replied.

'How long, Steve?' she shouted, her body shaking as she fought to control the urge to hit him. Melissa continued to bang on the front door.

'A few months,' he said, pusillanimously.

She snorted derisively.

'You lying, cheating bastard. I loved you, I trusted you more than anyone. I gave myself to you and this is how you repay me? Jealous of my commitment to work, jealous of my ability... You are a fucking male whore and one day you'll get what you deserve!' she shouted at him, before adding quietly: 'You've broken my heart. I knew I should never have let you in.' She looked him in the eyes; Steve bowed his head in shame.

Louise yanked open the front door and shouted at Melissa who was still wailing to be let in and banging on the door: 'Fucking shut up, bitch!'

Melissa backed away from the door as Louise stormed out through it.

'Don't ever come near me again Steve,' she yelled over her shoulder, 'and as for you Melissa...'

She drew back her right arm and punched Melissa in the face, catching her just below her right eye. Melissa screamed in pain.

'Steve she hit me! She hit me!' Melissa wailed, a red mark already swelling beneath her eye. Louise vaguely noticed that the elderly couple were still there, covering their mouths with their hands, looking aghast.

She walked quickly to her car and climbed in, her body still trembling with anger and rage. The engine roared as she drove away at speed, her tyres kicking up small stones and dust from the graveled drive way. A cloud of dust enveloped Melissa's naked form as she stood clutching at her face, whilst

Steve stood there dumbstruck, watching as she drove away.

As she veered away from the cottage, she continued to watch her beloved Steve in her rear view mirror, his image jumping with the motion of the car, trembling like her body. She exhaled deeply as she felt the first hot tear run down her cheek, its slow progression across her skin leaving a cool, wet trail. As soon as Louise was out of sight of the cottage, she pulled the car over, placed her head on her arms on the steering wheel and cried as she hadn't cried since she was a child.

Chapter XIII

It was early afternoon and the building was quiet. Not many people came in on a Saturday – unless of course they were working on a murder. DI Robert Scott sat hunched over his desk, sheets of paper strewn before him, highlighter pen poised over the sheet he was currently inspecting.

After tasking everyone with their duties earlier that morning, he had finished off the briefing by telling them that once their task for that day was done, they should go home, get some rest and that he didn't expect to see anyone back in the office until Monday, unless of course, there was a major break in the case. He'd arranged for some officers to cover the core team on Sunday, which meant they could all enjoy a day to themselves and try to get some sleep.

Robert was looking forward to his day off as he hadn't seen his wife since the case had begun other than to grunt at her as he rolled in and out of bed. Perhaps they could take a trip down to the coast if the weather was nice? The sea air would do them both good and he felt a hankering for real fish 'n' chips in paper, served and enjoyed as they should be on the beach.

Most of his detectives had rung in to say they were done for the day. Tony Jessop had taken a brief statement from another of David Saunder's former colleagues, nothing of any evidential value had come of it; Peter Jackman had made enquiries with the local taxi firms to see if Mr Saunders had booked any cab, he hadn't; Elizabeth Lane had returned to some of the pubs around the hotel, showing David Saunders' photograph to staff asking if anyone had seen him on the night in question - still waiting results; Greg Hampton had been sifting through Mr Saunders' client list and slowly contacting them in turn to ask when they had last seen him. The remaining five DCs under DI Scott's command were occupied obtaining statements from everyone else that had not yet been spoken to at the hotel.

It was unlikely that any of these tasks would in itself identify the killer, but any one of them could provide a simple, little, seemingly trivial clue which could help focus the direction of the enquiry. All the statements would be collated on Monday and any commonality, discrepancies or clues would be highlighted so that other investigative actions could be raised.

Robert rubbed his eyes wearily. The letters on the page were starting to blend into one as he felt his eyelids getting heavy. He just wanted to get through the latest lab and pathology report before he called it a day, ensured all his officers were off duty and went home to his wife.

His shoulders were tense and he stretched cat-like in the chair, arms above his head, back arched, trying to ease out the tension. He continued to read...

'The mutilation to the deceased probably did not occur post-mortem; the victim would likely have been semi-conscious, although probably drifting in and out due to the loss of blood and sentient, although to what capacity cannot be established....'

'Jesus Christ,' Robert said to himself aloud, imaging the agony Mr Saunders must have been in during his last few moments of life.

'The initial trauma appears to have been to the eye, and was likely made by a slim, cylindrical, pointed article administered to the eye with force. The blow initially pushed the eyeball back into the orbital socket, visible from the bruising to the brain in this location, before pulling the eye out of the socket. The optic nerve did not break, although it is stretched, presumably from when the eye was pulled out.

The eyeball itself is punctured; there is a deep, circular-shaped wound which penetrates through the sclera, aqueous humor and ciliary body. It is impossible to determine exactly how far into the eye the instrument penetrated, but it did not reach the choroid at the back of the eye as this is unmarked. Fluids from the eye, and blood, would have rapidly trickled into the orbital socket, quickly filling the deceased's mouth and throat. It is doubtful he would have been able to use his vocal chords as the fluid would have filled the buccal cavity and oesophagus, causing him to choke...'

'Poor fucking bastard,' Robert muttered, glancing up for a second to grab his white coffee, then deciding that his stomach couldn't quite handle the warm, milky fluid. He deposited the mug back on his desk. His brain was too full of bloody images, wounded eyeballs seeping vitreous humor, dangling from stretched optic nerves and lips bubbling out bodily fluids.

'Apart from this wounding to the eye, the rest of the deceased's face is unmarked. There is bruising to the skin around the deceased's wrists and ankles from where rope ligatures have been fastened. The bruising to the wrists is significant and indicates that the deceased was struggling to try and remove the ligatures pre-mortem...'

No fucking shit

'The deceased's torso and limbs have not been subjected to trauma. The genitals, on the other hand, have been completely removed; the penis and testicles have been cut away. The tearing to the skin and the lacerations to the bodily tissue in this area indicate that a bladed article, such as a knife, or other sharp edged tool, was used and the blade does not appear to have been serrated for the cuts are smooth. However, whilst the cuts are smooth, there is no precision in their infliction; multiple lacerations surround the area, which suggests hurried, rapid movements...'

Well, that was good at least, mused Robert. Imprecise incisions probably meant that the killer was lacking in experience. He just hoped it wasn't the handiwork of a serial killer in the making; the removal of the genitals smacked of 'killer's trophy' to him, one of the hallmarks of such killers. Mr Saunders' privates hadn't been found at the scene along with rest of him, so the killer must have taken them.

'Profuse bleeding would have ensued from this wound and it likely that this loss of blood and related body shock is ultimately what caused death.'

The report then went on to discuss toxicology. Blood-alcohol levels in Mr Saunders' body suggested he would have been pretty drunk, but not totally inebriated and there was no evidence of illegal narcotics, or other foreign bodies in the blood. Then at the bottom of the report was the usual caveat explaining that the details contained within it had been formed based on the evidence presented to the pathologist by the cadaver, there was always margin for error and that the evidence obtained from the autopsy was true to the best of the expert's belief and experience...blah, blah, blah. The usual 'arse-covering-you-can't-sue-me-if-I'm-wrong' blurb, with which Robert was only too familiar. The police had an 'arse-covering' caveat for everything they did; at least they did once they reached a certain rank – usually chief inspector level and above. Not so much protection was afforded to the officers on the ground.

Robert glanced up at the clock and noted that the afternoon was fast progressing into the evening. DC Lane hadn't called him yet to say how she'd got on with her pub enquiries, so he pulled out his mobile and dialled her number. Her phone rang a few times before going to voicemail, her clipped English accent telling the caller she was sorry she couldn't answer the phone but she would get back to them as soon as possible.

'Elizabeth, just wondering how you got on today with your enquiries. I'm assuming you didn't come up with anything, as if you had, I know you would have called. I'm leaving the office now but my mobile is on if you need to call about anything. By the way, when I said pub enquiries, I didn't mean go out on the piss, right? Only joking, although if you are, have one for me.'

He hung up the phone with a smirk. He had no doubt that Elizabeth had probably had a crafty drink or two, he certainly would have, but he also knew that she was professional above all else and would have made sure she got the job done first.

Robert placed the pathology report and autopsy photographs into his desk drawer, securely locking them away from prying eyes. If he got a move on, he'd have time to take Margaret out to dinner. He might even have a few drinks himself. He could certainly do with a moment to unwind.

Just as he was about to close the office door,

the phone on his desk started to ring. He stood motionless in the doorway, deliberating if he could reasonably pretend to himself that he hadn't heard it.

'Fuck it!' he swore, storming back to his desk, annoyed with himself for not leaving just a couple of minutes earlier. He was desperate for an evening with his wife and a good night's sleep.

He again briefly toyed with the idea of ignoring the call, but instead saw his hand reaching out to pick up the receiver.

'DI Scott, murder squad,' he barked gruffly into the handset.

The voice on the end of the phone was quiet and Robert was beginning to think it was a crank call when he heard a small sob and a whisper.

'Hello?' he said again, in a much calmer, more soothing voice. 'Can I help you?'

'DI Scott,' the voice eventually said after another brief pause. 'It's Mrs Saunders. I need to speak with you about my husband. There's something I think you should know.'

****

Elizabeth Lane was in the pub. She'd decided to have a drink after trawling around all the pubs within a mile radius of the hotel where Mr Saunders had been killed. DI Scott had told her to only visit the pubs within a half mile of the crime scene but she'd taken it upon herself to extend the radius of her task. She had so desperately wanted to find someone who recognized Mr Saunders and could provide some information, any information, relating to the night in question.

After hours of walking, jumping on and off the tube, and methodically traipsing around all the pubs meticulously marked on the map she had prepared earlier, and even to some that hadn't featured on it, she had finally given up and returned to the first pub on her list.

The Drunken Frog was barely a hundred meters from the hotel and it had seemed as good a place as any to call it a day and ring Greg to tell him to get down there for a little libation.

She'd spoken to him over an hour ago, but he had as yet failed to arrive. She called him again; he picked up on the first ring.

'Greg, get down here would you? I've been drinking now for an hour and a half on my own and the patrons of this fine establishment are starting to look at me funny. I think they think I'm on the pull!' Elizabeth moaned, mobile phone pressed against her ear with her shoulder, her hands circling the glass in front of her, wiping condensation from its surface.

'Well, unlike some people I know,' Greg replied over the phone, 'some of us have been busy working on a murder enquiry, not visiting pubs!' he teased.

'You cheeky git!' she blurted out, pretending to be offended.

'Yeah well you know, when you're an old sweat like me, you can't be taking any shit off young usurpers…' he laughed.

'Look Greg, don't piss me about, ok? I'm knackered, my feet hurt and I'm not in the best of moods. Too many rejections will do that to a person.'

'Thought you were used to rejection? Still single?' he teased her some more.

'You fuc…!'

'Now, now officer Lane. I hope you weren't about to use language unbecoming of a lady?' Greg butted in before she could finish her sentence.

Elizabeth sat open mouthed, thinking of a witty retort when Greg spoke again.

'What do you want to drink?'

'You know if you want to buy someone a drink it usually helps if you're actually in the pub with them, Hampton.'

'Turn around. I'm at the bar.'

She turned and sure enough, there he was smiling at her, mobile still stuck to his ear. He gave her an exaggerated wave.

'God, you're such a twat.'

She cut the call and got up to join Greg at the bar. He was still snickering to himself when she marched up to him and gave him a playful punch on the arm.

'It's been over an hour! What took you so bloody long?' she questioned. 'Seriously, that guy in the corner kept winking and smiling at me. I thought I was going to have to arrest him for being seriously weird.'

'Weird cos he fancies you? Hmm, then again, I see what you mean. Who in their right mind…?'

She dropped her jaw in mock disbelief: 'My God! How rude! I'll have another vodka as you're buying.'

Greg ordered their drinks and then the two detectives moved to one of the tables furthest away from the other punters to enable them to talk with relative freedom.

The Drunken Frog wasn't particularly busy

yet; there were enough drinkers to make the pub feel lively but not so many that it felt crowded. The clients were a mixture – business people in suits, couples in evening wear sitting cozily together, tourists in loose comfortable clothing, cameras slung around their necks talking animatedly with fingers jabbing at open maps spread on the table in front of them.

Greg and Elizabeth sat across from each other at a small two-person table towards the back of the pub. Elizabeth sat facing the entrance to the premises, as she liked to be able to see who was coming in and out. Greg sat opposite her and assumed his usual relaxed, open-legged posture, one arm draped casually over the back of the chair. They chatted amiably for a few minutes before the conversation came back to the murder enquiry.

'Did you give Robert an update yet?' Greg asked, taking a large gulp of cider and smacking his lips together appreciatively.

'What update? I didn't see the point of calling him for nothing.' Elizabeth sighed, 'Besides, he's probably buggered off by now, don't you think?'

Greg shrugged noncommittally.

'I just wish we'd get some sort of break through. He's got two young kids you know. What a way to lose your dad,' she continued.

'You going soft on me?' Greg asked.

'Stop pretending to be so untouched, Hampton. I know you are. I mean, the guy goes to work, tells his wife he's working late, and then the next she hears is us telling her he's dead and not only is he dead but he's actually been murdered. On top of that it looks like he was cheating on her and died strapped to a hotel bed, exposed and vulnerable, and then his sausage and brussels are hacked off never to be seen again.'

Greg spurted cider from the edges of his glass, gagging in mid-swig.

'I've never heard it referred to like that before, but I get the imagery. And you're right. I'm not untouched. Just don't dwell on it is all I'll say to you. We have no breaks at the moment, but that doesn't mean we won't solve this.'

'Yeah, I know. Just feeling a bit down is all. One of my lows, you know what I'm like.'

'A dip in the Great Elizabeth's bio-rhythms,' Greg smiled at her.

Elizabeth had struggled with depression for years and after a series of drugs, herbal remedies and counseling sessions, had decided she was better off without them, choosing instead to manage her 'episodes,' as she called them, by talking to Greg and working out. The exercise helped her focus her mind and unleash her inner anger. It did mean she had bouts of melancholy, but Greg was used to them and she had learnt how to manage them effectively to prevent herself from completely going over the edge.

'I was thinking, the penis thing is weird, right?' Elizabeth began.

'Oh here we go...' Greg rolled his eyes in mock boredom. He was also used to Elizabeth's sometimes random but variably interesting psychological theories. He could feel one brewing; she had that deep-thinking expression on her face.

'What would make someone remove the genitalia, the male genitalia, of the person they have killed? What fuels that desire? What purpose does it have?'

'Why does it have to have a purpose? The

killer is probably just a total nutter or was spaced out on some form of narcotic…' Greg dragged out the word nar-co-tic for effect.

'Don't be naïve. Everything has a purpose Greg, even if it's subconscious. And this murder was way to methodical to be the work of a drug-crazed loon and you know it. Look at the lack of clues for a start and the props that were introduced to the scene. It wasn't random, it was planned. The killer is smart, methodical and obviously disturbed. People aren't just born like that, they become like that…'

'Why do you have to theorise everything?' Greg asked with a sigh. 'And what are you getting at?' curious in spite of himself.

'Well, you know I love reading about psychology?'

'Trying to work out why you're such a nut, yes I know.'

Elizabeth shot him an evil look.

'Quite a lot of importance is put on sexuality in human development and the significance of genitals in this development. Look at Freud… he gave us the Oedipus complex, the Electra complex, the concepts of Penis Envy and Castration Anxiety…'

'The what and the what? And so what?'

'Well, look at the circumstances, Greg. Male killed and genitals removed. Is it castration anxiety being manifested via the removal of a fellow male's bits, thereby ensuring the safety of one's own penis? Or perhaps a latent homosexual who has been bullied or abused for his sexuality? Unable to come to terms with the conflicting emotions, does he resort to chopping off the offending appendages that he craves so much?'

Greg unconsciously pulled his legs together and sat up straighter in his chair.

'Or, is it a female with penis envy? Chop off the bits because "I don't have a dick and I want one because people with dicks seemingly 'rule' the world." Although you know my views on that! The penis is a powerful symbol, Greg.'

'You have truly lost it this time....' Greg shook his head. 'Where do you get this shit?'

'All I'm saying is that this is not our usual murder. It doesn't seem to have the same sort of motives we're usually trained to look for, you know? Money, jealousy, crime of passion, honour killing... Where does this one fit in?'

'Well crime of passion in the non-traditional sense springs to mind...'

Elizabeth ignored him.

'I think this is motivated by something on our killer's subconscious level because the usual motivations just don't seem to be there. And I think it's a woman.'

'Oh come on! How many female killers do you know other than the ones that are trying to escape abusive husbands or do it by accident?' Greg scoffed.

'As you ask I shall bore you with what I do know. Mary Ann Cotton here in the UK back in the 1870s. She killed over 20 people for their insurance money and was hanged in 1873. Traditional motive. From the Great US-of-A, Belle Guiness. She was never caught and she is reported to have killed over 40 people over two decades, usually for insurance money. Good going huh? Another traditionally motivated killer.'

Greg just stared at Elizabeth in amazement.

'You want more?' Elizabeth continued, 'Marybeth Tinning; she killed her own children, although to be fair she was diagnosed with Münchausen syndrome by proxy. But if you want a really interesting case, look at Mary bell, and I know you've heard of her.'

'Yeah I have. The 11-year-old girl who killed two little boys in the 1960s,' Greg said, intrigued.

'Actually, she was ten when she killed the first boy, who was only four, and eleven at the time of the other murder. It was 1968. Also, not only did she strangle the two boys, she also carved her initial 'M' on the second one's stomach and – get this – mutilated his genitals. Not a traditionally motivated murder, is it?' Elizabeth sat back smugly having proved her point.

'Fuck me. You're bloody scary you are,' Greg said to her. 'So, you think we've got another Mary Bell type killer our hands?'

'Well it's a theory and it's not beyond the realms of possibility, is it?'

'I guess not. Why did the Mary Bell girl kill the boys then?'

'That detective Hampton, I do not know, although Bell did allege that her mother had tried to kill her and forced her to engage in sexual acts with men when she was only four. I'm guessing that has to be a pretty big mind-fuck.'

'Ok, so I'm following the theory, but there is no evidence at all it's a woman. Women do not do this sort of thing. It could be a bloke with the same issues as the Mary Bell girl.'

'Except David Saunders is not gay and I doubt would have got himself all stripped off and strung up like that for a bloke,' Elizabeth retorted.

'Good point.'

'Thank you.'

'Still not convinced though.'

'Greg, it is just a theory I've been running over in my little mind. But I bet you twenty quid it's a woman.'

Greg shook Elizabeth's hand and then smiled sweetly. 'I do believe it is your round,' he said draining the dregs of his glass and placing the empty receptacle on the table between them.

'Good job I don't have penis envy, eh? Working with all you men! You'd all be wearing metal pants!' Elizabeth laughed to herself, as she trotted over to the bar, taking the empty glasses with her.

'Mad as a fucking mongoose,' Greg said to himself, shaking his head.

Chapter XIV

The flat was dark, shadows crawled across the floor taking possession of the room as the descending sun succumbed to night. The soft strains of Moonlight Sonata on repeat whispered through the living room, a mellow undertone to the increasing gloom.

A figure sat curled up on the floor in the farthest corner of the room, her legs drawn up to her chest, arms wrapped around them, hugging the limbs close to her body, shrouded in the darkness.

Louise sat, her eyes moist, old tears dried on her pale cheeks, her makeup smudged and messy. She couldn't feel anything other than a numbness that had settled over her like a comforting blanket. The anger had gone, driven out of her system during the long drive home.

She pondered the turn of events, wondering what she had done to deserve this. She felt as if things had started to fall apart since her promotion six months ago. The hours she spent at work had increased and she had been so focused on her work that during the time she did spend with Steve he had often told her she seemed distracted, like she wasn't really there with him. She was in the room, but her mind was elsewhere, he'd said. Was this why Steve had turned to Melissa? Had she neglected him a little too much? Was this all her fault? How many people would tolerate coming second to their partner's work?

Work. The only place she felt safe and in control. Or at least she had until Ben had asked her to draft up the 'list of doom'. Was she being punished by God for ruining the lives of others? Except Louise didn't believe in God. No God would have willingly put one of His subjects through her traumatic life. Her mother sent to a looney bin, separated from her sister as they were ferried off to different foster homes, the years of broken and damaging relationships... Why would any god put someone through that? The devout would argue it was His plan, but Louise knew you made your own luck in life, you had to account for your own actions, take responsibility for yourself and rely on no one. She'd started to rely on Steve, or at least to trust that she could rely on him, and look at what had happened. He'd gone off with that fucking bitch, Melissa.

Now as she sat on the floor musing over her life and the events of the past few days, she felt somehow at peace. It was like a mini-epiphany. She knew now that she would never trust anyone, never let anyone in - ever. From now on, she would be granite, her public face a façade that no one would get beneath, no one would chip away at. Oddly, she felt relieved at her realisation.

'You're on your own Lou. Just you against the world,' she whispered to herself.

Just like always.

Suddenly Louise caught a movement in her peripheral vision, a shadow passing in front of the window. She looked up sharply, but couldn't see anything. Probably just a bird flying past, she mused. She resumed her former position, head on arms, curled up in a safe little ball.

Then she heard it, a faint laughter, a male's voice drifting to her ears. She cocked her head wondering where the sound was coming from. It sounded too close to be coming from the street, perhaps it was coming from the communal corridor?

The laughter was getting louder, it sounded like it was coming from within her own flat. She felt the hairs rise on the back of her neck, felt anxiety grip her stomach and her extremities start to tingle in anticipation. Slowly she stood up, her breath catching in her throat.

The laughter was loud now, a deep cackle that sounded more malignant than jovial, sinister laughter that chilled her to the core. Moving slowly across the room she listened, trying to work out the source of noise.

The kitchen. It was coming from her own kitchen.

Fear gripped her insides and she began to tremble gently. She was alone in the flat, how could laughter be coming from her kitchen? How had someone got in whilst she'd been sat there? Unless they'd been in the flat all along. It wasn't something you did upon returning home to your sanctuary, walk through and look for strangers lurking in your wardrobes – or kitchen.

Mustering up all her courage, she moved slowly towards the sound, picking up a heavy, ceramic vase from the small glass table at the end of the settee, thinking that she could use it as a weapon if she had to. She tried to control her breathing, afraid the sound of her gasps would alert the intruder. She approached the threshold to the kitchen and with a deep breath, peered around the door frame, one hand holding the vase high above her head.

She saw a man stood with his back to her. He was tall, over six feet and looked muscular, she could see the swell of his biceps, the outline of his shoulder blades through the tight white t-shirt he was wearing. His legs were clad in dark blue jeans and his body moved in time with his laughter, large shoulders rising up and down as he cachinnated.

He turned suddenly to look at her, causing Louise to step back with a gasp. His eyes were pale blue and cold as ice, his hair thick and black, sprinkled with grey around the sides, his lips full and drawn back over perfect white teeth. Louise guessed he was in his thirties, probably the higher end.

Finding her voice she demanded: 'Who the fuck are you and how the fuck did you get in here?'

The man just looked at her and continued to laugh. Louise was spooked and took another step back.

'Get out! Get out of my home!' she shouted at him, her voice trembling, belying her fear, her hand still raised, gripping the vase tightly.

He stopped laughing and just stood looking at her. She decided she preferred the laughter to this creepy silence.

'What do you want? There's nothing here worth stealing. Who are you?' she asked again.

The man smiled and opened his hands showing her palms that were scarlet.

Oh my God. Is that blood?

He stepped towards her and Louise closed her eyes aiming the vase at his head. She heard the vase crash to the floor and felt shards of ceramic skitter across the linoleum, skipping over her bare feet. She opened her eyes. The man was gone. The kitchen was empty except for the shattered vase.

Louise shook her head in dismay and walked slowly into the kitchen, oblivious to the broken shards cutting the soles of her feet. She turned around full circle. He had vanished. Her breath escaped in a long, drawn out exhalation. What had just happened? Had she just had another full blown hallucination?

As the adrenaline seeped away she felt the pain in her feet, saw the small trail of blood she was leaving on the floor as she moved around the kitchen. She grabbed a chair and sat down looking at her bloody soles.

Tears burst from her eyes in a sudden unexpected torrent; she felt so alone and broken. She wanted to speak to Steve, to tell him what had just happened, to hear his reassuring voice. Instead she ran into the living room and grabbed her car keys not knowing where she was going, but just knowing she needed to get out of the flat.

****

'For God's sake Hampton. How many times? Read my lips - I - do - not -want - a -curry!' Elizabeth mouthed exaggeratedly.

For the past hour Greg had been dropping hints that he wanted to go to one of their favourite curry houses to finish off the night and he was still pestering Elizabeth to go with him.

'Now stop going on about it. You're getting on my nerves!'

After steadily drinking for the past five hours, the two detectives had decided to call it a night, both feeling decidedly merry. They had drunk copious amounts of vodka and cider, eaten bar snacks and dissected the case, discussing possibilities and options, Elizabeth devising and making up new theories as they went along. All in all, it had been a good night, a good occasion to unwind. Neither of them had realised how uptight they had been until the alcohol had kicked in.

'So, you're not coming then?' Greg asked, adopting the tone of a petulant child.

'No, I'm not.'

'Fine, I'll go on my own then, like a poor, friendless, rejected man…'

'If the cap fits,' Elizabeth giggled.

'Yeah, right! Well, I'm off then. What you doing? Going home from here?' Greg asked, wanting to make sure Elizabeth was going to be ok getting home.

'I'm going to jump on the tube and then get the mainline. I'll get the twenty past midnight train probably. Might grab a pasty - oooh or a hot dog!' she replied, happily.

'Come for a curry! You shouldn't eat those hotdogs from those carts. They're disgusting! If they get dropped the seller just picks 'em up and chucks 'em back on the grill, usually using the same hand he's just used to scratch his nuts, or wipe his ass.'

'How poetic. I know but they're perfect for soaking up the booze.' She grinned.

'Suit yourself. See you Monday then.' Greg gave her a quick squeeze and set off in the direction of the tube, turning round briefly to give Elizabeth a wave.

Elizabeth watched Greg wander off then turned around, heading in the opposite direction. At the corner of the street she noted plumes of smoke emanating from what appeared to be a hotdog seller's cart. Marvelling at the coincidence, she walked towards the smoke, salivating as the smell of frying onions hit her nasal passages.

The hotdog seller was fat, sweaty and grubby, streaks of carbon blackened his face as he wiped his dripping brow with dirty hands. He'd chosen a good location to ply his trade; a couple of hotels, including the one David Saunders had been murdered in, and three pubs that Elizabeth could see. Lots of drunk punters, *like me*, and hotel guests to sell his over-priced, unhygienic but yummy hotdogs to.

She walked up to him and ordered her food, noting that despite his fat, wobbly body, he actually had quite an attractive face, despite the baldness, double chin and hair poking out of his nose. She chuckled.

'You alright love?' he asked with a grin, his expression clearly indicating that he was used to drunken customers and their drunken antics.

'Yes, thank you. I was just thinking about beer goggles. You know when alcohol makes people more attractive.' She smiled back.

'I know all about that my love. You should see some of the things some of the guys around here take home with them. It's the stuff of nightmares.'

Cos' you're god's gift Mr hotdog man?

'I've woken up to a few nightmares in my time!' Elizabeth snickered again, playing along with the banter. 'You must see some sights of an evening stood out here watching the world go by?'

'You wouldn't believe some of it. People can be very funny when they're drunk.' He gave her a wink, and expertly flipped her hotdog sausage.

'Indeed, although they can also be very annoying when you're not pissed with them. My mate Greg is a prime example. Love him to pieces normally, but he annoys the hell out of me when he's pissed and I'm not!'

'He your fella'?' asked hotdog man.

'Greg? No, he's someone I work with and a really good friend.'

Hotdog man nodded his head.

'You here most nights then?' continued Elizabeth.

'Usually a couple times a week. I move around a lot you know?'

Trying to keep away from police unlicensed, unhygienic hotdog man?

Elizabeth was hit by a flash of inspiration. 'You weren't here on Wednesday were you by any chance?'

'Wednesday? Yeah I was as it goes,' Hotdog man replied, handing Elizabeth her hotdog. She reached out and took the food then placed it on the edge of the cart, fishing around in her handbag for the photo of David Saunders she had been showing around at the pubs earlier that day.

'I wonder if you can help me,' Elizabeth began, flashing her warrant card, 'I'm a detective…'

'Oh bloody hell. Haven't you got anything better to do than harassing innocent traders? I've tried to get a license but the council always says no. Don't report me, come on! That's entrapment that is, buying off me and then sticking me on. It's not fair, honestly, nothing better to do, no? Bloody hell!' hotdog man ranted, already beginning to close down the grill.

'No, no. Trust me, I couldn't give a shit that

you're illegally trading. I just really wanted to eat one. What you can help me with is something else.' Elizabeth raised a placating hand. Hotdog man looked skeptical. He wasn't a fan of police, they weren't to be trusted in his opinion.

'Just have a look at this picture would you? I know this is a real long shot, but have you ever seen him before?'

'I'm usually pretty good with faces but I do see loads of people every day.'

Hotdog man took the photograph from Elizabeth, and studied it. Elizabeth was impressed; usually people just gave the image a cursory once over, but not hotdog man. Perhaps he thought that by cooperating he could ensure Elizabeth didn't report him.

'Yes. I have seen him before.'

Elizabeth's heart jumped, her stomach did a somersault.

'Sorry, what did you say?'

'I said, I've seen him. I remember him because he was with this woman and they had a really weird conversation,' he replied, handing back the photo. 'What did he do?'

'It's not what he did, it's what was done to him.' Elizabeth answered, not wanting to give too much away. Her heart was pounding in her chest. Had she just found their first real significant witness?

'Oh, did he get attacked or something?' hotdog man asked, curious.

'Yes he did. Tell me about this conversation you heard,' Elizabeth suggested, switching into cop mode.

'He was talking to a woman, I think they were together, like a couple. I didn't get a really good look at her though 'cos she stood back from me, or rather she was walking next to him as they went past on the side furthest away from me, so I couldn't really see her. The guy, what's his name?'

'David.'

'David asked her if she wanted any food. I guess seeing me here made him think about it. I didn't hear her answer but I heard her voice, if you know what I mean. He then asked if she wanted one of my hotdogs and she told him to shut up, not to speak to her again unless he was spoken to and to keep walking. He said: 'Sorry mistress. Of course' and then she had a go at him again, telling him to shut up and not speak. It was weird, you know? The way she spoke to him, like he was a piece of shit on her shoe. Who talks like that?'

A murderer who is into bondage and domination.

'Do you remember anything else from the conversation?' Elizabeth asked, ignoring his question.

'No, that was basically it. He was trying to be polite and buy the lady some food and she told him to shut up and what not. I don't know if they'd had an argument or something but Christ! My old woman would never talk to me like that and I'd never talk like that to her,' hotdog man looked genuinely indignant at the prospect.

'So, this was as they were walking past you?'

'Yeah, they were walking towards The Majeste,' he pointed towards the hotel where David had been found murdered, 'and as they passed me they had that conversation. They paused briefly, you know, when he asked her about the hotdog and then carried on.'

'What can you tell me about the woman?'

Elizabeth asked.

'Well, I didn't really get a good look at her. I mean this section of the street is not exactly well lit, as you can see, and as I said she was walking on the other side of him, so he blocked my view, basically.'

Think man, think!

'Can you tell me anything about her at all? Age, height, skin colour, hair colour, anything she was carrying…?'

'She was tall, maybe around six foot, although she probably had heels on. Most women do these days don't they?'

He glanced down at Elizabeth's feet. Flats. How disappointing.

'She was white, I couldn't tell you her age as I didn't see her face. She was wearing a really long thin black coat and it had a hood. Now I think about it, I'm pretty sure she had the hood up. That's probably another reason why I remember so little about her,' he paused, thinking. 'She was carrying a bag, small rucksack size. It was down by her side. I think he - David – may have had a bag as well.'

'Anything else about either of them that struck you in any way?'

'Nah. That was it. Then they just went off towards the hotel. I didn't even see if they went in 'cos a customer came over.'

'Ok, that is great, you've been very helpful. This is where I work, call that number and arrange to come in and give a statement. You will give a statement won't you?' Elizabeth handed him her business card, and looked at him. In her experience if you told someone what they were going to do for you before you asked them if that was ok, they usually acquiesced.

'Your statement is extremely important. The man you saw was murdered that night. You may well have been the last person to see him alive,' she added, hoping the information would ensure his co-operation.

Hotdog man went pale.

'Jesus...' he whistled through his teeth. 'Murdered? Bloody hell.'

'So, you see it's important we get your statement as soon as possible.' Elizabeth added, 'Call me first thing tomorrow, ok?' Elizabeth decided that nothing would be lost in delaying the statement by a few hours so that she could take it personally when she was feeling a little less worse for wear.

Elizabeth was desperate to call Greg and tell him what she had just found out, but he was on the tube and wouldn't have phone reception. She thanked hot dog man once more and made him again promise to call her in the morning.

She was buzzing. This was a lead. She dialled DI Scott's number and waited impatiently for him to pick up. Instead the phone rang out and then went to voicemail. Elizabeth left a message and hung up, not sure what to do next.

She knew she should go home and try and sleep, but also knew this would be impossible. Still, she couldn't exactly roll up at the nick now, stinking of booze and fatigued, but nor could she wander around the streets all night waiting for morning. Besides, what could she accomplish tonight? The short answer was nothing.

She wanted to collect her thoughts and process everything hotdog man had told her. The train ride home would provide her with the perfect opportunity to do just that. And then she could call

Greg on the way as he would be off the tube by then. She was going to relish telling him he'd lost the bet and now owed her twenty pounds. She smiled to herself. The evening was just getting better and better.

****

Mark Faversham sniffed loudly, snorting the white powder up into his nose. The beat of the music from within the club caused the toilet cubicle doors to throb, accentuated every time the restroom door was opened, removing the physical barrier between him and the music. He felt good. He felt fucking good.

He'd taken a Viagra moments earlier and had now sniffed two lines of coke. The mix, 'sextasy', was guaranteed to get him horny, keep him hard and make him feel on top of the world. Coke on its own would keep him horny, but would give him 'limp dick', a well known side effect of coke use, hence the requirement to mix it with Viagra if he was to enjoy this as much as he should. Emboldened by the coke, he headed back out into the club.

Strobe lights blinked across the crowd, pulsating bodies, gyrating and dancing, moving with the beat. Everybody in the club was wearing clothing associated with bondage; PVC, leather, rubber, chains, collars, platform shoes, thigh-high boots. Some faces were painted, others were hidden behind masks and facial hoods. Some people wore dog-collars attached to long leads, crawling along the floor behind their masters, others were tied to crosses, spread-eagled and semi-nude, as an overweight dominatrix, sporting a tight PVC catsuit, offered people the chance to whip the prostrate subs.

Mark was in paradise. The coke had kicked in and he could feel the familiar surge of confidence begin to sweep through his body. He looked fit. His hair swept off his face, revealing his sharp jaw line. He was wearing tight leather trousers and a black PVC shirt, buttoned up to the top, his muscular frame rippling beneath the fabric.

He moved through the crowd, head bobbing to the beat, a smile on his handsome face. He took hold of a thin bamboo cane that the fat dominatrix offered him and methodically caned one of the female subs naked arses, feeling himself become hard as she moaned in pain and pleasure.

After a few minutes he moved on, heading to the dance floor, his eyes bouncing across the bodies in front of him, full of sexuality and lust.

Then he saw her.

Dancing alone, her red PVC catsuit like a second skin as it moulded to the contours of her athletic figure. She moved with slow, fluid movements, her hips rotating, arms raised, her hands running through her hair, which was long and black as the night. Mark stood mesmerized.

A small circle had formed around her, men and women alike watching her provocative dance. Mark moved towards her, the coke making him feel strong and confident. As he started towards her, she looked at him and continued her dance with her eyes on his, dark green with passion in their centre. She was dancing for him now and this excited him.

She rubbed her hands over her body and slowly pulled down the zip at the front of her catsuit, down between her breasts, almost down to her belly button, her hands all over herself. He could feel himself becoming more aroused, his penis starting to firm.

He stood still again, in a trance; she was hypnotic and now she was moving towards him, zipping the suit back up, lithe body swaying from side to side, her firm breasts outlined through the PVC, her small waist accentuated and her long legs exaggerated by the five-inch red heels she was wearing on her feet. She was tall and sexy and goddess-like. Mark couldn't move, transfixed like a rabbit caught in the headlights of the car that was about to cause its demise.

She was so close to him now he could smell her musky scent, dark and exotic. She wrapped an arm around his waist and danced around him, using his body as a solid prop around which she swayed and rocked.

'Mina?' he asked hopefully.

'Yes, Mark,' she replied, her voice deep and seductive.

She smiled alluringly and slipped a hand under his shirt, scratching his body with her long fingernails. Mark moaned in pleasure and pulled her into his body.

'No, no, no. You know you don't control me,' she derided. 'You do as I say.'

She leant into his neck, her lips less than an inch from his skin, her breath warm.

Mark closed his eyes, now oblivious to the other people in the club. He was only aware of this seductive, black-haired siren and the way she was making him feel.

'I think it's time we left,' she said to him, her hand rubbing against his swollen penis. 'Take me somewhere private where we'll be alone and won't be disturbed. I've got big plans for you.'

She grabbed Mark by the wrist and walked him through the club to the cloak room. Handing over her ticket, the receptionist gave her a long, black, hooded coat and a black bag. Mark did the same and was returned a thigh-length, black jacket. Simply putting on their coats allowed them to walk out of the club and appear normally dressed, all evidence of bondage and kink craftily hidden beneath the garments.

They emerged from the club into the fresh night air, and Mark was secretly relieved to see that the woman was equally beautiful in the light. Sometimes the darkness of the club could be misleading. He'd made that mistake before.

'Tell me where we're going,' she said to him, turning her face to look at him, her cool green eyes peering out from under her hood. Mark took the opportunity to admire her face.

'Richmond, my place. Is that ok for you?'

'You live alone?'

'My flat mate is away, so it'll be just us.' Mark grinned at her.

Mark raised his hand as a black cab drove into view, the yellow light on the dash indicating its availability for hire. They clambered in and Mark gave the address of his flat. Mina seductively leant back against the seat of the cab, her long legs set apart, her coat ensuring her catsuit could not be seen by the cab driver.

'Put your hand between my legs,' she quietly ordered Mark, 'under the coat.'

Mark did as he was told, his right hand snaking under her coat and resting against her crotch, awaiting his next order.

'Undo the zip, and put two fingers inside me.'

The design of the cat suit was such that, whilst the garment fastened with a long zip at the front, there was also a second small zip in the crotch area which allowed easy and quick access to the wearer's most intimate parts without the suit having to be removed. Mark felt the zip under his fingers and slowly inched it down before pushing his hand inside the garment, his fingers brushing against the smoothness of her shaved sex, the lips silky and soft to his touch.

He was so hard he felt he would burst. He wanted to kiss her, to pull her on top of him, to feel her firm body against his, but he knew he mustn't. She was in charge; having to exercise so much restraint was sweet torture.

He slipped his fingers into her and savoured her warmth and softness. She moaned gently as he pushed into her and pushed her hips up to greet his delving fingers. He sighed and felt himself losing control; as if she was aware of this, Mina suddenly pulled his hand away and raised it to her lips.

She looked at him as she opened her mouth and placed his fingers inside, gently sucking at his digits. Mark groaned in pleasure enjoying the sensation combined with the knowledge of where those fingers had just been, his arousal heightened by the fact they were doing this in a taxi, the driver oblivious to their antics.

Mina placed her hand on his crotch and began to rub, the movements in unison with those of her mouth around his fingers. Mark wasn't sure how much more he could take, he was desperate to feel her around him, to thrust up into her, hard and rhythmically. He closed his eyes and tried to focus on something non-erotic. He was relieved when the taxi pulled up outside his flat, pleased to have a moment to calm down.

He paid the taxi driver and showed Mina into the flat, watching her backside sway seductively from side to side as she preceded him into the building. With a quick look down the street, he closed the door behind them, hungry with anticipation and full of desire. He didn't know what she was going to do to him, but he knew for certain that it would be an experience he would never forget.

Chapter XV

DI Robert Scott was driving back from his meeting with Mrs Saunders. After answering the phone earlier in the office, he had quickly called his wife, Margaret, to explain that he would be working late after all, had grabbed the keys of one of the unmarked police cars and driven as fast as the roads would allow him, arriving at the Saunders residence in just under two hours.

Something in her voice had piqued Robert's interest; it sounded like an investigative lead. He knew he had to get to her as fast as he could; emotional people were susceptible to ambivalence, changing their minds in an instant and Robert wanted to make sure he got to Janet before she changed hers.

He'd arrived at the address and had been let in by a tearful Mrs Saunders, her eyes swollen and puffy. As soon as he'd crossed the threshold she had thrust a calling card into his hand. With a feeling of excitement in his belly, he'd inspected the card. It was a business card for a London venue, The Garden, and it declared proudly that all fantasies could be catered for, all fetishes indulged and all types welcome.

According to the card, The Garden was open five days a week from eleven o'clock at night to 6am the following morning. Something for the night owls. The card on its own did not mean a great deal.

So, David Saunders was in possession of a card for a bondage club? Big deal. However, if this was where he'd been on the night of his murder, one of the other club-goers could have been his killer.

Janet had led Robert through to the front room, the tea that had been politely laid out on the living room table during Robert's previous visit now replaced with a bottle of scotch and a glass, two fingers of the liquid inside.

As she ushered Robert in, Janet had gone over to the side of the room and retrieved another crystal glass, placing it on the table and telling Robert to help himself. He had politely accepted her offer and poured himself a small measure. He had then sat silently on the sofa opposite Janet, a sense of déjà vu as he noticed he was sat in exactly the same spot as when he had visited with DC Jessop.

'I am sorry to have called you like that. I was really distressed. And angry, you know? Then Megan came in and found me like that, it broke my heart for her and Charlie, I couldn't stop crying. I didn't know who else to talk to. I can't talk to my family about this, I don't want them thinking badly of David,' she had begun, tears once again brimming in her eyes.

'That's ok Janet. I'm glad you called me,' Robert had said, compassionately.

Janet looked at him, finished the dregs of her Scotch and poured herself another large measure. Robert wondered how many she'd had before he'd got there. He didn't blame her for wanting to drown her sorrows. If there was ever a time to throw one's self over board it was during a crisis like this.

'I'm sorry I was rude to you and the other detective before. He was so polite and kind. He was only doing his job I know, but when he asked me about David's sex life… I don't know, I felt like maybe I was being blamed for something.'

'Why did you feel that way Mrs Saunders?' Robert's voice was sincere and calming.

'I don't know how to talk about this stuff. It's so embarrassing!' Janet wailed in distress, bringing her hands up to cover her face.

Robert felt her misery. Janet was dealing with so much, and she was dealing with it on her own, whilst also having to be strong for her children.

'Is your brother here Mrs Saunders? Should I call someone to come over?' Robert was hoping that by diverting her thought processes for just a moment, it would allow Janet to regain some control of her emotions and assist her in imparting whatever it was she felt she needed to tell him.

'No it's fine. My brother had to go home; he'll be back first thing. The kids are in their room, sleeping, or at least pretending to be asleep. I have no doubt they'll come out to find me at some point. They both cry for him, especially Charlie who is that bit younger. He doesn't understand that his daddy isn't coming back.'

'This is a terrible time for you. I can only offer you my condolences and do whatever I can to try and make this less painful for you…' Robert trailed off. What a load of bullshit. What could he bloody do to make her feel better? It felt trite, but Janet seemed to be grateful for the sentiment.

'Thank you. You're very kind.' She downed her drink again and poured a third.

'The thing is, what I wanted to tell you, the young detective was right about David. He did enjoy… unusual sex.' She went silent.

Robert also stayed silent, waiting for more. It

only took an average of seven seconds before humans felt the urge to fill a pause in conversation with inane banter, usually a comment about the weather. Robert was well practised and knew how to use silences; indeed it was part of his interview technique and often caused suspects to begin rambling. They could hear the antique clock on the mantle piece ticking, its rhythmic clicks counting the seconds like a conversational chronometer.

'He liked to be tied up. And whipped,' Janet began, 'he liked to be dominated and told what to do. He wanted me to do things to him and he liked me to hurt him. I only 'played,' as he called it, a couple of times. I found it too strange, and quite frankly, I found it disgusting. That's not how I was raised. A man and a woman have sex because they love each other, as a way of showing their love. I couldn't see where this whipping and mistreatment of the man I loved could fit into that philosophy. I did try though. I tried because I wanted to keep David happy. He was a good man and once he re-alised how much I disliked it, he never asked me again.'

She sighed and took a sip of her Scotch.

'I was relieved. I never thought about what this could mean in terms of cheating, fulfilment, you know? Desires like that don't just disappear, do they? He must have still wanted to do those things but just couldn't do them with me. How could I have been so blind.' Janet hung her head and raised a trembling hand to her mouth.

Robert sat silently watching her, turning over possibilities and unanswered questions in his head. Was their killer a long-term partner of David's? Was it someone he indulged all his fantasies with? Was it a one-off thing? Was David a regular at The Garden? Was there club membership, were patrons photographed, did they pay a monthly fee, would anyone there be able to tell him anything …? So many questions.

'He stayed in London on a few occasions, he told me it was work, but now, who knows? He could have been doing anything, going to that club.' She pointed at Robert's hand which was still holding the card, her face a picture of disgust. Robert remained silent.

'He used to have all the gear, you know? Trousers, shirts, collars, ball gags, rope... the lot. After we fell out about the bondage stuff, he told me he had thrown it out. Who knows if he did or not. Maybe that's what he had in his gym bag and maybe that was why he always left it in the car? I am so stupid aren't I?' Janet snorted contemptuously. 'Stupid idiot wife. Can't keep her husband happy, trusts him so much she doesn't even look in his gym bag and never disbelieves him when he says he's got to stay up town for work. No wonder men cheat on us all the time. We're so stupid.'

'Janet, you're not stupid and not all men cheat, and of those that do it's rarely because they can't get what they want at home, it's simply because they can,' Robert replied, hoping what he was saying would reassure her. To be honest he didn't have a clue why men cheated. He'd been faithful to his wife from the day he'd met her.

'You mentioned you rowed with David about the bondage sex. Can you remember when this was?' Robert asked, hoping to get an idea of how long David may have been frequenting The Garden.

'Oh that was years ago. We were still living at

the old house then and Charlie was just a baby. I'll be honest, it was a hard time for me. I had post-natal depression after Charlie was born and I was rowing with David over pretty much everything, not just the bondage. We both thought our marriage was going to end, but then we just clicked back into place, just like when we first married.' A wry smile spread across her face at the memory.

'How long have you lived here?'

'We moved here two years ago, when David got his new job with PR International in London.'

'Would you have the days he stayed up in London marked in a diary by any chance?'

'No. I didn't make a note or anything.'

'What about the frequency?' Robert continued.

'Well he stayed up there now and then, really. Maybe once every three or four months? Something like that. It wasn't so often that I really felt his absence, if you know what I mean?'

'I do. Janet, I need to ask you some pretty embarrassing questions. I hope you'll answer them and not feel that I am just prying into your private affaires.'

'Yes, it's ok. I have prepared myself for this. I won't throw you out again, don't worry,' Janet smiled at Robert and he smiled back. It was the first time she had genuinely smiled and it lit up her face.

'It's not the first time I've been thrown out of someone's house and I'm sure it won't be the last,' he replied, his eyes crinkling with good humour.

Janet leaned forward and reached out for the bottle of Scotch, then changed her mind and settled back in her chair, looking at Robert like an inmate on death row waiting for the guards to come and collect her on judgment day.

'Can you tell me exactly what David liked you to do to him? The reason I'm asking is because if he was seeking the same gratification elsewhere, this could tell us something about the person who was maybe doing it to him. Do you understand what I mean?'

'Not sure.'

'What I mean is, from what I understand, there are some people who dominate, some who like to be dominated, some who do both, some who like to be hurt, those who like to do the hurting and so on… The more I know about David's preferences the narrower our pool of potential suspects could become. The more I know, the better I can hunt for the person who murdered your husband,' Robert explained.

Janet's eyes welled up again at the word 'murdered' but she retained control of her emotions.

'I see. This is so embarrassing. Will all of your colleagues have to know? I can't bear to think of us becoming the canteen joke, I know how it can be at work. It's oh so funny when it's not happening to you.'

'Janet, some of my colleagues will have to know aspects of this conversation, but it will not become public knowledge in any way. I give you my word I will do everything in my power to protect yours and David's good name.'

Janet seemed satisfied by this. She sighed.

'Ok. David told me he was a 'sub', he liked to be dominated. He usually wanted me to tie him up. He taught me the knots so that the rope wouldn't tighten once it was done up and so that I wouldn't cut off the circulation. Then, he liked me to use a thin cane on his chest and…' Janet stopped, the words catching in her throat. This was not the sort of thing she was comfortable talking about.

'It's ok Janet. I assure you I am unshockable. When you've done as many years as a police officer as I have, you've pretty much seen and heard it all,' Robert prompted. Janet nodded, but couldn't meet Robert's eye as she continued.

'He also liked me to cane his genitals. Sometimes he wanted me to tie him face down and cane his backside. He also had this rubber whip that he liked me to use. He liked me to wear really high heels and press the heels into him. Sometimes he'd ask me to say things, and slap him. I didn't like doing it at all, but I wanted to try and keep him happy.'

'Did he ever want to dominate you?'

'No. Always me dominating him. I am a strong woman and I have no problem putting my point across or holding my ground in everyday life, but this was too strange for me. We only did it maybe six, seven times in all. At least, only that many times with me,' she said sadly.

'Last time we were here, DC Jessop asked whether David had any homosexual tendencies. I know this must be very distressing, but are you sure he didn't?'

Janet looked at him and for a moment Robert thought she was going to throw him out again, but instead she simply said: 'I am one hundred percent positive he didn't.'

Robert nodded. 'I am sorry, but I had to ask.'

'It's ok. If any of this can help your investigation, I am willing to answer your questions.'

'Had you ever heard of The Garden? Did

you ever go to any of these sorts of club with David?'

'No I didn't. He asked me a couple of times if I would be willing and it normally sparked a row because I wasn't prepared to do that sort of thing in public. At home, just the two of us was hard enough.'

'Janet, this information has been very useful. Is there anything else at all you want to tell me, or think might assist me?' Robert asked, sensing that the conversation was coming to a close.

'That's it. If I think of anything else, I'll call you.' Janet had offered him a weak smile, formalities were exchanged and Robert had left.

Now Robert was pulling onto his drive way. The living room light was on so he knew that Margaret was still up. He pulled the keys out of the car's ignition and sat for a moment, looking at his house, his mind mulling things over.

He took his phone out of his pocket and noticed he had a missed call from DC Lane. As he was about to dial his voicemail facility, he saw the kitchen light flick on and then saw Margaret's silhouette through the net curtains.

Robert watched her for a while moving around the room, at the fridge, by the sink, taking something out of the cupboard. He couldn't imagine being without Margaret; if she was taken from him, he wouldn't want to continue living.

He returned the phone to his pocket suddenly overwhelmed with a need to hold onto his wife and tell her that he loved her. Whatever Elizabeth had to tell him could wait until the morning. He jumped out the car and walked to the front door. Nothing was going to stop him seeing his wife tonight and enjoying a few hours with her. Nothing

****

Mark Faversham had hastily thrust a couple of tenners through the cabbie's window after the taxi had dropped him and Mina at his apartment, quickly opened the front door and made his way into the bedroom as ordered by the raven-haired goddess. He hadn't even stopped for breath.

Now he was gagged and bound, his arms and legs stretched painfully, spread-eagled across his king-size bed, completely naked. He'd been lying here a while now. He didn't know where Mina had gone.

For one brief moment he hoped that she wasn't robbing him, removing his flat-screen TV and state of the art stereo system as he lay here powerless and vulnerable. He almost chuckled at the thought of being stuck, tied to the bed, his manhood on full display until Peter came back on Monday. How long could a human go without water again? He reckoned he'd probably survive until Monday night but it would be bloody agony. He wouldn't even be able to shout for help, the ball gag preventing any form of speech other than grunts. As Mark was pondering how he could escape from his bonds should the need arise, he heard the bedroom door open.

Then suddenly, she was there, standing at his side, sporting long, black rubber gloves, a mini skirt that just skimmed the bottom of her arse cheeks and a sexy corset that finished below her perfect breasts. He felt himself becoming aroused as he admired her.

So, that was what she had in her bag - a

change of clothes. He'd never seen such a beautiful woman or felt quite as aroused as he did now. He wondered what other delights she kept in her bag.

Mina moved towards him, smiling provocatively, her skirt revealing tantalising flashes of her femininity as she sashayed towards the bed. She had something behind her back, which Mark hoped was a whip. He guessed he'd find out soon enough.

She leaned over him and kissed his forehead, her breasts hanging inches from his gagged mouth, her body sliding onto the bed and over him so that she was straddling him, her long legs circling beneath his torso, pulling him tight up against her naked sex. He winced as she squeezed her strong legs around him, his arms pulling against the ropes that bound him.

Mina, brought her right hand forward and showed him what she'd been hiding. It was a metallic circular object, about the size of a two-pence piece, with little needle like prongs around the circumference. It reminded mark of an old-fashioned doctor's implement you might find at a museum.

The circular wheel was fastened to a black handle, which Mina now held in her hand. She placed the wheel against his chest and gently wheeled it across him from nipple to nipple. The prongs pricked his flesh, leaving a little trail of polka dots against his skin, but not breaking the surface. He groaned. It was an exquisite sensation; he could feel the heat of her intimate part against his swollen penis, sensuous and gentle, and he could feel the prickling across his skin, painful and distracting. He was loving it.

Then Mina stood up and looked down at

him, towering over him, one hand against the ceiling so she could steady herself as the mattress molded around her feet. Mark looked at her, confused. As he gazed up at her in the dim light, she looked different, her face looked different, but he couldn't explain how. Was it her eyes? Where was that seductive gaze that had so captivated him? Where was that provocative smile? She looked - evil.

Mark felt his heart rate increase, a feeling of apprehension washing over him, rising from the very pit of his stomach. He'd seen live mice dropped into cages with hungry snakes; the mice knew their end was coming as the scent of the predator reached their olfactory organs. They would hunch and tremble, waiting for the inevitable to happen, sometimes with a pathetic little squeak, just before the snake struck. This was how he felt now. He was the mouse and she was the serpent. Somehow he knew this would be his death bed.

As if reading his mind, Mina chose that moment to reveal a silver knife, the blade long and sharp; it looked like a boning knife. She grinned and laughed as Mark began to struggle violently against the restraints strapping him to the bed, his breath escaping in grunts. Mina dropped down onto his chest, holding the knife within inches of his right eye. He stopped moving.

'That's better,' she whispered, 'no one likes a coward.'

She taunted him, repeatedly moving the knife closer to his eye and then dramatically pulling it away. Tears started to form in Mark's eyes, sweat beaded on his brow.

'You fucking pathetic creature,' she snarled, 'look at you! Think a dick makes you a man do you?

Fucking joke, that's what you are, all of you.'

She moved down his body, the knife trailing down his chest but not cutting the skin. She took hold of his manhood in her left hand and tugged at it playfully. It remained limp in her hand.

'Imagine, if I'd had one of these, my life may have been totally different. What do you reckon? Do you think he would have left me alone?' she asked Mark, touching the knife gently to her pouting lips.

Mark grunted and tried to scream, but the ball gag prevented him from making any coherent sound.

'I can't hear you!' Mina mocked in a sing-song voice.

'This is for all the years of pain and suffering.'

She pushed the knife deeply into the tender skin underneath Mark's testicles, then tugged the knife up towards his penis in a semi-circular motion. Mark cried out in agony, the sound muted and terrible from behind the gag, his body started to shake with adrenalin.

He tried desperately to free himself from the ligatures binding his wrists and ankles, the ropes biting into his flesh.

Mina withdrew the knife. 'I'll finish that later,' she said.

She got off the bed, Mark rolled his head to look at her, his eyes wide, tears trickling down his cheeks. His mind was reeling. He knew he was going to die. He thought it was supposed to be a moment of clarity and serenity, the moment before you slipped from this world into the next. That's what people said, wasn't it?

But all Mark Faversham could feel as he lay

there, blood draining from the gash between his legs, was the pain, the burning, overwhelming pain. His eyelids felt heavy. He guessed it wouldn't take him too long to bleed to death.

Mina moved to the head of the bed and looked at Mark's face; he forced himself to focus on her as he felt himself drifting into unconsciousness. From under half-closed lids, as his body bled and his life was slipping away, Mark saw Mina raise her arm above her head. He could just make out the point of a metallic object as she drove it down towards his eyeball. He felt his eye pop as the orb was forced into his skull.

And then, thankfully, sweet oblivion.

Chapter XVI

Today was going to be different. Today, she was not going to take it lying down. Literally. Today she would fight and protest and she would keep doing it until he left her alone. She didn't care if he hit her, as she knew he inevitably would, she was going to make him see. She was older now and stronger and she'd endured this for long enough. That bastard was going to get what he deserved.

She'd been working on her implement for weeks and she knew exactly where she was going to put it. She was almost looking forward to his visit.

During one of the nights he had kept her locked up, she'd managed to prise off one of the metal struts that supported the bed frame; the bed that represented fear and pain, the bed she'd come to hate.

She'd made her hands raw as she'd twisted and turned the metal support, wriggling around under the bed trying to get purchase as it slipped between her sweaty palms. She'd needed to be quick; he could be back at any moment. It had taken her three days to get it free, spending a few minutes on it at a time between the visits he'd arranged for her.

She remembered the feeling of exaltation as it had finally snapped; she'd held it against her chest and cried with relief. She'd been clever and removed one from the middle of the bed frame so that he wouldn't see, then she'd hidden it under the mattress. It had given her a feeling of power knowing it was there, even when they were doing those things to her.

Then she'd needed to sharpen it. It wasn't much use to her blunt. She could have tried to smack him over the head with it, but she knew she wasn't strong enough to inflict any pain on him that way. What she needed was a nice sharp, jagged edge. So, she'd spent hours twisting and grinding the metal against the concrete floor beneath the bed so he wouldn't see the marks on the floor; hours of blood, sweat and tears had been spent honing the sharp metal point she had crafted.

And now she was satisfied she could inflict some damage, give him some serious pain, just like he'd given her over the years.

Now she was ready to kill him.

Chapter XVII

Louise hated doctors' surgeries almost as much as she hated hospitals. She hated the smell of the strong antiseptic most medical establishments used, that pervasive and cloying smell which seemed to scream: 'They're all sick or dying, but don't worry! I'll protect you from their evil germs!'

Admittedly the GP's surgery didn't smell like that, but Louise's dislike of doctors was so intense she almost believed it did. She glanced around the waiting room eyeing up her fellow patients, wondering how many of them were genuinely ill, how many thought they were ill and how many just wanted a day off work.

What category do you fall in?

It had taken her all her courage to call the surgery first thing that morning to make an appointment with Dr Ross, her assigned doctor who she had only visited once in the last three years. Now she sat there, legs tightly crossed, trying not to bite her fingernails.

Also in the waiting room was a young woman with a baby girl (*I wonder… immunisations?*); a young man with a terrifying cough (*smoking?*); a teenage couple looking even more scared than Louise (*pregnant?*); a middle-aged man with an enormous stomach who wheezed every time he moved (*obesity!*); a collection of elderly people talking amongst themselves (*the ravages of old age…*) and Louise (*fruit-*

loop, head case, lunatic and mad woman…).

The baby girl started crying, loud, ear-splitting shrieks. Her young mother cooed softly whilst caressing the girl's face and gently bouncing the infant on her knees. Louise couldn't help but smile; the scene was touching. A young mother tending to her offspring, clearly concerned about her child's health and welfare.

Louise didn't remember her mother much, but she did remember that the times she had been around she'd been gentle and kind. She'd had a great smile. Her 'second mum' as she'd called her foster mother, had also been kind and patient with Louise, trying to help her settle in with her new family, replacing the family she'd lost. That was until they had fallen out many years ago, Louise didn't remember what over, and they'd lost all contact with each other. Louise hadn't bothered to try and resurrect a relationship with either of her foster parents; did that make her ungrateful?

'Mr McEvoy! Room three please!' the sprightly receptionist chirruped out from behind the reception desk.

The man with the huge stomach rose and wheezed his way down the corridor.

At the sound of the receptionist's voice, Louise's heart leapt, afraid she was about to be called next. She regretted coming, wanting to be anywhere than where she currently was, but she had promised Ben.

Besides it couldn't do any harm to discuss her visions with a professional, could it? The one in the kitchen on Saturday had been the last straw. It had seemed so real, felt so terrifying. She could still hear the man's malign laughter echoing in her head.

Even more concerning than the vision itself was the fact that she couldn't remember what she'd done after leaving the flat. Where she'd been and what she'd done escaped her. So was she experiencing blackouts on top of visions?

Maybe it's epilepsy?

That's why you're here Lou, to get the doc's expert opinion.

But what if he says I'm mad and sections me like they did mum?

Isn't it better to know one way or another?

Dunno…

Louise sighed. The baby girl was still crying and her mother was starting to get embarrassed, her cheeks tinged scarlet, as some of the other patients began to tut unhelpfully. Louise glared at some of them, feeling her own misery brimming and tears beginning to well in her eyes.

'It's not the baby's fault,' she said out loud. 'She has no control, bless her.'

She smiled at the child and the young mother smiled back at Louise, grateful for the support. A couple of the older patients turned away from Louise and resumed their conversations.

It's not her fault, it's not your fault, it's not her fault, it's not your fault, it's not your fault, it's not your fault, it's not your fault….

Although Louise knew it wasn't her fault that Steve had cheated on her, she couldn't help but think that maybe she had pushed him towards Melissa, or at least away from herself. If she was honest, she hadn't always been nice to him, she'd been difficult and pedantic, but she just couldn't help herself. She knew it was only because she was subconsciously testing him, to see how much of her shit he would take before he ran away. They always ran away, eventually. That was why she needed to test them out first, see whether the next one would abandon her like the last one, like her father, like her mother, like everyone she'd ever known. As Louise sat there in the doctor's surgery, weeping softly to herself, she felt lost and alone. So alone.

Shifting to sit up straight in her seat, she sniffed the last tears away and wiped the moisture from her cheeks. Fuck it. So Steve had cheated - she'd survive without him. So Melissa had stolen her man - she'd get what she deserved in the end.

Louise realised that there was little point worrying and ruing the things that were beyond her control. She couldn't turn back time and she couldn't take away the pain Steve had caused her. But she could carry on and she could show him, and that bitch, that they would not break her. Louise smiled to herself as she hardened her resolve.

No pity, no fear and no weakness.

'Miss Jackson! Room 1 please!' the receptionist called out.

Louise stood up, smoothed herself down and then headed for the front door. At the reception desk she smiled at the happy receptionist.

'Sorry to waste the doctor's time. I suddenly feel much better,' she said, pulling up her collar and stepping out into the morning sunshine. The receptionist watched her leave, dumbfounded.

Nothing wrong with you girl, nothing at all.

****

'Derek, can you come into my office please?' Ben Matthews poked his head into the writers' office.

Five writers, including Derek Cooper, were currently in the room tapping away on their keyboards; they all stopped and looked up as Ben spoke.

Quickly, realising that Ben did not have a general communication to give them, the writers looked at each other, shrugged and then continued typing. Obviously on a roll, Ben mused. Derek hit ctrl, alt, delete and locked his machine as he got up slowly to follow the boss into his office.

The writers were notoriously suspicious of everyone around them, always protecting their content from prying eyes in case they should be plagiarised, sabotaged, deleted... A particularly paranoid type of person, Ben had come to realise. Derek was no different; he was secretive with his writing, giving nothing away until his deadline was met and the piece was as good as complete.

Ben preceded Derek into his office and sat down; Derek followed his example and sat across from Ben, the large glass desk separating them. Ben moved a large bundle of files from the desk so as better to see Derek and, therefore, ameliorate communication, something he had learnt from Louise and her knowledge of body language.

Although he had rehearsed what he was going to say over and over in his head all night and on his journey into work this morning, Ben was unsure how best to launch the conversation.

Derek sat looking at him, his eyes enlarged by the thick lenses of the glasses he wore perched on the tip of his nose. His greying hair was wild and unruly, tufts protruding from behind his ears where he'd tried unsuccessfully to gel it back; his forehead was high, giving him the air of lofty intellect and his eyes were sharp and bright. Derek looked every bit the stereotypical eccentric writer. Derek shifted in his seat and then spoke, tired of waiting for Ben to begin.

'Would it help you if I say I know why you've brought me in here?'

Ben was taken aback. 'I'm sorry?'

'The whole country is in a recession, with virtually no industry untouched, cut backs and redundancies abound. I presume you've brought me in here to sack me.'

Ben sat open-mouthed, wondering how in the world Derek had deduced the purpose of the meeting.

'How did…?' Ben began.

'I've been paying attention. You've been growing gradually more tired looking, you've been snappy and rude to most of the staff, obviously something's been on your mind. And I noticed you called two private meetings with your little shining star, Louise. You would only let your gentle manners slip if the problem you faced was seemingly insurmountable, and you would only summon Louise if you needed her help, in this instance I'm guessing it was to help you decide who to sack. Now, I wonder why I'm here sitting opposite you?' Derek said coolly, a slight sneer tugging at his top lip.

Ben was astounded at Derek's perspicacity.

'You are right that I have brought you in here to offer you redundancy. The company is failing and I am being forced to make sacrifices if the business is to stay afloat. You are very perceptive, but you're wrong about Louise. Yes, I did tell her about the magazine's problems and I did ask her to give me an indication as to who she thought we could afford to loose, but the ultimate decision is mine and mine alone. This is my company and I accept full responsibility for who I have decided to sack,' Ben replied.

'Ah,' Derek clearly didn't believe him. 'So what's going to happen to the little angel? Who else has she decided needs to vacate the premises?'

Ben was unimpressed.

'Derek, I don't appreciate your tone or insinuation. Louise will remain on staff, but there are nineteen other people that I have the unfortunate task of dismissing today. This is difficult for all of us. You are not being singled out for any reason other than that your personal performance record is inferior to that of others working for this publication. You are a good writer, and it is with a heavy heart that I have to let you go.'

Derek shook his head.

'"Have to let me go". It sounds like I've got a choice, when I clearly haven't. Why not just have some balls Ben and tell me you're sacking me, none of this euphemistic bullshit designed to placate me and soothe my ego. I'm a big boy, I can take the truth. Louise wanted me out didn't she?'

'Jesus Derek, what is it between you two? She was promoted six months ago because she is of superior calibre, it was nothing personal.'

'Yeah, until you two got involved. Everybody thinks she got promoted over me because you two were, shall we say, fornicating,' Derek sneered.

'I do not have to explain myself to you or defend my honour against your spurious and malicious accusations. You're fired, get your stuff and leave. You needn't bother submitting your last assignment,' Ben said, his voice rising on a par with his anger.

'I'll go Ben, but I want to know what my redundancy package is. You can't just sack me because you're failing and not provide some form of recompense. I have always submitted excellent articles and they have always been on time.'

'You have submitted adequate articles that have needed editing and you have always submitted them on time after being chased for them at least twice. You'll be getting four months' pay up front.'

'Not bad. Thank you boss - oh sorry, you no longer merit that title do you? I'll get my things and be gone by lunch.'

Derek rose and looked as though he was about to leave, when he turned suddenly and said: 'Any chance you can give little Miss Sunshine a message from me Ben? Tell her she'll get what's coming to her, would you? She may think she can come in here, throw her weight around, sashay about barking orders, raise her skirt for the boss in order to get what she wants, but in the long run, those who deserve shall reap the rewards.' Derek smiled and strode out of the office before Ben had a chance to reply.

'What the...?' Ben was shocked.

It appeared as though the seemingly meek and mild mannered Mr Cooper also possessed a darker, more sinister side to his character.

Ben wearily rubbed the back of his neck and let out a deep breath, shaking his head in amazement at the man's gall. Now he understood what Louise meant about arrogance. This was the longest interaction Ben had ever had with the man and it was now clear to him that Derek Cooper really was an arsehole.

'Good riddance,' he muttered under his breath.

One down, nineteen to go. He hoped they wouldn't all get as personal as Derek, although Ben did anticipate a full spectrum of emotions to be played out in his office today. God he felt tired, and miserable, and mean, and loathsome. The harbinger of doom, as portrayed by Ben Matthews. He reached forward and grabbed the telephone on his desk, punching in a single digit.

'Jenny, it's Ben. Can you please come up and see me in my office? Yes right now please.' He hung up and leant back in his chair.

He wondered briefly how Louise was getting on at the Doctor's, assuming she had actually gone. He would call her at lunch time and find out. Even though it was Ben himself who had practically ordered Louise to go to the doctor's that morning, he really wished she was here with him. He could do with an ally.

There was a gentle knock at the door as Jenny timidly entered the office. Ben smiled at her sadly.

'Jenny, please take a seat. I'm afraid I have some bad news...'

Chapter XVIII

'Oh Ben, fuck off!' Louise cursed as her mobile phone vibrated on the table next to her for the third time in half an hour. She moodily shoved the device into her handbag, not wanting to talk to Ben yet and figuring that if the phone was out of sight, she would feel less inclined to answer when he called back again, which she knew he would.

Louise guessed he was calling to find out how she'd got on at the doctor that morning and she wasn't quite ready to lie to him yet, although in theory it would only be a half lie. After all, she had been to the doctor's - she just hadn't physically seen the doctor.

After leaving the GP's surgery, Louise had headed to her local library determined to research for herself what could be causing her hallucinations. What could a doctor really tell her that she couldn't find out for herself through books and the internet? Without wanting to trivialise the years of training and academic studies that GP's had to undertake, they were not specialists. They would have to perform tests, maybe refer her to a psychiatrist, ask her loads of questions relating to mental health, work/life balance, diet and God knew what else, and Louise would have to answer truthfully if she really wanted their help. She could just imagine the conversation:

Doc: 'How many units of alcohol do you

consume each week Ms Jackson?'

Louise: 'Oh really, hardly any doctor! Probably two glasses of wine a week, what's that? A unit or two?'

Liar, liar, pants on fire! Try a bottle a night...

Doc: 'And what about sleep? Do you sleep well as a rule?'

Louise: 'Oh like a baby. Always get my eight hours.'

More like four if you're lucky.

Doc: 'How about eating? You eating ok? Regular, healthy meals?'

Louise: 'Yes doctor, of course. Plenty of fresh veg and fruit. I understand the importance of my five a day.'

Usually, left overs for breakfast, like pizza...

Doc: 'Well Ms Jackson, there doesn't appear to be anything wrong with you.'

Louise: 'That's great, sorry to have wasted your time.'

Louise had been at the library for just over two hours and after spending the first thirty minutes trying to find the relevant book section, had instead settled for a bit of internet research first to get her started. She also knew that she couldn't answer the phone to Ben in the library without incurring the wrath of the fearsome-looking librarian and so had the perfect excuse to hide out and appease her conscience when she had to tell him why she hadn't answered the phone.

So far her internet research had proved very interesting and somewhat alarming. As far as she could tell, she was either suffering from psychotic depression, had eaten something that had poisoned her, was developing Parkinson's disease, was bi-polar or schizophrenic, had Hoigne syndrome, had taken narcotics, had epilepsy or was simply suffering from sleep deprivation. She liked the latter option best and it did kind of fit with her general lifestyle, she supposed.

Louise had always been a bad sleeper. From the age of thirteen she had suffered from night terrors, waking up in her dreams, her brain thinking she was awake although she was actually still asleep. The terrors would range from thinking she was being suffocated by paranormal forces, whilst feeling actual pressure on her chest as if she was being pinned down, to seeing white shadows at the foot of her bed and hovering above her. The only commonality in the dreams was that she could never turn on her bedside lamp despite her fingers jabbing furiously at the 'on' button, and she could never vocalise the screams that were desperately trying to escape her. And she always tried to scream for her mother to come and save her.

Steve had said that sometimes she would just thrash and thrash in the bed and that when he put his arms around her she would go limp, as if all the fight had suddenly drained out of her. He also said that sometimes she made gargling noises which were pretty horrific and had scared him shitless the first time he'd heard them as he'd thought she was choking.

The frequency of the terrors had diminished over the years, and now she didn't experience them more often than maybe once or twice a year, but she still had nightmares or immensely vivid dreams almost every night. Louise had just come to accept them as part of her normal nightly routine, but she knew that her brain was staying far too active to be healthy. Could this really be the reason why she was having these visions?

She felt immensely relieved to read that this could well be the case. It would mean that she wasn't a nutter like her mother, even though lunacy was supposed to be hereditary, at least in part. It would mean that she could sort the problem by herself without having to consult with the medical profession and have them judge her, test her, analyse her, treat her like an object to study and pick apart.

It also meant that she was not broken and therefore, did not need fixing with drugs or behavioural therapy. Louise felt like laughing. All she really needed was to stay off the booze, learn to chill out and perhaps pop the odd sleeping pill now and then.

Louise was smart enough to know that not everything you read on the internet was true, but when there appeared to be an over-arching consensus between sources, confirmed or not, you could pretty much guarantee that there would be at least some kernel of truth in what was being said.

With the sleep deprivation hypothesis firmly rooted in her mind, she disconnected from the library internet and headed towards the book shelves indicated on the screen for further research. She felt her bag buzz as her phone went off again. She knew it was Ben without even looking.

Just give me a few more minutes and I'll be all yours Mr Matthews…. Now though, I have some reading to do.

****

Sweat was dripping from Elizabeth's brow, trickling down her forehead into her eyes. She quickly grabbed her gym towel and rubbed it over her face, not even breaking her stride as she continued to pound on the treadmill. She was seven kilometres in and only had three to go until her run was complete. She'd set the gradient to 1 so as to recreate the outdoor running experience and was running at a speed of ten kilometres an hour, not that fast but not bad for someone who had just finished a ten hour shift and had very little sleep the night before. This was her release; it was how she got out pent up anger and energy. It was her opportunity to gather her thoughts, process the day and settle her mind.

Today had been nuts. James Wilton, hot dog man, had come in to the station and given a statement, after giving her some bullshit excuse about not being able to make it in on Sunday because his dog was ill and he'd been trying to find a vet. Elizabeth had told him to cut the crap and concentrate on remembering Tuesday night.

She'd pushed him hard, testing his recall, trying to get as much detail as possible without making him feel pressured into giving her an answer which could have caused him to resort to false memory. The difficulties of eye witness testimony were well documented and Elizabeth wanted to achieve best evidence.

An E-fit had been considered, but Mr Wilton's recall of the suspect's features wasn't good enough and so the idea had been dropped.

Once Mr Wilton had gone, his statement had been copied and distributed amongst all the detectives on the team. They'd gone through it line by line looking for clues and avenues for exploration, brain storming and discussing theories.

Elizabeth had told the team what she had read about female killers, including Mary Bell, and had suggested that some digging could be done around historical cases of serious sexual abuse against female children reported around twenty-five or thirty-five years ago.

She was working on the premise that killer's usually stick to an area they are familiar with when committing their first murders and the notion that most serial killers are in their twenties or thirties when they start their murderous activities proper. She was also assuming that this was a serial killer in the making given the removal of a 'trophy' from the scene.

The anticipated torrent of arguments had ensued: there was no evidence this was a serial killer, but if the murderer was a serial killer, they couldn't know for sure that this was the first murder and if that was the case they couldn't say where the killer's 'comfort zone' would be; without further details, any checks on child abuse cases would be futile as there would be no variables with which to wheedle out the 'potentials' from the 'definitely-nots'. How could they try and guess an approximate age for the killer on which to run the checks?

Elizabeth had suggested that it still couldn't do any harm to have a look to see if any of the girls in question were traceable, residents in the area, were known to police or had other details linked to their names. She would only look at those who had a date of birth that put them in the age range of twenty-five to thirty-five years of age and she could eliminate any victim that wasn't white; James Wilton had noticed the killer's skin colour from her hands.

DI Scott had supported her and said she

could pursue that line of enquiry if she wished, but he didn't want her wasting too much time on it, as per the proverbial needle in a haystack. Elizabeth had been happy with this and had felt somewhat vindicated at having the DI's support. She knew it would take her ages to get hold of and sift through the names; she suspected there would be hundreds, maybe even thousands, but what else did they really have to go on at the moment? And what harm could it do to obtain this information alongside other investigative avenues?

Then the conversation had turned to the bondage club seemingly frequented by David Saunders, The Garden. They'd performed the usual checks on the business, including a good old-fashioned internet trawl, and had discovered that the club opened at 11pm every night, except Sunday and Wednesday, and continued into the early hours.

According to the Garden's website, some nights there would be guest performers and there was a diary of events. Every night of business club-goers could expect a 'BDSM play area', a comfortable, laid back atmosphere to be enjoyed with like-minded people and an array of alcohol from around the globe.

'What does BDSM actually stand for?' DC Matt Awcock, had asked.

'It stands for Bondage, Domination and Sado-Masochism,' DC Tony Jessop replied, 'I only know that because I did a bit of research on bondage after this case began.'

'Oh yeah? Sure you did!' joked Elizabeth, 'you look like a bondage freak to me. Reckon you're wearing PVC underpants.'

The team had all laughed and cracked a few

jokes at Tony's expense.

'Well, we do have to visit the club for a witness trawl. I don't want us to go in heavy-handed though, so I only want a few officers to actually go into the club. I think this would be a good assignment for Tony and Elizabeth, given that you both seem to know so much about the alternative lifestyle,' DI Scott said, a mischievous twinkle in his eye.

'What?' the detectives had said in unison, Tony looking horrified.

'I'll do it guv, no problems. I'm always up for broadening my horizons,' Elizabeth had said cheekily, once she had recovered from the shock, then to Tony: 'Don't worry Tone, you can be my plaything.'

She lent in to him and gave his knee a squeeze. The team sniggered.

'Good. The club doesn't open until eleven as you know, so I'm going to dismiss you two now, go and chill out for a few hours, then come back here for ten thirty. Greg, Matt you two can come back as well. We'll trawl the punters going in and out of the club. The rest of you, go home and get some quiet time. We'll hand over any actions to you in the morning so I want you fresh,' Robert declared, a plan of action clearly formulated in his mind.

'Er, guv, one small thing,' started DC Julian Bradshaw, who was still looking at the club's website. 'There is a really strict dress code. People in normal clothes, i.e. our two adventurous detectives, won't get in unless they're wearing something that is either "rubber, PVC or in keeping with the alternative lifestyle,"' he read off the site.

'No fucking way! I am not doing that,' Tony

stated. 'I am not walking about in public dressed up like a bloody freak from the circus.'

'That seems a bit close-minded Tony. Do you always judge people so superficially?' Elizabeth asked challengingly.

'I don't care what you say about diversity and 'alternative lifestyles', this is not something I believe in or understand or want to be involved in, in any shape or form.'

Robert intervened: 'No one expects you to go in dressed like the regular clientele. Just badge it and explain what you're doing to the manager or whoever is in charge. I'm not going to force you Tony, but I do need two detectives to go into the club and trawl for witnesses. Who's up for it?'

'Guv, I've already said I'll do it,' Elizabeth replied, slightly surprised by Tony's strong reaction.

'Thanks Elizabeth, who else?'

'Count me in Guv. I don't mind, I'm not easily offended and actually find all this quite interesting. It'll be something to tell the wife!' DC Julian Bradshaw, or JB as he was usually known, declared. 'Besides, I would be more than happy to accompany the delightful Elizabeth,' he smiled at her and she blew him a kiss.

'Great, that's all sorted then. Greg and Matt can witness trawl outside the club with me… Actually Tony, you can come on that too if that doesn't offend your sensibilities?' Robert asked, a little annoyed at the detective's recalcitrance.

'Fine,' Tony said sullenly.

'Ok sorted. In that case go off and do whatever it is you've got to do. Elizabeth, JB, Greg, Matt and Tony, back here for 22:30hrs please. The rest of you, have a good evening.' Robert had concluded the debrief.

It was now 18:30hrs. Elizabeth only had one kilometre to go until her run was complete. She glanced down at the treadmill's console and noticed that her work phone which was balanced on it was ringing. She hit the stop button on the machine, tugged her headphones out of her ears and answered the device. She suspected it was probably JB wanting to discuss their evening assignment, but it wasn't; it was DI Scott. He sounded irate.

'Elizabeth, I need you to come in asap. We've got another body and it looks like it's our bondage killer's handy work.'

He barked out the address to her, which she committed to memory, and then hung up.

Holy shit, another one.

Elizabeth dashed off the treadmill and bolted into the changing room, ignoring the wobbliness in her legs. She knew she didn't have time to shower, so in less than five minutes she was out of the gym and running to the tube, heart pounding and mind racing. This, she knew, was bad news. Two murders so close together, if they didn't catch this killer soon, Elizabeth knew there would be more bodies. It was only a matter of when.

****

'I come baring gifts!' Louise said to Ben as he opened his front door to let her in. She was holding two shopping bags containing dinner and wine.

After eventually leaving the library, Louise had finally returned Ben's calls and asked if she could come round to see him in the evening. As a sweetener, and a virtual guarantee that he wouldn't say no, she'd told him she would prepare dinner and bring suitable refreshments.

Ben had of course agreed. After the day he'd had, he could really use some friendly company, he'd said, adding that he also wanted to know how she'd got on at the doctor's. Louise had stayed quiet on this subject whilst on the phone; she still wasn't quite sure what she was going to say to him about that.

'Hello you,' Ben said, adding, 'I don't think I've ever been so glad to see your smiling face.'

He put his arms around her and hugged her to him, Louise's arms stretched out to the sides as she tried to hold onto the shopping bags whilst being subjected to Ben's bear hug.

'Ah Ben, you missed me, huh?' Louise replied into his chest, thinking to herself how strong he felt and how surprisingly comfortable she was in his grip. She was disconcerted by the feeling and broke free from his grasp, slipping past him into the hall way. He closed the door behind them and followed her into the kitchen.

Neither Louise nor Ben had noticed the black car parked a short distance away, or the occupant sitting in it, observing them from the shadows.

Chapter XIX

Elizabeth made it to the crime scene in good time, arriving simultaneously with the scenes of crime officers. She gave them a quick wave, noting that once again Becca was on shift. This would be nice for her, she mused, two crime scenes relating to the same killer. Several uniformed officers were standing at the entrance to the block of flats, taking details from residents as they came and went, and Elizabeth could make out at least three marked police vans parked in the vicinity.

She approached the officers and flashed her warrant card, identifying herself to them. The officers looked at her somewhat quizzically, noting that she was red-faced and sweating but Elizabeth wasn't bothered and didn't feel inclined to give an explanation; she was used to people looking at her strangely.

She hadn't exactly been popular at school; too many brains and too many looks her mother had said. She'd always had an athletic build, was never able to gain weight and had always far surpassed her peers in intellect.

Unfortunately, her fellow pupils had not admired these qualities but had resented them; Elizabeth had been a threat and had subsequently been bullied for pretty much all of her school life. Quizzical looks were, therefore, nothing to her.

She jogged up the stairs to flat number 6 on

the third floor. Another uniformed officer stood at the door holding a scene log and controlling a cordon. Through the door, Elizabeth spotted Robert sitting in the living room with a handsome looking man with thick, dark hair, tanned skin and chiselled features.

Robert caught Elizabeth's eye and waved her in. She identified herself to the uniformed officer at the door, gave her details to be noted on the log and walked in to the living room towards where Robert was sitting, dropping her gym bag by the front door as she did so. Robert stood up and met her half way.

'We've got another one. This is Peter Reiley and his flat mate, our deceased, is Mark Faversham. I haven't got much out of Peter yet as he is still getting over finding the body. Apparently they have known each other since they were kids. I haven't looked at the crime scene yet either, or at least nothing further than a cursory glance through the bedroom door. Looks pretty fucking messy.' Robert spoke quietly, not wanting Peter to over-hear him.

'And this is definitely the same killer?' Elizabeth asked.

'Looks that way. Peter told me that the body is tied to the bed in the same manner as David Saunders.'

'Christ.'

'Yeah, I know. Elizabeth, I'd like you to take Peter down to the station and get his statement. He won't be able to come back to the flat for a while, and I'm sure he'd rather not stay here anyway, so once you're done see if there's anyone else he can stay with.'

'Of course.'

'Thanks. When you're done, go home and get some rest, ok? I still want us to visit The Garden at some point, but obviously that won't be tonight now. If there's any change, I'll call you.'

Elizabeth smiled at him in acknowledgement then went over to Peter Reiley to introduce herself and talk him through the process.

Robert left her to it and walked to the front door where he could see the scenes of crime officers putting on their white investigation suits. He walked over to Becca and asked for a suit for himself.

'I'm coming in this time Becca. I need to get a feel for this killer,' he said by way of explanation.

She simply nodded and handed him a suit which he quickly put on. He walked back through the living room towards the bedroom, noting that Elizabeth and Peter Reiley had left and wondered how they had managed to slip by without him noticing.

Becca entered the bedroom first and gave a running commentary as she did so, her comments being noted by another crime scene officer who stood on the threshold. As she proceeded through the room, Becca placed round plastic steps onto the floor to mark the path that she was taking into and around the room; this path would be used by anyone who entered the room from now on so as to limit disruption to any potential evidence. This was known as the common approach path and would demarcate the most unlikely route the suspect would have taken to enter and move around the room. It was as a simple as passing over the threshold to one side instead of straight through the middle, sticking close to the walls when navigating the room and approaching the bed from the bottom instead of the top or sides. Of course, it wasn't perfect because you never knew where a suspect may have been, or what they may have touched, but it provided a starting point for entering a crime scene.

Robert followed Becca in, scrutinizing the scene as he went. The room was large and masculine. A big black wardrobe with glass-fronted doors was positioned on the left side of the room, taking up most of the wall space; the window next to it was covered with heavy, black and red curtains. Under the window was a black, plastic laundry basket and in the left-hand corner, there was a chair with a high back, black in colour, with clothing slung over it.

Next to this, pushed up against the back wall was Mark's king-seized bed, grey sheets and pillows stained red from dried blood; to the right of the bed, a bedside cabinet complete with black shaded lamp and reading books.

Propped up against the right-hand wall was a conspicuously clean mountain bike and gym weights; also to the right of the doorway was a chest of drawers supporting a sophisticated stereo and what appeared to be family photographs. Above the bed there was a large black and white photograph of New York city.

Robert mirrored Becca's steps and moved towards the bed to look at the body. The smell was atrocious, the body bloated and pale. He looked at the face. Again, the left eye was seriously damaged, but on this occasion remained within the orbital socket. Dried blood caked the right side of Mark's face and his mouth hung open. He had bruises and cuts around the sides of his mouth. His hands were tied to the bed headrest, his wrists rubbed raw and bloody where he had tried to break free. Again the torso appeared unscathed. As Robert's eyes descended down the length of the body, he mentally prepared himself for what he was going to see.

Mark's penis and testicles had been removed in full; all that remained was a bloody, gaping, circular wound, with jagged edges and flaps of skin hanging loose in places.

As Robert stood there, regretting the pasty he had grabbed on his way to the scene and which was now doing pirouettes in his stomach, he tried to visualise the killer, tried to imagine the setting.

He saw a man, a professional man, allowing and wanting himself to be tied up for sexual thrills. A man who trusted an apparent stranger enough to allow her to render him totally powerless and vulnerable. Why did he trust her? From what he'd read trust was paramount in S&M. You had to be sure the person you were with would stop when asked and not go beyond the agreed rules. How could you guarantee a stranger wouldn't turn out to be a deranged killer? Enough said.

Robert visualized a killer, a female, standing proud over the prostrate figure on the bed, beautiful, strong, athletic. If these men allowed themselves to be lured away by someone, she would have to be pretty damn spectacular, he mused. These were not stupid men, they were successful and both David Saunders and Mark Faversham appeared to take care of themselves physically. Both would have been considered attractive to the opposite sex and would, therefore, be able to pick and choose the women they wanted to spend time with.

He saw her standing over Mark, a dark, faceless form taunting him, a blade in her hand, enjoying his fear, enjoying his pain, relishing his impotence. He could feel Mark's fear.

This murder hadn't been reported until Monday evening when the body had been discovered by Mark's flatmate, so presumably no one had heard any screaming at the time of the murder. Robert liked to think that people would still call Old Bill if they heard the cries of a person in need, so working on that assumption, he could assume that no one had heard anything, or at least nothing they felt worthy of note.

The neighbours were being spoken with to establish if they had indeed heard anything out of the ordinary, but Robert already knew the answer. They wouldn't have heard any screams because Mark had been gagged, the cuts and bruises around his mouth evidenced this theory. He suspected that in keeping with the alternative bondage lifestyle the killer had been able to easily gag Mark under the pretext of sexual play, the real motive being much more sinister and deadly.

Robert looked again at the gash between Mark's extended, stretched legs, the removal of the male organs rendering his body disturbingly androgynous. Was that the killer's plan? There was no doubt that if you wanted to emasculate a man, removal of his dick was a pretty fucking effective and sure fire way to do it. So, what was this killer's problem? What was her motivation? And why did she damage the eye? What part did it play in her scenario?

As the questions tumbled around Robert's skull like dirty laundry in a washing machine, he watched Becca, tweezers in hand collecting fibres, hairs, anything she could find from the bed around the corpse. Collecting fibres, collecting hairs, collecting… souvenirs, just like the killer.

Robert had seen enough. He could feel the tension building behind his eyes, a dull throb beginning to knock gently from the inside of his skull. He signaled to Becca that he was leaving and exited the room. He removed the paper suit he'd been wearing and bundled it up, placing it in a plastic disposal bag brought by the SOCOs.

He walked out of the flat and gave the uniformed officers their instructions, leaving a uniformed inspector in charge of the scene. He also left them his phone number in case they needed to get in touch with him.

Ordinarily he would have stayed at the scene until the SOCOs had completed their examination but he needed to get out of the flat, get some air. He was confident the officers remaining behind were more than competent to manage the crime scene.

Robert was acutely aware of how desperate they now were for a break in the case. And they needed one fast, or the body count would only continue to rise. Maybe something would arise from this latest crime scene? Robert doubted it. This was a clever, meticulous killer. He began to make his way in the direction of the police station then changed his mind. The club would be open in a few hours. It was time to go hunting.

****

The smell of sizzling steak filled the kitchen, the crackle of the burning oil forcing Louise and Ben to talk loudly in order to be heard. The kitchen was large and chic with black granite work tops, chrome handled red units, state of the art appliances and pale grey mock-stone flooring. Louise loved it; it reminded her of a show home she had once seen, modern, sleek and un-lived in.

Although Ben did of course live in this house, it was obvious he was scrupulous with his cleaning efforts. What else does a single-man living on his own without so much as a pet cat do of an evening? Don the marigolds and have a good scrub of course. Louise chuckled at the thought.

'What now Ms Jackson?' Ben asked amused, giving her a sideways glance, one eye trained on the steaks he was poking.

'Nothing.'

She smiled sweetly and raised her wine to her lips feeling better than she had in weeks. She wasn't sure if it was the company, the wine or the fact she had discovered some kind of explanation for the weird things that had been happening to her lately. She didn't even feel that bothered about Steve tonight.

'Should you be prodding the steak like that?' she asked, peering into the frying pan.

'I like to keep moving them about so they don't burn. I let the oil get really hot before I put them in. Brown on the outside, nice and pink on the inside.'

'I see. Is that a technique the gourmet chefs use then?'

Louise leaned one hip against the work top her arms folded beneath her breasts, right hand clutching the stem of the wine glass. Ben ignored her jibe and carried on cooking.

'Aren't you supposed to be sorting out the potatoes? Scoop out the centers and mix them with the cottage cheese,' he ordered.

Louise placed her wine on the counter and began to do as he bid. She was struck by the ease with which they were cooking and preparing dinner together, the picture of domesticity.

'So, Louise, you still haven't told me what the doctor said.' Ben looked up from the steaks, one eyebrow arched quizzically. 'Any reason for that?'

'No, no reason. Just thought I'd wait until we were sitting down for dinner.'

Actually, I don't want you to be pissed that I didn't go...

'Well, tell me now. I was trying to call you all day to find out how you were.'

'I know, I'm sorry. You see the thing is I didn't actually go to the doctor's today, or rather I went but I didn't stay to see the doctor.'

The truth is always better than a lie

'Oh Lou, why not? You promised you would.' Ben stopped poking the steaks altogether and looked at her, unimpressed.

'It's ok Ben, I went to the library and did some research. I think I know what it is that's been causing these hallucinations, visions or whatever they are. It's just simple sleep deprivation.'

'Sleep deprivation? That sounds like bollocks to me.'

'No honest, I spent hours looking it up. You'd be surprised how many books there are on the subject,' Louise said earnestly.

Ben looked at her as if she had just declared that she was in fact a man, his expression a contortion of cynicism and scepticism wrestling with amazement and disbelief.

'Louise, you cannot just read a few books and self-diagnose. This could be serious,' he began.

Louise held up a placating hand and said: 'Look, I know what you think and I understand what you're saying but Ben, I am fine. Honestly. I was a little perturbed by it all at first but now I understand it's nothing more than over work, lack of sleep and too much pressure. I'll go to the chemist tomorrow and get some sleeping tablets, herbal ones at first and if they don't work I will go to the doctor and explain that I can't sleep.'

'I just cannot, will not, explain to a doctor what is happening or they will think I'm mad. You know what I told you about my mother. I will not have them cart me off to some loony bin too. I will not let them poke and probe around inside my head, bouncing around their theories. You know they have to formulate some sort of diagnosis to put on your record and which doctor is going to say it's only sleep deprivation? They're always so scared of getting sued that you just know they would run tests "just to be on the safe side."'

Louise used air quotations to expound her point.

'And you just know they'd find something wrong. They always do! Nobody has a perfect upbringing. They'd be all "so tell me about your childhood? Tell me how you were affected by the death of the pet goldfish." She waved a hand in front of her face dismissively, her eyebrows drawn together in a tight frown, lips pursed in annoyance.

'It's all crap that psycho-babble you know? There is symbolism and meaning in anything and everything if you want there to be and of course, it is all subject to personal opinion and belief,' she finished, sounding somewhat like a petulant child.

'Not a fan of doctors are you?' Ben stated

after a brief pause.

'No I'm bloody not. Look what they did to my mother? Fucking wankers!' she concluded.

'Ok. I won't mention it again. Let's just enjoy dinner and talk about things that won't set either of us off. How does that sound?' Ben extended his hand and Louise shook it.

'Sounds like a bloody good idea to me.' She smiled wearily, feeling like she had already had to justify herself to one skeptic and wondering how many others she would have to convince of her sanity.

As the conversation moved onto more trivial matters and their laughter filled the kitchen, neither of them noticed the man standing in the shadows beyond the kitchen window, collar upturned, darkness enveloping him in her impenetrable embrace. He stood watching until the pair moved into the dining room and turned off the kitchen light.

Then he slowly turned and walked away into the night.

Chapter XX

From the outside the club didn't look particularly special. The tall, imposing entrance revealed no clues as to what could be going on inside. It certainly didn't look like a 'den of iniquity', which was how Robert reckoned Janet Saunders would have described such a place.

The front door was grand; a high, wooden, studded door with a large brass knocker on the front. It was open, and led into a small vestibule where a further, equally grand door prevented nosey parkers like Robert from glimpsing the inner sanctum.

There was a large bouncer on the inner door wearing a full-length, leather coat over black slacks. He reminded Robert of a character from the Matrix movie. All he needed were the frameless, rectangular glasses and the look would have been complete.

As Robert stood there, he wondered how people knew to come to this place. There was no sign, there was no audible music, there wasn't even a venue name over the door. In fact Robert had only worked out that this place was indeed the Garden when he had checked out the neighbouring buildings and discovered that they were all commercial premises that operated in the day.

He leant against a lamp post, watching the entrance to the premises, a true personification of an old-fashioned detective cliché. Now all he needed to complete his look was a Columbo-style mac and a cigar. He didn't have a cigar but he did have a cigarette, which he lit with his cheap throw away lighter. If he didn't have expensive smoker's paraphernalia he could just about convince himself he wasn't really a smoker.

A few people had emerged from the venue and a few had gone in since Robert had commenced his vigil fifteen minutes earlier. Most had been dressed in keeping with social expectations, regular clothing seemingly concealing the fetish apparel beneath, but a few had chosen to be more overt with their garb, sporting PVC trousers and tops, the women exposing swathes of cleavage and leg. Club-goers had presented a form of invitation to the bouncer and this appeared to be enough to secure them entry.

Now, where does one get an official invite?

Robert wasn't really sure what he was looking for as he stood there, leaning up against his trusty lamp post, a cloud of cigarette smoke enveloping his head. He should have been at home with his wife, but instead he had chosen to stand in the street like some sort of naive voyeur, sneaking peeks of a practice with which he was unfamiliar.

He shook his head to himself and was about to turn away to go home, when he heard the club door open again. He looked towards the door, the portal to the other side, and saw a tall, well-built male step out into the street.

He had waist-length, black hair, pale skin and the sort of rugged features one expected of a rock star. He was wearing a short, black leather jacket over a deep red t-shirt and shiny, black trousers. He had an immense presence about him, the type of energy that would cause people to look at him and take heed when he entered a room, which was probably why Robert felt himself being drawn to him.

The man drew a cigarette from a pocket of his jacket and put it between his lips. He checked his pockets repeatedly searching for something to light it with. Robert could just make out whispered expletives as the man continued to fumble through his various pockets for a lighter. As if sensing Robert watching, the man looked up and then, noticing Robert's lit cigarette, strode towards him. As the man approached, Robert extracted his own lighter and offered it to the man. The stranger took it and nodded appreciatively.

'Cheers. Thanks very much.' His voice was deep and gravelly; he even sounded like a rock star.

'No problem,' Robert replied, nodding back and exhaling another cloud of smoke.

The stranger looked Robert up and down, and then looked back at the entrance.

'You going in, then? Or are you just... enjoying the view?' the stranger asked, with a wry smile. He ran a hand through his thick hair and squinted at Robert as if trying to work him out.

'No, no, not going in. I don't have an invite,' Robert replied, thinking fast, 'and I don't know how to get one.' Perhaps he could use this unexpected encounter to his advantage?

'You don't know how to get one?' The stranger seemed unconvinced and Robert guessed he was going to have to play the part of a frustrated husband who needed new kicks without his wife's knowledge.

Margaret, forgive me my love. This is just work, I

promise.

'Well, no. I'm new to all this, or rather, I've never been able to try it out. My wife isn't exactly open-minded, if you know what I'm saying.'

'Ah.' The stranger seemed uninterested and began to turn his back on Robert. Fearing he was about to lose a potential source of information, Robert changed tack.

'I'm guessing I could probably find out more online, but my wife shares the computer and I wouldn't want her finding out. Any papers or mags you can recommend?'

'There are a few,' the stranger said, turning back to face him, 'but seriously, online is best.'

'Why's that?' Robert asked, hoping to appear earnest.

The stranger eyed him again and then asked: 'So, what are you?'

The question was clearly a test to check Robert really was interested in the bondage scene. Why all the secrecy? Robert mused, but then he supposed the social stigma surrounding bondage was probably enough to make anyone at least a little cautious. Look at Tony Jessop's reaction.

'I'm a switch. Or at least I'd like to be. I want both subservience and to be subservient,' he replied, hoping he sounded convincing enough for the stranger to let his guard down, or at least let it down enough so Robert could find out how the hell someone could get into this exclusive club.

'I see. So how'd you find out about this place?' the stranger asked, clearly suspicious.

'I found a card in the back of a cab.' Robert dug out his wallet and produced the card Janet Saunders had given him for the stranger's inspection.

He looked at it and then back at Robert.

'You need to get yourself online. There are loads of sites where you can find out where the next event is going to happen. Some of them get moved around. Lots of people don't like these sorts of clubs, they get fucked off with 'freaks' frequenting their area. This place is invite only, and you can only get an invite on the club's website. It's open most nights, just some nights have special guests and activities. And some nights you want to go somewhere else, you know?'

Robert couldn't imagine what sort of guests and activities would be on the agenda in a place like The Garden.

'Wow, I didn't know people were so hostile. But then as I said, I haven't been able to experience it yet,' he said.

'Yeah, sometimes people are really aggressive. That's another reason for the invitations. You kind of need to know who's coming and going cos the stuff in there is private. Don't want any ol' fucker coming in. And no head cases,'he added

'I get it. But what about someone like me who's never been to anything like this before? Have I got to sign up or something?' Robert asked.

'Yeah, you need to set up a user name and so on. Piece of piss.' The stranger threw his cigarette onto the floor and crushed it beneath his big black boot. Robert quickly offered him another one from his packet, wanting to keep the man talking for as long as possible. He took it and lit it from the flame held in Robert's hand. Robert lit another one too.

'These events are held regularly then?' Robert injected a note of excitement into his voice, which wasn't entirely faked. He was getting excited at the prospect of learning how to become part of this world, to become part of the killer's world.

'Yeah. As I said, this place is open almost every night. Others just spring up as and when. Depends what you're into really.'

'I wish my wife was willing to try this with me. Is that going to be a problem, me turning up on my own?'

'Not necessarily. Everyone in there is liberal. It'll all depend on what you want or what you want to do.' The stranger was grinning at him now. 'After all, it is about fantasy, right?'

Robert smiled back. 'I'm hoping to find that out.'

'What would you have done if you hadn't been able to speak to me?' the man asked.

'I was thinking about mustering up the courage to ask the guy on the door,' Robert lied.

'He wouldn't have told you anything.'

'Then I guess I would have just continued this miserable existence.'

'Miserable, huh? Well, get yourself online and get signed up.'

'Yeah, I'll do that.'

'When you get in there you'll think you died and went to heaven. You've never seen anything like it.'

'I can't wait. Hey, just curious, are most people regulars, or do people come from all over?'

The stranger looked at him quizzically, obviously wondering why he had asked the question.

'I'm just worried about the wife finding out, you know? All the same faces. What if I bump into someone on the street when I'm with her?'

The explanation seemed to satisfy the

mystery man.

'I see. There are certain rules. You don't discuss anything that happens inside a club, you don't tell anyone your real name, unless you really want to, and you don't acknowledge each other outside the club. You're not alone in your predicament. Lots of people can't tell their partners where they're going of an evening.'

Shit. That was going to make for difficult, uncommunicative witnesses and would mean that obtaining the registration information of those that downloaded invites would probably be as good as useless if there was no requirement to actually use your own name.

'Anyway, I've got somewhere to be. Thanks for the light and the cigarette.'

Obviously the conversation was over. Robert smiled.

'Thanks for the chat. You have no idea how much you've helped me.'

****

Louise was laughing so much that her sides actually hurt. She was sat on the sofa in Ben's living room and the pair were giggling like a couple of teenagers that had just performed an infantile prank. The bottle and a half of wine she had consumed probably had something to do with her bout of giggles, but Louise wasn't complaining. It felt so good to be laughing.

Her world had been turned upside down by Steve's infidelity, especially because it was with that bitch Melissa, and then he had lied to her face at the cottage. He was no better than the other men she had known in her life; a liar, a cheat and selfish. She felt wounded and emotionally bereft.

That on top of the 'list of doom' she'd compiled for Ben and the visions of the last few days, it was little wonder she felt pretty damn miserable; she certainly hadn't felt much like laughing recently. Now though, she was having a great time.

As their laughter subsided, they sat back and rested their heads on the large cushioned sofa-back, side by side, relaxed in each other's company. Louise looked at Ben and smiled, almost setting off another fit of chuckling as he grinned back.

'Thanks for letting me stay over Ben. I promise I'll be the perfect guest. I won't throw up in the spare room and I'll even put the toilet seat back up for you,' she joked.

'You're very welcome. I don't like the idea of you sitting home alone pinning for numb nuts. The man is not worthy of your tears,' Ben replied. Louise nodded.

'Like I said, thanks. I don't really want to go home for a bit anyway as it goes.' Louise reached towards the coffee table to pick up her glass of wine and almost slid off the sofa.

'Oops,' she sniggered, picking the glass up with a wavering hand and settling back against the sofa cushions. Ben laughed then looked at her quizzically.

'Why's that?'

'Oh, it's just I had one of my vision things in the flat and it was fucking creepy. I thought I saw some bloke in my kitchen, he was just stood there laughing at me and he had blood on his hands. I actually threw a vase at him, can you believe that? I threw a vase at a vision! Ha!' She started laughing again. 'I threw a vase at a vision!' Ben smiled despite himself; the mental imagery was actually quite funny.

'The really weird thing about it though, is I don't know what I did afterwards, after I broke my vase. I left the flat but I don't know where I went, who I saw or even what I did. I woke up in my flat though, so I guess I can't have gone far. I guess I probably just went for a wander to clear my head or something.' She looked at Ben, trying to work out what he was thinking.

'Had you been drinking?' he asked, glancing at her glass of wine.

'Nope. Not a drop.'

'Well Ms Jackson, you are one strange cookie,' he teased.

'Don't I know it! Come to think of it, I don't really know what I did after coming back from Cornwall either.'

Louise frowned, trying to recall events.

'Nope, don't remember.'

'That's a bit worrying Louise. I wish you had spoken to the doctor you know. Would you go if I came with you?' he asked, genuinely concerned. Louise was touched.

'No, I really don't want to go. They'll just think I'm a loon. Seriously. I'm just going to take it easy for a few days. I will take you up on that offer for some time off and just relax. I'm sure it's just stress. I need to get over Steve. Bastard. But I tell you, I am so glad I punched that bitch Melissa. I've been wanting to do that for ages, even before I knew she and Steve, that she and Steve, well…' her voice trailed off. She didn't feel like laughing anymore. She suddenly felt hollow and alone again.

Ben reached out and took hold of her hand, giving it a gentle squeeze.

'It must have been awful for you, seeing her like that and finding out as you did. The man really isn't worth it Louise. You're better off without him.'

'Thanks Ben. I don't know what I'd do without you right now.' She smiled at him sadly.

'Personally, I think the man's a fool. He was lucky to have you.'

Louise looked at him. He was gorgeous, he was kind, he was considerate. She couldn't imagine him ever hurting her. She slid closer to him on the couch and looked into his face. Suddenly, she moved forward and kissed him, her lips against his, her body pressing against his side. She was surprised when Ben firmly but gently pushed her away from him, his hands on her shoulders pushing her back.

'Louise. Don't,' he said gently.

Louise looked down and felt tears welling up in her eyes. She felt so lost, so alone, she just wanted some affection. And now here she was crying again.

'I'm sorry, I've made a twat of myself.'

'No you haven't, honestly. I think you're amazing, but this isn't right. You're not in a good place right now, your head is all over the place. And you've had a fair few glasses of the ol' vino.' He smiled at her and gently wiped a tear off her cheek. 'I could never take advantage of you.'

Louise looked at him, her eyes sad and moist. It broke Ben's heart to see her looking so vulnerable. She was a beautiful woman both inside and out. He wished he could make her pain go away, protect her from the world.

'I'm so sorry Ben. So sorry.' She began to

sob.

'Come on, it's alright. It doesn't change anything between us, ok? I'll always be here for you.'

As he spoke Louise turned her body into his and buried her head in his chest, her hot tears dampening his shirt. He wrapped his arms around her and held her, letting her cry against him. He didn't know how long he held her, but eventually her body stopped shaking and he could no longer hear her crying.

'Louise?' he whispered softly in her ear. She didn't respond. He said her name again but she still didn't stir. He could tell by the rhythm of her breathing that she had fallen asleep, wrapped up in his arms.

Ben gently moved Louise off him; she didn't wake. He picked her up off the sofa and carried her up stairs to the spare bedroom, twisting and turning his body as he negotiated his way through the house, ensuring Louise's legs and head didn't come into contact with anything. She didn't move, still dead to the world, a mixture of alcohol and exhaustion. Upstairs, Ben gently placed her on the bed in the spare room, laying her on her side, and then pulled the duvet up around her. She looked so peaceful. He hoped her slumber would be equally serene.

Chapter XXI

She could hear his footsteps in the room above, hear him pacing around, clanging pots together, dishes being picked up and put down. She could hear muffled voices, a female's and a male's, the conversation sounding animated as always. She heard stomping footsteps, lighter than his, and then heard a door slam.

A car engine started up moments later and then she heard the crunch of its wheels on gravel as it drove away from the house.

She sighed to herself for she knew what this meant, her body involuntarily tensing in a conditioned response; he was alone and so would be visiting her soon.

Today, though, she was ready for him and she was almost excited by the prospect of his visit. The weapon she had carefully crafted over the past few weeks was ready, its point sharp and lethal. She held it now in her right hand, her thumb gently rubbing the shiny, metal surface, giving her comfort.

She slid it beneath her body, hiding it from view, as she heard his footsteps approaching the basement door. This was it, soon he would feel pain just like she had felt over the years, soon he would be nothing more than a shell, just like she had learnt to become when they did those things to her and made her do those things to them.

She smiled as she thought about what life would be like when she was free of him. It would certainly be better than this present existence.

The basement door opened and his heavy steps caused the staircase to creak as he descended. The basement was gloomy, the two small, rectangular, frosted-glass windows, which sat just above ground level, insufficient to dispel the shadows, but as he opened the door at the top of the stairs he flicked on the light, the single naked bulb now casting a weak radiance around the room. He looked at her and slowly approached the bed.

'What are you smiling at bitch?' he asked, his gruff voice sending shivers down her spine.

She hadn't realised she was still smiling and she was afraid now he would sense what she was planning, sense that there was something different about her. She made her expression blank and closed her eyes afraid that he would see her intentions in them.

'I said what the fuck are you smiling at bitch?'

He was leaning over her now, his face inches away from her own; she could smell his breath and it made her feel sick. She continued to lie motionless, arms by her sides, her legs straight and pulled together. She felt him move away from her face and briefly opened her eyes to see he had moved to the foot of the bed and was taking off his shirt and unfastening his belt, his muscles flexing as he disrobed. She quickly closed them again, afraid of making eye contact.

'So, we're going to be quiet today are we? You know I don't like that, I prefer it when you protest, make noise and put up a little bit of fight. It makes it more fun.'

She could feel his weight on the end of the bed, his hands touching her legs, the contact making her jump.

'That's more like it you stupid fucking bitch.' He laughed, the sound grating and unpleasant.

'Now open your eyes, you know I like you to see me when we're riding.'

She could feel his weight moving up the bed, his naked body hovering inches above her own. She slowly placed her arm under her back and pulled out the weapon, palming it so he couldn't see. She tried hard to keep her breathing regular, to calm herself down, she didn't want him suspecting anything was different.

'Open your eyes bitch, or I swear to God I will make this so painful you'll wish you'd never been born. Open your fucking eyes,' he demanded.

She wanted to obey him so he wouldn't hurt her but she knew she couldn't; he would see her murderous intentions in her eyes if he looked in them, he would see that she was so scared yet so excited about what she was going to do. She wasn't quite ready, her courage wasn't quite there, she just needed a little more time.

'For the last time, cunt, open your fucking eyes!' he shouted in her face. She felt spittle land on her cheeks and his breath moving her hair.

She opened her eyes and looked at him, her gaze penetrating and full of hate. He saw it then, something in her large green eyes besides her shattered innocence, there was a darkness he had never seen before, something different. The girl had changed.

'What's going...' but before he could finish the question she seized the opportunity, took advantage of his proximity and his moment of hesitation.

She raised the metal spike she had crafted and rammed it into his left eye with all the strength she could muster; she screamed at the top of her lungs as she felt the spike connect with his eyeball, felt a gentle pop as it penetrated through the tissue.

He yelled in agony but she was unrelenting, she rammed her fists upwards, against the spike, again and again, driving it deeper and deeper into his skull. He rolled onto the mattress, lying on his back, and she quickly straddled his chest, holding on with her legs as he tried to protect his eyes and get her off him; she continued to beat at the spike, unable to stop, even though her hands were becoming bloody and sore from the repeated contact with the rough end of the metal strut.

Eventually, he stopped screaming and his struggling became feeble. She slid off him and pressed her feet against his body, using her legs like levers to push him off the bed. He fell with a thud onto his side, the momentum of her push propelling him onto his stomach, the spike piercing ever deeper into his skull, and then over onto his back where he finally came to rest, the metal strut standing proud in his eye socket like a flag of accomplishment at the North Pole.

He twitched and spasmed as the last life drained out of him, a pool of blood collecting around his head as it ran in rivulets from his ears and eyes. She had done it, she had killed him. She felt tears well up in her eyes as she realised that she was free, he couldn't hurt her anymore, he would never put those filthy perverted hands on her ever again, he would never again take her riding, never again sell her out to other men for their pleasure. She had won, she was victorious and he had paid with his life.

She stopped crying, using the backs of her bloodied hands to wipe the tears away, crimson smudges marking her cheeks, and ran to the bottom of the stairs where she listened intently for a moment for any noise; all she could hear was her heart pounding in her ears. She took one last look at his ugly, bloodied body and then she ran up the stairs, ran as fast as she could away from him, away from the cellar and out to freedom.

Chapter XXII

Louise turned the key in the lock of her front door wearily. She felt like shit. In fact, she felt like shit that had been run over by a 7-ton lorry. She padded into the flat, throwing her keys onto the small table by the front door. It was 8:30am, but the West-facing flat was still dark, the strengthening sun rising on the opposite side of the building. The flat looked how Louise felt. Depressed.

She'd woken up from her drunken slumber just after six thirty, sweating and scared. She couldn't remember what she'd been dreaming about but upon opening her eyes and momentarily forgetting where she was, the room unfamiliar, she'd experienced a moment of true fear. Upon remembering where she was, she'd rapidly calmed down, until the memories of the night before began to float back into her consciousness.

What had she been thinking? She'd made a pass at Ben, got drunk and told him way more than she should have. She felt vulnerable and didn't like knowing that he knew so much about what had been happening to her. She wished she could turn the clock back and erase the night, suck the words back into her mouth and that stupid kiss. She hoped she hadn't ruined their friendship.

She'd got up then, gingerly, her head pounding, pressing her fingers against her eyes in a vain attempt to massage away the pain. She'd wandered through the house calling out for Ben, receiving no reply. In the living room she'd found a note, scribbled in Ben's hurried, spidery scrawl.

Gone to work. Help yourself to anything you want in the fridge etc. Take as much time off as you need. Will call you later. P.S - How's the head? x

She hadn't taken up his invitation to raid the fridge, preferring instead to just get out of the house as quickly as she could, away from the reminders of last night and her embarrassment.

She'd gathered up her stuff and headed down to the tube to make her way home. The service was always slow that early in the morning, as the city began to crawl back to life, but for once she hadn't minded. She was in no fit state to hurry anyway; it was taking most of her concentration just to navigate the stairs and subways.

And now she was home. She flopped down on the sofa, kicked off her shoes and rested her head against the back rest. She sighed. What a mess she had become, a drunken, exhausted mess.

The mixture of emotions she was feeling was confusing; she was sad about Steve, angry about Melissa, furious at herself for hitting on Ben, scared about the visions and perplexed by her lack of memory. All in all, the combination of these various sentiments just left her feeling depressed and deflated. She didn't recognise herself.

There was a knock at the front door, strong, purposeful. She opened her eyes and considered getting up, then decided that she couldn't be bothered.

Just some peace, that's all I want!

'Miss Jackson?' a voice called out. 'Open the door please!'

She frowned and leaned forward in her seat.

Who the fuck - at this time?

She didn't recognise the voice.

The knocking continued.

'Miss Louise Jackson! Open the door please. It's the police!'

Now she was worried. What the hell had happened?

She pushed herself off the sofa and went to the front door, opening it rapidly, startling the two plain-clothes officers that stood before her brandishing their warrant cards as identification.

'Miss Jackson?' the first copper asked, returning his badge to his jeans pocket as he spoke.

He was about 40 years of age with thick sandy-blond hair, blue eyes and a muscular physique. Stubble littered his chin giving him a rugged, masculine look, but the dark circles under his eyes indicated that he hadn't shaved due to a lack of time caused by an early start rather than for aesthetic purposes.

Cute.

'Yes, that's me. What's wrong? What's happened?' she asked, alarmed.

The second officer spoke now: 'We're from Devon and Cornwall police, we're here to investigate an allegation of assault.'

He was younger than his colleague and almost polar opposite in terms of appearance; overweight, dark haired, dark eyed and clean shaven.

Not so cute.

'Assault?' she asked, confused. Then the penny dropped. 'Ah. I think I know what this is about.'

The second copper spoke again: 'I am

arresting you on suspicion of assault against Miss Melissa Vines. You do not have to say anything, but it may harm your defense if you do not mention…' He prattled off the caution.

Louise bowed her head and began to snicker to herself, she couldn't believe this was happening. The whole situation was ridiculous and she couldn't help but wonder when her life would get back onto an even keel. What else could happen to her?

'You can't be serious. Melissa called you guys? You've had to come all the way up here for this?'

'Yes. Please come with us. We're going to take you to the local police station for a chat on tape. They know we're coming,' the cute officer said.

'Fine. Just let me put my shoes on. I can't believe this. Did she tell you why I hit her?' Louise asked.

'Please don't discuss this with us now Miss Jackson. There'll be plenty of time for that at the station. You are under caution,' the second officer reminded her.

She looked at him, considered making a snide retort, then thought better of it. She pulled her boots on, picked her keys back up and closed the front door. In the hallway the second officer placed her in hand cuffs, taking hold of her arm as if she would flee from him.

'Is that really necessary?' she asked him. 'Where exactly am I going to run to and why would I?'

'No offence Miss Jackson, but I don't know anything about you. You'll be wearing these until we get to the station. You could be storing bodies under your floor boards for all I know. The cuffs stay.'

She shrugged. 'Fine. Lead on.'

The officers escorted her out of the building and towards the unmarked police car on the other side of the road. She felt like a criminal. How much lower could she sink?

****

The briefing room was buzzing. DI Scott had called everybody in. The congregating detectives knew he must have something big to tell them as he had gone back on his word about most of them not needing to come in until the afternoon. Despite their tiredness, they were all chirpy and excited, hoping that maybe there had been a break in the case.

Elizabeth yawned widely, not bothering to cover her mouth.

'Dear God, it's like looking into the jaws of hell,' Greg declared, frowning with disapproval.

'I'm too tired to care about your sensitivities, *Monsieur* Hampton. I was up most of the night taking a statement from our latest victim's gorgeous flat mate, whilst you were most probably snoring your big fat head off,' she replied, moodily.

'Oh really? I'll have you know I also had a late night.'

'Yeah, but you weren't working. Let me guess... pub?'

He grinned at her, his silence speaking volumes.

'Yeah, see? No excuse. Self-inflicted equals what?'

'What?'

'No sympathy, that's what,' Elizabeth stated smugly.

Greg pouted at her and feigned disinterest.

'What do you think the guv's got to tell us?' JB asked as he slipped into a seat behind them. He looked exhausted, his face drawn and pale, his eyes red rimmed.

'No idea, but it had better be good,' Greg said.

'You know it will be,' Elizabeth retorted. 'He wouldn't have brought us in early otherwise.'

'Yeah you're right. It must be a lead,' Greg proposed.

'I bloody hope so. This case is a nightmare. I don't think I've ever worked on one that has been so forensically challenged,' JB declared. 'Have you?'

'No, this killer is definitely in another league,' Elizabeth said. Greg nodded in agreement.

'Elizabeth would know. Ask her what happens to all her boyfriends and why we never see them again once she's introduced them to us? In her freezer, that's where you'll find them...' Greg teased.

'When did you look in my freezer?' Elizabeth asked, in mock surprise.

The detectives laughed together, enjoying the moment of light-heartedness.

Robert walked in and an anticipatory hush descended upon the room. All eyes were on him trying to assess from his demeanour whether the news they were about to hear would be good or bad, whether it would mean another long day for them, or whether they would be able to go home and spend some time with their families.

Robert's body language wasn't giving much away. He walked straight over to the 'brain board' as they called the white board at the front of the room, which was covered with pictures and diagrams, theories, names and places, all pertaining to the bondage killer enquiry. It was fully up to date, photos of Mark Faversham included, the board having been updated by Becca first thing that morning.

'David Saunders, Mark Faversham. Both into bondage, both highly successful. One married, one single. Different ages, same ethnic background. Both fit and healthy, both wealthy. Both were tied up and mutilated, both had a sharp implement delivered to the eye. One was killed in a London hotel, the other in his own flat. Trophies, in the form of the victims' genitalia, were taken away from the scene in both cases. Both men appear to have placed a significant amount of trust in the killer. The question is why? Why did these men let a stranger come back with them?' Robert paused for effect.

He had their attention and he could see their minds turning over what he had said, pondering possibilities.

'Perhaps she was just too good to resist?' said JB.

'Or I'm guessing that maybe because she's a woman they don't feel threatened by her,' said Tony.

'Or maybe they had met before,' murmured Greg.

'The truth is that it could be any one of those things or a combination of all of them. There's a code of conduct in these places, you don't engage with each other out of role, people don't give their real names and secrecy ties all the participants. Basically, you don't blab,' Robert said, amused despite himself at their surprised faces. 'How do I know this?'

'The question was going through my mind

guv,' Elizabeth smiled.

'Well, I went to the Garden last night. I didn't go in and I hadn't actually intended on going there, but I stood outside for a while just watching the comings and goings. I got into conversation with a club-goer and had quite an interesting chat.'

Elizabeth and JB looked at each other.

'I thought you wanted us to go there?' JB asked.

'I did, maybe still do, but once I'd left the Faversham crime scene I wanted to go out and get some perspective. I just wanted to see the place with my own eyes.'

'What else did you find out?' Tony asked, guessing there had to be more to follow.

'I found out that to get into the club you have to have an invite, which you can only get online. We know David Saunders frequented the Garden at least once because his wife found the club's business card in his suit pocket. We don't know where Mark Faversham went Saturday night, but we do know it was a bondage club in the city because he told his flat mate, but I'm going to assume that wherever he went also requires an invite of some sort...'

'I get it - the internet guv. That's what you're saying isn't it? That's the link between our victims and the killer?' Elizabeth asked. A murmur went around the room.

'I think it's an avenue we definitely have to pursue,' Robert replied.

'Just because you have to download an invitation doesn't necessarily mean there's a link between the victims and the killer,' Greg started, 'It just means that they all have access to the internet as does almost every UK household.'

Some of the officers nodded in agreement.

'But are you thinking there are forums, or online chat rooms?' Elizabeth asked Robert.

'Possibly, we need to check it out. It's not something I've ever looked at online so I don't know what sort of sites exist.'

'I guess that would make sense. The killer logs on, starts chatting away to a potential victim and then suggests meeting in one of the clubs. She's the one in control then isn't she? Because at the end of the day, they have to trust her, sure, but she also has to trust them and know they're not going to hurt her. Otherwise she could be putting herself in danger. God the irony!' Elizabeth declared.

'So what do you want us to do guv?' Greg asked, already confident he knew the answer and that it would mean a lot of hard work.

'We need to get both of the victims' computers forensically analysed. I want each machine thoroughly checked, deleted files, saved chat messages, previous internet history, anything and everything contained on those machines is to be looked at,' Robert began. 'I've arranged for an officer from the high-tech crime unit to come over and assist us with this. He'll be seconded for the duration of the enquiry.'

'What about their phones? I'm guessing we'll be checking Saunder's phone again and submitting the latest victim's?' Tony asked.

Mr Saunders' phone had already been checked for messages and contacts, but now it would be subjected to a more thorough analysis, including deleted messages, saved files, images, videos and email correspondence. Mark Faversham's phone had yet to be analysed, but it would be subjected to the same barrage of analysis.

'And I'm guessing we're going to want the call data for the phones too to see if there are any common numbers between the victims?' JB finished.

'Yes definitely,' Robert agreed.

'Just thinking, and you've probably already thought of this, but would it be worth us getting the undercover super computer snoopers on board, given this latest development?' Greg suggested.

Elizabeth and JB nodded in approval.

'The covert online investigations team? Absolutely. In fact give them a call after this briefing Greg and tell them the situation. We may need their services, depending on what we find on the computers. If there's any evidence of a chat room or forum that both our victims used, then certainly we will begin that process.'

'But there may be loads of sites, forums and what have you. The killer could use more than one?' Elizabeth piped up.

'True, but hopefully the computers will give us something to work with,' Robert replied. 'By the way Elizabeth, how are you getting on with the database of names of care children?'

'It's coming together slowly. It's not complete yet as I'm still waiting for several councils to provide me with the data I need.'

'Ok, good work. One last thing, Tony can you do some digging around this club's website. The guy told me last night that apparently you have to register if you're to get an invite to one of the clubs, so the company that runs the website must have a database of users. We'll probably need a court production order to get the information released and

I expect that most people don't provide any real details when signing up, but see what you can do, ok?'

'Sure, I'm on it,' Tony said

'Elizabeth can you find out if there is any council CCTV that covers the street the club is on? Get that downloaded as a priority.'

'Of course.'

'Right team. Let's get moving on seizing those computers. Two of you to go to the Saunders' house, two of you to Faversham's, two to prep and brief the high-tech guy and the rest of you crack on with the other enquiries. Don't forget to call the IT department before you begin searching for any sex-related sites or they're going to think you're all surfing for porn. I don't want Professional Standards thinking I run a team of sex addicts who can't even wait to get home to get their porn fix.'

Everyone laughed at this.

'Guv, what about the visit to the Garden?' Elizabeth asked.

'We're going to hold off for now. Let's see what else we can dig up first. Besides, from what I gathered yesterday, they're not going to be forthcoming witnesses. We may follow it up later.'

Elizabeth was a little disappointed. She looked at JB, a mischievous smile tugging at her lips.

'That's a shame. I was looking forward to seeing your little puny chicken legs enveloped in PVC,' she joked.

'Sadly it is not to be, and that pleasure shall have to be saved for you for another day,' JB laughed.

'Ok everyone. Back here for five o'clock please,' Robert barked.

The detectives filed out of the room like pupils dismissed from class, each one hoping that the day's enquiries would bring them one step closer to the bondage killer.

Chapter XXIII

The police interview room was hot and stuffy, the two Devon and Cornwall officers, Louise and her duty solicitor crammed into the small room, sitting on chairs bolted to the floor. In fact, everything in the room was pinned down; even the three-deck tape recorder was fastened to the table. A thin black strip of plastic stuck mid-way up the walls circled the room. This apparently was an alarm; if it was touched it would send an alert to the custody suite and the interview room would suddenly fill with highly-strung officers, brandishing batons and looking for trouble. At least that was what the officers had told Louise upon entering the room. She'd been tempted to press it just to see what would really happen.

Earlier, they'd transported her to the police station, handcuffed and humbled. Louise hadn't even wanted to look out the window as they'd driven her through the streets of London to a local police station, such was her embarrassment. The police officers hadn't bothered trying to speak to her so she'd spent her time gazing at the car's carpeted floor, counting the crumbs and bits of debris that were collected there.

Louise had felt so broken and alone during the journey to the police station; she'd wanted to cry but pride had prevented her from giving in to her tears. How had her life become so fucked up? She had been sailing along quite happily, loving her job, her man, her life in general and then, suddenly, she'd been betrayed by that same man, her career was in jeopardy and she was sitting in the back of a police car wearing handcuffs.

The custody sergeant booking her in at the station had been friendly, exercising that cop humour which was dry yet affable, in a bid to put her at ease. It hadn't worked; she'd still felt scared and alone. He'd asked her if she wanted anyone advised she was at the police and she had considered calling Ben; ultimately she'd decided against it, her shame from the previous evening still causing her cheeks to burn.

And now here she was, sitting in the interview room, looking across the table at the officers, the tape machine whirring quietly in the background. They'd already done the legal part of the interview, her rights, entitlements... blah, blah, blah.

She'd tuned them out; her solicitor had explained all this before the interview began. Now they were telling her why she had been arrested and asking her for her account.

'Ms Jackson, can you tell us what led up to the events described by Ms Vines? We've told you what she's saying, what the allegation is, anything you want to say to that?' the cute officer asked her, the ugly one seemingly taking notes, or doodling; Louise couldn't tell.

'Well, I had just driven down to Cornwall, thinking that it would be a nice surprise for Steve... He'd been pretty off with me because I couldn't go away with him. He always said I put my work before him and I guess, with hindsight he was right. The company I work for is -'

'Which company is that Ms Jackson?'

Louise didn't appreciate ugly cop's interruption. 'Why do you need to know that?' she asked.

'So we can follow up, test the veracity of your account,' he replied, looking at her sternly.

Cute cop didn't appear too amused with ugly cop's interruption either, judging from the way he way looking at him, his lips pursed, one eyebrow raised.

'Well, maybe it would be a good idea to let me finish my account before you 'test for veracity'. What do you reckon?' Louise stated, snidely.

Ugly cop looked back down at his notes.

Obviously not used to interviewees with an IQ over 100.

'Please go on Ms Jackson,' the good looking officer encouraged, amused, a slight smile pulling at his lips. His colleague was young in service and too arrogant for his own good; it was entertaining seeing an interviewee putting him in his place.

'As I was saying,' she resumed, 'the company I work for is struggling and I needed to attend an event with my boss. We were hopeful it would drum up more business and it was because of this event that I couldn't go away with Steve. We had a big row, but we did actually make up before he went away.'

The memory of their make-up sex and the mysterious woman's face at the window came back to her in a flash, the images startlingly clear and bright. She stopped talking briefly and shivered. She looked back at the cute officer, hoping he hadn't noticed her stalling. She was definitely not revealing any of that to the police. He didn't appear to have noticed, probably assuming she was just taking her time to recollect events as they had happened.

'As soon as I got down there I kind of guessed something was wrong. All the curtains were drawn but the door to the cottage was open, so I went in, and I noticed two wine glasses in the kitchen. This made me immediately suspicious; I just knew he had another woman there - '

'Has he cheated on you before?' again it was ugly cop interrupting her flow.

How fucking rude!

'How is that any of your business, or even relevant, and where do you get off interrupting all the fucking time?' Louise could feel herself getting angry.

'Hey, no need to swear at me. You've obviously got a temper...' he almost whispered the last few words.

'Are you intentionally trying to antagonize me? I'm here, being totally honest with you and you're just trying to make me feel worse than I already do. You're purposely trying to rile me! I'm trying to tell you what happened, perhaps even manage to elicit a single iota of empathy from you, and all you do is interrupt me, patronise me and treat me like I've committed the worst crime of the century!'

Louise's solicitor gently touched her arm. 'He is allowed to ask these questions Louise,' he said quietly. 'Although officer, I think it would be respectful of you to at least allow my client to answer one question at a time.' This time he injected authority into his voice.

Cute copper intervened: 'Ms Jackson, I'm

sorry my colleague's questions are upsetting you and that you feel you are not having sufficient time to respond. There is no time limit on this interview, so please take all the time you need.'

She cocked her head slightly, her face suddenly taking on a harder, darker expression, her eyes glinting.

'Are you in a committed relationship?' she asked.

'Ms Jackson, I am asking the questions here,' cute copper replied, his eyebrows raised for emphasis.

'Look, I know you're in charge, you're the boss and I'm the lowly criminal, but please, do me this one courtesy and talk to me like a human being. Are you in a committed relationship?'

Louise's designated solicitor looked at her beseechingly, wondering what on earth his client was going to say next.

Cute copper sat back in his chair, a slight smile again twitching at the corners of his mouth. He put his pen on the desk, seemingly deliberating if he was going to respond.

'Yes. I am.'

Louise smiled back at him: 'And how would you feel if you walked in to find a man lying in your girlfriend or wife's bed? Not only is he lying there but he's taunting you, telling you you're not good enough for the woman you love? Telling you that he is better than you and can please your woman more than you can?'

'Louise…' the solicitor began, turning in his chair to look at her straight on.

'No, I'm curious,' Louise turned away from him, 'to hear what the officer has to say,' she finished.

He looked at her and Louise noted the compassion in his face. This man didn't want to be here, probably had better things to do; he was just doing his job and he didn't agree with what his job was requiring him to do at that precise moment. This glimmer of humanity warmed Louise.

'I would beat him to a pulp,' the officer replied dead pan, 'and once I'd finished with him I would throw her out of the house faster than you could say 'call the police'. That is in an ideal world of course. But Ms Jackson, we don't live in an ideal world, do we?' he leaned forward.

She also leaned forward: 'No, we don't.'

'So, you can't go around punching people, even if you feel you have just cause, can you?'

'No, and I really wish I hadn't hit her, I should have hit him instead. Takes two to tango, doesn't it officer?'

Are you flirting with this man, in front of his idiot colleague and your solicitor?

Ugly copper interjected: 'So in summary, you admit to hitting Ms Vines, are demonstrating remorse and wish you had hit your ex instead. That about right?'

Louise and cute cop were still looking at each other.

'Ms Jackson? Is that right?' repeated the second officer.

'Yes,' she said without taking her eyes off cute copper, her eyes searching his face.

He returned her gaze: 'I have no further questions Ms Jackson. This interview is concluded,' he said abruptly.

He turned off the tape recorder and stood

up, leaving his colleague wondering what the hell had just happened.

'I suspect your solicitor will want to have a chat with you. We'll be in the custody area when you're ready,' he finished before exiting the room, the second officer trailing after him.

What just happened? Who the fuck did I just turn into? Since when do I use my sexuality as a tool?

Louise was genuinely perplexed. She couldn't register what the solicitor was saying; something about a caution, nothing to worry about, not a conviction... She heard herself answering him but her mind was elsewhere.

The room was spinning, she couldn't focus on anything; the solicitor's words were coming to her as if through a thick wall and slowed down like an audio tape in a dying cassette player. Suddenly she fell forward, her head and shoulders collapsing onto the desk in front of her as blackness engulfed her.

****

'Post for you Ben.' Vanessa swung into Ben's office, one hand on the door frame, the other holding a wad of white and brown envelopes.

Vanessa had been in charge of the post for as long as Biztalk had been in operation. She was doing her morning rounds, delivering and collecting the various correspondence that needed to be both sent out and distributed to the various departments within the building. She smiled as she placed Matt's post on the desk, her neat dyed-red bob bouncing around her head as she flounced into the room.

She was known as the 'Little ray of sunshine' for her small stature, upbeat disposition and ever-present smile. At 50 years of age, and with a curvy, slightly rotund frame, Vanessa was seen as something of a mother figure by the younger members of staff. She always made time to give advice, engage in chit chat and listen to people's worries.

Ben looked up from his computer. 'Morning Vanessa. Chirpy as ever I see.'

'Indeed, which is not what can be said for you, by the looks of you,' her voice was gentle and deep, her concern genuine.

Ben's eyes were red rimmed and puffy, the dark circles beneath them betraying his tiredness. Grey stubble peppered his chin and cheeks and his hair was dishevelled. He did not look good.

'Hmmmm…' he grunted, returning to his work, clearly not in the mood to talk.

'You ok, Ben?'

Vanessa slunk into the chair opposite him on the other side of his desk and looked at him, trying to make eye contact. Ben didn't look up and continued tap, tap, tapping on his computer keyboard.

'Let's just say,' he replied eventually between taps, realising that Vanessa was in no hurry to leave his office, 'that I have been better.'

He stopped typing and reached for the post Vanessa had placed on his desk.

'You want to talk about it?'

'Not particularly, no. In fact Vanessa, I don't mean to be rude, but I could really do with being alone right now and cracking on with what I've got to do.'

He began shuffling through the post, prioritising which envelope he would open first.

'No problem Ben, I'll leave you to it. Do you want me to make you a nice cup of tea?' she asked, standing up and heading towards the door. Vanessa firmly believed that a good cup of tea could solve even the most problematic situation.

'Vanessa, you are an angel, but no thank you.'

'You know where I am if you change your mind.' She left the room, a vague scent of perfume wafting after her.

Ben looked at the envelopes, they were all printed except for one which had been hand-written in capital letters. He picked it up and opened it with an old-fashioned silver letter opener, an expensive gift from Louise last Christmas.

As he opened the envelope two grainy photos fell out face down onto the desk. Ben looked at them quizzically and turned them over.

The first image showed Ben kissing and hugging Louise in greeting the night before. They were standing on his door step, his arms wrapped around her.

'What the...?'

Ben turned over the second photograph, his breath catching in his throat. The image had obviously been taken by a long-range lens as it lacked some clarity but it was obvious that the people in the image were Ben and Louise.

The picture must have been taken through his hallway window and it showed him carrying Louise up the stairs, her head resting against his chest, her legs dangling over his right arm. Perplexed Ben reached into the envelope and withdrew a letter from within. The letter, unlike the envelope, was typed.

As he read, Ben's mouth dropped open in disbelief. He could feel rage and indignation swirling through him in eddies of pique. He looked down at the signature of the sender and let out a snort of rage.

It was signed 'DC'. There was only one person that Ben knew with those initials, only one person who would harbour enough hate to attempt to blackmail him. It could only be Derek Cooper.

****

Louise was sat on a long bench pressed up against the wall at the back of the custody suite. She had just been seen by the police force medical examiner after her blackout in the interview room. Cute cop sat next to her, a Styrofoam cup of water in his hand.

'Here, drink this.'

He handed Louise the water and she drank it gratefully. Her throat felt parched and she still felt slightly light-headed and woozy.

'Thanks,' she mumbled.

The cute copper leant back against the wall, his legs stretched out in front of him.

'Well, I've never had that happen before. Never had a prisoner pass out in interview.'

'A prisoner? Jeeze… And there I was thinking it was all about being innocent until proven guilty.' Louise downed the last of her water and leant forward, her elbows on her knees.

'Well you did admit punching Miss Vines,' the officer leant in and spoke softly, 'not that I blame you.' He smiled at her and Louise was grateful for the suggestion of allegiance, even if he didn't really mean it. 'Unfortunately, that is just what we call people in our custody - prisoners. Nothing personal.'

Louise nodded. She wasn't really interested anymore. She wasn't in the mood to flirt, to play games, to answer back. She just wanted to get out of the custody suite, go home and have a nice, long, soak in a hot, bubbly bath.

The medical examiner had told her she'd had a faint, probably brought on from the stress of the last few days and the current police investigation. She hadn't argued, what did she know? Stress - the silent killer.

She couldn't help but wonder if the blackout was in some way connected to the hallucinations she'd been having. After all, this wasn't the first one she'd had. How else could she explain having absolutely no memory of her return trip from Cornwall?

'I'm sorry about my colleague's behaviour. He's new and overzealous. He hasn't yet learnt how to speak to people amicably, whilst maintaining a degree of authority,' cute cop continued.

'What, like you?'

Cute cop ignored the question and stood up. He walked over to the custody desk and began a conversation with the smart-looking custody sergeant.

Louise hung her head and closed her eyes. Her solicitor had already told her what would happen next. She'd been advised that if she admitted punching Melissa she would be offered a caution, given that it was her first offence and it wasn't particularly serious in the scheme of things. A caution suited Louise as it wasn't a conviction and was not something that would automatically have to be declared if she needed to take a new job, something that was beginning to look more and more likely, given the potential imminent demise of Biztalk and her freakish spell of bad luck.

'Miss Jackson, could you come over here please?' The custody sergeant beckoned to her.

Slowly she stood up, her legs felt like jelly and she almost swooned. She walked up to the custody desk and tried desperately to listen to what the custody sergeant was saying, but her brain was simply not taking it in. She was proffered a piece of paper and asked to sign it, which she did unquestioningly. Apparently, that was it. The case was complete, she was free to leave and her property was returned to her.

She walked slowly out of the custody suite, the big custody door clanging shut behind her. The fresh air felt fabulous against her face and she inhaled deeply.

She switched on her mobile phone and felt it vibrate gently in her hand as it alerted to her to a missed call and a new voice mail message. Louise glanced down and noted the caller ID. It was Ben. Although she knew she should at least listen to the voicemail and find out what Ben wanted, she just couldn't face it at that moment. She simply wanted solitude. She wanted to go home and recompose. Louise glanced up the road and noted the familiar red and blue circle of a London Underground roundel indicating a tube station in the distance.

She returned her mobile phone to her pocket, pulled up her collar and was just about to head off when she heard someone calling her name. She turned and saw an attractive young female with long blonde hair, a tight figure, wearing a dark grey suit, waving at her. The woman walked briskly towards her.

'Louise? My god, I can't believe it's you! I'm Elizabeth Lane. We went to school together for a couple of years at Northborough High.'

The woman extended her hand and Louise took it, initially confused, until memories of her school days floated back into her consciousness.

'Busy Lizzy? Oh my god!' Louise smiled warmly as she remembered her old school colleague from all those years ago. 'What on earth are you doing here? How long has it been?'

They shook hands firmly and Elizabeth motioned with her head to the police station.

'Well believe it or not, I now work here. I'm a detective. Been a police officer for eight years now.'

'No! Seriously? Busy Lizzy *has* been busy, hey? Who would have thought?'

'I know it's crazy isn't it! What about you? What brings you here? I didn't even know you were in London? It's been over 15 years since we spoke.'

'15 years. Time sure flies, huh? Unfortunately, I wasn't here by choice, I was an unwitting guest,' Louise replied.

'Ah, I see.'

The women then heard someone shouting for Elizabeth. Tony Jessop was standing outside the police station, holding the door open with his foot.

'Elizabeth, phone call. Sounds important. It's the council,' he shouted.

'Oh great! I'll be right there!' Elizabeth shouted back at him.

She turned to Louise: 'Look, I would love to catch up with you. I'll be honest, I saw you coming out of the interview room earlier, so I kind of guessed you weren't here by choice. You don't look that different. Give me a call later, ok, and we'll arrange a get together, if you fancy it?' Elizabeth reached into her suit pocket and produced a shiny business card with her details.

'Well, I just might do that. Detective.' Louise took the card and shook her head. 'This is surreal.'

Elizabeth frowned not knowing what Louise meant.

'I have to run. Call me ok?' and with that Elizabeth turned on her heal and jogged back towards Tony, who was still holding the door open. Louise watched until Elizabeth and Tony disappeared from sight.

Biztalk going down the pan, hallucinations, being arrested and now a blast from the past. Whatever next?

Chapter XXIV

Elizabeth thanked the caller on the end of the phone and hung up, smiling widely.

'Well, my list is almost complete. That was the last borough council to respond to my request. Just got to add the details to my Excel spreadsheet and I'll have a list of all the names of white females that were put into care after experiencing sexual abuse in London and whose date of birth would now make them anywhere between twenty five and thirty five,' she said to Tony, who was busy reading witness statements relating to the killings, reviewing the evidence, looking for clues that may have been missed. He put the papers down.

'You're putting a lot of faith into a lot of assumptions Elizabeth. I'm pleased you've got all your information but I am not convinced anything will stand out from it. I mean we don't even know the age of the killer, or that she was put in care, sexually abused or that she lived or lives in London.'

'Yeah I know, but it's one hypothesis of many. I read that most serial killers begin honing their skills in their mid to late twenties so based on that and the fact that our killer now has two bodies to her name, I'm going to assume she is somewhere in that age bracket. Some assumptions can be deduced from the logical application of psychological probabilities, Tone,' Elizabeth retorted.

'Just don't pin all your hopes on it, is all I'm saying.'

'Well, thank you for the advice and don't worry, I won't. It's just an idea. I know it may well come to nothing, but it's something to explore and, by keeping myself busy, I keep out of mischief.'

'Hmmm, indeed.' Tony looked up from the papers scattered across his desk. 'Who was that woman you were talking to earlier?' he asked.

'The one outside?'

'Yeah.'

'Oh just someone I knew at school. We used to hang out, smoke cigarettes and make fun of the boys. She was only at my school for a couple of years, but we had a lot of fun during that time. Weird actually as we didn't know each other that well in reality but we just ended up larking around together. I haven't seen her in over 15years. The last time I saw her I was 15 or 16 I think.'

'She was hot.'

'Yeah, she always was popular with the boys.'

'You seeing her again are you?' Tony probed.

'What's it to you? She could be married for all you know and have a litter of sprogs'

'Is she? And does she?'

'How should I know?'

'You'll let me know when you find out won't you?'

'Jesus Tony, what am I? Your pimp or something?'

'Just a little friendly favour Elizabeth, that's all I'm asking,' Tony winked at her.

'God I hate it when you do that.'

'What?'

'Try and use your charm and good looks on me. I'm impervious, you know.'

'No you're not, you love it. Go on, just one little favour. You never know, she could be the woman for me.'

'And there I was thinking that was me. Hmmm... well, if she calls, I'll see what I can find out for you. But, just don't pin all your hopes on it, is all I'm saying,' Elizabeth replied smugly.

'Touché Ms Lane.' The pair laughed and continued laughing as the office door swung open and Greg came sauntering in, followed closely by an officer neither recognised.

'This is Elizabeth and Tony,' Greg began, the officers all extended hands and exchanged formalities. 'And this is Ian. He's come over from the covert unit at headquarters to assist us with the online investigation. I'm just showing him around and filling him in on the investigation thus far,' Greg said by way of introduction.

Detective Constable Ian Burell was a tall, imposing man in his late 40s. He had peppered grey hair that was cut close to his scalp and this, along with his tailored suit, rendered him the epitome of distinguished. His eyes were dark and intelligent, his hand shake firm and strong. Elizabeth liked him instantly. He seemed solid and reliable. Tony disliked him immediately. He seemed smug and arrogant.

In Tony's experience, a lot of officers that worked out of the force headquarters building, especially those involved with the covert side of policing, had over-inflated opinions of themselves, the fact that they frequently brushed shoulders with high-ranking officers in the corridors of power seemingly pandering to their sense of self-importance.

This coupled with the Force's biased budgetary spending for projects initiated by those working at headquarters, as if working in that building somehow guaranteed that all their proposed projects were marks of genius, served to really get up Tony's nose.

'So, this is where the investigation is being run?' Ian remarked conversationally, his eyes taking in the strewn papers and glowing computer screens.

'Yes, we set this office up as the incident room. It's the only one in the building fit for purpose to be honest,' Tony replied. 'We don't have the same luxuries as you guys over at headquarters. There's a lot less funding over here.'

Elizabeth looked at Tony, surprised at his brusqueness.

'I think you'll find that's the same everywhere. There's never enough money in the pot, is there?' Ian replied, failing to be antagonized by Tony's comment. 'Is this where I'll be working?' Ian addressed his question to Greg.

'No, you're going to be upstairs with the computer geeks, on the fourth floor.'

'Only fitting that an officer from headquarters be located upstairs above us lowly minions,' Tony mumbled.

Ian looked at him and said: 'You get overlooked for a job at FHQ or something? You got something you'd like to share?'

'No. I just don't like the way you lot come over here and lord it like you're some sort of big shot. We have the same rank, we do the same job, you just get all the funding, praise and overtime.'

'Listen, I know about this investigation, I have been briefed. I know that you have jack shit to go on and this is why your DI requested I come over. I am here by invitation mate so I suggest you get used to it,' Ian retorted, becoming annoyed.

'Tony, what has got into you?' Elizabeth whispered from the corner of her mouth.

His mood had completely changed; two minutes ago they had been sharing a laugh, and now Tony looked as if he was sucking on lemons. The two men stood facing each other in a pose reminiscent of a Mexican stand-off. Who would draw first? The local sheriff, or the stranger that had just wandered into town?

'Tell you what Ian, let me show you upstairs,' Greg said, diffusing the situation.

'Good idea,' Elizabeth concurred. 'Nice to meet you Ian. Looking forward to working with you on this enquiry and getting some results.'

'Nice to meet you too. Hopefully the computers will reveal a little gem we can use and give this case a break.' Ian smiled at her and then followed Greg out of the office.

Elizabeth turned to look at Tony.

'Tony! What was that all about? You don't even know the guy!' Elizabeth demanded.

'No, but I know his type. Think they're better than all of us.'

'What's up with you? You haven't been yourself the last couple of days... You blew up in the briefing, you're getting all hot and bothered now. Want to tell me what's going on?'

'Nothing's going on, I'm just tired. And I guess a part of me didn't want FHQ involved in this.

You know how it is, they come over here, we get a break in the case and no matter where that break originated from, it's always down to the FHQ officer's great work. They all look out for each other over there, little boys club, that's what it is. I bet they're all bloody masons!'

'Oh Tone, you are funny sometimes. It doesn't matter who gets the recognition as long as the job gets done right? We're all on the same side.'

'Well you would like to think so but that's not the way it seems to pan out. In my experience this department always gets overlooked.'

'Come on, cheer up! Tell you what, how about I buy you a nice cold pint after the briefing this afternoon? Would that make you feel better? Then you can tell me what's really got you grumbling.'

'That's not a bad idea. I could do with a drink.'

'Perfect. Now will you please get the stick out of your ass and relax a bit?

'I'll try,' Tony said.

'That's all I ask.' Elizabeth smiled and the detectives got stuck back in to their paper work.

****

The room was dimly lit, illuminated solely by a television in the corner of the room. Images from the device scurried across the walls and danced across her pupils as she watched the evening news on mute. She quietly raised a glass of red wine to her lips as she watched, a gamut of emotions thrilling through her at the headline emblazoned across the bottom of the screen, big bold letters proclaiming

'Breaking News' and 'Murder.' She smiled to herself; this was her work, her vengeance, broadcast to the nation.

Two photos then appeared on the screen of the men she'd killed, smiling and posed, presumably with the reporter providing a brief narrative of their lives as an accompaniment to the images.

Although she was personally more interested in their deaths, she found herself intrigued by what sort of men they might have been in life. Adulterers, weak, idolising. Dead. That much she did know.

She pointed the remote control at the TV and turned up the sound, no longer satisfied to watch the report in silence.

'...successful and much respected businessman, leaves behind a wife and two children...'

Adulterer, weak, idolising. Dead.

'The murder of Mr Saunders occurred only five days before the discovery of the body of the second male believed to have been murdered by the same suspect. The second victim has been named as Mr Mark Faversham, and his body was discovered by his flat mate on Monday night, two days after police believe he was in fact murdered. He was single and worked as an investment banker in the City...'

Ok, so not an adulterer, but still weak, idolizing and dead. She nodded her head and raised her glass towards the TV in an insincere apology at incorrectly labeling him an adulterer.

The camera settled back onto the somber visage of the young reporter relaying the story, his eyes wide, hair swarming around his head in the breeze, as he valiantly tried to retain his composure and ignore his unruly mop.

'...so far no connection has been made between the two victims, it is not known if they were known to each other or why these men were targeted. The murders have been linked, police say, due to consistencies in the MO, the manner in which the men were killed, although they are not prepared to say exactly what that MO is at this stage...'

As the camera panned out, she could see that the reporter was stood outside the police station where the case was apparently being investigated. Just as she was starting to get bored of the missive and was about to turn the volume back down, the young reporter introduced a police officer who was purportedly in charge of the investigation. She watched again, intently.

'Can you tell us anything else about the victims at this stage?' the young reporter asked.

The camera moved to the right a little and the officer came into view.

His face was round, his hair receding and a small, double-chin provided evidence of a slightly overweight body beneath his expensive-looking suit and perfectly knotted tie. He had a certain gravitas about him, probably due to his deep voice and she eyed him up curiously; so this was the face of her enemy. This was the man who was leading the hunt to find her.

She felt a sudden jolt of fear, an explosion in her chest as she wondered what he knew about her. Did the police have any leads? Had they worked out how she found her victims? Had she left any clues behind? She'd been careful at each crime scene, rubbing the bodies with antiseptic gel and carefully wiping the surfaces she may have touched prior to putting on her PVC gloves, effectively scrubbing away any traces of her DNA and fingerprints. But what if she'd missed something?

'Both the males that were murdered were successful in their chosen fields, they were both described as being popular and well liked. We do not know at this stage if there is a link between them but we do know they were both killed by the same killer judging by the manner in which the bodies were found and the way they were killed.'

The banner at the bottom of the screen gave the officer's name as Superintendent Meadows.

'Are you in a position to elaborate on the way in which the bodies were found? Or even tell us how they were killed?' the young reporter asked.

'Both males died from stab wounds. That is all I am prepared to say at this time.'

Stab wounds? That's quite the euphemism…

'Are you close to identifying the suspect?'

'We are pursuing a number of leads and are hopeful we will identify the culprit soon. Meanwhile, I ask that if anyone knows anything about these murders that they contact us. Any information will be treated in confidence. That's all for now.'

Superintendent Tim Meadows looked as if he was about to walk away when the reporter piped up.

'Just one more question please sir, what about the killer? Can you tell us anything at all about the man responsible for this?'

Meadows looked at the reporter and paused.

'I didn't say we were looking for a man.'

He then turned away from the reporter and strode back towards the police station.

'Does that mean the suspect isn't a man? Sir!

Sir! Are you looking for a woman then?'

The reporter fired questions at Meadows's back as he disappeared back inside the police station.

The camera swiftly focused back on the reporter who excitedly began paraphrasing what Meadows had said.

'And as you just heard, the police have not said they are looking for a male suspect in this case so the killer could be a woman. I suspect the police may even be suggesting that the murderer is in fact a woman given this observation about gender. This is an interesting development and one which potentially puts a new slant on...'

The reporter continued to speculate as to what exactly Meadows had meant, prattling on and hypothesizing, his voice now annoying her. She returned the TV to mute, wanting silence so she could think.

So they had pieced together that the killer was a woman. She wasn't that surprised as it was only a matter of time and she was actually glad that Meadows had stated this on national TV. Her message would be all the louder to the world now that they suspected a female killer.

Female killer mutilates, emasculates and humiliates male victims. Of course the press didn't know that yet, but they would soon enough. She was a messenger and she was only just getting started.

****

Elizabeth and Tony were sitting together in a quiet pub drinking cider when the news report came on. The TV was on mute so as not to inconvenience the patrons but the yellow subtitles running across the screen spelt out the reporter's words all too clearly for them to see. They sat opened mouthed as their boss revealed that the killer was a woman, bewildered and perplexed as to his motives.

'That can't have been cleared by the DI,' Elizabeth stated incredulously.

'Fuck. What's he doing? We don't want the press knowing that!' Tony said.

'Give me your phone,' Elizabeth demanded.

'Huh?' Tony continued to look at the TV screen, transfixed.

'Give me your phone. Mine's died. The DI needs to know about this.'

Tony handed his mobile to Elizabeth and she furiously searched through his contact list to locate Robert's number. Finally finding it, she dialled.

****

'Who the fuck does he think he is?' Robert fumed into the telephone held to his ear, Elizabeth's loud, animated voice booming from the ear piece as she detailed the news report she had just seen. 'Fuck's sake!'

Robert grabbed the remote control for the large TV that hung on the incident room wall and switched it on.

'What channel?' he barked.

He found the correct channel and watched in horror as the gleeful reporters continued to update the public with the latest development that the killer was a woman. Even the banner at the bottom of the screen was now proudly declaring: 'Police hunt for woman killer after two males murdered.'

'That man is a fucking liability.' Robert hung up the phone, Elizabeth's voice still audible right until he hit the 'end call' button.

He sighed deeply and shook his head. Not only did they have two murders on their hands with fuck all to go on to occupy their every waking moment, they now had to contend with a media frenzy and the sensationalism this would bring, potentially boosting the killer's ego, and also tipping the killer off as to the stage they were at in the investigation.

As if that wasn't bad enough the news about it being a female killer would also undoubtedly elicit the usual influx of calls from the lonely and insane purporting to be the killer, and reports of 'sightings' from concerned neighbours, friends and family members.

Meadows had just unleashed hell on Robert and his team; Meadows's motives were irrelevant. Thanks to him the nation, and the killer, would now be watching their every move, results would be expected and they would be expected soon.

'Fuck it,' Robert said to the empty room whilst snatching up the handset of the phone on a nearby desk. He couldn't do anything about the shit storm Meadows had created but he could give the man a piece of his mind. He didn't give a toss that Meadows outranked him and could easily hang him out to dry. Meadows needed to know what he'd done and Robert intended to make sure that he did.

Chapter XXV

Elizabeth gently rolled herself to the edge of the bed and gingerly put a toe onto the bedroom floor, glancing back over her naked shoulder to see if her movement had awoken Tony. Still flat on his back, snoring softly, Tony was undisturbed by Elizabeth's stealthy manoeuvres as she attempted to extricate herself from the bed and serpent-like duvet which enveloped her.

She continued to slowly push herself off the bed until she was finally free of the duvet's clutches and standing naked by the side of the bed. She let out a quick breath of relief. It was awkward enough that she had drunkenly fallen into bed with a co-worker, without having the awkward morning conversation about what had happened and to let Tony see her 'au natural' with her breath smelling like a vat of old apples. She wanted to cut and run, take the cowardly way out and simply get out of there as fast as she possibly could.

She didn't really known how it had even happened. They'd been drinking and watching the news getting gradually more annoyed with the news report, then they had moved on to a curry house, downed more drinks, and then, when they should have parted company at the tube, they'd started kissing. Elizabeth didn't even know who'd initiated the kiss.

Before she knew it, they were in Tony's flat,

clawing at each other, pulling frenziedly at each other's clothes, overcome with an overwhelming passion. And now here she was trying to creep out of her colleague's flat without being spotted, without having to face him, trying to regain some semblance of self-control.

She reached down and gradually picked up all her clothes which were strewn at various locations across the bedroom floor, testament to the night of unadulterated passion she had shared with Tony, the garments akin to route markers demarcating where their passion had begun and ended. Just as she was about to scurry cross the threshold and make good her escape, Tony's voice startled her:

'And where do you think you're going Ms Lane?' His voice was gruff and gravelly, full of morning huskiness.

She peered over her shoulder, feeling colour rising to her cheeks as she blushed. Tony was propped up on one elbow looking at her, a knowing grin on his face.

'Er, I was fleeing the scene of the crime?' Elizabeth said sheepishly, her unkempt hair falling into her eyes.

'So I see, trying to leave without saying goodbye. I'm going to start thinking you only wanted me for my body. Best you come back here.' Tony tapped the bed with his palm and pulled back the bed covers, inviting her back in.

'Tone…' Elizabeth began.

'I know, it's a bad idea, we're colleagues, we're working closely together. But we're also young free and single. And to be honest, you do have a great arse,' he smirked. 'So what's really the harm?'

Elizabeth shrugged and walked over to the

bed, dropping her clothes back onto the floor as she crawled under the covers into Tony's warm arms. She was disconcerted at how good it felt to have his arms wrapped around her, to feel his warm breaths caressing her neck, his firm, naked body pressed up against hers.

'So, what's the big deal Elizabeth?' he whispered into her ear, his hand running up and down her leg, over her stomach and up towards her breasts. 'Hmmm?'

'It's just, I don't know. It feels... odd. I mean what is this really? It's just a drunken fumble, right?'

'Do you want it to be just a drunken fumble?' Tony's hands stopped rubbing her body.

Elizabeth rolled over to look at him.

'Do you?'

'Oh no you don't. I asked that question first.'

'I don't know. I had never thought about the possibility of you and I getting together. I mean you're gorgeous, funny, intelligent and a huge pain in the neck, but I just thought we were buddies.'

'Well, we are buddies, buddies who have just moved into the buddies-who-have-sex club. I would like to do this again. I wouldn't mind hanging out with you more, see how things go.'

'You're such a bloke. Hanging out? Do I have to eat spicy wings, drink beer and burp too?' Elizabeth asked. Tony laughed.

'Now that is entirely up to you! Tell you what, let's keep this to ourselves, see how things go. You never know, you may end up falling madly in love with me.'

'Hmmm... then again I may end up

murdering you and framing the bondage killer,' she sighed. 'Ok, let's see where this takes us.'

'Good. I like the sound of that.'

Tony kissed her on the forehead and glanced at the clock on the bedside table.

'You know we don't have to be in the office for at least another hour.'

'So what?' Elizabeth teased, coquettishly.

'You know what...' Tony pulled Elizabeth to him and kissed her hard on the mouth, his erect penis pressing against her thighs. She kissed him back no longer embarrassed, no longer confused. All she knew was she wanted this man and she wanted him now. To hell with the consequences, whatever they may be.

****

Louise felt better than she had in days. After returning home from the police station she had turned off her mobile phone, taken a long, hot bath, dressed in her most comfortable lounging-around-the-house clothes, and then curled up in front of the TV, wrapped in a duvet, cradling a glass of her favourite red wine.

She'd watched hours of mindless shows before falling asleep around 10pm, the drama of the last few days catching up with her and smothering her in weariness. She had not stirred until eight o'clock the following morning, her slumber not even interrupted by dreams.

She still lay on the couch, eyes closed, savouring the warmth and comfort. She stretched languorously and gradually forced herself to sit upright. She flicked the TV on to watch the morning news then she got up and padded into the kitchen to make herself a cup of coffee. Just as she flipped the switch on the kettle, yawning widely, her front door bell rang.

'Holy mother fuck!' she exclaimed the noise startling her.

As she walked over to the door she decided by process of elimination that her morning visitor was most probably Ben given that she had not returned his calls or spoken to him since the morning she had left his house.

Can't be the police as they've already been, Steve...? I think not. Melissa? Oh I wish!

She glanced through the peep hole and saw Ben standing there, one arm pressed up against the front door, his face looming large in her small circle of vision.

'Shit,' she said quietly to herself. She hadn't heard the external door bell ring so she guessed he must have snuck into the building on the heels of one of her neighbours.

Ben, unimpressed by her lack of contact, was now standing on her doorstep, patiently waiting to be let in. She could no longer avoid him and this briefly frustrated her. She'd had enough of people getting involved with her life, causing upset to her routine and simply inconveniencing her.

I could pretend I'm out or in the shower?

No. Come on Louise. It's Ben! He's always been good to you. Let him in, you stupid cow.

'Ben...' she began as she swung the door open. He raised a hand.

'It's ok,' he said, 'I just wanted to check you're alive, that you hadn't slipped over and cracked your head open or something, or that you weren't

241

injured and unable to get to the phone. Now I see you're ok, I shall leave. And by the way I didn't appreciate you blanking me.' Ben turned around, about to walk away but Louise reached out and grabbed hold of his arm, preventing him from leaving.

'Ben, come in. Let's talk. I am so sorry for letting you down. I should have called you, but I had a hell of a day yesterday you wouldn't believe it,' she said. 'Please come in. Let me at least explain.'

'Lou, there is always an excuse with you.'

'Yeah, but this one's bloody good, I assure you.'

Ben shook his head and rolled his eyes. 'Alright, fine.'

As he walked into the flat he noticed a slight smell in the air, an unpleasant smell that he couldn't place. He crinkled his nose as he sniffed the air.

'What's that smell Louise? I don't mean to be rude.'

'Smell? I hadn't really noticed. It's probably the sink getting blocked again. It's a bit of a crappy design, more of an S-bend than a U-bend. It keeps getting clogged. I'll whack some bleach down it later and give it a good ol' plunge. Here, I'll open the windows to let some fresh air in.'

She opened the living room windows and they moved into the kitchen where Louise made them both coffee. Ben placed his morning paper on the kitchen table and listened incredulously as Louise animatedly told him about what had happened the previous day with the police, from the moment they had arrived at the front door to finally leaving the police station and running into her old school acquaintance Elizabeth; she didn't tell him about passing out in the interview room. Hallucinations, passing out, periods of time she couldn't account for... This was not something she really wanted to share with anyone, not even Ben. What he didn't know couldn't hurt him.

'I think it was quite probably the weirdest day of my life. I'm not that surprised that Melissa called the police on me, she is one horrible bitch after all, but I was quite surprised to meet someone I used to know at the police station. We went to school together for a couple of years in Hertfordshire in our early teens, got into trouble together and used to cause mischief wherever we went. When I moved away from the area, Elizabeth and I lost touch. I can't believe she's become a police officer,' she smiled. 'People always surprise you, don't they?'

'That they do. I should have listened to you about Derek for example. That man is dangerous,' Ben said, reaching into his pocket to show her the letter he had received. Louise looked at him curiously.

'What's he done now? I presume he didn't take too kindly to being made redundant?' She sipped her second mug of coffee peering at Ben over the rim.

'Something like that. Read this and tell me what you think.'

Ben handed her the envelope and waited as Louise looked at the contents.

'These pictures are from the other night! Is he fucking stalking you? My God Ben, that's seriously creepy. He must have been lurking outside like some kind of fucking voyeur. Jesus.'

'Read the letter,' Ben said.

Louise read, shocked and disbelieving. What had she done, what had Ben done to make this man hate them so much? It wasn't like he was being fired without remuneration, and Biztalk was making legitimate cuts in order to stay afloat. It was nothing personal, a rational person would realise that. She read:

NICE PICTURES DON'T YOU THINK ? YOU HAVE BEEN LYING TO EVERYONE ABOUT YOUR RELATIONSHIP. PURELY PROFESSIONAL? I THINK NOT. WE ALL KNOW WHERE GOING UP THE STAIRS LEADS... I KNEW SHE WAS BEHIND ME BEING MADE REDUNDANT BUT YOU LIED TO MY FACE AND SAID IT WAS NOTHING TO DO WITH HER. COWARD. THESE PICTURES ARE ALL THE PROOF I NEED TO SHOW THAT YOU TWO ARE IN A RELATIONSHIP AND THAT YOU CONSPIRED TOGETHER TO SACK ME. YOU HAVE BEEN BULLYING ME AND DISMISSED ME SIMPLY BECAUSE YOUR 'GIRLFRIEND' DOESN'T LIKE ME. THAT'S UNFAIR DISMISSAL... SEE YOU IN COURT. DC

Louise's mouth dropped open and the colour drained from her cheeks.

'Lying, crafty, evil fucker!' she exclaimed.

'Indeed.'

'Fucking bullying? Fucking bullying? What the fuck!' she shouted jumping up from the kitchen chair, getting angrier and angrier the more she studied the letter.

Ben reached out to take the correspondence from her but Louise moved it from his grasp, reading parts of the letter aloud, whilst pacing around the kitchen. '"We all know where going up the stairs leads." I can't believe this Ben. "Dismissed me simply because your girlfriend doesn't like me." Oh he's fucking got the "don't like him" part right.' She paused. 'This is all my fault. I should never have come round to yours. And I tried to kiss you.' She raised a hand to her forehead, a sharp pain in her head causing her to gasp.

Ben took her by the arm and forced her to sit down, extricating the letter from her grip as he did so.

'Calm down Lou, it's not worth getting that worked up over. We just need to plan what we're going to do next.'

He waited for Louise to respond but she remained silent, her head bowed, her shoulders gently heaving. Ben thought she was crying.

'Lou? It's ok. Look at me. We'll sort it out. Lou?'

She raised her head and looked at him her eyes clear and angry, they looked almost wild, her whole face and demeanour seemed different.

'Lou? I…'

'Fucking men. Fucking MEN!' she shouted. Ben was startled.

'Whoa…'

'Always causing fucking problems, always getting what they want, always manipulating, getting their own way,' Louise fumed. 'He will not get away with this Ben. He'll get what he fucking deserves, you mark my words.'

'Lou, please! Calm down. I wouldn't have let you read it if I'd known it was going to upset you this much.' He placed a placating hand on her arm.

245

'It's ok, we will work this out. And it's not your fault.'

Ben sounded calm but he was shaken. He'd never seen Louise lose it before and it was actually quite terrifying. He had glimpsed another side to her, a darker side, which he hoped he would never see again.

Louise let out a deep breath and stretched her arms in front of her, then rotated her neck and shoulders easing the tension away. She breathed in and out deeply.

'Sorry about that outburst Ben. I just get so wound up, so stressed. I can't believe what is happening here. A few days ago my life was happily ticking along, I had no real worries beyond getting publications out on time and now Biztalk is struggling, people are being made redundant and let's not forget it is because of me; my own job is in the balance too if the company goes down the pan; my boyfriend, the one man I thought I could trust, has cheated on me and broken my heart; I've been arrested by the police and processed like a common criminal; and now this. Derek fucking Cooper. I know it's not all about me Ben and this is affecting you too, but I feel exhausted.'

Ben took her right hand in both of his and squeezed to show he understood. Louise seemed calmer now, more like herself. He was stunned by the rapidity of the change from red-hot temper to calm and collected. Had she always been like this?

He tried to think back to previous occasions when he had seen her in a mood and decided he'd never before seen her anywhere close to such a rage. But, he supposed, she'd never been in a situation like this before. He made a mental note to keep a close eye on her over the next few days fearing that she was heading for some sort of breakdown.

'Lou, I know this is a difficult time for you and I am so, so sorry about asking you to help me with the downsizing. If I'd known things would turn out like this, I promise you I wouldn't have asked you to do it. I also shouldn't have let you know what Derek was up to, you don't really need to know I guess. After all it is me he is threatening to sue not you.'

'Yes but it involves me too doesn't it? I am a part of this whether I want to be or not.'

'In all honesty, yes.' Ben sighed. 'I thought about taking this letter to the police and trying to do him for blackmail, but if you think about it, he's not actually blackmailing me, he's simply telling me of his intentions. The fact he has the photos is creepy but he's not using them to try and extort money from me - he's going to go through the courts.'

Ben rubbed his head and face, he was exhausted too. He hadn't slept for days, the worries of the future keeping him awake at night. The company, that he had worked so hard to build, was teetering on the brink of collapse, a former employee was threatening to sue him and he'd roped Louise into it by simply being her friend.

'Right, let's think about this. What's the worst he can do?' Louise stated, her brain running through options and ideas. 'We can legitimately show that redundancies are necessary for the survival of Biztalk, we can show that he is one of the least productive staff on the books and would therefore be a candidate for redundancy, we can show that he has a personal vendetta against me...You know I don't think this is actually that bad Ben when you stop and think about it. It just means we're going to have one ugly fight.'

'An ugly, costly fight. What if I lose? Think of the costs. Maybe I should speak to him and find out what his price is?'

'Ben! No, you can't! You cannot give in to this bastard. He'll want reinstating for one and there is no way that can happen.'

'You're right, you're right,' Ben agreed.

'I say go and find yourself an awesome lawyer and wait for the court summons to come through. He could be bluffing after all.'

'I don't think so somehow, he's obviously thought this through. Why else would he take the pictures?'

'Hmmm... I guess this means we shouldn't really see much of each other over the next few days or weeks?' Louise asked.

'Fuck that Louise. I will not let him dictate my life and you shouldn't either.' Ben rarely swore and his use of the expletive made Louise realise just how upset he truly was over the whole thing.

Louise smiled at him.

'I'm glad you said that. You're the only person I can talk to at the moment.'

Ben answered something but Louise could no longer hear him, her attention was drawn to the front cover of the newspaper Ben had placed on the kitchen table. The headline mentioned something about murder and two photographs of the victims occupied the front page. The man on the right looked familiar to her, she racked her brain trying to work out where she had seen him before.

'... I don't know how much a lawyer will cost but I guess I might be able to find one of those no win, no fee firms…' Ben continued.

She had definitely seen this man before.

Where dammit? Where do I know that face from?

She picked up the paper and began to read the article.

'Lou, are you listening to me?'

'I know this guy,' she said.

'Which guy?' Ben asked quizzically.

She turned the paper round so Ben could see the front cover.

'This guy. The second victim, "Mark Faversham."' She read his name from under his photograph. 'He's the guy! He's the guy that spoke to me that day at the tube station. The one who said: "Your secret is safe with me." What the fuck?' she looked at Ben beseechingly, her face knotted with confusion.

'You sure?'

'Yeah!'

She glanced up and saw that at that precise moment the TV was also showing a segment on the murders of the two men. She raced into the living room, grabbed the TV remote and turned up the volume, listening attentively to the news report. Ben followed her out of the kitchen wondering what had suddenly grabbed her interest.

'Holy fuck. Two guys murdered, by a woman they reckon! My God and he spoke to me like he knew me. How did he know me Ben? I swear I'd never seen him before that day.'

'Maybe he mistook you for someone else?' Ben offered.

'Yeah maybe. Do you think I should tell the police?'

'Tell them what? That he spoke to you?

Doesn't really advance any investigation does it?'

'No I guess not, especially as I don't even know where he is supposed to know me from. Jesus, this is all so weird. I feel like I'm living in some sort of twisted parallel universe.'

They stood there together watching the segment, both wondering what had happened to their nice, ordered lives, what had happened to their rosy futures which had seemed so certain up until a few days ago. Louise's brain was doing somersaults, her mind was reeling. As if things weren't odd enough already.

A noise by the front door broke their reverie.

'Postie,' Louise said.

On cue the letter box opened and several envelopes were pushed through, pattering to the ground in an untidy heap.

'Shall we get out of here?' Louise asked. 'I could really do with some air to clear my thoughts.'

'Good idea,' Ben concurred.

Louise grabbed a jacket from the hook on the wall next to her front door, stooped to collect the envelopes, placed them on the small table that held her keys and opened the front door. She didn't inspect the post she had received for if she had she would have seen that one of the envelopes had been hand written in a tight floral script, a hand writing not dissimilar to her own.

For now though the post was ignored and she headed out the door with Ben, chatting about a great café down the road where they would be able to get a fabulous fried breakfast, she was in the mood for stodge and whatever happened, her life couldn't get any stranger. She didn't know then how wrong she was.

****

DI Robert Scott sat outside Superintendent Meadows's office, unimpressed at being made to wait, he kept catching Meadows's PA's eye and it was getting embarrassing. She was a good looking woman, but he wasn't looking at her because he fancied her, which is what she probably thought, he was simply looking at her because he was bored and her head was blocking his view out the window.

'Shouldn't be much longer now, sir,' she said politely as Robert caught her eye once again.

'No problem,' he muttered, swiftly looking away. He was so angry about the news report he'd seen the night before, and further infuriated by Meadows's failure to take his calls that he had stormed over to Meadows's office first thing after his morning briefing to confront the man, who now seemed to be studiously avoiding him, probably hoping that if he made Robert wait long enough he would eventually waft away like a bad smell. He'd already been waiting for 15 minutes, his leg angrily twitching as he sat, quietly fuming.

They'd already had 22 crank calls since Meadows's big-mouthed report, 22 calls his officers had to look into, 22 calls that were wasting his officers' time, 22 calls that would probably take them precisely nowhere further forward.

That morning his officers were following up other various lines of enquiry, none of which Robert honestly expected to yield results. At the moment the victims' computers were the best sources of potential evidence that Robert could think of; he hoped it wouldn't take Ian long to find some commonality between the two machines. All they needed was a site name, a user name, anything which could link both victims to the killer.

The killer. He wondered what she thought about the news report, would she be pleased, pissed off or indifferent? Would she be proud, gloating? He decided she probably didn't even care. After all to be committing murders of this sort she most likely possessed a supreme arrogance believing that she wouldn't get caught; she was certainly exceptionally careful at the crime scenes not to leave a trace.

He wondered how she had received Meadows's revelation that they knew the killer was a woman? Maybe she would come after Meadows? Perhaps he should consider offering Meadows some form of security detail? Ultimately, Robert decided that Meadows would just have to take his chances, after all it was his own silly fault if he wanted to go and have his huge head broadcast into the living rooms of the unsuspecting British public.

He briefly pondered how guilty he would feel if Meadows did indeed end up being a victim and decided that the worst thing about that scenario would be seeing the boss's flabby body sprawled naked on a bed, no cuts between his legs as, let's face it, the boss had no balls. Robert chuckled to himself, the thought cheering him up immensely.

The door to the office opened and Meadows's considerable bulk loomed large in the doorway.

'Robert, come in.'

Robert followed his boss into the spacious office and followed his example, sitting himself at the circular table in the corner of the room. There was a large mahogany desk at the back of the room which boasted a state of the art computer, a mountain of paper work, which Robert suspected Meadows may have just put there to make himself look important, and a couple of photographs of Meadows's wife and daughters.

'I guess you're here because of the press release?' Meadows initiated the conversation.

'Yes. I had to come and see you, face to face, to see if you have any idea at all of the shit storm you have created by revealing the killer is a woman? To see if you have any inclination as to the extra amount of work you are causing my detectives? To see if you actually even care about this enquiry at all?' Robert's tone was measured; he was trying very hard not to lose his temper.

Meadows looked at him for a moment, annoyed with Robert's blatant lack of respect for his rank.

'You think my comments to the press have anything to do with your office receiving crank calls? Even if I hadn't suggested that maybe the killer was a woman, do you really think you wouldn't still have had crank calls, time-wasters calling up trying to do their civic duty? Wake up Robert. This isn't about what I said at all, it's about the fact I organised a press release without you.'

'That's bullshit and you know it. I don't give a shit about the fact that you did this without consulting me. For all I care you could go on national TV and do naked cartwheels outside the front of the station, if that would make you happy. What I do have a problem with is that you have revealed a hugely significant detail far too early in this enquiry. You have put us under the spotlight and are exerting a massive amount of pressure on us to get results when you know too well that we are currently clutching at sweet FA.'

'I would like to remind you who you are talking to inspector. What I say goes. You will simply have to deal with this as best you can. The media were due a release and I gave them one. You are assuming that you will not get any positive leads from this which, I would suggest, is quite close-minded.'

Robert shook his head in disbelief. 'How can you be so arrogant? Don't you care that this is prejudicing our enquiry? Oh no that's right, you're looking for your next promotion. What do you care about solving crime?' Robert could feel his temper rising, he swallowed hard to try and keep it under control.

'How dare you come in here talking to me like that! If you're not careful I will pull you off this investigation altogether and let headquarters run this enquiry instead.'

'Don't threaten me, sir, it's not necessary. You know you have made this enquiry a hell of a lot harder by that TV appearance. My team is already working exceptionally hard on this case and now on top of what they've already got to do, they're having to deal with this shit.'

Meadows thought about this. He knew that the press release would probably shake the team up a bit but in his mind that wasn't a bad thing. He had thought it might give them more focus knowing they were under the microscope and scrutiny of the public, he hadn't even considered the additional work load it could generate. Robert was a difficult man to manage, stubborn and outspoken, but he was also an excellent detective with a natural instinct for tracking down criminals and an excellent manager; his team were very loyal to him.

'Robert, are you saying you are unable to handle this enquiry now?' Meadows asked, antagonistically.

'No, that is not what I'm saying. I am saying that I am now under resourced; my detectives are being pulled in too many directions. I need more people.'

'Fine. I will second three officers from Headquarters to your team for the duration of this enquiry. Their role will be to follow up the telephone leads. Better?'

Robert was perplexed, it wasn't like Meadows to try and be helpful; he felt instantly suspicious.

'That would be helpful. What's the catch?'

'No catch. Maybe just pay me a little more respect next time. We are on the same side and I do want the same result as you, despite what you may think,' Meadows said.

'Right, right. So you're not thinking that if you have more officers on the team you'll be able to take the credit when this is solved? And if we fail, well that'll be the fault of my officers and my head will be on the chopping board instead of yours?' Robert asked knowingly.

'That's particularly cynical Robert, even for you.'

'Is it?' Robert didn't bother to wait for Meadows to respond, he'd had enough of the man for one day.

He got up and headed out of the office, roughly pushing the door open. As he walked past the pretty PA, who was looking at him quizzically, he heard Meadows's office door slam shut in his wake. He'd let Meadows's officers deal with the cranks and he would be grateful for their assistance, but he was dammed if he was going to let that man believe for one moment that he didn't know what he was up to. If it wasn't bad enough having to try and second-guess the killer, Robert also had to try and second-guess his boss; it was exhausting.

As he left the building and began his journey back to the police station, Robert decided it was time to attempt to break in to the bondage world. The Garden needed to be visited, they needed to try and break through the veil of anonymity that protected the clientele. He wasn't expecting a friendly welcome, but what the hell, it wasn't as if this enquiry was still under wraps, Meadows had seen to that. At this stage, they really had nothing to lose.

Chapter XXVI

The group of detectives stood outside The Garden like a group of underage teenagers trying to buy alcohol from the local corner shop; excited, slightly nervous and desperately hoping to get what they had come there for.

Robert, JB, Elizabeth and Tony had put themselves forward for the witness trawl. Although each of them was exhausted from the amount of hours they had put in over the past few days, each of them was also desperate to try and find a witness or clue that could help them crack the case. This was what being a police detective was to them; it wasn't just a job - it was their lives.

'What? You're coming too?' Elizabeth had asked when Tony had also volunteered earlier in the evening briefing. 'I thought you were totally against the alternative lifestyle and wouldn't be seen dead in a place like this?'

'That was before I knew it meant I would get to spend the evening with you,' he'd replied, whispering into her ear. She'd smiled and wondered at the warm feeling his words had conjured in her midriff.

'You do realise I won't be changing into rubber for this outing don't you?' she'd said mischievously.

'I know, but I have a very vivid imagination.'

They were each armed with a photograph of

David Saunders and Mark Faversham which they were going to show to people in the club in the hope that someone might recognise either of the two men. They still didn't have a photo of their killer, but if they were able to find a good enough witness who had seen either of the men with the killer, they could potentially produce an accurate e-fit picture of her, assuming of course their memory and descriptive skills were good enough.

'Ok, here's the plan. We go into the club and spread out, one in each corner of the club, we will show pictures to as many people as possible and then get out of there. Once we've done inside the club we will come back out and show the pictures to punters going in. Once we're happy the club is pretty much at capacity, we'll bugger off and get some well earned sleep,' Robert said.

'If you feel like you're making headway with anyone in there, ask them about regulars, female regulars, anything you think could be useful. I don't want us to reveal too much though, the media haven't got hold of the fact that there is a bondage element to these murders yet and I would like it to stay like that for now.'

'What do we tell the people in there then? They're bound to ask why we're trawling here in particular?' JB asked.

'Just say it was one of the last places David Saunders was seen alive. We don't actually know if Mark Faversham was here on the night of his death, but we're showing his picture too as it is likely he was,' Robert replied. 'Just use your common sense people, go with your gut. If you think it's worthwhile divulging more information about the case do it, but don't get carried away.'

'No worries guv,' Elizabeth said.

'One last thing, I don't know what goes on inside these clubs. If you observe any criminality, such as drug taking, drugs changing hands, I want you to ignore it.'

'Really?' asked Tony.

'Yes, we are here to solve these murders, that is it. This audience will be hostile enough without us arresting them for having a bit of white,' Robert stated.

'You're the boss,' Tony acknowledged.

'Right, we ready?' Robert asked.

The group confirmed they were and marched up towards the front door of the venue. Robert pushed the heavy outer door open and the detectives made their way into the vestibule area, congregating there like underage teenagers who had been caught trying to buy alcohol at the local store whilst truanting and who were now waiting to be seen by the school principle.

The strains of loud, hardcore music could be heard emanating from the club beyond and the pulsating lights of silver strobes periodically flickered out from underneath the door. The burly bouncer that Robert had seen previously eyed them up suspiciously as they made their way towards him, his long black coat swishing around his ankles as he turned to give them his full attention.

Robert approached the man and presented his badge, explaining that they needed access to the club as part of a murder investigation. Elizabeth looked at Tony as they waited for Robert to secure them access; he looked nervous, furtive almost, like he was afraid to be seen there.

'You alright Tone?' she asked quietly, gently

touching his arm.

'All good Elizabeth, all good.' He smiled back at her.

Elizabeth could hear the bouncer muttering about how it wasn't really appropriate, he didn't want trouble in the club, the guests would be threatened by their presence and that they would not be well received. Robert was doing his best sweet talking, explaining that they wouldn't be long, they wouldn't harass the guests, they just needed to bottom-out this line of enquiry and did he really want to obstruct officers in the execution of their duty, an offence he could get arrested for? Just when Elizabeth thought they were going to have to step it up a notch and get heavy-handed, the bouncer stood back and swung open the thick, wooden door that led directly into the venue.

Elizabeth felt a rush of adrenaline surge through her as she crossed the threshold into the club, the knowledge that at least one of the victims had probably been here on the night he was murdered, as had the killer, coupled with the novelty of being in such a place as The Garden provided a heady, exciting mix, making Elizabeth feel quite exhilarated.

She wondered briefly how it must feel to be able to enact one's fantasies in a semi-public domain where everyone was like-minded, where everyone had something in common. It must be a liberating experience, she concluded.

Upon passing through the inner door, a set of wide-carpeted stairs led down to the actual club area and from her raised position at the top of the stairs, Elizabeth surveyed the club, eyes sweeping across the venue, quickly scanning the environment for any immediately obvious threats or suspicious activity.

She had once been told by a career criminal that police officers were always betrayed by their eyes when they were trying to be covert; it didn't matter how they dressed, their eyes would always dart around looking for signs of trouble, whereas Joe Bloggs, who ordinarily didn't give a shit about his surroundings, just wanting to get to where he was going, do what he had to do, would usually just look straight ahead or at the ground. Tonight though it wouldn't be their eyes that gave them away as Old Bill, their whole attire and demeanour screamed copper and never had any of the detectives felt so exposed.

The venue was larger than it appeared from the outside. A large, square dance floor assumed pride of place in the middle of the room and it was heaving with scantily-clad people dancing, gyrating and performing erotic behaviours which fell just short of full-blown sexual acts. Around the edges of the dance floor circular podiums supported bare-chested men and bare-breasted women wearing the tiniest thongs Elizabeth had ever seen, some of whom were dancing, some of whom were simulating sex and others who were presenting their bare flesh to other party-goers to whip and cane.

The right-hand side of the club was made up almost entirely of a long, wood-topped bar behind which Elizabeth could make out at least six bar staff, all appropriately dressed for their surroundings, looking harassed as they hurried to serve the thirsty customers who kept on coming, unrelenting like Medusa's serpents; where one once was, another appeared.

The left-hand side of the room comprised a seating area, large plush sofas and armchairs, littered with writhing bodies in various states of undress, women straddling men, their bare breasts pressing against the men's chests; men lying on top of half-naked women, moving their hips between the women's legs, tongues licking up and down their bodies and between their breasts, as others looked on.

The back of the club led to the toilets and a large sign flashed green neon: 'Play Area'. From what Elizabeth could see, this section of the club comprised a number of crucifix-style constructions, which people were tied to being happily flagellated by others.

There was also a pen in which people crawled around on all fours like animals, dressed from head to toe in latex, some sporting dog collars, some horse-like manes, and from which they were selected for either a whipping, caning, or a pseudo-sexual act.

Elizabeth was not a prude, but she felt herself blush being surrounded by so much sex and sexual energy. She didn't know where to look without feeling like a pervert, she'd never seen anything like this before in all her years as a police officer or in all her years of sexual experimentation.

The whole place and all the people within it were there to feed desire, fuel fantasy and satisfy sexual needs. It was a world removed from anything Elizabeth had ever experienced and she couldn't help but feel a little aroused herself as she slowly picked her way through the people to the back of the club. She wondered how her male colleagues were rating the experience.

As she moved across the room, people stopped and looked at her, clearly perturbed by a suited female in their midst and undoubtedly wondering what the fuck the police were doing in their club and hoping they weren't there to spoil the party. The crowd weren't hostile towards her, but Elizabeth could feel their discontent.

She glanced round and saw that Robert had wasted no time getting stuck in. He was over by the seating area and was flashing the photographs around to anyone who would bother to look at him for a few seconds.

Tony and JB were still at the front of the venue mingling and talking to people that were standing around the dance floor. Elizabeth decided that the best place for her to begin would be at the bar; the bar staff would likely have served David Saunders and the killer that night, so she figured this was as good a place to start as any.

She pushed her way to the front of the queue of people waiting for drinks, ignoring the protestations directed at her back, only having to turn once to give her best evil stare at a particularly vociferous patron.

'Police business,' she mumbled as she pushed her way through. She stood at the bar for about a minute before a female member of bar staff came over to serve her.

The barmaid was wearing a strapless mini-PVC dress that just covered her buttocks, just held in her ample bosom and only just held together by a zip that ran the full length of the front of the dress.

She had a curvy, womanly figure; long, blonde hair that was wound into thick dreadlocks that hung halfway down her back, and a multitude of piercings through her lips, nose, right eyebrow and ears. Her eyes were painted black, contoured like an Egyptian queen's, and her lips were scarlet; she looked amazing and oozed sex appeal. Elizabeth felt veritably dowdy in her presence, her lack of makeup, plain, black suit and neatly-tied hair a stark contrast.

'What can I get you?' she asked; even her voice was sexy, like honey on velvet.

'I was hoping I could show you a couple of pictures. I'm investigating a double murder and the victims are thought to have been here before they were murdered.' Elizabeth spoke loudly to make herself heard above the music and across the bar.

'Figured you were a rozzer. Not exactly the place for suits is it?' she asked, looking Elizabeth up and down.

Elizabeth said nothing.

'Show us your pictures then,' the barmaid said, realising she wasn't going to get any small talk.

Elizabeth passed the photos across the bar to the barmaid who scooped them up quickly, her long, black fingernails scratching the bar top. She glanced over them and slowly shook her head.

'Nah,' she said disinterestedly, then: 'Oh jeez, these are the guys that have been in the news, right? I recognise them from the TV.'

She slid the photos back towards Elizabeth; Elizabeth left the pictures where they were, face up on the bar.

'The first guy was murdered two Mondays back,' she said, her finger tapping David Saunder's photograph. 'The second guy on the Saturday just gone.' Elizabeth tapped Mark Faversham's picture. 'Were you working those nights? Have you seen either of them here?'

'Sure was. I'm always here but no, I've never seen these guys in here, or if I have I don't remember.'

Elizabeth nodded, and asked: 'Could you please quickly show these pictures to the other members of staff working tonight?'

'You've picked a pretty rotten time for this. Can't you see how busy we are?' the barmaid asked incredulously, turning on the attitude.

'Yeah I can see that, but we're talking about two dead bodies here so I'd appreciate some help.'

'Fine.'   the   barmaid   picked   up   the photographs and walked along the length of the bar, showing the pictures to her fellow workers as she went.

Elizabeth looked around the club again as she waited for the barmaid to return. The venue was so busy she wasn't surprised that the barmaid didn't recognise either of the victims; she must serve hundreds of faces a night and neither of the victims was particularly distinctive.

Elizabeth saw that Robert was now making his way back towards the front of the club whilst JB was still busy chatting to people around the dance floor; he even appeared to be having a laugh with some of them, which was typical of his happy disposition - nothing could faze him. Tony had moved further away from the dance floor closer to the front of the club and he looked like a cat on a hot tin roof; he kept glancing at the bar and then glancing away. He was talking to a buff man sporting an impressive green Mohican, wearing leather trousers and a thick silver chain around his neck.

Elizabeth thought at first that maybe he was looking for her, looking to be rescued, so she raised her hand, but when Tony didn't acknowledge her, she turned to see if she could spot what he was looking at behind her. It wasn't immediately apparent to her what was catching his attention. She shrugged and turned back to the barmaid who was at that point returning with her photographs.

'Sorry, no one recognises either of them, apart from seeing them on the news. Wish I could help.'

'No worries, thanks for looking. What's your name?' Elizabeth asked.

'Charlie, and you're welcome.'

Elizabeth smiled and turned to move away from the bar when she heard Charlie mumble something which she couldn't quite make out.

'What was that?' Elizabeth asked.

'I said I do recognise someone here tonight though.'

'Who?' Elizabeth's breath caught in her throat. Could this be a potential witness, a clue at last?

'That guy.'

Charlie pointed to where Tony was standing with the man with the mohican.

'The guy with the green hair? You've seen him before?' Elizabeth asked.

'No, not him. Your mate in the suit. The copper. I've seen him in here before.'

'What? You sure about that?' Elizabeth was confused.

Why hadn't Tony mentioned this to her? Was this why he had acted so defensively and refused to come here initially? If he had been to The Garden before why hadn't he shared his knowledge to help the enquiry?

'How do you know him ?' Elizabeth asked, still unsure if the woman was being honest.

'Best you ask him that love. I don't kiss and tell.'

Elizabeth was lost for words and before she could think of anything else to say, Charlie had moved to a different section of the bar to serve customers.

Elizabeth looked at Tony, who finally looked at her and caught her eye. He smiled at her and she smiled back tentatively. What the fuck have you been up to Tony? What else are you holding back?

Robert was signalling that it was time to leave the club and Elizabeth was glad. She suddenly felt claustrophobic, even though the venue was anything but small. She needed to get some air.

As she watched Tony move towards the door, Elizabeth couldn't help but wonder what sort of man he was. She thought she knew him but clearly she didn't know him at all.

****

Mina had spotted them from the moment they had entered the club and her immediate reflex had been to bolt, get as far away from them as she could. However, her survival instinct also told her that if she bolted they would spot her as easily as she had spotted them.

She knew that they didn't actually know who she was, that they didn't have any images of her, for if they did, they would have broadcast them by now asking the concerned public to call in and tell them who she was. This made her feel powerful.

She was here, right in front of their noses and they didn't have a clue. She looked totally different from the last time she had been here and she'd used another fake name when signing up for her invite, provided another anonymous email address for the invitation to be sent to. They had no idea who she was or what she looked like.

She watched them from the back of the club as the four officers starburst out and began showing their photos, trying to hunt her down. She held a vodka in her hand and slowly swirled the mixture in the glass, walking slowly around the back of the club, keeping in the shadows, skulking like a fox stalking a hen coop.

The female officer walked to within four meters of her, and Mina couldn't help but turn her face away, turning her back on the woman who was trying to catch her. She kept a vigilant eye on the copper near the seating area and noted the location of the other two, before moving towards the toilets. She was starting to feel insecure, her confidence was wavering. She needed to check her reflection, to make sure her disguise was still intact. She didn't like the feeling of paranoia the officers' presence was invoking.

Quickly, she slunk into the ladies toilets and went straight to a mirror over one of the many sinks. About ten other women were by the basins, checking their appearance, applying makeup, brushing their hair and checking their clothes, and she did the same as them; just another woman there to have fun - not a killer who was meeting her next victim.

Tonight she was wearing a short blonde bob that curled under her chin, brown contact lenses, dark brown eyebrows, heavy black make up and black lips. Her outfit tonight was different too, less dominatrix but still in keeping with the bondage theme.

She was wearing a black and purple corset that sucked in her already small waist and pushed up her breasts, black PVC leggings which emphasised the contours of her muscular thighs, and black patent ankle boots with seven-inch spike heels. She hardly recognised herself so was confident no one else would either. She gave her outfit a quick once over and then returned to the main club area her confidence renewed.

She looked around, again noting the positions of the police officers as she moved towards the play area, which was where she was meeting her next victim, Daniel Taylor.

They had been in contact over the internet for a few days and Mina had described to him what she would be wearing; he had done the same. She recognised him now as he walked towards her, cutting straight across the dance floor. She liked his confidence, liked his arrogance. Soon he would be begging her for mercy and all his self-esteem and confidence would be irrelevant. She hoped he cried; the idea of big, strong men crying and beseeching turned her on.

Daniel was wearing dark green combat trousers and a black PVC shirt, open to the fourth button, his hairless, muscular chest just visible beneath. He had spiky, black hair, tanned skin, was about six feet tall with toned arms, long legs and broad shoulders. Mina liked what she saw.

She could already visualise him fastened to a bed, powerless and prone, victim to her whims and fancies. She could feel herself getting aroused

He walked over to her and said, 'Mina.'

No doubt, no hesitation, he was strong and masculine.

'Mistress to you. Daniel,' she replied nonchalantly, swirling her drink one last time before knocking back the last sips in one large gulp.

'Drink mistress?' he asked, leaning into Mina and breathing in her scent.

Mina put her hands on his hard chest and scratched her nails painfully down his body making him wince and groan as she pondered this.

She was enjoying watching the coppers hunting for her, enjoying having them in such close proximity, but she was also keen to get started on Daniel, keen to feel another kill; the urges were becoming so much stronger and closer together these days.

'Make it quick, vodka neat, no ice. You'll have the same, but a double for you,' she purred into his ear, biting on the lower lobe, her hand rubbing his groin which she was satisfied to find was already hard.

'Yes mistress.' He sighed with pleasure as she touched him and then hurried off to do her bidding.

Mina smiled to herself, it was all too easy. These men were so gullible, so easy to manipulate. It was easy to be in control when men were thinking with their small heads. They didn't realise how weak this made them.

She looked at Daniel at the bar; he was standing close to the female copper who was in conversation with the blonde, dreadlocked barmaid. The other copper was still in the seated area, but she had momentarily lost sight of the other two across the dance floor.

She tried not to let this worry her, reminding herself that she was in control, they didn't know who she was, they weren't about to jump on her and arrest her. They came back into view as the crowd changed shape, both engrossed in conversation, both busy being copper-like.

She smiled again relishing the feeling of superiority, the feeling of being untouchable. She was God. She had the power to decide who lived and died. She felt omnipotent and awesome.

She turned her smile on Daniel as he returned with the drinks, pressing her body up against his, gently moving her hips against his firm manhood.

'So, slave, where are we going tonight? Where are you taking your mistress so we can have some fun and be undisturbed?' She kissed his exposed chest and ran her tongue across his nipples.

'My sister's place, she's away so we'll have it to ourselves,' Daniel replied, breathlessly.

This woman was amazingly hot, he couldn't believe he had got so lucky. Her body and outfit were the stuff of wet dreams. He imagined what her beautiful mouth would look like sucking on his cock, imagined her looking up at him with those big, brown eyes. He felt his penis swell at the thought.

'Good. And you're sure we'll be undisturbed there? I have plans for you, things I want to do to you, things no other woman will have ever done to you, things that you'll never experience again.'

'Totally... undisturbed... yes,' he panted as she continued to arouse him.

She smiled at him before kissing him hard on the mouth, her tongue stabbing at his, her hands

271

all over his body.

'We could go over to the seating area,' he breathed. 'Just play for a bit?'

'You do as I say, don't forget that,' she warned.

'Of course.'

The female copper was looking at someone beyond the dance floor and Mina followed her gaze to the other copper talking to a man with green hair. Mina could sense that something was wrong, it was how she had survived so long, being able to read people and their intentions.

'I think it's time to go slave. I just need you to collect my bag on the way out.'

She handed him her cloakroom ticket and together they progressed through the throng of bodies towards the exit. Mina pulled Daniel's arm around her and used his body as a partial shield from the female copper. As they passed the male copper talking to the man with the green Mohican she turned her face into Daniel's chest, looking for all intents and purposes like a woman who'd had too much to drink and was being escorted from the venue by her caring man. At the door as Mina turned to face forward again, she almost walked straight into the copper who had been over by the seating area.

'Excuse me,' he said as they went to walk past him. 'Have you seen either of these two men before?' Robert thrust the photos into their faces, forcing them to stop and have a look.

'No mate, never seen them,' Daniel replied.

'What about you?' Robert turned his focus on Mina; she returned his gaze and for one panic-stricken moment she thought he knew, thought he could see into her soul and recognised it for what it was, a dark place full of murderous thoughts and depraved ideas.

'No, don't know them,' she replied, pleased to hear that her voice was not betraying her fear, her tone remaining stable and clear.

'You sure?' Robert asked her again, looking at her intently. She was beautiful and he couldn't stop himself from staring at her.

'I told you no. Now if you don't mind, we've got somewhere we need to be.'

Mina stared at him, her face devoid of expression. This was another skill she had developed over the years - a perfect poker-face that revealed nothing about her thoughts and feelings.

'Certainly.' Robert stepped aside and the couple walked past him into the vestibule. Mina could feel his eyes on her back, she forced herself to keep walking and to not turn round.

'I'll meet you outside, slave,' she whispered to Daniel.

Robert watched as the woman left, not sure why he was being drawn to her, whilst also trying not to notice the contours of her body and tight arse as she sashayed away from him.

The man she was with removed something from the cloakroom and then left the club. Robert saw him reconvene with the woman outside on the pavement, glimpsing her through the front door as it swung shut.

'Alright guv?' JB's voice came from behind him at the top of the stairs and Robert turned round, just as Tony and Elizabeth caught up with him.

'That is quite a place, eh?' he continued, 'I had no idea people could do some of the things I saw in there! What did you think Elizabeth?'

'Yes, quite a place.' She looked at Tony.

He was quiet and she wondered what was going through his mind. Robert spoke to the bouncer and showed him the photographs, he shook his head so Robert thanked him for his help.

They walked out of the club into the cool night air and Robert scanned the area to see if the beautiful blonde and her friend were still in the vicinity; they were nowhere to be seen. He turned to his team, and asked them one by one what they had found out, if they had any leads or potential witnesses. They each told him what he already knew, the trip had in essence been a waste of time. They all looked deflated and exhausted. He decided to call off the witness trawl.

'Let's call it a night, we're all tired and I don't think there's much point us continuing this. I would have thought the staff and the bouncer would have been the best people to help us, more so than the patrons really, and as they all drew a blank, I think we can knock it on the fucking head.'

'Good idea guv, I'm shattered and starting to forget what my wife looks like. If I dash off now, I may be able to catch her before she goes to bed, or at least before she goes to sleep,' JB said.

The detectives mumbled their goodbyes and set off in different directions. Elizabeth quickly strode off towards the tube but Tony caught up with her, quickening his pace to match her stride.

'Where you going so fast? Not even a goodbye? I was hoping you'd come back to mine,' he said earnestly, reaching out to take hold of her hand.

'I don't think so Tony. I don't know who the fuck you are. Leave me alone, ok?' Elizabeth snapped at him, pulling her arm away roughly. Tony recoiled, momentarily shocked by her outburst.

'Whoa… what have I done?' Tony asked, suspecting he already knew.

'I'm not entirely sure,' Elizabeth began. 'What have you done? Anything you want to tell me about that place? Anything you think maybe you should share with this investigation?' She was angry now and quickened her pace even more.

'I see. Let me explain, would you? Elizabeth!'

'Fuck off Tony, I don't want to hear it!' she shouted back at him,

She felt hurt and betrayed, although she didn't really know why. They'd only slept together once, Tony didn't owe her anything or have to explain his sexual past to her, but still she felt he had abused her trust by not telling her of his familiarity with the club, that he had intentionally stultified the investigation by not revealing what he knew about the bondage scene.

'Elizabeth, come on, don't be like that!' Tony stopped walking and watched as she skipped down the steps to the London Underground, annoyed with himself for volunteering to come to the club tonight. He had worried something like this might happen, but on balance he had decided that it had all happened long enough ago to not really matter anymore. Clearly he had been wrong and now he had some explaining to do.

Chapter XXVII

It was late morning and Tony had just arrived at the police station. He was dreading seeing Elizabeth, unsure as to how she would react to his presence, but hoping she would at least allow him an opportunity to explain.

He really enjoyed Elizabeth's company, she was a good laugh and they had great sex, he had hoped they could forge some sort of real romantic relationship; now he just hoped that he hadn't fucked it up for good.

As he entered the office he could hear Elizabeth laughing, her good-natured cackle resonating around the room. He should've guessed she would make it into the office before him, sometimes he wondered if the woman ever slept. From the office threshold he observed her in conversation with Greg, still wearing her running gear, hair scraped off her face into a long ponytail, her face ruddy from exercise. She looked amazing, especially for a woman who had just run to work.

As if sensing his gaze, she turned and looked at him, her friendly expression changing to one of disappointment. This didn't look good. She resumed her conversation with Greg without so much as acknowledging his existence.

Tony sighed and walked over to his desk, simultaneously switching on his computer and scooping up the post that had been left on his work station. He opened the envelopes distractedly as the computer booted up, his eyes still on Elizabeth, waiting for an opportune moment to talk to her in private.

A few moments later, Tony saw that Elizabeth was leaving the office. He quickly jumped up and pursued her down the corridor, hoping to catch up with her before she went into the ladies locker room to shower.

'Elizabeth!' he called after her. She turned briefly then continued walking along the corridor to the changing rooms.

'Elizabeth, please wait.'

This time she stopped and turned to face him. She leant against the locker room door, folding her arms across her chest as she waited to hear what he had to say.

'Elizabeth, let me explain. It's not as bad as you're probably thinking,' he began.

Two uniformed officers were walking towards them, their police radios crackling. Tony lowered his voice: 'Can we go somewhere quiet so I can tell you about it in private?' he asked as the officers walked past him.

'No. You can tell me here, or you can fuck off,' Elizabeth said, matter-of-factly.

'I don't really want to discuss this in the corridor.'

'Well then we won't discuss it at all,' Elizabeth shoved open the locker room door and went inside. She was surprised when she heard Tony's voice behind her.

'You can't be in here!' Elizabeth said firmly, quickly scouting round the room to check there was no one else in the vicinity. The locker room was empty. 'Get out Tony!' Elizabeth put her hands on his chest and began pushing him back towards the door.

He took hold of her hands and said: 'No, you need to hear what I have to say. Stop treating me like I have done something terrible! All I have done is held back some information and I didn't do that for nefarious reasons, just because it's no one's business.'

Elizabeth dropped her arms to her sides and looked at him. His eyes were wide, his expression sincere, she decided she should at least hear him out and she was curious despite herself to find out how Tony was involved with the club and the barmaid, Charlie.

'I just don't understand why you never mentioned anything about this. How come you were known by one of the barmaids in that place? How can you have been to a bondage club and then not share any of that knowledge with this enquiry Tony? It could have saved time, it could've helped.' Elizabeth was full of questions.

'How would it have helped? We wouldn't have been any further forward if I had said to everyone, "Oh hey, I know what it's like in a club, I've been to one,"' Tony countered.

'But you must have known about the invitation thing? That would have made us look at the computers much earlier.'

'Look, I never obtained an invitation, I didn't know one was needed. When I went to the club I went with a girl I was seeing, she was into bondage, she wanted to take me to a club and she sorted it all out. I only went out with her a few times, this was about a year ago, and I only went to the club once.'

'Ok, then explain how the barmaid knew you. There's no way she would have remembered you if you only went in there once. You're not so bloody amazing that you leave an indelible mark on the memory!' Elizabeth challenged.

Tony tried not to be offended.

'The night I went to the club, the girl who took me there turned into a compete psycho bitch, we argued and she tried to hit me, so I ended it there and then. She was a strange woman, which is probably what attracted me to her in the first place, I thought she'd be fun, you know be a challenge. I like unusual women.' Elizabeth rolled her eyes and then stared at him, one eyebrow raised, willing him to get to the point. 'I'm not saying you're strange and that's the reason why I like you. I'm just saying that this woman, she did not react in a normal, rational way,'

'Get on with it Tony.' Elizabeth sighed.

'Sorry.' Tony realised he was digressing. 'After the argument and I told her it was over, she left the club. I was relieved she left so readily as, like I mentioned, she was a complete psycho. I decided to stay for a bit, to make sure I gave her enough time to put a bit of distance between us…'

'Yeah, I'm sure that was the reason you stayed,' Elizabeth interjected cynically. Tony ignored her insinuation.

'…so I went to the bar, ordered a drink and just started chatting to Charlie because she happened to serve me. I spent about three hours in the club, talking to her when she wasn't serving other customers. We had a bit of a spark and so when she finished her shift, we went back to her place and well, you can imagine the rest. I didn't see her again after that, I didn't go back to the club and I really thought that as this happened a year ago she wouldn't remember me, or recognise me or whatever. I certainly did not expect her to start chatting to you and for it all to come out like this.'

Elizabeth considered what he had said, biting her lip thoughtfully.

'What about this psycho woman? She psycho enough to kill?'

Tony laughed emptily: 'Oh don't worry, she moved to America not long after we broke up. She's long gone. Besides, she was nuts, but I can't imagine she could kill. She fainted once at the sight of blood when I cut my thumb.'

'So, you only went once and that was with this psycho woman who arranged everything, you then ended up falling into bed with the barmaid, and after that one-night stand you never saw her again or went to the club again? That makes you sound like such a chauvinist. And you didn't reveal your knowledge of bondage to the investigation because...?' Elizabeth asked, not yet ready to let Tony off the hook.

'What knowledge? I don't really know anything about it, do I? I could maybe have mentioned I'd been to a club but I still don't see how that would have helped and it's not exactly the sort of thing you brag about is it? Can you imagine if the rest of the team knew? I'd never hear the end of it. I honestly did not think that I could offer any insight or ideas that could've helped this investigation. If I had thought otherwise I would have said something because believe it or not I would like us to solve this case. You're not the only one who gives a shit about the job,' Tony concluded.

'Ok, you've said your piece. I still wish you had at least confided in me so I didn't have to find out that way.'

'I'm sorry Elizabeth. In my defence though, we have only just started sleeping together, it's not like I know everything about you either.'

'Sleeping together? You think it's going to happen again?'

'I hope it does,' Tony replied.

For a moment Elizabeth didn't say anything as she digested what he had said to her, she just looked at him, her eyes impenetrable; Tony couldn't tell what she was thinking.

Finally she said: 'I need to shower Tony. You'd better leave.'

Tony sighed: 'So that's it? Just because I have a past?'

Elizabeth remained mute as she turned her back on him and padded over to the showers. Deciding there was nothing more to be achieved Tony left the locker room angry with himself, with Elizabeth and with the world in general.

****

Denise Taylor was humming to herself as she put the key in her front door and opened it, generally pleased with life and the world in general. Her boyfriend of five years, Ryan Murphy, had just proposed to her and she had accepted, thrilled that he had finally popped the question. Mrs Denise Murphy, she liked the way it sounded.

The previous evening Ryan had come to the restaurant where she worked as head chef and ordered a plate of risotto. He had then hidden the ring within the dish and sent it back to the kitchen, demanding that the staff inform the chef of how dissatisfied he was and that he expected a personal apology from her; he did not expect to find the chef's jewellery on his plate. His waiter, Adam, was in on the gag, as were the rest of the staff; they all knew Ryan and what he was planning.

'A ring in his fucking risotto? What the...?' Denise had said when the offending platter had been returned to her kitchen. She'd plucked the ring off the plate, remarking how much she liked the design.

When Adam had told her about the request for a personal apology, Denise had snorted and refused, stating she was far too busy and that the ring certainly hadn't come from her fingers so she had nothing to apologise for.

'I really think you should speak to this guy Den, he's not happy and I understand he works as a food critic,' Adam lied. 'Just explain to him so that we can get rid of him, eh?'

Denise had bad-temperedly smacked a few pans about and spouted a few expletives before shouting at the sous-chef to cover for a few minutes. She had followed Adam out of the kitchen, the ring in her hand, ready to fight her corner.

Adam led her to where the man was seated; he had his back to them as they approached and Denise hadn't recognised him straight away.

'Good evening sir, I understand there's been a problem with...' she began politely, stopping as the man turned to face her and she realised it was Ryan.

'Ryan, what the bloody hell are you doing here?' she had asked perplexed.

'Did you find your ring?' he asked, smiling.

'My ring?'

'The one you carelessly left in my risotto. You'll have to take better care of it in future.'

Then he had dropped to one knee in front of all the customers and staff and asked her to marry him. She'd been so shocked that words had failed her, the 'yes' she desperately wanted to say lodging in her throat.

'Den, will you be my wife?' Ryan repeated, starting to worry that this might not have been such a good idea.

'Of course I will!' she had eventually exclaimed, so happy she thought her heart would burst.

The restaurant had erupted in applause and she had never felt so happy in her life. She hadn't gone back to work after that, the sous-chef had taken over and she had spent the evening with Ryan sipping champagne and talking about their future. They'd spent the night together at Ryan's, wrapped up in each other's arms, blissfully happy.

Now she was home and she couldn't wait to tell Daniel her good news. She hoped he was in as she felt ready to burst, barely able to contain her excitement; she hadn't told any of her friends or family yet as she had wanted to savour the moment with Ryan before letting others into their happy, joyful world. As she opened the front door she noted that it was not double locked which meant that Daniel should be home.

'Dan!' she called as she stepped into the hallway, dropping her keys into the pot they kept on the table by the door; she noticed that his house keys were in the pot, the big voodoo doll keyring she had given him hanging over the edge.

'Dan! I have news!' she trilled, excitedly.

She continued humming as she progressed through the house to the kitchen. Where was her bloody brother? A quick look around the kitchen satisfied her that he wasn't lurking in there. Denise progressed into the living room, passing various family photos and culinary certificates that hung proudly on the wall.

Daniel's boots were lying near the sofa as if they had been hurriedly kicked off; his combat trousers and a PVC shirt were also strewn across the floor. He had clearly been eager to undress.

In the past four months, whilst Daniel had been staying with her, Denise had never known her brother to leave his clothes lying around; he was normally the perfect house guest. She wondered why he had stripped off in the living room and not cleared up after himself; she wondered why he had been wearing a PVC shirt. She wondered what his wife would think.

Daniel's home, which he shared with newly-pregnant wife, Caroline, was in Lancashire but he was currently staying with Denise in the week, travelling home at weekends, whilst completing work on a large-scale construction in London for which he was chief architect. The project was set to last a further four months, much to Denise's chagrin, as she was enjoying having her brother around and didn't want him to leave.

She didn't like seeing the clothes lying around, however, as they were making her suspicious that Dan had been with a woman. She didn't like cheats, considering it completely ignoble. She left the living room and continued to the foot of the stairs, shouting up towards the landing, hoping to hear Dan answer back. She was met with silence. Denise slowly walked up the stairs, listening for any noises, any signs of movement.

As she crept up the stairs she felt the hairs on the back of her neck stiffen and her flesh shivered with an unease she didn't understand; she sensed something was wrong, something had happened to her brother. At the top of the stairs, she shouted for her brother again, but this time she didn't expect a reply.

She walked down the corridor to the spare bedroom that Dan was using during his stay and stood in front of the door; it was only now that she detected a faint, unpleasant smell, which appeared to be emanating from within. Gingerly, she opened the door, quietly saying: 'Dan, you in here? You alone?'

She poked her head around the door frame, her eyes flitting across the various bedroom furniture and paraphernalia, seeking her brother, her gaze eventually settling on the bed at the far-side of the room. It took her a second to register what she was actually looking at, her brain refusing to accept what her eyes were telling it.

She saw a man's body, bloodied and blue, stretched across the bed, the arms and legs pulled taught by rope ligatures fastened to the four corners of the bed. Even before her eyes made their way up to the man's face, Denise knew it was her brother who lay there, torn and lifeless, the distinctive eagle tattoo that he had had inked on his thigh when he was 17 was still partially visible beneath the layer of caked blood that had dried on his leg.

Denise felt tears pricking her eyes as she registered that this blood-stained mess in front of her was all that remained of her wonderful, fun-loving brother, the brother who had looked out for her their entire lives and who had always put her first.

She looked at Daniel's face and saw that his left eye had been pushed back within his skull, his mouth open wide in a silent scream; her gaze moved back down his body and Denise realised that not only had Dan been murdered, he had been brutally mutilated for between his legs there remained nothing but blood and gore.

She raised her hands to her face, sobs racking her body, and dropped to her knees, shaking with shock. Yesterday had been one of the happiest days of her life, but now Ryan's proposal would always be tainted by death. She couldn't help but think that if she had been at home, instead of at Ryan's, her brother may not have been murdered, he may not have been tied up and left dead and undignified. Maybe this ghastly murder could have been prevented? She would have to live with that guilt for the rest of her life.

****

The investigation team were gathered in the incident room for their afternoon briefing. Elizabeth and Tony were ignoring each other, sitting at opposite sides of the room, concertedly trying to avoid eye contact, although Tony was finding it harder than Elizabeth to pretend she was invisible, occasionally glancing in her general direction.

All the detectives working on the case were present, including Ian Burrell, along with three other officers, two men and a woman, that nobody knew but who Greg guessed were also from Force Headquarters as they seemed quite friendly with Ian.

The room was packed and everyone, except the newcomers, looked worn out.

Robert began the briefing by raising the thorny issue of the press release Meadows had conducted without his knowledge or approval on Tuesday. Since then, Meadows had appeared on TV a number of times, asking the public to assist if they had any information "no matter how trivial it may seem" and the phones had been ringing off the hook.

The media department was working overtime trying to keep the reporters satisfied and trying to find suitable material to release to the press - there wasn't much of it. Robert had managed to intercept one of the release writers and had given him strict instructions that no matter what Meadows said or did, nothing was to be released about the victims' penises being removed or the fact the victims had been tied to their beds. The man had turned a strange green colour and had given Robert his word.

'We have three officers joining us to help with the telephone calls resulting from the media appeals,' Robert explained, indicating the three officers at the back of the room with Ian.

The officers looked slightly uncomfortable as all eyes turned on them and they introduced themselves as Alicia Lewis, Richard Monahan and Mick Brown.

'You're all detectives working out of headquarters, right? Did the boss explain what he wanted you to do here?' Robert checked.

'Yep, that's right. We've been told to lend a hand with the phone calls only, but if there is anything else you need us to do, we're happy to help,' said Mick.

Alicia smiled but Richard looked like he wanted to be anywhere other than where he was at present. Tony couldn't help but smirk; it wasn't often that FHQ officers got made to do the grunt work. He hoped it might serve to bring them down a peg or two.

'I know the circumstances surrounding our involvement are less than ideal,' Alicia felt compelled to say, 'and for what it's worth, I don't think Mr Meadows should have revealed that the killer is a woman either. I also know that we're probably here as a punishment for his mistake, but as Mick said, whatever you may think, we really are happy to help. It's actually nice to get away from headquarters for a change.'

'Thank you for that,' Robert said, 'and welcome to the team. I'm sorry you were chosen to fix the problem the boss created.'

'It is what it is,' Richard mumbled.

'Indeed. Right, how are we getting on with the council CCTV?' Robert asked, dismissing Richard, disappointed by his sullen attitude.

'We have managed to get some images from the street where James Wilton, the hotdog seller, said he saw David Saunders and the killer. Two council cameras service that street and we have obtained images from both. However, the images are really poor quality; the image from the first camera, which is the better placed camera, is too grainy for any possible identification to be made and it's a little out of focus. The second camera is also no good as its range is too far. It's at the wrong end of the street basically, and all you can see are two figures walking along the top of the image,' JB said.

'Typical,' Robert grunted.

'I know. They're never where you bloody need them. As for footage from outside the club on the nights the two victims were killed, again there a couple of cameras that cover the immediate area, but none of them directly cover the club. The footage from around the streets that lead to the club has been looked at but the suspect hasn't been spotted on any of it. It's difficult not knowing which route she may have taken, which direction she came from and also not having a specific time.'

'Are any of the current images suitable for enhancement?'

'Certainly none of our own imaging software is up for the job, although we have tried, and I have tried to outsource it but unfortunately, when the images are this poor there's not a lot that can be done.'

'Ok, can we get the cameras moved? If they're rotated in any particular direction can we get any better shots of the club?' Robert asked.

'I went up to the council building and had a look at the coverage myself. We can get good coverage of the closest tube station and two shots from the junctions of two of the streets adjacent to the club. I did ask if it would be possible to leave one of the cameras on the tube station for example, in case she went to the club again on foot, and I was told that they could do this, but that would only be until an emergency call came out from any of our uniformed colleagues. The CCTV operators then move the cameras about trying to locate the officers, or the incident in question. They had four calls whilst I was there. The cameras, I would say, are too hit and miss,' JB finished.

Robert nodded, thinking about the stunning blonde he had seen the night before. He hadn't seen which way she had turned upon leaving the club but she had left the area quickly leaving Robert to surmise that she may have hailed a taxi. He couldn't explain what it was about this woman that was captivating him so, he couldn't tell if he was suspicious of her or if he simply fancied her.

'Could we maybe get permission to install our own covert camera in the environs of the club?' Greg suggested.

'No. We won't get the authority for that, it'll be deemed too intrusive. It'll capture too many people and besides we'd be working on the proviso that she's going to go back to the club and that she met with both victims there, which while we suspect it, we can't categorically state that it's the case. The intel wouldn't be strong enough to support our application in this instance,' Robert replied. 'What about your list of abused girls Elizabeth? And what about the rope the victims were tied up with?'

Tony looked at her. She had changed into a charcoal grey suit, applied a little makeup and her hair was now fastened in a bun. He couldn't help but visualise her in his mind's eye as he had seen her in his bed the previous morning, her hair tousled, her face makeup free, lips slightly parted, sweat running down her naked body as they made love with abandon. As if guessing what was on his mind, Elizabeth suddenly turned and gave him her most disapproving look causing Tony to lower his eyes to the floor.

'I have my list from the council guv,' she replied. 'I just haven't had a chance to go through it yet. I shall get on it ASAP. As for the rope, it could have come from anywhere. I am told by the scientists at the SOCO labs that there is nothing distinctive about it, there are no features that we could use to trace it to a particular shop or batch and that it is commercially available in any sex shop and on the internet. So, not much use to us really.'

'Kind of what we expected then,' Robert said. Elizabeth shrugged in agreement. 'Ok, now Ian. Please tell me you have some good news for us.'

'Well actually I think I do. I've managed to establish that both victims have used the same internet chat room. They have each used a number of different sites and it's no surprise that there is some cross-over on both computers as this is quite a specific fetish in a specific city. However, there is one site in particular that they have both used repeatedly, and both used leading up to the day of their murder. This makes me think that they may have used this chat room to converse with the killer.'

A murmur of excitement rippled around the room. One of the incident room telephones began ringing so JB got up to answer it.

'I'm in the process of trawling through deleted files, old internet files and cookies to see if I can find any old web logs or chats that may have been saved by either of the victims. It's taking a little while because although I can run software to automatically trawl the two machines, I need to physically go through the reports it creates to look for commonality. It's a bit tricky when you don't have any keywords or names to look for, I'm just comparing words as and when they come up... It's an imperfect system, but I'm confident I'll get a username pretty soon,' Ian said, confidently.

'This is excellent news, good work Ian. Can

you give an estimated time frame at all?' Robert asked.

'No, I can't say, I wouldn't want to raise any expectation, but I am making good progress.'

'Would it help you to have another pair of eyes going through the reports with you?'

'Thank you but no, it's easier for one person to go through the material to be honest.'

'Ok good stuff.'

JB was thanking the caller on the end of the phone; he did not look pleased.

'JB? What was that about?' Robert asked him as he retuned the receiver to the cradle. JB shook his head and said: 'We've got another body, same MO. Discovered by his sister this afternoon when she returned home after spending the night away.'

'Holy fuck,' Elizabeth said.

'That means...' Tony began.

'Yeah. It means this guy was killed last night. The night we were in the club.'

Chapter XXVIII

Louise stood looking out of her kitchen window, one hand holding back her net curtain, the other pressing a telephone to her ear. She looked at the bus stop where she had seen, hallucinated, or imagined the weird man with crooked teeth over a week ago now.

Today there was a handful of people waiting in the small shelter and today the sun was shining. No strange people out there, she mused, or at least no obvious ones; you never knew what was lurking in the dark recesses of people's minds. People would never fail to surprise, disappoint or impress, it was part of the human condition and Derek Cooper was a perfect example of this. He was also the topic of the conversation Louise was having with Ben.

'So, you haven't heard anything further about his plans to sue?' Louise asked, dropping the curtain and moving into the living room, where she plonked herself down on the couch, curling her legs up under her.

'No, so far nothing,' Ben said, 'It's early days though, isn't it?'

'Yeah I guess so. I don't know how long these things take.'

'Me neither. You'll never guess what though,' Ben said

'What?'

'Derek is actually here at the moment. He's

in the office.'

Louise sat up straight and felt anger flushing to her cheeks. 'What? What for? What's the fucker up to?' she questioned.

Ben paused before responding and she guessed it was because of her angry rant the previous morning.

'It's ok Ben. I'm calm. I won't have another outburst,' she reassured.

'Well, he reckons he left some stuff here and that he has files he needs on his computer.'

'I can't believe you let him in Ben! What were you thinking? What if he's trying to infect the network with a virus or something, or steal next edition's headlines?' Louise was immediately suspicious.

'I knew you'd disapprove, but there is nothing to be gained in being difficult, that would just be playing into his hands. And don't worry, I have Sam in IT monitoring his every key stroke to see exactly what he is up to. If he tries to plant a virus or sabotage next month's issue, Sam will shut him down immediately.'

'Don't you just love technology! It always freaks me out when the IT geeks monitor a machine you're working on remotely. They did it on my computer once to help me with a persistent fault and I was very excited to see my cursor moving about seemingly opening applications on a whim!' Louise giggled and Ben loved the sound; at that moment she sounded like her old self again.

'He's also here to ask the other writers and some of the other staff out for a drink with him apparently. I'm not invited of course.'

'Is anyone actually going to go?' Louise

asked, appalled at the notion of anyone wanting to sit and socialise with the man.

'Yeah, I think so. Maybe they just want to check he really is leaving,' Ben joked. 'Although I suspect it's more likely because they want to know all the gossip. I'm sure he'll be bending their ears about his plans to sue me and his unfounded suspicions about us.'

'Great,' Louise snorted.

'I think I'm going to get a lot of funny looks here tomorrow.'

'Should I come back to work do you think? Show them that it's all a load of bollocks? Doesn't me being off make it look like we have something to hide?'

'Well that's really up to you, but I personally think you should give yourself a bit more time. After everything you've been through in the past week, I think you're entitled to some time off.'

'I am actually starting to feel a little better,' Louise admitted, 'and I've been getting a bit more sleep lately.'

'Good, that settles it then. At least take the rest of the week off and then see how you feel about coming back next week.'

'Sounds like a plan,' Louise picked up the remote control from the coffee table and turned her TV on, switching over to the evening news and muting the volume. She read the headline scrolling across the bottom of the screen: 'Third victim of female suspect found, killer still at large.'

'Bloody hell, have you seen the news?' she asked.

'No, I've been at it all day,' Ben replied.

'There's been another murder, that woman

killer has killed another guy, someone called Daniel Taylor,' she read the headline to Ben.

'That's quick work, three murders in just over a week. Guess that makes her a serial killer now, huh?'

'Yeah, I guess so. Did I tell you I know one of the officer's working on this enquiry? We went to school together for a couple of years.'

'You did mention it,' Ben replied.

'She gave me her card and said to give her a call so we could have a catch up some time. I don't know if I want to call her though, I'm not sure we'd have anything in common now.'

'Ok, now I know you really are not yourself! You would normally jump at the chance to talk personally to someone working on a live case like this.'

Louise laughed. 'Yes I guess I would. I don't expect she could tell me anything anyway.'

'Probably not. Don't you want to meet up with her, just for old time's sake?'

'Hmmmm... dunno. What if she thinks I'm weird?'

'Well, that's a given Louise,' Ben teased.

'Oi! Cheeky bastard!'

'Only joking,' Ben's deep, throaty laugh made her smile.

'You know what, I will call her and see if she can see me tomorrow night. Why not eh? Could be fun to remember the old school days.'

'There you go! That's better. You mustn't shut yourself away Louise, or you'll turn into some old recluse.' Ben was only half-joking this time. 'Oh, looks like Derek is leaving the building. Halle-fuck-ing-lujah! Now I can go home and not worry about the place being burnt down, or my office being desecrated by a pissed off former employee.'

'Good! Hopefully he'll trip going down the stairs on his way out and kill himself. That would solve all your problems, wouldn't it? If he died?' Louise stated.

'It sure would, but knowing my luck he'd only sustain an injury and would then sue me for that too.'

Louise laughed and then said: 'Thanks Ben,'
'What for?'

'For being a friend, for listening and for cheering me up,'

'No problem,' he sounded chuffed on the other end of the line; Louise wished she could see his handsome face.

'Right, I'm going to head home now Lou. Give me a call if you want to chat at any point, ok?'

'Ok, Ben. Bye for now,' Louise hung up the phone, feeling almost happy.

She picked up Elizabeth's card and rang the mobile phone number printed on it; the call went straight to voicemail so she left a slightly rambling message about meeting up, apologising for the short notice, hoping Elizabeth was ok and that it would be good to catch up if she was available, but she would understand if she wasn't as Elizabeth likely had other plans as it would be a Friday night, or she would probably be too busy working on the murder enquiry… Louise hung up the phone feeling like an idiot and hoping Elizabeth wouldn't think she was some sort of lunatic.

She watched the news for a little while longer, shaking her head at the depravity of the world, feeling sorry for the families of the dead men.

She wondered how it must feel to have someone you love taken away from you in such a violent manner. Louise had lost her whole family when she was just a young girl, but at least none of them had been murdered, and she didn't remember them anyway. She wondered if it felt similar to being cheated on, the end result was the same after all, you still ended up sad and on your own.

When someone was murdered they were taken away from you - they didn't intentionally leave you, they didn't mean to cause you any pain or misery, it wasn't their fault their life was snatched away and that their families were left behind bereft and grieving. Cheats knew exactly what they were doing, the pain they would ultimately cause, so in some ways Louise opined that losing a loved one to a murderer had to be easier than losing them to the bitch they worked with; at least their love hadn't waned, you would always know they'd loved you.

Louise was starting to feel morose at these thoughts bouncing round her head, images of Steve and their happy times together plaguing her. She sighed and picked up the post that had arrived the previous day to distract herself, casting her eye over the envelopes as she shuffled through it. Bill, bill, letter from the bank, unwanted flyer and a handwritten envelope from an unknown sender. The handwriting was pretty, almost calligraphic; someone had taken some effort to produce handwriting this neat.

The letter intrigued Louise, but just as she was about to open it, her mobile phone bleeped, alerting her to an incoming message. Louise dropped the post back onto the coffee table and picked up her phone. The message was from Elizabeth and it read: 'HEY! GOT YOUR MESSAGE. CAN'T TALK RIGHT NOW, BUT I CAN MEET YOU TOMORROW ABOUT 7PM. COME TO THE DUKE OF YORKE PUB NEAR THE POLICE STATION. ANY PROBS, DROP ME A TEXT. E'

Louise smiled and quickly tapped out a reply confirming that she would meet Elizabeth there, feeling a little excited but also a little nervous about the prospect of reminiscing with an old school friend.

Abandoning the post yet again, Louise prepared to head out, suddenly feeling the urge to go for a walk in the evening sun, wanting to clear her head and hoping to get some fresh perspective on her life.

****

Denise's house was swarming with police, her driveway and garden were cordoned off with blue and white police tape, officers in white suits were milling around and four uniformed officers stood in front of the cordon, keeping the media and nosey neighbours at bay. Other officers, including those in uniform and detectives from the investigative team, were conducting door-to-door enquiries, interrogating the neighbours about anything they may have seen or heard the night before.

Denise was at the police station giving her statement to Tony; her fiancé was with her trying to comfort her as best he could. She was understandably distraught; it would be bad enough finding a stranger in that way, but to find your own brother in that prone position with the blood and the filth of death all over him, must have been horrifying. She would certainly be suffering many a sleepless night as a result.

Greg and Robert were standing in the hallway, watching the scenes of crime officers work in the bedroom. They were all wearing the required sterile suits to ensure they didn't contaminate the scene in any way.

Upon arrival they had both scouted around the house trying to get a feel for the killer's movements, trying to piece together which rooms the killer may have been in, which items of furniture she may have touched.

Nothing had immediately struck them except for the fact that the victim had undressed in the living room; there was no realistic way of narrowing down the scene to expedite evidence recovery. Obviously the bedroom was the primary crime scene, as was the victim's own body so they took priority.

The spectacle in the bedroom had been macabre, with the body displayed in the star-fish shape that was now synonymous with this killer's MO, Daniel's penis and testicles hacked away by a furious hand, his left eye ball punctured and forced into his skull, blood and body fluids all over the bed and floor around it.

Although this was the third crime scene of this kind Robert had attended, they weren't getting any easier to stomach, no easier to push out of his head when he closed his eyes at night. It was an unfortunate truth that once something had been seen, it could never be unseen, never be erased from one's memory.

The scenes of crime officers were almost ready to remove the body from the bedroom and they signalled to Robert that this was so. He nodded acknowledgement.

'Three victims in such a short space of time. This woman is getting way too confident,' Greg said, as much to himself as to Robert.

'Yeah, and she's now officially a serial killer, not that that's any surprise. She's been collecting trophies from the beginning.'

Greg nodded and unconsciously placed one leg in front of the other in appreciation of what those trophies were.

'She's spiralling isn't she? I mean usually serial killers start slow don't they and then build up momentum as they get better at it, used to killing?'

'You sound like Elizabeth,' Robert said.

'She's rubbing off on me,' Greg agreed.

Daniel's body had been placed into a white cadaver bag and was now being carried into the corridor. The detectives stopped talking and lowered their heads in respect for the dead man. Robert did not recognise the man in the bag; he'd had a good look at the man's face when he was still in situ. He'd been hoping for a spark of recognition or a gut feeling, but instead he had just felt sorry for the victim, his sister and his family.

Again, as with Janet Saunders, the family had to deal with the fact that not only had Daniel been murdered in an extremely gruesome way, but he had been leading a double life in which he indulged his sexual fetish. Also, he had cheated or had been about to cheat on his pregnant wife. Robert couldn't imagine how anyone could deal with so much pain.

He'd also been angry with himself for not paying closer attention to the male companion of the beautiful blonde from the night before. Was this him, the big, strapping man he had briefly spoken to in the club, lying here in this bag, degraded, withered and lifeless? He wished he could recall the man's face, but no matter how hard he tried, all he could see was the woman's pulchritudinous visage and her amazing eyes.

He felt his stomach somersault as he thought of her; he was becoming more and more convinced that he had been in the presence of the killer that night in the club and he was becoming more and more convinced that the stunning blonde was the culprit. He had nothing to base this gut feeling on, no evidence, no reason to suspect her, but he had a nagging suspicion in the back of his mind. He hoped he wouldn't have to carry the guilt for Daniel's death if his gut feeling turned out to be founded.

Once Dan's body had been carried past them Robert said: 'Let's go Greg. There's nothing to be achieved by us being here. Don't know about you but I could seriously use a drink.'

Greg was only too happy to leave the gruesome scene and readily agreed with his boss's suggestion. As the officers left the house to hunt for the nearest pub Robert couldn't help but wonder how many more men would have to die before they caught this murderous woman. So far she had not made any mistakes, had not left any significant clues at any of the scenes and the frequency of the murders was highly disturbing, her need to kill clearly as strong as it was obsessive.

Robert jumped as he felt his mobile phone vibrate in his suit jacket pocket; he extracted the device and squinted at the caller ID - it was Ian.

'Guv,' Ian sounded out of breath and animated, 'I've got it, I've got a name!'

'Fuck me, what is it?' Robert looked at Greg, a grin spreading across his face triumphantly.

'It's Mina. Our killer's name is Mina.'

****

Derek Cooper was walking alone towards the council car park which was located near the Biztalk premises, having parked his car there earlier because of its convenient proximity to his old office.

He hadn't really needed to collect anything from his former work place, he'd only gone there to wind Ben Mathews up, to see how he'd react. He'd been disappointed by Ben's placidness, hoping that his presence might have elicited an angry reaction from the man he was intending to royally screw over. Instead Ben had simply asked him what he wanted and then told him to be as quick as he could, unperturbed by Derek's audacity.

After whiling away a few hours messing about on his old computer and talking to former colleagues, Derek had left the office and headed to a nearby watering hole; some of the Biztalk staff had followed him, sneaking out when they thought Ben wasn't looking, feeling somewhat traitorous for fraternizing with their boss's enemy and not wanting Ben to catch them shame-faced.

After a pleasant and what Derek considered successful evening drinking with his former colleagues, Derek was now heading home. The evening had turned out better than he expected be-cause most of his colleagues appeared to sympathize and support his claim of unfair dismissal, although not all of them had agreed that he should sue over it.

They had, however, proved to be a captive audience, listening to him open-mouthed as Derek told them all about Ben and that bitch Louise, and recounted what he had seen them doing at Ben's house, embellishing every detail as he did so. "Never let the truth stand in the way of a good story" was the mantra he had learnt early on in his journalistic career when he had been employed by a local rag. He was a little more discerning now, less likely to twist the truth to make it fit with the angle of the piece he was writing, but it was still a motto he liked to apply in situations such as this.

The honest truth was that Derek had no idea if there was anything going on between Louise and Ben or not, but it suited his purposes to believe there was, and he found it much easier to spit his venom at the woman if he convinced himself that she had been promoted over him because of romantic liaisons with the boss.

He didn't want to admit that she had been promoted because she was better at the job than he was, more likeable, more talented and definitely less megalomaniacal. What did he care if the woman was actually competent? That job should have been his and he would never forgive her for taking it away from him.

And then he'd been singled out for redundancy above all of the other writers purely because Louise didn't like him. Bitch. He hadn't liked her since the day he met her, waltzing around like she owned the place, best buddies with the boss almost as soon as she had started working there; he'd been there a lot longer than her and that should have afforded him some sort of superior hierarchical status.

Now though, Derek had found a way to make all this work in his favour and the irony was that Louise had unknowingly granted him that opportunity when she had put him forward for redundancy. He had guessed that she was the voice in Ben's ear and Ben's face during their confrontation had confirmed it. He smirked to himself as he thought about his revenge; a court case could quite easily ruin Biztalk and then they'd all be out of work.

Derek was a little surprised that Ben hadn't yet proposed a meeting with him to discuss how the matter could be kept out of court, to see if Derek had a price, but then Ben Mathews was known for playing hard ball. He was probably waiting to see if Derek was bluffing. He'd find out soon enough.

Derek walked into the car park and headed down toward the lower subterranean level. The car park had been rammed full when he had arrived there earlier that day and the only space available had been on the lower level; he didn't like parking down here as a rule, finding it dingy and malodorous, the stench of old urine and human waste pungent in the stale air.

He wrinkled his nose as he descended the ramp, his head still full of thoughts of revenge and a big fat payout. There didn't appear to be anybody else in the car park, no signs of any tramps or wasted drug addicts. Only a sprinkling of vehicles were located in this section of the car park, but Derek noticed that an old Ford Mondeo was parked close to his Nissan; he hoped the driver had left him enough room to get into the driver's seat.

He grumbled under his breath and as he did so he heard a soft clanging sound from the rear of the car park, as if someone had dropped something metallic.

He turned swiftly, holding his breath, but he neither saw nor heard anything. He felt goose bumps rising on his skin as he scanned the shadows for the source of the noise, sensing there was someone there, lurking in the darkness. After a moment, unable to discern any figure in the gloom, Derek continued hastily towards his vehicle which was only a few meters in front of him, a sixth sense urging him to get away from the car park as fast as he could.

He reached his car and fumbled to put the car key into the driver's side lock, his hands shaking. He heard a movement behind him, footsteps running towards him, but Derek didn't turn around, instead he desperately tried to get his car door open. The lock disengaged with a pop and Derek swung open the door, the metal smashing into the Mondeo beside him. As the door swung open, Derek saw the silhouette of a hooded-person reflected in the glass of the window standing behind him, causing him to gasp with shock, surprised that someone had been able to get so close to him so quickly.

Derek prepared to confront the person, knowing that the only reason someone would be standing so close to him in this dark, smelly car park, would be a sinister one; he suspected it was probably a junkie preparing to mug him, or a thief trying to steal his car. He turned in one fluid movement hands raised, fists clenched as he prepared to act in self-defence, but he hesitated when he saw who was standing behind him.

'You!' he exclaimed, his sentence cut short as he was hit hard in the face with a metal object. The impact knocked him off balance and he fell onto his knees between the two cars, the assailant looming large over him.

'Don't hurt me, don't hurt me!' he wailed, his voice high-pitched and full of fear.

Derek looked up just as his attacker stabbed downwards with a sharp metal implement, the point connecting with his left eye and bursting the eye ball, aqueous humor, blood and tears streaming down his cheek. He screamed in terror and pain as the spike was yanked upwards, causing the eyeball, still stuck to the end of the spike, to be pulled halfway out of his orbital socket. Blood and fluids started to trickle down the back of Derek's throat, making his screams guttural and gasping.

He fell onto his back and the assailant straddled him, raising the metal spike high above Derek's face, holding it there for a moment like an executioner about to deliver the fatal blow. Derek briefly caught another glimpse of the assailant through his right eye and he noted she was smiling, eyes wide and hungry, face contorted into an expression of sheer glee, relishing this murderous endeavour.

Derek knew then that he was going to die, that his last breaths were going to be taken on this dirty, stinking car park floor. He speculated briefly as to how he would be discovered, whether his body would be frisked for his wallet, his watch and gold bracelet removed by a drug addict looking to score their next hit. He wondered how long he would lie there before he was found. Would anyone care that he was dead?

As he felt his life forces draining away, he tentatively raised his hands above his face to shield his eyes from the blow he knew was coming. His hands were easily knocked aside by the assailant as the metal object was again rammed forcefully into his left eyeball. Derek thought he heard the assailant laugh and then the world went black.

Chapter XXIX

Mina felt exhilarated, her heart was pounding in her chest and her senses were alert. She was crouched in the shadows of the subterranean car park, her long, black, hooded coat assisting in her camouflage.

She didn't have to wait too long before she heard her next victim descending into the subterranean car park, muttering under his breath and completely oblivious to her presence as he headed towards his car. She shifted her weight onto her other foot and as she did so, lost grip of her metal weapon; it dropped onto her toe before gently rolling to the floor, its resonance diminished by the prior contact with her shoe.

She held her breath hoping the sound wouldn't give her away. She saw the man looking around the car park trying to locate the source of the noise and swore at herself subvocally.

Fuck it, stupid fucking creature.

After a few tense moments the man seemed satisfied that he was alone and continued towards his vehicle. Mina gently picked up the weapon and waited until she was sure his back was turned and he was occupied with opening the car.

She was pumped. This was killing outside her comfort zone, this was killing of a totally different kind. It was too public and too risky and she knew there were too many variables that she couldn't control and which could ultimately lead to her capture, but she was so excited that none of these things mattered enough to stop her.

She saw the man hurriedly trying to get his keys into the driver's door so she knew she had to act fast. He was clearly on edge and if she didn't move soon she would lose this opportunity.

With a quick glance around to ensure they were still alone in the car park, she ran as swiftly and quietly as she could towards the man's back, surprised she was able to come right up behind him before he even looked round. She was sandwiched between him and the Mondeo, she raised her hands above her head preparing to strike him, when he pulled open the driver's door and quickly spun round to face her. He said: 'You!' and then she struck him as hard as she could on his left cheek causing him to fall to the ground between the vehicles on his knees.

He began begging her, pleading with her not to hurt him and she felt so powerful, so strong, that she relished the sound of his terrified voice. As he looked up at her, his eyes full of fear, she struck downwards with all her strength, ramming her weapon into his left eye. He fell onto his back and she dropped onto his chest straddling him and continued her assault on his eye and face.

She savoured the feeling of awesomeness she was experiencing as his cries turned into animal-like squeals; she laughed a sinister evil sound as the man passed out beneath her. She stopped attacking him, placing her hands on his chest as she allowed herself a moment to catch her breath. Killing was strenuous work.

Once her breathing had slowed and Mina

felt herself coming down from the kill, she stood up and quickly cast an eye around the car park. It was still empty, no one had come running to the man's cries.

Luckily for her, London was a noisy city, her victim's wails lost in the cacophony of roaring engines, police sirens, car horns and thundering tube trains overhead. Mina still had to perform her ritual on the body. Usually she liked to sit and look at the body for a while before doing this as she liked to relive the moment when the body became a mere vessel and its life force ebbed away.

Her first kill in that hotel room had been so exhilarating, so terribly satisfying, that she had needed time to fully take in what she had done, what she had accomplished. She had taken a man's life and it had felt good. Then she'd sat at the foot of the bed for over an hour, looking at the corpse, thinking how weak and vulnerable he looked.

She had only intended to take a trophy from the first victim, as a reminder as to why she was killing, to remind herself of the hurt and pain that fuelled her need. But when she had killed the second victim in his home, she had wanted to mutilate him in the same way – she had discovered it was fun emasculating the victims in this manner and she enjoyed it. Not only were they dead, they were no longer men and she loved the feeling of empowerment this gave her.

By the third victim, she was already visualizing his demise and the desecration of his flesh before she'd even met him. So now it was a necessary part of her killing ritual and although this current kill was well and truly outside of her usual killing parameters, she couldn't resist the urge to cut him up too. Tonight though, she didn't have time to sit and reflect.

Mina knew that at any moment someone could come striding down the ramp into the subterranean car park and so she had to do this quickly. She removed her mobile phone from her pocket and took a couple of pictures of the man lying prostrate at her feet; if she couldn't take the time to enjoy looking at her handiwork now, she would admire it later at her leisure.

She then knelt down besides the body and deftly undid his belt and fly; she quickly pulled down his trousers and pants and looked at the small, shriveled appendage that lay between his legs.

She pulled her boning knife from her pocket and removed the glove from her left hand; she liked to feel the flesh when she cut it away, she liked the feel of the skin against her palm. Mina didn't worry about fingerprints as she would only be touching the part of the penis she would be taking away with her.

She grabbed hold of the man's testicles, squeezing them hard in her left hand and pulled them upwards so that she could insert the knife beneath them. She began carving upwards towards the man's stomach in a circular motion, moving the knife in and out as she progressed through the skin and flesh. The man seemed to rouse a little as she made the cuts to the most sensitive part of his anatomy, his body twitching and shuddering, but Mina knew it was simply his body's last futile attempt to cling on to life. As if on cue she heard the male's raspy death rattle as he finally made the transition from living to dead.

Mina's knife was very sharp and she rapidly cut a semi-circle through the man's flesh, across his pubic hair, and then continued slicing down the opposite side, back down towards his testicles. As she cut, Mina delighted in the blood which spurted from the wounds she was making, the scarlet fluid trickling along her knife blade and over her hands, making both the knife and the flesh slippery, and difficult to hold onto.

As she reached the inside of the man's right leg, almost completing her circle and the full removal of the man's genitalia, she heard loud voices, a group of people laughing. The sound momentarily terrified her.

She froze and held her breath, the voices were coming closer.

Fuck, fuck, fuck, fuck…!

Mina could feel panic setting in but she knew she had to stay calm, she had to remain in control. She quickly slashed through the final bit of meat and promptly put the quivering flesh into her pocket, wiping her hands on her coat to remove the worst of the blood as she did so. She pocketed the knife and silently pushed herself up onto her toes so that she was crouching out of sight, her head just below the window of the dead man's car.

It occurred to her then that she could just get in the man's car and drive away; the keys were still clutched in his lifeless hand. But if she took the car, she would have to dispose of it and she would leave all sorts of evidence in it, whether it was hairs, DNA or clothing fibers. She supposed she could drive it into the country somewhere and torch it as that would get rid of the evidence, but what if she was picked up on traffic cameras or ANPR cameras? It was too risky. She could get pulled over by some Bobby and then she would have some real explaining to do. Also, if she removed the car she would be leaving the body on full display and she had wanted to hide it in the boot before she left.

She was starting to become furious with herself, she should never have started this, she should never have performed a killing outside of her comfort zone, she should have stuck to her plans and only killed in private. She had known this was too risky from the outset but her ego had convinced her she'd be ok, she was untouchable. This is what happened when you acted without meticulously planning things through - things went bloody wrong.

Fuck, fuck, fuck, fuck!

Mina carefully raised her head and peeked through the driver's side window of the dead man's car; she saw four pairs of feet descending the ramp to the subterranean car park, two sets of high heels, clicking loudly on the concrete floor, supporting slim, feminine legs, and two sets of smart shoes, peeping out from under the hem of smart trousers belonging to two men.

Her heart was pounding in her chest and her extremities were tingling with adrenaline. For the first time in a long time she didn't know what to do. The group would be on the subterranean level within a matter of seconds so she had to make a decision and she had to make it fast. Did she stay here, crouched between the cars, hiding with a dead body and blood on her hands hoping they were going to one of the vehicle's on the others side of the car park, or did she get the fuck out of there now, leaving the body where it was instead of finishing up and securing the man's body in the boot of his own car?

Mina scanned the car park looking for an

alternative exit, somewhere she could flee to before it was too late and the group spotted her in all her evil glory. The women's laughter was high-pitched and echoed around the car park and still Mina waited, undecided, like a condemned woman deciding between lethal injection or death by firing squad.

Finally, after frantically scouring around the car park for an escape route, she espied a green fire exit sign on the wall behind her. The feet were almost at the bottom of the ramp as the group came ever closer.

With one last look at the dead man by her feet, Mina leapt up and ran as fast as she could towards the fire exit, the sound of her steps masked by the women's shrill laughter. She slipped slightly as she ran towards the exit, so put her arm out to steady herself, pushing against the boot of a car parked near the fire exit to regain her balance. She bounded across the threshold and into the shadows just as the group rounded the corner and came fully into view.

Mina stood out of sight within the fire exit doorway and watched for a moment as the group moved across the car park. She quickly shrugged off her long coat and rolled it into a ball so that she could shove it into the plastic bag she had brought with her for that purpose, along with her gloves and weapon. She withdrew a pack of tissues from her trouser pocket and wiped her hand removing the last traces of blood that had not come off on her coat and once she had finished, threw the dirty tissue into the bag too. When she was satisfied that she was as clean as she was going to get and would pass unnoticed by the rest of the world, she walked swiftly but calmly up the fire exit stairs.

Mina exhaled a deep sigh as the realization of how close she had come to being seen hit her. A few more seconds and it would have been too late, she would have been caught red-handed at the kill site, blood on her hands and a lump of human flesh in her coat pocket.

She pulled the plastic bag close to her body and continued her ascent out of the car park, ensuring she kept her head lowered so that her face would not be captured on any CCTV cameras. As she reached the top step she heard a faint scream rise from the subterranean level of the car park. So, they'd found him.

Mina smiled to herself as she emerged from the car park fire exit and into the cool night air; she felt truly invincible. She had murdered a man in a public car park, left his body lying in plain view, had been interrupted in her ritual, but still she had been able to act quickly enough to avoid being found at the scene and remain a faceless killer.

Mina glanced around her, looking up and down the street for any obvious signs that she was being scrutinized or followed; apart from a few late night revelers heading home the streets were pretty quiet. In a few minutes however, these streets would look very different; soon they would be crawling with police and emergency services. Mina did not intend to hang around until that happened.

She spotted a taxi heading in her direction, so she raised her arm to hail it. It pulled over at the curb just as she heard the first sirens wailing in the distance. She gave the cabbie an address that was different to her own but close enough that she could walk the last bit of her journey and settled back into her seat. She closed her eyes and let her mind drift. This was her fourth victim. And in a couple of days, she would be meeting with victim number five.

Chapter XXX

Elizabeth was tired and was now regretting arranging to meet Louise for drinks. They'd had another long day in the office and right now all she really wanted was to go home, crawl into bed and go to sleep; she wasn't in the mood for making small talk with someone she had known over fifteen years ago and who she probably had nothing in common with anymore. But still, she had extended the invitation and so she shouldn't complain that Louise had taken her up on it.

After Louise had left her the slightly strange and verbose voicemail the day before, Elizabeth had sent her a text agreeing to the meet and had suggested the time and place, something else she was now regretting. She should have thought about it more carefully and arranged to meet Louise closer to home; she could have saved herself some travel time meaning she would be able tuck herself into bed sooner, and besides as the pub was so close to the police station it was half full of coppers. If she'd wanted to be surrounded by police, she would have stayed in the office. And it was Friday night to top it off, so the place was heaving.

She took a swig of cider enjoying the cool refreshment and leant back in her seat mulling over the day as she waited for Louise to arrive.

They weren't much further forward but now they did have a name, or at least an alias, which was a bloody good start. The name was being run through every single intelligence and suspect database they had access to and was being touted around all the local 'snouts', or covert human intelligence sources as they were officially called. Elizabeth preferred the reference 'snout' as she had little respect for grasses, although she knew they did sometimes come through with valuable nuggets of information. She just resented that they had to be paid or offered a way to avoid jail in order to give up those nuggets. What, alas, had become of civic duty? Was it too much to expect the local shit bag to rat out his mates just because it was the right thing to do?

Elizabeth raised her hand in acknowledgement to two men that had just come in, recognizing them as two of the uniformed officers that worked out of the station. They gave her a wave back and proceeded to the bar to order their drinks. Elizabeth remembered her uniformed days; she had been so full of zeal and ideas, thinking she could help the community, really make a difference. But somewhere between then and qualifying as a detective she had become jaded, exhausted by the seeming lack of humanity in the people she met.

Elizabeth had learnt that the world could be a very cold and cruel place; after dealing with so many shitty people, day in and day out, she sometimes found it difficult to remember that there were also decent people out there, people who did have morals and values and who would put themselves out to help someone in need. It was just that in her profession they were difficult to find.

She thought about the bondage killer and wondered what had happened in the woman's past to make her turn out as she had. She had almost

certainly been sexually abused given the sexual element to these murders and she was almost certainly
a London resident or at least very familiar with the
city. So far Elizabeth had not found anything useful
in the lists she had procured from the council. There
wasn't a great deal she could do with the names on
the list when she had nothing to compare them to.
She had looked at victims that had lived close to
where each of the three murders had taken place but
nothing had jumped out at her. Even though she had
no evidence to base it on, working solely off gut
instinct, Elizabeth was convinced the killer's name
was on her list; she just had to work out which one it
was.

Mina. It was an unusual name and of course
it didn't feature among the names she had been
supplied, that would have been too easy. The name
would be released to the press in due course once
they, or more precisely Ian, were able to show
categorically that it was the name the killer was using.
The name had been found on both David Saunders'
and Mark Faversham's computers; now they needed
to see if it also appeared on Dan Taylor's laptop.
Coincidence could then be eliminated; Elizabeth
didn't know what the odds would be for the name to
appear on three different computers of three otherwise unconnected victims if it didn't relate to their
mutual killer, but they had to be infinitesimal. Ian
was currently taking the brunt of the pressure from
the enquiry; Elizabeth wasn't sure if he had even
been home since he had been seconded to the
investigation. Now that was dedication for you.

Elizabeth glanced at her watch, noting that it
was ten past seven; when she looked up she spotted
Louise strolling in to the venue as if on cue, her eyes

scanning the room as she tried to locate Elizabeth's whereabouts. Louise looked radiant; she was wearing a low-cut, tight-fitting sky blue top, which displayed her pushed-up cleavage to the hungry eyes of the males in the vicinity and a pair of black trousers that clung to her thighs and arse.

She was wearing high heels and so towered over most of the women in the place, the additional three inches extending her height to just under six feet. Her dark blonde hair was swept up into high ponytail that hung to the middle of her back and it was clear that she had taken some time to apply her makeup for she looked immaculate. Not for the first time that week, Elizabeth felt decidedly shoddy in her work clothes.

As she had mentioned to Tony just a couple of days before, Louise had always been popular with the boys, and clearly, from the appreciative glances thrown her way by the male patrons and the jealous stares of the females, she had not lost that appeal over the last fifteen years.

Elizabeth stood up and waved to catch Louise's attention; Louise smiled at her and picked her way through the groups of punters milling within the establishment, slowly making her way over to the table Elizabeth had been guarding for them for the last twenty minutes.

'Well, busy Lizzy, here we are!' Louise said by way of greeting.

'Indeed! Who would have thought, eh?'

'I know! I never thought something positive would have come out of me being arrested!'

'Well, I've just about finished this one,' Elizabeth said, indicating her pint glass, 'so sit down and I'll get us a drink then you can tell me what you've been up to for the past few years. What do you drink these days?' Elizabeth asked.

'Wine is my favourite tipple of late, so a glass of any dry white would be awesome thanks.'

'Coming right up. You look great by the way,' Elizabeth added as an afterthought.

'Cheers. You too. I like your suit.'

Although Louise was smiling when she said it, Elizabeth had a feeling she didn't mean it and was just being polite.

'Thanks. Back in a sec.'

Elizabeth disappeared to the bar and Louise settled back in her chair and took in her surroundings. This all felt so surreal to her; here she was sitting in a pub with a woman she went to school with a decade and a half ago, not really sure why she was here and wondering what on earth they would talk about. How did you catch up on fifteen years in a few hours? She also felt strangely nervous being so close to the police station and she was pretty sure a lot of the people in the pub were police officers; they had that quiet confidence about them.

Louise glanced at the bar and saw Elizabeth laughing with the bar staff as she handed over the money for their drinks, clearly known to them. She looked good too and not all that different to how she had looked all those years ago, just a little leaner and with a few soft lines around her eyes and mouth. From the way she carried herself it was apparent to Louise that Elizabeth possessed a lot of that copper confidence and knew how to handle herself; she couldn't imagine Elizabeth being afraid of anything.

As Elizabeth returned to the table, Louise heard her mobile phone ringing in her bag; she quickly rummaged around looking for the device.

'Sorry, this is rude,' she said to Elizabeth. 'Let me just see who it is and turn it off.'

'Oh don't worry about that. My phone is always going off at inopportune moments and unfortunately I always have to answer it,' Elizabeth smiled.

Louise removed the phone from her bag and looked at the caller ID; it was Ben. She wondered what he wanted; they'd only spoken a day ago and they weren't in the habit of calling each other that often. Assuming that Ben was only calling to check up on her again, Louise pressed the reject button, silencing the call. She then turned off the phone and slid it back into her handbag. Whatever it was, Ben could wait. Tonight Louise wanted to forget about her troubles and the strangeness of the past few days; she just wanted to have a few drinks and let her hair down.

'So,' Elizabeth asked, when Louise had finished silencing her phone and returned her handbag to the floor beneath her feet. 'What have you been up to?'

****

Ben hung up the phone and smiled to himself. Louise had rejected his call and had by that gesture unwittingly told him all he needed to know; she was out with company, which was actually the reason he was calling her in the first place, to make sure she had gone to meet her old school chum and hadn't decided instead to recluse herself in her flat. If Louise was at home she would have just let the phone ring out so that she could pretend she hadn't heard it; because she had in effect hung up on him, he knew she was out and didn't want to appear rude to her friend. Ben marveled at how well he knew the woman.

Just as Ben settled down in front of the TV in his sitting room, a cold beer in hand, he heard the front door bell ring.

He grumbled to himself, annoyed at the intrusion and wondered who the hell would be visiting him on a Friday after seven o'clock in the evening. He just wanted to unwind and gradually ease himself into the weekend, was that too much to ask?

Ben stepped over to his front window, swigging from his beer bottle, and pulled back the edge of the curtain so he could peek at his evening visitors. A uniformed officer and a man in a suit stood on his front step, patiently waiting for him to answer the door. Surprised and worried Ben hurried to the door to let them in.

'Good evening. Are you Mr Ben Mathews?' the man in the suit asked.

'Yes, I am. What's happened?' Ben studied the man's face trying to read it for an indication as to what could have happened to warrant the police turning up at his house. The man in the suit flashed his warrant card and said:

'I'm Detective Sergeant Maddox, this is PC Howitt. We're from the City of London Police. Can we come in please?'

'What's this about?' Ben asked.

'It involves one of your employees and it is a sensitive matter. Can we come in?' DS Maddox asked again.

'Yes, of course. Come this way.'

Ben stepped aside to let the officers into his

home and they then followed him into the living room. Ben turned off the TV as he walked past it and invited the officers to sit down.

'I'm sorry to disturb you Mr Matthews,' DS Maddox began. 'This is about one of your employees, Mr Derek Cooper. He was found murdered late last night in a car park on Rampton Street.'

'What?' Ben couldn't believe what he was hearing, he was stunned. 'Murdered? He was in the office only yesterday.'

Ben shook his head and brought his hands to his face in shock. Derek Cooper had been murdered on Rampton Street, close to the BizTalk offices, after drinking with former co-workers; he wondered who would do such a thing.

'Why? How?' Ben asked, so many questions filled his head.

'A motive hasn't been established yet. He was struck about the face with a sharp object, maybe a knife, and he sustained some trauma to other parts of the body. It looks like it was a blow to his eye that ultimately killed him, but we're waiting for a full report from the coroner,' DS Maddox explained.

'Jesus. I can't believe it.' Ben shook his head.

'It must be a lot to take in Mr Matthews, but I would like to ask you some questions. Do you need some time to digest this?'

'No, it's fine. Anything I can do to help.'

'Can you tell us about the last time you saw Mr Cooper?' the detective asked. The PC remained silent, taking notes in his pocketbook.

'It was yesterday afternoon, he had come to the office to collect files, paper work… to be honest

I'm not entirely sure what he was collecting. He is actually a former employee; I made him redundant on Monday. I need to downsize the company you see. He came in about three, was in the office for a good few hours and I know he was planning on going out for drinks with some of my staff. I wasn't invited so the last time I saw him would have been about six thirty yesterday evening.'

'I see, and what was your relationship with Mr Cooper like?'

'Well, before I fired him, it was fine. I never really had any dealings with him. But when I told him I was making him redundant, he took it very personally. I received a letter on Tuesday, which he must have hand delivered to the post room, and it contained photos of me and a female co-worker. The pictures were taken to make it look like we're having a relationship, which we're not, and the letter suggested that Derek was going to sue me for unfair dismissal because of the romantic liaisons he thought I was having.'

'Why would that give him grounds for unfair dismissal?'

'Because he wanted to suggest that the female in question had put me up to it for a personal vendetta and that it wasn't actually related to his performance,' Ben clarified.

'Right, I understand. We did find some photos in Mr Cooper's car, and meeting you now, I realize that the man in those pictures is you. Who is the woman?'

Ben really didn't want to tell the officers any more than he had to, he didn't want to give them Louise's name. The last thing she needed was more police sniffing around her and more unsettlement.

'Do I have to tell you?'

'You don't have to, but it would be helpful for us to know who she is. We will need to speak to her too to corroborate your story.'

'Am I suspect?'

DS Maddox paused for a moment before answering.

'No. But you are so far the only person we have spoken to who has any sort of motive for wanting Mr Cooper dead.'

'What, you think I'd rather see him dead than fight him in court?'

'I'm just making an observation.

Ben sighed, 'Her name is Lucy Jamieson,' he lied.

'Thank you. Do you know which members of your staff went out drinking with him last night?'

'No, no idea. As I mentioned, I wasn't invited.'

'The car park in question is close to your offices isn't it?'

'Yes it is.'

'Do many of you staff park there?'

'The majority of my staff commute by public transport because I have a system in place whereby they can have a loan for their rail card or whatever, and then pay it back in installments directly from their monthly pay.'

'Would you be able to provide me with the names of all your employees and their dates of birth? We'll need to speak to all of them, especially the ones who saw him last night,' DS Maddox said.

'Yes, I can get that for you. I'm guessing you don't want to wait until Monday to get that information?'

'You guess right. The sooner we can speak to all potential witnesses the better'

'Well, we can go to the office now and I'll get you a list if you want? I don't have access to the HR records from my home computer,' Ben suggested helpfully.

'That would be very helpful Mr Matthews. PC Howitt will go with you.'

'Just wondering before we go, why did you come to see me if I'm not a suspect and I wasn't a witness?'

'We found documents relating to Biztalk in Mr Cooper's car and we discovered you were the owner of the business from your website. Given the proximity of your offices to the crime scene we supposed he had been coming from work and as such you became someone we needed to talk to, as are all your employees.'

'Oh right. So you suspect one of my employees may have done this?'

'All options are open at the moment, we can't say anything for definite at this stage.'

'Jesus.'

Ben felt his blood run cold. Could one of his staff, someone he knew, actually have murdered Derek Cooper?

'Ok Mr Matthews, I think we're done here unless you have any questions?'

Ben shook his head: 'No, not at the moment.'

DS Maddox gave Ben his card and told him to call if he thought of anything else. Ben thanked him and got up to get his office keys; he wasn't really listening anymore to what the officers had to say.

All he could hear was Louise's voice in his

head, repeating over and over what she had said to him hours before Derek Cooper had wound up dead. *"Hopefully he'll trip going down the stairs on his way out and kill himself. That would solve all your problems, wouldn't it? If he died?"* Louise's words now took on a sinister edge. *"That would solve all your problems, wouldn't it? If he died? ...solve...your problems... if he died?"*

They'd joked about it but now it had happened. Was it just a dark coincidence that she had uttered those words and now Derek was dead? Or was there more to it than Ben wanted to believe? He thought back to the way Louise had reacted when he had told her about the letter Derek had sent him, the way she had flown off the handle. He had felt like he was momentarily talking to someone else; he'd glimpsed a darker side to her.

As much as Ben didn't believe it was possible and he couldn't begin to fathom that Louise was involved, he found himself wondering: could Louise have something to do with Derek's death?

****

Louise and Elizabeth were having a great time; the drinks were flowing and the conversation was easy, any shyness washed away by the alcohol. They'd talked about their school days, reminiscing on old teachers and pupils and wondering what had become of them all; they'd talked about places they'd travelled to, people they'd met and they talked about how they had ended up in their current professions. Elizabeth told Louise she had done well to get into such a coveted position so quickly; Louise told Elizabeth she couldn't believe she had become a police officer.

'I thought you'd become a doctor or something,' Louise said. 'You were so adamant you were going to fix people.'

'Well, I kind of do fix people as a copper. I help mend lives by catching the bad guys,' Elizabeth giggled into her drink. 'God that sounds really pretentious! I mend lives; I'm amazing don't you know!'

The women laughed.

'You're working on that female serial killer case aren't you?' Louise asked

'Sure am. Never seen anything like it.'

'How's the case going?'

'I can't really tell you Louise, as much as I'd like to. And I swear that is not me being pretentious again!'

'I understand, I'm just curious, you know? It fascinates me. This killer is a woman and that's really rare isn't it? Especially if she's acting alone, cos don't most women killers have a partner of some sort?' Louise asked, genuinely interested.

'Well, I'm no authority but from what I have read and studied over the years, yes, our current killer would be rare; she's killing so violently, taking trophies from the bodies and appears to be working alone. Don't think I've ever read a case that is similar to this one; the closest I could think of was Mary Bell. And oi, you're making me say too much.'

'I've heard of Mary Bell, the killer child right? That's seriously creepy isn't it, a killer that is a child?'

'You're telling me!' Elizabeth agreed.

'So, are you guys close to catching her, this bondage killer?'

'Louise, you know I can't tell you that.'

'I don't want details, just wondering if the men of London still need to be running scared.'

'We're getting closer,' Elizabeth said. 'Actually, I'm really excited because we have a name, well, we have a nickname.'

'Wow, that's great news then, isn't it? So you should work out who it is soon?'

Elizabeth was about to reply when her work phone started to ring; Tony was calling her.

'Hold on Louise I need to get this; it's work.' Louise nodded and smiled, indicating she didn't mind.

'Tony, what is it?' Elizabeth asked, there was a pause and then she said, 'If it's not work related Tony, I'm not interested.' She paused again as she listened to what Tony had to say. Louise looked at her curiously.

'Tony, like I said, if it isn't work related, I'm not interested. I'm out with a friend at the moment, ok? It's none of your business who, so go away.' She hung up the phone, huffing loudly. 'Bloody men.'

'Tell me about it. My whole life would have been a hell of a lot easier if there were no men in this world!' Louise concurred. 'That your boyfriend?'

'No, yes, oh I don't bloody know. It's complicated,' Elizabeth took a large gulp of her drink. 'We work together, we slept together and now I don't know what we are. He wasn't totally honest with me about something and now I don't know what I should do. I don't want to bore you with the details.'

'I don't mind. I enjoy a good man bashing every now and then,' Louise smiled broadly, displaying her perfectly straight, white teeth.

'Nah, you're alright. You're single, right?'

Elizabeth asked.

Louise's smile dropped and her facial expression changed to one of hatred. She didn't answer Elizabeth straight away, she instead stretched her arms in front of her and rolled her head as if easing away tension in her neck. Elizabeth watched her, wondering what the hell she was doing.

'Yeah. I'm single. Newly single. The guy I was with cheated on me with a member of his staff. They'd been having an affair for months and I didn't suspect a thing,' Louise eventually answered, her voice low and dull.

Despite the alcohol whirling round her brain, slightly distorting her judgment, Elizabeth was surprised by the quick transition in moods Louise was displaying. Just a moment before she'd been as metaphorically high as a kite, but now she had suddenly crashed back down to earth.

'I bloody caught them at it in a romantic country retreat which had been booked for me and him. Fucking bitch had the nerve to suggest I wasn't good enough for him. So I hit her and that's why I was at the police station on Tuesday, for assaulting her. It's a joke really. They can break my heart and they don't get fucking arrested for that,' Louise looked like she was about to cry.

'Sorry Louise, I didn't mean to upset you,' Elizabeth said gently.

'You haven't upset me. It's fucking men that upset me. They're only happy when they're sticking their dicks into something, especially when they're sticking it somewhere they shouldn't. It's why they like to cheat so much, cos they know they shouldn't be fucking doing it. They don't care about the pain they're causing or going to cause. The world would

332

be a better place without men in it.'

'I don't know as I agree entirely with that statement, but I can see why you would think that after your boyfriend cheated on you. Sorry to hear that Louise. They're not all bad though, there are some good ones,' Elizabeth said.

The atmosphere around the table had changed, it was now charged with tension and Elizabeth felt like leaving. She wasn't quite sure how this had happened. They'd been merrily chatting away, happily talking rubbish, and now all she wanted to do was to get away from Louise as quickly as she could.

'You're wrong Elizabeth. They're all bad, they all have a rotten core. All they want is to fuck you. Once they've done that, they get bored and they leave you for someone else,' Louise was getting angrier with every statement.

'Women cheat too; women can be cold, calculating bitches. Why do you feel so much hatred towards men?'

'Because they're fucking pigs!' Louise almost shouted.

'Whoa, ok. I think we should move on from this topic. It's clearly upsetting you and this was just supposed to be a nice quiet drink,' Elizabeth said calmly, trying to placate her. Louise looked at her angrily for a second and then her face changed as she broke into a sheepish smile.

'You're right. I'm sorry. I don't know where that came from.'

'No problem Louise, it's probably the alcohol amplifying your feelings. Shall we call it a night?' Elizabeth asked, hoping Louise would say yes.

She no longer wanted to sit here with this

man-hating woman, who clearly had deep-seated issues regarding the male of the species.

'Yeah, that's probably a good idea. I've had too much wine already.' The women stood up and gave each other an awkward hug.

'Was nice catching up with you Elizabeth. Sorry about getting worked up at the end there.'

'Like I said, no problem. I understand why you feel that way in light of how your boyfriend treated you. You going to be alright getting home?'

'Yes officer, I'll be fine,' Louise snickered and raised her hand in a fake salute.

'Good. You take care of yourself, ok?'

The women parted company and walked off in opposite directions. Elizabeth glanced back over her shoulder to check on Louise, but she was already out of sight, lost amidst the Friday night crowds.

Chapter XXXI

Tony reached out his hand and felt Elizabeth's warm body lying next to him. He groaned contentedly and rolled his body up against hers, enjoying the feeling of their skin touching, and wrapped an arm around her chest, pulling her close.

Elizabeth was still sleeping a blissful, alcohol-induced slumber and Tony had no inclination to wake her, she looked so cute curled up on her side, her hair strewn across the pillow like octopus tentacles, her lips slightly parted.

He was pleased she had come round to his flat last night, even if it had been after eleven thirty when she'd knocked on the door. She had forgiven him and that was the main thing.

He'd answered the door in his boxers and as soon as he'd let her in, she'd pushed herself roughly against him, driving him back against the wall, her mouth pressing against his, her hands all over his body. She'd then grabbed his arms, spun herself around so that her back was to him, put both his hands between her legs and rubbed her arse against his already swollen penis.

He'd bitten her ear and pulled her hair, jerking her head backwards exposing her neck so that he could bite that too. She'd gasped with pleasure and continued to writhe against him for a few moments longer.

Then she'd moved away from him briefly to

remove her suit jacket and blouse, revealing a sexy red lace bra, before dropping to her knees in front of him, one hand pushing his torso, keeping him against the wall, the other yanking down his boxers and exposing his manhood. It had felt so good when she had taken him in her mouth he had had to concentrate hard on something non-sexual to prevent himself from coming there and then.

She'd looked up at him, erotically licking his shaft, her eyes full of lust. 'Elizabeth,' he'd murmured, holding her face gently between his hands as she continued to pleasure him.

She'd then stood up and removed her trousers, giving him a good view of her toned figure and the red lace underwear set, she looked hot as hell.

'Get on the floor, Tone,' she had ordered and he had happily obliged.

She'd stood over him for just a second, giving him a glimpse of her femininity through her racy red thong and then she dropped down onto him, straddling his waist and rubbing herself against him.

Finally, she had held her knickers aside and pushed him inside her; she had been so ready for him, that he had entered her easily. She'd begun moving up and down his shaft, slow then fast, slow then fast... not knowing her rhythm he hadn't been able to match her motion so he had relinquished all control to her.

She'd leant back, grinding her hips against him as she came and he'd stiffened inside her as he allowed himself release in unison with her. She had then lain on top of him for a while, her body hot and sweaty, and he had gently caressed her back.

Finally, she had looked at him and smiled,

and said: 'Hi Tony. How are you?'

They'd both laughed as they'd unraveled themselves from each other's embrace and got into bed. And now it was 8am and here they were, snuggling together, not a care in the world.

'Hmmmm,' Elizabeth mumbled, taking hold of Tony's arm and pulling it tighter around her. 'That feels nice.'

'How's your head?' Tony asked her softly, his face pressed into her hair.

'Um…' Elizabeth raised herself on one elbow and blinked sleepy dust from her eyes. 'Fine, I think.' She grinned at Tony. 'Who was a naughty boy last night Mr Jessop?'

'I think you'll find you ravaged me, actually. You were in charge.'

'You complaining?' she teased.

'Not at all. Feel free to come round here for a booty call anytime.'

Tony pushed himself up, kissed her tenderly on the mouth and then pulled her back down into the duvet with him, rolling onto his back so that she could lay on his chest.

'So, how did it go with your friend last night?' he asked. Elizabeth chuckled.

'It was a female friend Tony, actually it was the one you saw the other day outside the nick.'

'What the super hot one? And you didn't invite me!' he asked feigning incredulity.

Elizabeth smacked him on the side and said, 'Oi! That is out of order. Besides she's way out of your league,' she drew out the 'way' to emphasize by just how far.

'What would I want her for anyway, when I have you,' he kissed the top of her head.

'Who says you have me? I just needed a shag.'

'Charming! So did you ladies have a good catch up? You knew her from school didn't you?'

'Yeah, feels like a life time ago. It was nice reminiscing; we mainly talked about the past and what we are now doing in our adult lives; she's an editor for some company or other, I can't recall the name. Actually, I don't think she gave me the name. She's still as funny and smart as I remember her to have been back then. And she's still got a way with the boys,' Elizabeth raised her head to look at Tony and narrowed her eyes. 'Don't say anything,' she warned.

'What? I didn't say a word,' Tony replied defensively.

'Hmmm… yes, well. Best you get her out of your mind. It was going great, we were having a laugh and just talking shit, you know how you do when you're getting close to having one too many…'

'Close? You may want to revise that statement!' Tony interjected.

Elizabeth ignored him and continued: 'Shortly before we called it a night, we got onto the subject of men and Louise became really… I don't know how to describe it really… aggressive, I guess. She totally snapped and the whole mood changed.'

'Women and their mood swings.'

'Don't be so bloody sexist Tony. I know plenty of men who have mood swings... you want me to give you examples? Because I could always mention how weird you were when Ian came over from FHQ?'

'Ok, ok, point made. Sorry. So what do you mean exactly about her manner changing?' Tony replied

'One minute she was absolutely fine, I asked her if she was single and then she did this weird stretching and head rolling thing and her manner totally changed, her voice, her mannerisms. She said that all men were bad to the core, were all cheats and were 'only happy when they were sticking their dicks into something.' Her words, not mine. She went from funny, laughing and joking to almost rage within a split second and without any sort of warning. I'm sure she only reacted like that because her break up is so recent and she found her ex in bed with an employee apparently.'

'Ouch, that's got to hurt,' Tony agreed.

'Yeah, but I dunno, it was just strange. Made me feel really uncomfortable, like I didn't want to be near her. I felt as if I was talking to two different people. Does that sound crazy?' Elizabeth raised her head to look at Tony.

'Not really. It's alcohol though isn't it? It has the capacity to change even the sweetest person into a blubbering mess, or an irate pugilist, or a rampant nymphomaniac with an urgent booty call,' Tony said, mischievously. Elizabeth laughed.

'Guess so. Not sure I'll meet up with her again though, think she's a bit unpredictable. I'd be afraid of saying anything that might set her off.'

They lay for a moment lost in thought, when Tony said: 'Just thinking, your friend, didn't you tell me the other day down the pub that she was fostered and used to live in London?'

'Yeah, that's what she told me at school. She was fostered out at age 8 or 9 and used to live in London, before that she lived on the outskirts somewhere, can't remember where though. Why?'

'You know why…'

'Oh my god, of course, my list. She could be on it if she was sexually abused. Bloody hell Tony, can you imagine that?'

'You could have been fraternizing with the enemy,' Tony said, only half joking.

'Right come on Tone, get up. We've got work to do.'

Elizabeth threw back the bed covers and practically jumped from the bed, a flurry of legs and arms as she dashed across the room heading for the bathroom.

'Elizabeth, seriously? Now? We don't have to be in for ages yet!' Tony called after her. He heard her phone ringing in her bag. 'And you're phone's ringing,' he added.

'Ignore it! And yes, I mean now!' He could hear that she was in the shower and the idea of her lathering up, covering her body in white, bubbly foam started to make him hard. Just as he was considering quitting the warmth of his bed for the warmth of the shower, his phone began to ring too. Tony took the call and then rushed into the bathroom to join Elizabeth, bumping her out of the water jet with his body, startling her.

'What the…?' she asked, soap bubbles slithering down her body.

'We've got to get to the office asap…'

'Yeah, I know,' she interrupted grumpily, annoyed at Tony's invasion of the shower cubicle.

'No, I mean, the boss is asking us to go in. It'll be him who called you just now. We're now investigating four murders. We've got another body on our hands.'

****

There was a loud rip as Louise tore open the first item of post she had neglected to open for the past three days. It was a very unexciting generic letter from the bank offering her special rates on a credit card. She screwed it up and aimed it at the waste paper bin; the ball of paper bounced off the rim into the centre of the room. Louise ignored it and began opening the second letter which she was anticipating would share the same fate of the first.

It was a beautiful day, the sun had full reign of a clear blue sky and a gentle breeze periodically blew through the open living room windows. When she had got up an hour or so earlier Louise had vowed that despite her wine headache, she was going to get on her running shoes and head down to the canal for a nice long jog in the sunshine.

But first, once she'd finished with the post, she was going to call Ben. He had tried to call her five times last night and had left two voicemails asking her to call him as soon as she could. His missives hadn't given her any indication as to what he wanted to talk about.

Louise scrunched up the second letter and threw it at the bin, missing her target again. She picked up another envelope and turned it over; this was the one with the pretty handwriting. She ripped it open and extracted a piece of A4 paper that had been carefully folded in four. The letter was also handwritten, which surprised Louise. Who hand wrote letters these days? She read:

Dear Louise,

It's taken me a few days to decide if I should get in touch with you, but after careful consideration and deliberation, I decided that I had to tell you what happened last week — I couldn't forgive myself if I didn't and besides, it was part of the postmortem instructions I received. I hope this letter reaches you because I got this address off the internet on one of those people finder websites; it's scary what you can find out online. I couldn't find a complete postcode but hopefully the partial one I found will be sufficient to get this letter to you.

I just wanted to let you know that our mother died last week of a heart attack. I was contacted by the prison she was remanded at and they told me she'd died in the prison hospital. Apparently she had put me down as her next of kin. They also sent me what I guess can best be described as her will. She didn't own anything so her only instructions were that you and I had to be informed of her death. And that is why I am writing to you, to carry out her last wishes.

I don't know what you know about our mother, what you remember, so I hope this doesn't come as too much of a shock for you. I did think that maybe I should just leave the past in the past and not write to you, but now that I have written this letter I feel a weight off my mind, so I know I have done the right thing.

Your sister, Michelle Blackmoore

Louise was dumbfounded, her hands started shaking. Was this a sick prank?

Her mother had died years ago and she had been locked up in lunatic asylum, not a prison. She read the letter again, the words blurring on the page, tears brimming in her eyes, as she read each line over and over, a multitude of questions assailed her. If her mother hadn't died when she was a girl, why had she been told that by her foster family? And why had they told her that her mother had been sectioned instead of sent to prison? It didn't make any sense.

Her mother had experienced a break down after her dad had left, that's what she had always been led to believe. She hadn't been sent to prison! What could she have done that would cause her to have been locked up for over two decades? Had her foster parents lied to her for all those years? And if so why? To protect her?

She couldn't even ask them to find out as she had lost contact with them many years earlier after a series of rows had finally escalated into full blown familial warfare with many harsh words exchanged, each of them adamant they were in the right and equally adamant that they would not be the first to apologize and make peace.

Louise's head was reeling, she couldn't think straight, she needed answers. Everything she thought she knew was in jeopardy, everything she had believed about her mother seemingly a lie. What was her past? Was there any truth in anything she had been told? Was this letter really from her sister, or was someone simply trying to make her life more tumultuous? Only one person could answer these questions; Louise needed to speak to Michelle.

She picked up the envelope and studied the postmark; the letter had been posted four days ago from a postbox in Kent. So, Michelle was living in the Garden of England, knowing which county she was in should make her easier to find. It was time for Louise to do some tracking of her own.

****

The briefing room was packed with officers working on the bondage killings after Robert had called a full briefing, telling everyone to get in 'as fast as they fucking could.' Everyone was now present, including Tony and Elizabeth who had arrived at the station 10 minutes apart to ensure they did not become fodder for the gossip mongers. They didn't want anyone to know they were sleeping together yet, and they didn't want to give anyone the opportunity to suggest their conduct was unprofessional.

Robert was standing at the front of the room with his back to the waiting detectives, scribbling on the white board. He wrote the name Derek Cooper and then turned to face the room. Apparently, Meadows had also been invited to this briefing, or he had got wind of it and invited himself, because he sat close to where Robert was standing, reading a handful of documents and looking important.

'Thank you all for coming,' Robert began, 'I know it was short notice and some of you were off for the weekend. There has been a development in our case... I think you all know by now that Ian identified a nickname for our killer? The name she uses when contacting victims online is Mina.'

There was a murmur of agreement around the room; the revelation of a name had travelled fast among the group of investigating officers and was not news to anyone in the room.

'What you don't all know, however, is that we are now investigating four murders, instead of three.'

This time a series of exclamations bounced around the room as those who hadn't already been advised of this over the phone expressed their dismay.

'The fourth victim,' Robert continued 'was a man called Derek Cooper and he was actually murdered on Thursday night. The body was found in a car park by a group of friends who had been to the opera.'

'Why the fuck didn't we know about this Thursday night then guv? 'scuse my language,' said a voice from the back of the room.

'The body was found shortly after midnight on Rampton Street, which falls within the jurisdiction of the City of London Police, not us. At first they had no reason to suspect that their dead body was linked to our three dead bodies because, although Mr Cooper's genitals were also missing as is typical of our killer's MO, we have not released that fact to anyone. As far as they were concerned it was just an isolated case. It is only when they started to do their intelligence checks that they found our intelligence files and so realised the murder was connected.'

'So, we know this is our killer because the genitals were removed and we know it can't be a copycat because nobody knows that our killer does this to the bodies, but you said the body was found in a car park. That's very different, isn't it? A bit too public?' Greg asked. 'The previous three murders all occurred in private places.'

'Yes, this is the bit which doesn't fit with our killer's usual behaviour. I haven't come up with any reasonable hypothesis as to why she chose to kill this man in a public car park, and he wasn't wearing bondage gear. It doesn't look like she picked him up in a club. I'm open to any suggestions as to why you think this might be.'

The room was silent as the detectives thought about this for a moment.

'Give it some thought,' Robert said, 'it may become clear as we find out more about this victim.'

'What have the City of London Police established about this murder and what have they done thus far?' Elizabeth asked.

'DS Maddox has submitted a full handover report and package and I spoke with him last night and first thing this morning. He told me that Mr Cooper had driven into London to visit his former work place, a company called Biztalk. He had just been made redundant and told the boss, Benjamin Matthews, that he needed to collect some old files he had been working on. He stayed in the building for a few hours and then went out to have some drinks with his former colleagues. He was then found dead, lying between his car and a car belonging to a lady called Alison Stuart, by four people who had just been to the opera.'

'Murdered just like that out in the open...' Greg shook his head in wonderment then said: 'Does it look like he was targeted specifically, guv, or does it look like an opportunistic killing?'

'I don't know and again please let me know your thoughts. At the moment, we have to play catch up a little bit as we need to get ourselves up to speed with what City of London Police have done already. They've covered a lot of ground; they've spoken to the boss of Biztalk and several of the company's employees. They have given me a list of all the employees at the company, they have obtained the car park CCTV but it hasn't been viewed yet. They conducted a full forensic survey of the scene and have spoken to the poor sods that found the body. I need you all to read the various statements and reports they have already collated to make sure you are fully aware of all aspects of this latest murder.'

Robert paused for a moment and began sifting through various papers that were placed on the desk beside him.

'This is a list of all the Biztalk employees along with their phone numbers. I want each of you to call a couple of the employees and find out who the victim was drinking with, then I want urgent statements from those people. JB can you please take the list and divide it up amongst everyone here. I need a team to attend the deceased home to retrieve his computer - Ian you can coordinate that please. I want a couple of you to view the CCTV asap - Greg, I'm putting you in charge of that. I also want a couple of you to visit the scene and have a good look round, see if you can spot any other council CCTV cameras, any business premises that may have CCTV on the streets or may have been open at that time of night - Elizabeth, can you sort that out please?'

Robert concluded the briefing and the officers filed out of the room, keen to begin the enquiries they had been tasked with; Meadows and Robert left the room together and Elizabeth overheard Meadows saying something about the need for another press release and that he thought the name should be released to the public. She didn't hear Robert's reply, but saw him shaking his head.

Although Elizabeth knew she should get straight on with visiting the crime scene, as she had been requested, there was one thing she wanted to do first, just to ease her suspicious mind. She walked quickly into the adjacent incident room and flopped into her chair at her desk, calling out for Tony to join her.

'I'm going to run Louise's name through my database, what do you reckon? Will she or won't she be on my list of names?' she mused, drumming her fingers on the desk as she waited for her computer to boot up.

'God, I don't know… You know how I feel about this list, that it's a great big stab in the dark with too many 'ifs' and 'buts'. But if your hypothesis is correct and she was sexually abused, resided in London at the time and was fostered out, then yes, I guess there's a good chance she'll be on it,' Tony replied.

'Jesus, I feel nervous!' Elizabeth loaded up the Excel spreadsheet she had populated with all the names she had received from all the London Councils and selected the finder tool. She typed in LOUISE JACKSON and hit the find button. After a couple of seconds searching the Excel dialogue box opened and read: 0 matches found.

'Well, that's that then. She wasn't sexually abused and therefore, does not fit the profile of our killer,' Elizabeth said, disappointed at the anti-climax.

'That's probably a good thing isn't it? I don't think it would be very nice to find out that the person you used to go to school with and were drinking with last night is a killer.'

'Maybe there's a problem with my database? Maybe the councils didn't give me all the names?' Elizabeth said hopefully.

'Or maybe she's not on the list for a reason Elizabeth. You have no reason to suspect her other than the fact that you didn't like the way she spoke about men.'

'I guess you're right. God how suspicious am I? Thinking about it now, I can't actually believe I thought she could be a murderer! No more cider for me, it does things to my head,' Elizabeth said, making light of the situation and masking her disappointment.

'Let's go find JB and see who he wants us to

speak with from Biztalk,' Tony suggested.

'Yeah, alright. You want to come to the crime scene with me after that?'

'Yes, I'd like to see where this latest murder happened.'

Despite what she had just seen with her own two eyes, that Louise Jackson's name was not in her list, Elizabeth couldn't help but wonder if this was because she had made a mistake when compiling her list of names. Perhaps one of the councils had missed some names off their registers, or perhaps she had omitted some of them when copying them over to her excel spreadsheet? Elizabeth didn't know why she was suspicious of Louise, she just knew that she should listen to her gut, and right now, her gut was telling her that Louise was one dark horse.

Chapter XXXII

The drive to the address Louise had found for her sister had taken longer than the anticipated two hours predicted by the satnav, an accident on the A20 out of London adding almost an hour to her journey.

Sitting in the subsequent traffic jam with nowhere to go and nothing to occupy her mind, Louise had been unable to escape the thoughts that were running circles in her head. She was confused, there were too many questions, too many things she did not know, too many long-held beliefs, which could all be false if the content of the letter was true.

She had tried hard to recollect various events from her past, various people she had met and known over the years, to see if she could remember anything that could help her make sense of this madness. Nothing came to mind. She felt as if she had been sucked into one enormous cyclone of turmoil, from the moment she had seen the strange man at the bus stop to the moment that letter had fallen through her letter box, and it didn't seem ready to throw her back down to earth yet.

She just wanted it to stop, she needed it to stop; she was losing sight of who she was, not recognizing the woman who was currently experiencing this life. What had happened to her? Louise knew that too many life disturbances could unbalance even the most resilient of minds; she didn't know how much more she could take.

She was now parked in front of a pretty, little semi-detached house in the village of Lydd. Floral hanging baskets adorned the front of the property, pink, yellow and blue flowers blooming resplendently in the sunshine. A neat patch of grass and two colourful flower beds lay behind a low wall that enclosed the front garden and separated it from the pavement and roadside. It was a pleasant looking property and it was obvious that the owners took pride in their home. Louise had driven past the house three times before mustering the courage to finally park in front of it.

She had been sitting here for half an hour, running through the questions she wanted answering, imagining how this conversation might go. Louise looked at the house again and wondered what the woman inside would look like; would she recognize her as her sister? Was she even home? There were no cars on the drive so Michelle could be out. Louise hadn't considered what she would do if there was nobody home, but she was adamant she was not going home until she had answers.

Exhaling deeply, Louise stepped out of her car and slowly made her way up the driveway towards the front door. It was now or never; she couldn't sit there all day like some amateur stalker.

She was finding it hard to breathe as the nerves kicked in, her heart beating so hard in her chest she thought it might break through her ribs and jump out onto the perfectly trimmed lawn. She wiped her sweaty palms against her jeans and tried to calm down by forcing herself to breathe deeply. A gold door bell was affixed to the left of the door and

Louise pushed it with her index finger, her hand trembling.

She shifted nervously from one foot to the other as she waited for the door to be answered. Just when she was beginning to think that there was nobody home, she heard movement behind the front door. Louise heard a lock being turned and then the door was pulled open, a woman carrying a young child on her hip stood in the doorway looking at Louise curiously.

'Michelle Blackmoore?' Louise asked.

'Yes?'

Louise didn't recognize this woman at all; she did not bear any of the features that Louise recalled from her childhood sister. Michelle was slightly overweight from child bearing and she was considerably shorter than Louise at five feet two inches tall. Her dark brown hair was cut into a chin-length bob, most of it pushed behind her ears, the ends curling up towards her mouth. She had a pleasant and attractive face, with big grey-blue eyes and a small slightly upturned nose. She was wearing black jogging bottoms and a baggy, green T-shirt spattered with baby food and paints. The boy she was carrying had bright blonde hair which stuck up all over his head and he squirmed in his mother's arms to get a good look at their visitor. He had multi-coloured paints on his face and hands; mother and son had clearly been bonding over a creative finger-painting endeavour.

Louise didn't know what to say, her mouth went dry and her throat seized up – no words would come out; she wasn't prepared for children and here in front of her was her nephew. Seeing her sister standing before her was more of a shock than Louise had anticipated and all the questions she had devised on the journey down and whilst sat outside the house abandoned her.

'Can I help you?' Michelle asked, a flicker of annoyance on her face at the unexpected guest.

'Michelle, I'm Louise Jackson. You wrote to me a few days ago,' Louise said finally finding her voice.

Michelle's mouth dropped open and her eyes widened in disbelief.

'Oh my god. I... Louise! What are you doing here? How did you find this address?' she asked, dismayed.

'I found you the same way you found me. The postmark on the letter you sent was from Kent so it made it a lot easier for me to find you. You're right, technology is wonderful. I paid a small fee to get your full address off of one of those people finder websites. It was easy as I knew the county you lived in, your full name and of course I remember your approximate age.'

'But why are you here? I didn't give you my address for a reason. I didn't want to see you,' Michelle said coldly.

'Can I at least come in for a few minutes?' Louise asked, hurt despite herself. She hadn't expected a fanfare and cartwheels, but she had expected a basic level of hospitality instead of outright rudeness.

After a moment's consideration, Michelle reluctantly stepped aside and told Louise to head out to the garden at the back of the house. Louise stepped into the long corridor that led to the kitchen and through the kitchen windows Louise could see an average-size garden complete with child's play area and sand pit. A set of stairs led up to the first floor on the right and to the left Louise glimpsed a large, plush living room, furnished to a high standard.

Photographs of the family hung on the corridor walls and from these Louise established that Michelle was married and had two children, one of which was just a baby. Louise wondered where the other child was. As if reading her mind Michelle said from behind her: 'Melody is upstairs sleeping.'

Louise passed through the kitchen where a number of dishes sat next to the sink waiting to be washed and stepped out into the garden. She could see where Michelle and the little boy had been playing, a large waterproof mat spread across the grass next to a set of garden furniture, paper and paints strewn about its surface.

Michelle sat the little boy on the mat so that he could continue playing with the paints and pulled a garden chair over for Louise and then one for herself. She repositioned a baby monitor on the garden table. The women sat around the mat watching the boy for a moment.

'What's his name?' Louise asked, not sure how to begin; she had so many questions.

'Kyle,' Michelle smiled at the boy who was contentedly rubbing his hands in the paints, making as much mess as he could. 'Have you got any children?'

'No. I'm not married either.'

'It's a wonderful feeling. It makes you feel secure and loved and wanted. Having children gives you a sense of purpose and makes you realize you're needed. Everyone needs to feel needed,' Michelle said sagely. 'Especially people like us.'

'What do you mean?'

'People who had their childhoods destroyed and their families torn apart. It makes for a very insecure adult.' Michelle crouched down and tweaked Kyle's ears making him giggle.

'Michelle I am so confused. I don't remember anything from my childhood. I barely remember my teenage years. I vaguely recall our mother, but I have no memory whatsoever of our father. I have no idea what happened to our family. And it seems that everything my foster parents told me is a lie. This is why I had to come and see you. I was hoping you would explain things to me,' Louise said, her tone hopeful.

Michelle looked at her and there was something in her eyes, a wariness that Louise didn't understand.

'What did your foster parents tell you?' Michelle asked.

'They told me that our father left when we were little more than babies and that our mother hadn't been able to cope with his departure or raising us on her own. She had a mental breakdown and was sectioned in a mental hospital and a short while later they told me she had committed suicide. I never questioned them as I didn't think they would have any reason to lie.'

'Have you spoken to them about the letter I sent you?'

'No, I don't talk to them anymore, we fell out years ago. I don't even remember over what – probably something really stupid. I have no desire to speak to them again and from their lack of contact, it's pretty clear that they don't want to talk to me either.'

Louise ran a hand across her face and over her hair; she could feel a headache settling in behind her eyes.

'That's harsh. I still talk to my foster parents. I don't know what I would have done without them - them and my husband, James.'

'I guess you were the lucky one, huh?' Louise said, feeling slightly jealous that her sister seemed to have it all worked out and was living a comparatively normal and peaceful existence in her perfect home with her perfect family.

'Yes, I definitely was the lucky one Lou.'

Michelle reached out as if to touch Louise's hand then pulled away when she realized what she was doing. Louise was shocked both by the gesture of tenderness towards her and by the use of her abbreviated name; the only people to ever call her Lou were those that were close to her such as Ben and Steve.

'You know, sometimes things are better left buried in the past. If you can't remember certain things, it is undoubtedly for the best,' Michelle said.

'You may be right, but something is happening to me at the moment. I feel like my life is spiraling out of control and I need help. I need answers. Please tell me what you know,' Louise begged.

Michelle pursed her lips and shook her head, clearly reluctant to tell Louise what she wanted to know. Finally she spoke.

'Our father didn't leave us when we were babies, he lived with us in that horrid house on the outskirts of London until I was 11 and you were 8. He was not a nice man, he used to beat mum black and blue, and when he had finished beating her, he would usually set about beating me too. He never hit you because you were of no use to him if you were ugly. You were such a beautiful child; I see now that those looks have remained with you into adulthood,' Michelle said, her voice wavering. Recollecting the past was taking her back to a time she would rather forget.

Louise listened attentively and tried hard not to interrupt, her dismay at what she was hearing evident from the bewildered, confused expression on her face.

'He would take you away for days, sometimes weeks and mum and I wouldn't see you until he finally brought you back. He used to say you were staying with his parents and having a great time. You always looked well and you weren't bruised so mum wasn't too concerned. You have to understand that she was a shell; there was no fight left in her, no fire. She was a broken woman.'

Michelle began to cry, her tears glinting in the sunlight as they gently rolled down her cheek. Louise was stunned, disbelieving her sister's words as much as she knew them to be true. She felt something moist land on her hand and only then realized that she too was crying.

'The day we got taken away by social services, mum and I were heading out to do some shopping. We didn't know where you were as dad had taken you away again. We drove off, but then mum realized she had forgotten her purse so we headed back to the house. Then we saw you. You were naked and covered in blood, and you were running out of the house crying. I don't know what had happened to you. Mum shouted at me to stay in the car, she ran to you and then carried you into the house. She was gone for what felt like forever and I just remember being so afraid; I didn't know whether I should go in and look for you both or if I should just stay sitting in the car waiting for you. I waited and I waited and then the police turned up.'

'There were loads of them, they had dogs and guns. A policeman opened the car door and picked me up; I can still remember how strong his arms felt.'

Michelle crossed her arms across her chest and unconsciously smoothed her hands over her biceps.

'He carried me away from the house, but as I looked over his shoulder I could see mum coming out of the house. She had blood all over her and they were placing her in handcuffs. You were holding onto her legs and wouldn't let go. You were much cleaner and dressed; mum had cleaned you up.'

'The police tried to take you away from her but you wouldn't let go. You were screaming and crying and kicking out at the officers. You wouldn't let anyone touch you. I shouted for you and you heard me. When you saw me you let go of mum and ran over to me. The policeman that was carrying me scooped you up too and put us in his police car. They then drove us to a 'safe place' as they called it, which basically meant a hostel where we would be looked after by social services.'

'There were loads of kids there and we stayed there for about three weeks before you were sent to your foster home; I stayed a couple weeks longer before I was also found a foster family. I don't know why they separated us. I used to cry for you but eventually, I suppose, I just forgot about you. My new family had their own children and they were very good to me, treating me like a full blood sibling.'

Michelle bent down and picked Kyle up, placing him on her lap so she could cuddle him and derive comfort from him. Louise felt even more isolated by this action.

'It wasn't until I was much older that my foster parents explained that our father had been murdered by our mother and that she was in prison. Apparently the way our father was killed was so vicious there was no hope of mum ever being released – she never gave a reason to the courts as to why she murdered our father, and I never knew the full details of his murder, nor did I want to know.'

'I went to visit her in prison when I turned twenty-one. I'd had years of counseling and therapy by then, and I finally felt strong enough to go and see her. She looked like a new woman, it was quite surprising. Prison was a better place for her than our old family home. I think she was just so relieved to be free of him and to know that he couldn't hurt any of us anymore.'

Michelle fell silent and returned Kyle to the mat; he was getting fidgety and grumpy, his mother had spent too long talking and not enough time giving him the attention he wanted. Louise couldn't speak, words failing her for the second time that day.

'That's all I can tell you Lou. It's all I know.'

'Do you know where he used to take me? Or what he did to me?' Louise asked, disgusted and appalled by the sad, twisted story Michelle had just recounted.

'No. I don't think he took you to see relatives though and I can guess what he did to such a pretty child as you.'

Louise felt sick. The idea of anyone doing that to a child was abhorrent; the idea that a parent could do that to their own flesh and blood was execrable. She stood up and ran over to one of Michelle's perfect flowerbeds and vomited onto the flowers. Michelle went over to her.

'Lou, I am so sorry. You should never have come here. The past should have been left in the past. I shouldn't have told you this.'

'Yes you should. I came here looking for answers and that's what you've given me. I needed to know Michelle. I don't remember any of this so it's as if you're talking about someone else.'

Only she wasn't. The little girl described in Michelle's harrowing tale, was her. Louise stood upright; the wave of nausea was passing. She glanced towards Kyle who was looking at her quizzically, and then looked at Michelle who was standing beside her.

As Louise looked at them she felt herself getting angry; why couldn't she have this life? The doting husband, the beautiful children, a stable family home? Why did things always go wrong for her?

Louise wiped the side of her mouth with the palm of her hand and breathed deeply.

'Thank you for telling me the truth Michelle.'

Michelle simply nodded and walked back over to her son.

'I'll get out of your way now,' Louise said quietly, her mind still trying to process what she had just heard.

'That's probably for the best. You've got a lot to take in.' Michelle picked Kyle up and turned to face Louise.

'I don't want to see you again, Lou. I don't mean to sound cold or hard, but it's taken me a long time to get my head on straight and to get myself together. I don't want reminders of the past and I don't want to go through this again. I hope you understand?' Michelle said, tears in her eyes. Louise looked at her not knowing what to say or how she should feel.

'I understand. You've done well for yourself, you don't want some woman turning your life upside down, you know in the same way a letter about your mother dying when you thought she was already dead might,' Louise said matter-of-factly. She was starting to feel angry and resentful again. 'You sent me a bolt out of the blue Michelle and expected me to handle it, so forgive me for coming to see you to get a few answers.'

'Louise, I did what I thought was right.'

'You did it to assuage your conscience,' Louise spat. 'Did you really stop to think about how that letter might make me feel? How do you think I feel now, knowing all I believed was a lie? That I was an abused kid? Fuck!'

'Don't swear in front of Kyle!' Michelle said angrily.

'And now you are telling me that you don't want to see me! That's fucking rich! What choice did I have in any of this? What about what I fucking want?'

'Louise please! Calm down. Don't take this out on me! I did what you asked and told you the truth!'

'You are the same as every other cunt! It's all about you, isn't it? Poor little Michelle had it so hard, but at least she didn't have to worry about daddy's dick. That was saved as a special treat for her little sister.'

Louise was in a rage.

'Louise, stop!' Kyle started crying, the raised voices scaring him.

'No I won't fucking stop! You're unbelievable! You send me a letter which shatters my world, you then tell me about our incestuous father, murderous mother and that no one knew any of this, and you expect me to what? Be happy? Just walk away without feeling anything?'

'Get out of my house,' Michelle said firmly, bouncing Kyle on her hip as she tried to soothe him.

Louise went quiet and stared at them, her eyes hard and unfeeling. Michelle unwittingly took a step back; she was afraid by what she saw. The hairs on the back of her neck rose and she felt herself leaning away from her sister. Louise looked evil, her face was different somehow. It was as if she had slipped a see-through plastic mask over her face; her features were in essence the same, but they were distorted.

'Louise, you're scaring my son. I want you to leave.'

As Michelle watched, Louise's face changed again, the lines softened, her pupils dilated and her mouth relaxed. Her voice changed in pitch slightly and her stance became non-threatening. Now she looked like the woman Michelle had been conversing with earlier that afternoon.

'I'm sorry,' Louise said softly, shaking her head, 'I don't know where that came from. I'll see myself out.'

Michelle watched Louise walk away until she

reached the front door, then she followed her, Kyle still sobbing in her arms. She went into the living room so she could keep Louise under observation from the window. Louise didn't look back; she simply got into her car and drove away.

Once the car was out of sight, Michelle went to the front door and for the first time since she had lived in her house, pulled the security chain across the door. Her encounter with Louise had spooked her; she hoped they would never meet again. She wasn't a psychiatrist but she had lived through enough depravity to know that there was something terrifying lurking in her sister's soul.

****

Greg had been watching the CCTV from the car park on Rampton Street for just over an hour and it was making him sleepy; it was difficult enough scouring CCTV when you were well-rested, but doing it whilst sleep deprived was torturous.

The digital footage he had retrieved from the City of London Police was contained on five DVDs, and each DVD held the footage of about four cameras. The first difficulty Greg was presented with was trying to work out which part of the car park each camera was pointing at because they did not have handy names such as 'ramp' or 'car park level 1', they were simply numbered 'Cam1', 'Cam 2' and so on.

Then Greg had to contend with timing discrepancies, as the times displayed on the monitor for each respective camera were wrong. The time on the camera he was looking at now was three hours and eleven minutes slower than it should have been, reading 20:05hrs, when in fact the time of the recording was 23:16hrs.

Greg was struggling to find the approximate time of the murder on the footage and so had just decided to watch all the footage at high speed, which was why it was taking him so long. He finally came to the end of 'Cam 8', which was the last camera on the second DVD. Nothing. He ejected the disc and inserted the third disc, yawning widely.

He opened up the file for 'Cam 9' and hit fast forward; then he sat back in his chair and put his feet on the desk, his eyes never leaving the monitor. This camera presented a long-shot of the middle section of one of the car park levels; there were two cars parked close together in the middle of the shot, and a couple of others dotted around the vicinity. To the left of the image Greg could just make out what appeared to be a white line on the floor circling round a pillar, which possibly demarcated a ramp to one of the levels. The multi-story car park had three levels, so Greg wasn't able to tell which level he was looking at.

The footage skipped along, cars drove in and out, people came and went, the speed of the frames making them look like they were waddling akin to old fashioned movies that were shot at sixteen frames per second instead of the modern day twenty-four.

Greg yawned again and stretched; the time on the monitor was approaching 23:00hrs. As Greg watched he saw a man walk over to a vehicle, then stand at the driver's side door; he appeared to be fumbling with something in his hands. The angle of the camera was such that Greg could see the man's left-hand side and his upper body over boot of the car which was parked at a forty-five degree angle to the camera.

Suddenly, from nowhere Greg saw a flurry of movement as a dark figure skittered across the screen towards the man. The man then dropped down between the two vehicles; Greg didn't see where the figure went.

He twisted in his seat, putting his feet back on the floor and quickly stopped the footage. He rewound it until he could see the man walking towards his car and then he hit playback, the footage now playing at the correct speed.

The man arrived at the driver's side door and then from the right-hand corner of the screen, a figure all dressed in black ran towards him. The man's back was turned to the figure, so the person was in effect running towards the camera and if they hadn't been shrouded in black, the camera would have picked up their face.

Greg watched intently at what happened next. The man turned to face the figure and from the motion of his head, it became clear to Greg that the man had been struck in the face. He then fell to the ground and the figure dropped down to his level. Greg couldn't see what happened at ground level as the car was blocking his view, but he did see a raised hand holding a sharp pointed metal object, striking downwards, repeatedly. For a few minutes there was no movement and then Greg saw the black figure stand up and run off to the right of the screen towards a fire exit.

'Jesus,' Greg mumbled, glancing around the office. Almost everyone was out following up their various enquiries, but JB was sitting a couple of desks away.

'JB, come check this out! I've found it on the CCTV.'

JB hurried over and stood watching as Greg replayed the footage.

'Holy shit! Have you tried the other cameras yet to get a facial shot?'

'Not yet. The timing is wrong on this camera. What time was the body found?'

JB scanned the report.

'The call came in at 00:04hrs,'

Greg skipped forward until the moment when the group of friends found the body. He watched as the women screamed, grabbing hold of their men, the men turning their backs to the corpse. One of the men pulled out a mobile phone, dialed a number and put it to his ear; the time on the monitor read 23:37hrs. The camera was twenty-seven minutes out.

Greg rewound the footage again and replayed it; he wanted to work out exactly what time Derek Cooper had been murdered. Knowing that the camera was 27 minutes out he was able to work out that Mina had begun that attack at 23:48hrs and had fled the scene at 00:02hrs. She had spent fourteen minutes in total attacking and mutilating the body; she certainly hadn't wasted any time.

'Greg! Look at that!' JB suddenly exclaimed, excited. 'Watch the car by the fire exit!'

They watched the footage again, slowing it down so that they could watch it frame by frame, and saw Mina put a hand onto the boot of a grey Ford Focus parked next to the fire escape.

'Fuck me! She touched the car.'

'Yeah and look,' JB pointed at the screen, 'she's not wearing a glove on that hand.'

The detectives smiled at each other and leapt into action. JB quickly logged onto a computer so he could run a check on the Police National Computer to find out who the car belonged to.

'Give me the VRM,' he shouted to Greg.

'It's Romeo 3, 3, Papa, Quebec.'

'PNC shows it as registered to a Mr Ethan Jubozi with an address in Eastham. Let me just do a quick check on that address and see what phone numbers are listed for this guy. Here we go, I've got a mobile.'

'Fantastic, give it here.'

JB read out the number to Greg, who punched it into the desk phone. He gave the thumbs up to indicate to JB that the number was ringing.

As Greg spoke to the owner of the vehicle and explained that they needed to examine his car as a matter of urgency, JB called the SOCO team and gave them Mr Jubozi's address, detailing the exact location where Mina had touched the vehicle. Greg hung up the phone at the same time as JB.

'Fucking awesome. He's only too happy to help and for once we have some good news! He hasn't driven the car since Friday evening when City of London Police released the crime scene, and it is currently sitting in his garage. He knew about the murder because, obviously, when he tried to get his car out of the car park on Friday morning, it was cordoned off,' Greg said happily.

'And SOCO are on their way and should be at his address in an hour. They said there's a good chance of getting a good print lift from the vehicle because the metallic surface is an excellent material for capturing DNA and prints,' JB said.

'We need to tell the DI,' Greg said. 'Where

is he?'

'Dunno. Probably still talking to Meadows.'

'I'll call him.'

'No need, I'm here.' Robert's voice came from the back of the office as he strolled in. 'What you got?'

Greg and JB told Robert what they had seen and the actions they had taken. Robert was overjoyed and applauded them both for their good work. Now they just had to wait to hear back from SOCO to see if they were successful in lifting a print, and then to see if the print was held on the national database. They were finally on the killer's tail and they were close. As long as those prints came back with a match, they would know the identity of their killer within the next 24 hours.

Chapter XXXIII

The evening briefing had been short but highly animated, everyone had been so excited about the potential fingerprint sample on the Focus; even Meadows had cracked a smile. The DI had asked the core investigative team to come back early in the morning, even though it was a Sunday, and to be prepared to attend the suspect's address to arrest Mina and perform a thorough search of her home.

He had warned them that it could potentially prove to be a very long day and that they would need to be prepared to work into the night to get the suspect remanded and charged; despite their fatigue, no one complained.

The case needed a break and finally, almost two weeks after the first murder they had their best lead yet. The DI hoped they weren't being premature in preparing to execute an arrest the following morning; he just had a good feeling that they would get a suspect ID sometime that night and so wanted to be ready to react accordingly.

The Scenes of Crime Officers had attended Mr Jubozi's house and examined his vehicle, descending upon it like a flock of vultures on a decaying carcass. Becca had called Robert to confirm that there was a suitable fingerprint sample in the area Mina had touched and that even more importantly it was of sufficient quality for a speculative search of the fingerprint database. If

Robert had been more athletic he would have done back flips around the office.

Becca told him that Mr Jubozi had been planning to get the car washed later that evening because he didn't like the thought of it having been sat in a crime scene, so they were lucky Greg had spoken to him when he had. Becca ended the call by saying she was not going to go home until the sample either got a hit or came back as negative, and she hoped Robert realised how badly this murder enquiry was affecting her love life. Robert had sympathised and told her she was a 'fucking star' for being so dedicated.

For the rest of the briefing they had discussed what else had been found on the CCTV and the short answer was: nothing. Despite the multitude of cameras that covered the car park, they hadn't been able to get a good shot of Mina's face on any one of them, she was so camera aware. Even when she had been running up the stairwell to exit the car park, she had been sufficiently composed to remember to bow her head, keeping her face obscured.

Greg had tried his best to print off some photos that could be used for identification purposes, but even in the best shots, Mina's face resembled a grainy blob rather than a human visage. Greg had bemoaned the fact that there had not been any suitable CCTV footage in the entire enquiry.

After the briefing the DI had taken the team to the pub, buying the first two rounds to thank them all for their commitment to the job. There had been a lot of back patting and joviality.

Elizabeth had left the pub after the first round, making up an excuse about needing to be elsewhere. She text Tony as she left to invite him over to her flat so they could have their own celebrations. Tony had stayed in the pub for one more round before taking Elizabeth up on her offer and making his way to her flat. They'd had a rampant sex session before finally collapsing exhausted on Elizabeth's sofa.

Now, Tony was in the kitchen making cups of hot chocolate, humming to himself, and Elizabeth was sitting naked on the settee, her laptop on her knees as she prepared to do some research. Tony popped his head out of the kitchen to ask her if she wanted milk to be added to her drink, but stopped, frowning, when he saw the computer.

'Don't you ever stop?' he asked. 'What are you doing now?'

'I am doing some open source research on Louise Jackson,' Elizabeth replied without looking up.

'Errr… why?'

'There's just something about her that is bugging me,' Elizabeth replied.

Tony came out of the kitchen and sat beside her, placing the two hot chocolates he had made onto the coffee table in front of them. He placed a hand on Elizabeth's naked thigh and moved it slowly up towards her hips.

'You sure you want to do that now?' he teased.

Elizabeth picked his arm up by the wrist and theatrically dropped it onto his lap.

'As much as I would love for us to continue shagging like bunnies, if I don't check this out now, I'm not going to be able to sleep.'

Tony sighed exaggeratedly.'Ok, fine. I'm

hurt you can resist my charms so readily, but hey, I'll survive. So, what have you found out so far?'

'Give me a chance. This laptop isn't exactly modern and my wifi is a bit slow.'

Once the internet search engine had loaded, Elizabeth typed LOUISE JACKSON into the search bar and pressed enter. The computer slowly whirred into action; Elizabeth reached forward for her mug of hot chocolate and took a sip.

'Oooh, good chocolate Tony,' she drawled, appreciatively.

'I aim to please.'

After a few more seconds the screen blinked as the search engine returned its results. Elizabeth read out some of the web page descriptions: '"Louise Jackson, Scotland; Louise Jackson, Hull; Staffordshire"... Bloody hell there's loads of them.'

'Do you know where she was born?' Tony asked. 'It would help narrow things down a bit.'

'No, I don't know. I'll type in the school we went to as well see if that can refine the results.'

Elizabeth's fingers danced across the keyboard as she entered in the name of her old school. After another wait, some more results pinged up in her browser.

'Ah, this looks more promising. "Louise Jackson, former alumni of St Martin's Secondary School." Elizabeth clicked the link.

'That sounds posh.'

'It was a bit I guess. Great school. I had a lot of fun there.'

'You're not supposed to have fun at school in your teens. You're supposed to hate it, refuse to go and act all surly.'

'There's a list of former students here... Ah,

372

there's me. God, reading through these names is taking me back a bit.'

'Any pictures on there? Bet you were a cutie,' Tony said.

'I don't need photos Tone, I need a date of birth.'

'You're not going to find her date of birth on the school website. They wouldn't publish that.'

'Hmmm… No I guess they wouldn't. Ok, so let me go back to the search again and try something else. Let's try: Louise Jackson, London.' Elizabeth typed rapidly.

A number of entries appeared on the computer screen and she set about the laborious task of going through them one by one. Tony rested his head on the back of the sofa as he waited for Elizabeth to get a match, intending to only rest his eyes for a few minutes, but instead promptly fell asleep, his lips slightly parted, gentle snores alerting Elizabeth to his slumber.

She smiled at him, amused, and then continued with her research. There were a lot of Louise Jacksons in London and without photographs it was difficult for Elizabeth to know if she was looking at the right person.

Finally, Elizabeth found an entry that sounded promising. There was a profile on a business networking website relating to a Ms Louise Jackson who gave her profession as writer/editor for a business publication in London. There was a small box in the right-hand corner of the screen where a photo could be uploaded; Louise Jackson hadn't posted a photo of herself but in small writing just below the box was a date of birth.

'Bingo,' Elizabeth said under her breath.

Just as she was about to quit the page and begin a new search with the date of birth she noticed the name of the company Louise Jackson stated she worked for: Biztalk.

Elizabeth was surprised; that was the name of the company the latest victim had worked for. She had read the list of employee's names provided by the company owner, Ben Matthews, and she was sure she hadn't read Louise's name on the list.

How had she missed it? Because it wasn't on the list. Now, why would the boss fail to include her name? She made a mental note to see if she could find out.

Elizabeth began another search this time including both the name and date of birth she had obtained from the business network website. She scrolled through various pages until she found an entry pertaining to a deed poll name change.

Elizabeth opened the page and read the entry: 'Louise Jackson, formerly Louise Adams name changed by deed poll'. The date of the name change was 23 years earlier.

Excited, Elizabeth opened her spread sheet containing the list of names she had compiled for abused girls, which she had saved on her own computer as well as her one at work. She typed in the name Louise Adams and froze in amazement when the computer indicated a hit.

'Fuck me,' she exclaimed softly.

There it was in front of her eyes; Louise Adams, a.k.a Louise Jackson, had been a victim of sexual abuse as a child. The cards were beginning to stack up against her.

Elizabeth cast her mind back to the evening she'd spent with Louise. Louise had asked her about the murder, she'd asked a few questions saying she was fascinated by the fact the killer was female. Had she asked Elizabeth anything more than any other member of the public would have? Had she been more eager for any of the details of the case? Probably not. In Elizabeth's experience people were always intrigued by police work, especially murder cases. But then it hit her, something Louise had said. Elizabeth couldn't believe she'd missed it at the time and that she was only remembering it now.

"So, are you guys close to catching her, this bondage killer?"

Those were the exact words Louise had used.

How had she known about the bondage element to the killings? It hadn't been released to the media, nobody beyond those connected to the enquiry knew. Had she been careless in what she said to Louise? Had she said it during the conversation?

Elizabeth shook her head; she knew she hadn't. She ran through what she knew in her head: Louise somehow knew that bondage was involved in the murders, she was an employee of Biztalk, she was a victim of sexual abuse and she'd turned into some man-hating psycho during her evening with Elizabeth. It was all circumstantial but as far as Elizabeth was concerned this was good enough reason to suspect that Louise Jackson was Mina.

'Tony! Wake up!' she shook him violently, startling him. 'I know who the killer is!'

****

Ben was not happy. He'd been trying to call Louise since Friday night and she had not bothered to answer or return his calls. He'd left a couple of messages and sent her a few texts, initially just asking her to call him because he had some news for her, as he still didn't know if she was aware of Derek Cooper's murder, and then asking her to call him because he was worried that she hadn't been in touch. Clearly, his pleas were falling on deaf ears – or something had happened to her. Either way Ben wanted to find out and it was frustrating him that she was ignoring him. He considered going round her flat again but decided that ultimately he shouldn't feel responsible for her, regardless of their friendship, and that he couldn't keep spending his time chasing after her. And if he was totally honest – he was pissed off.

Recently, Louise had been presenting Ben with a dilemma; her behaviour was out of character and as such he felt warranted medical attention, but on the other hand, she was still the beautiful, intelligent, charismatic woman he had hired to work for him all those years ago. What should he do? Should he try and convince her again to seek medical help or should he just leave her be?

On top of this, for the past twenty-four hours he had not been able to think of anything other than Derek bloody Cooper and Louise's words about how Derek's death would solve all of Ben's problems. She'd spoken that phrase and suddenly, as if her utterance had been an evil spell, Derek was dead. The internal conflict was agonizing and Ben just couldn't decide what he should do. The question kept spinning round inside his mind, like a filthy sock in a washing machine, round and round, sullying his thoughts and tainting his opinion of Louise, the woman he used to think he knew so well.

Could Louise kill? Ultimately, it came down to whether he believed she had the capacity for that kind of rage and violence.

Before Wednesday morning, when he had visited Louise in her flat, Ben would have happily answered no to that question, without doubt or hesitation. But, after seeing the way she had reacted to Derek's letter and photographs, the way she had snapped, Ben couldn't help but think that maybe she did. If only she would answer the bloody phone! He felt sure that he would be able to tell from the tone of her voice and the way she reacted to the news about Derek if she was in some way to blame.

Ben was also worried about the police investigation into Derek's death. When the police had come round to his house the previous evening, he had lied to them, not wanting to give them Louise's name. He had been trying to protect her but he knew it was a stupid thing to have done. As soon as he'd heard the fake name 'Lucy Jamieson' leave his lips he'd wanted to suck the words back in, but at the same time he knew that it was too late; the lie had begun.

If he told the officers that he'd lied and then given them Louise's real name, the police would have been even more suspicious about her role in Ben's life and their involvement in Derek's death. They would have wanted to speak to Louise urgently and most probably would have arrested Ben; he was pretty sure DS Maddox had been itching for an excuse to take him in for questioning. He'd then gone to the office with the uniformed PC to access the HR records for Biztalk and when the computer system had populated a list of all his employees, Ben had quickly deleted Louise's name from the list before handing it to the officer.

He was up to his neck in lies and had probably committed a number of offences by lying to the police. If they found out about Louise, which they inevitably would, he would have to lie again and pretend it had been a glitch in the computing system and he would have to suggest that DS Maddox must have misheard him when he gave the name.

And why had he done all this? Because he had experienced a moment of utmost stupidity and had thought he was helping Louise – the woman who was now ignoring him and throwing his assistance back in his face – and because he loved her.

It had come as quite a shock the moment he had realized he had fallen for her somewhere along the way. It was when he had left her sleeping in his spare room, looking so angelic and small, that he had begun to fully understand his feelings for her. It was why he had lied for her, why he felt so strongly that he needed to help her, to protect her.

And now he felt like a fool. Had he fallen in love with an illusion? Was he really that gullible? Ben hadn't cried since he was a young boy but now, with all these mixed emotions and confused thoughts whirring through his head, he felt tears of frustration, pain and anger brimming in his eyes. He needed to speak to Louise. He needed to know she was ok and to let her know what he had done for her. He picked up the phone and tried to call her one last time.

****

The ringing phone was strident, its piercing

tone cutting through the darkness like a bomb through a tranquil meadow. Robert jumped at the sound then jumped again as Margaret jabbed him painfully in the ribs.

'Do you have to have that thing so bloody loud?' she asked, annoyed at having her sleep disturbed.

'Sorry darling.' Robert flicked a button on the side of his mobile, silencing the phone. He saw from the caller ID that it was Becca. This meant one of two things – either they now had a name for their killer, or it was back to the drawing board.

'It's important Mags, got to take this one.'

'Never marry a bloody copper,' she mumbled before rolling over, turning her back on Robert and taking most of the bed clothes with her. Robert gently patted her on the side and then answered the phone.

'Becca, tell me what I want to hear,' he said without preamble.

'I've got a hit. Your killer's name is Louise Jackson.'

Chapter XXXIV

At the top of the stairs leading out of the basement she stopped and listened for a moment. All was quiet, she was alone. Her breathing was still hurried, coming to her in ragged gasps, and her body was shaking. She was naked, but there was so much blood on her, that she appeared clothed in crimson. She looked around the kitchen; it was neat and tidy, just as it had to be to keep him happy. She had heard him in his rages, knew how he resorted to violence if things weren't just so. Not anymore. He wouldn't hurt anyone ever again. She felt a small flicker of pride beneath her fear of the unknown. What would happen now?

She hadn't been stood there long when she heard a car driving towards the house, the sound of its approaching engine a welcome sound to her young ears. It meant salvation. She dashed out of the house via the kitchen door which led directly onto the driveway, screwing up her eyes as she was temporarily blinded by the bright sunlight.

When she opened them again she saw her mother running towards her, so she began running towards her mother, oblivious to the pain of the gravel against the soles of her bare feet. Her mother lifted her up and began sobbing uncontrollably, her mother's tears falling onto her scarlet body, dripping down her skin, creating white channels.

Her mother took her back inside the kitchen and stood her up in the kitchen sink, which she filled with warm water. She handed her a dish cloth and said: 'Louise, stay here. Try and wash the blood off,' before descending into the basement.

After a moment's silence, Louise heard her mother scream in anger, an ear-piercing, frightening noise, followed by the dull sound of her mother attacking the body. Thump, thump, thump. Louise froze. Did this mean she hadn't killed him and he'd still been alive?

She heard her mother coming back up the stairs so resumed washing herself, using the dish cloth to wipe blood from her skin, staining the water in the sink a bright pink. Her mother came back into the kitchen and now she was spattered with blood; she was almost as bloody as Louise.

'He's dead Louise. You killed him. My darling, precious girl, I am so sorry, so sorry. I couldn't protect you. I tried, I wanted to. I told him to leave you alone and to not take you away from me. I thought you were with his parents, not locked in the basement. My poor girl, I am so sorry. You were here all along,' her mother cried against Louise's head, gently rubbing her back as much to soothe herself as to soothe Louise.

'He beat me so badly I couldn't help you. The basement was off limits to me — if I attempted to go down there he would hurt me so badly. I hope one day you'll forgive me my darling, precious daughter.'

They held each other for a while, Louise standing in the bloody, tepid water, reaching up to wrap her arms around her mother's neck and her mother embracing her against her bosom. Eventually her mother broke away and cradled Louise's face in her hands.

'Here's what we're going to do my darling. You are never, never going to speak of this. You are going to put it out of your mind and pretend it was all a bad dream. Do you understand?'

Louise was confused, but she nodded in agreement anyway because she knew that's what she had to do to please her mother.

'I have his blood all over me, my fingerprints are all

381

over the weapon you used to kill him because I removed it from his eye and attacked him again with it. We will clean you up, wipe all evidence off of you and we'll make it look like I did this, ok?'

Louise couldn't speak, she was so afraid and bewildered. She understood what her mother was saying but she couldn't respond. Her mother was going to take the blame for killing that monster and Louise didn't know why. But she was happy to know she wasn't in trouble and that she wouldn't be punished for what she had done.

Once Louise was clean her mother carefully plucked her from the sink and then followed her upstairs to the bedroom she usually shared with her sister. It was a pretty room with pink walls and yellow stars; the colour of the walls was similar to the colour of the water in the sink and Louise liked it.

They found some fresh clothes for Louise and once she was dressed her mother crouched down to her level and said: 'Do you remember what I said Louise? You must never, ever breathe a word about what you did. If anyone asks you, you will either say nothing or say that I did it, ok? Mummy did it. Mummy murdered daddy. You understand?'

'I understand mummy,' Louise had replied.

'That's my beautiful girl.' Her mother had stroked her face and smiled at her, a sad, pitiful smile. 'You will not be punished for this Louise, mummy will. It's what mummy deserves for not protecting you. I'm sorry, I'm sorry...' her mother began crying again. After a few minutes she pulled herself together, and dabbed her eyes with the edge of her blouse.

'I'm going to call the police now Louise. They will be here soon. They will arrest me and take me away. I may never see you or Michelle again, but you have to understand, I love you and I will always be thinking of you. You are my special, brave girl and I will love you always, you know that Louise?'

Louise nodded again and reached out for her mother, practically climbing up her body so she could be in her arms.

'Louise, careful the blood.' But it was too late, blood had already transferred from her mother onto Louise's clean clothes. Not that it mattered now, the police would know it was simply transferral from their embrace.

It hadn't taken the police long to arrive after her mother had placed the telephone call, the sound of their sirens and screeching tyres frightening Louise and further adding to her trauma. She hadn't wanted to be taken from her mother and had only released her grip on her mother's legs when she heard Michelle shouting for her.

'Remember Louise. You never speak of this, you must forget it. It's just a bad dream.' Her mother had bent down and whispered in her ear just before Louise ran to Michelle.

She had never forgotten her mother's words; she had never said anything about her daddy, what he used to do and the other men he used to sell her out to. She never told anyone that when daddy was supposedly taking her away to stay with a relative, he actually only took her downstairs to the basement where he could keep her locked up and use her at his leisure. She had promised her mother she would never speak of it and it was a promise she would always keep. Her secret was a heavy burden which Louise struggled to carry. Luckily, she could rely on Mina.

Chapter XXXIV

Louise didn't know where she was going, she was not consciously thinking of her destination; she was just driving. She'd been on the move for hours, her knuckles white as she gripped the steering wheel, her hair flailing around her head and across her face as the wind from the open car windows howled through the vehicle.

Louise was looking at the road ahead but she could not see it; she couldn't see anything beyond the torrent of memories tumbling through her brain, each one more painful than its predecessor. She remembered now. She remembered everything and the pain ripped through her like a circular saw through timber.

Since leaving her sister's house she had simply driven round and round through the evening, into the night and now into the early hours of the morning, thinking about what her sister had said, only stopping to refuel when the brightness of the fuel light on the dashboard had caught her eye, cutting through her reverie and bringing her momentarily back to the present.

Each time she thought about the conversation she'd had with Michelle, another memory was triggered, and then another and another. She wished she could slow the memories down but they came at her in an unrelenting onslaught as her mind finally gave up trying to protect her from the painful truth.

She felt as if she was watching scenes from a despicable horror movie as the images played behind her eyes, and she had a strange sense of detachment from her body; she felt as if she was no longer in charge of it and had no influence over its actions.

Louise was scared, she was angry and she was hurt. She was scared of what her recollections would mean for her future; how could she go back to her normal life now? She was angry at what those men had done to her and the fact that no one had protected her, and she was hurt that someone could do those things to her, a small, innocent child who was held captive in a basement and abused by men who paid her father for the privilege. She couldn't fathom how anyone could do that to a young girl, how they could do it to her, and she felt the pain she had suffered as a child manifest afresh.

She had recognized some of the faces in her memories; she'd recognized the old man with the crooked teeth she'd seen at the bus stop almost two weeks ago - he'd been one of the men that had abused her. The man she'd seen in her flat was a depiction of her father and the woman she'd seen at the window, looking at her with such sad, sorrowful eyes, was her mother. She realized now that she had been slowly falling apart, her mind gradually leaking repressed memories, trying to test her mental robustness, the memories manifesting as twisted hallucinations.

Louise let out a loud cry as she remembered the kitten, Sunshine, and what that bastard had done to it. In the small time she had with that kitten, she had fallen in love with it and the cat had reciprocated, nuzzling her and purring. He wouldn't even allow her to bond with an animal, totally depriving her of any form of emotional connection with another creature, keeping her emotionally isolated and withdrawn. The cat had helped her though, as it had given her the courage to fight.

She recollected crafting the tool she had eventually used to kill him and now instead of sobbing she cackled gleefully as that day came back to her. She recalled the way his body had felt when it seized up in agony; she remembered the sound his eye had made when she had popped it in his skull and she remembered the sound of his dying breaths. Her hand had been raw for days afterwards but no one had known how she had hurt herself. They'd just smiled at her and tended to her wounds, prattling on, totally oblivious to the fact that she was a killer child.

That day her mother had made her promise she would never speak the truth, never tell the secret they shared – even Michelle had not known the truth. Her mother had taken the blame for Louise's actions, seeing it as a small penance for the years of abuse Louise had suffered.

It was true that her father had been an evil, vindictive, violent man and Louise's mother most probably had been afraid he would kill her and Michelle if they'd tried to help, but Louise still couldn't forgive her for allowing that monster to do what he had done to her. Had she known that he sold her to other men too?

Louise was horrified by her recollections, disgusted by the conduct of those that should have protected her, but she was equally sickened by some of the memories of her own actions. As much as she was glad she had murdered her vile father, she was shocked that she had been able to commit such a brutal crime. She also remembered now why she had fallen out with her foster parents all those years ago and the thought of what she had done made her want to vomit.

She remembered how she had stolen a puppy from outside a shop where it had been tied up, waiting patiently for its owner to come back out, quickly unfastening the dog's lead and running with it back to her foster home. The puppy had been full of life, bouncing around her feet, its tongue playfully licking her legs.

She had taken the animal into the garden shed, stood it on a garden chair and then tied rope around each of its limbs. She'd then tied the rope to the four legs of the chair. At first the puppy had simply licked her and nibbled gently at the rope, enjoying the attention and the game, but then Louise had yanked the ropes hard, pulling the poor animal's legs apart, causing it to fall onto the seat on its stomach, legs painfully pulled in four directions.

The puppy had yelped and squealed in pain so Louise had taken more rope to tie around its muzzle, effectively quieting the animal. It lay there, prone, helpless, whimpering, its eyes wide and full of fear.

Louise had then taken hold of her foster father's shears and placed the puppy's tail between the blades. She'd then violently closed the blades, severing the animal's tail, reducing it to a bloody stump. The dog had wriggled violently, straining to break free of the ligatures that bound it and Louise had just watched, mesmerized by the blood.

She'd then taken hold of a hacksaw, intending to remove the dog's head, but before she had had a chance to make the first cut, the shed door had been pulled open by her foster mother, alerted by the dog's yelps, and the hacksaw had been violently wrenched from her hand. Her foster mother had slapped Louise hard around the face and ordered her to get out of the shed.

Louise remembered being shocked by the slap, her foster mother had never resorted to any form of physical violence, she was such a gentle woman, and then she remembered staring at the woman, her eyes full of hate as it dawned on her that the woman would not let her finish her task; she needed to kill the puppy.

She had run out of the shed and into her bedroom, grabbed a duffle bag and begun filling it with clothing. Her foster mother had eventually followed her into the bedroom and they had rowed heatedly. Louise had called her foster mother all the names under the sun and her foster mother had called her evil and said she needed to seek professional help.

Louise had pushed past her, duffle bag slung over her shoulder and she had run into the kitchen, where she had turned the gas on. Her foster mother had pleaded with her to turn the gas off, to calm down, they needed to talk. Louise had simply looked at her and pulled a lighter out of her pocket, threatening to burn the place down. Eventually her foster mother had given up trying to reason with Louise and had run out of the house, jumped into her car and driven off. If Louise was going to blow the house up, she was not going to be around to be caught up in the conflagration.

Shortly afterwards, Louise had also left the house. She had left the gas on but she had decided not to ignite it – she didn't really want to die.

That had been the last time they had spoken. She'd never seen either of her foster parents again nor had she thought about the incident; she didn't know what had happened to the puppy.

Louise realized now, in this moment of clarity as she was driving to an unknown destination, that there was something very wrong with her.

As startling and horrifying as all the revelations were to her, this realization was the most shocking for her - the knowledge of what she had become. It had taken her some time to connect the dots, to piece it all together, but now she knew. She was a killer. She was an evil, sadistic killer.

She was Mina.

Guilt washed over her, her body jolting with adrenaline, as she saw the faces of the men Mina had murdered – David Saunders, Mark Faversham, Daniel Taylor, Derek Cooper – all dead because of her, killed by her hands. Louise felt afraid then powerful, disgusted then proud, ashamed then delighted, a whole gamut of emotions swirling through her.

She was also perplexed. How could she have seen the photos of the victims on the news and not realized then that she was responsible? How could her memory be that repressed? How could Mina take control of her so completely? Who the fuck was she?

She was the young girl that had been molested and abused for years, emotionally starved and deprived of love, transformed into a mere shell; the young girl who had developed a secondary, stronger, sinister personality to take over when Louise could no longer cope. She began to sob at the wheel, her vision becoming blurry.

'I can't, I can't, I can't...' she said repeatedly to herself as her mind fell apart and she broke down. 'I can't take anymore of this.'

She pummeled her forehead with her left hand and screamed as she did so, the years of agony and torment audible in her cries.

'I am Louise Jackson, I am Louise Adams, I am Mina, I am Mina, Mina, Mina...'

Her voice faded out and her tears dried as Louise finally gave up and disappeared within her own mind. Mina was in charge now and she would take care of Louise just like she always had.

****

It was six-fifteen in the morning and the team was now only ten minutes away from Louise Jackson's flat. They'd convened at the police station at five am to discuss this morning's actions. Robert, Tony, Louise and Greg were travelling in an unmarked car to the residence, following behind a marked police carrier which contained a team of burly Operational Support Unit officers, or OSU, who would be making the entry into the premises and checking it was secure before Robert and his team went in.

They would also assist in the searching, allowing the investigative officers more time to look at the surroundings and the items recovered. The rest of the team, including the officers from Force Headquarters, were at the station on standby.

Elizabeth was very quiet in the car, not only because she was extremely tired having stayed up all night, but also because she felt quite nauseous knowing she had been drinking and socializing with a killer. She had always believed she would know when she was in the company of a vicious murderer, that something about them would give it away. She certainly hadn't suspected Louise at all that night. She felt sick. She'd shared details of her life with her and had discussed the case. Had that been Louise's plan all along? To get Elizabeth to reveal what she knew? Elizabeth cracked the car window open a little and raised her face into the draft. As if sensing her discomfort, Tony reached a hand across the back seat and touched her gently on the thigh. She turned and smiled at him appreciatively, grateful for the contact.

'Right, this is it,' Greg said as he pulled the car to the curb, parking behind the marked carrier.

The block of flats looked well maintained, housing eight stories and perimetered by trimmed hedgerows. The officers disembarked the vehicle and made their way through the front gate, single file as they approached the front door, the OSU officers following up the rear. There was a panel of buzzers for the various flats to the left of the door. Louise lived in flat 3 on the ground floor; Robert pressed the buzzer for flat 10. No answer. He pressed the buzzer for flat 7. After a short pause a weary voice said:

'Who is it?'

'The police. Let us in please,' Robert replied.

The occupant of flat 7 needed no further explanation; the lock on the door buzzed as the occupant granted them entry into the block.

Now the OSU officers went into the lead, armed with an enforcer to break Louise's front door down. They all moved swiftly and quietly down the corridor until they were stood outside Flat 3. Robert nodded to the first OSU officer that they were ready; everyone was pumped and ready for action.

The OSU officer swung the enforcer and slammed it into the front door, breaking the lock with one blow and sending the door flying back on its hinges. He shouted: 'Police!' as his colleagues rapidly filed past him into the flat and spread out through the various rooms.

The investigative team followed the OSU into the flat, their hearts sinking as they heard the OSU officers shouting 'Clear!' as they swept through each room looking for the suspect.

Louise was not at home.

Then the smell hit them, a thick, pervasive odour, akin to perishing food.

'What the fuck is that?' Robert exclaimed. 'Jesus, let's get some fucking windows open.'

Everyone gagged at the smell, it was so pungent.

'Can anyone tell where that smell is coming from?' Robert asked.

'We'll start searching the place Guv,' the sergeant in charge of the OSU team said. 'Lads! Three of you to start in the living room, three in the kitchen, one of you to maintain the search record book.' The officers set about their task, grateful for the gusts of fresh air wafting into the flat through the open windows, dissipating the smell somewhat.

'Fuck it!' Robert exclaimed, turning to his team. 'She's not here.'

'I'll go ask the neighbours,' Elizabeth said, turning on her heel, pleased to have an excuse to leave the flat and the malodorous, stagnant air within it.

'Ok, and Elizabeth. Good work. I know you

worked out the identity of the killer before the fingerprints came back. Tony told me.'

Elizabeth blushed then said: 'Not quick enough though unfortunately. I still ended up having drinks with the woman.'

Before Robert could respond, Elizabeth walked out of the flat to see if she could rouse any of the neighbours who might know where Louise was, or when she had left. Robert watched her leave; he understood how she felt.

The officers made quick progress through the living room, seizing a number of items including Louise's laptop computer, hard drive and memory sticks. Robert was struck by the austerity of the flat – it felt unlived in. There were no photos on the walls or cabinets, no knickknacks or paintings... the place had no personality. It was purely a functional residence where Louise simply slept and ate – nothing more. It was not a home.

The officers searching the kitchen looked in the cupboards, behind appliances and in the fridge and freezer. Once they were sure there was nothing of interest in the room, they left the kitchen and moved into the bathroom.

Robert wandered into the kitchen once the search team had moved out and leant against the kitchen counter. Elizabeth soon returned to the flat and found Robert in the kitchen. Greg was in the bathroom with one half of the search team; Tony was with the other half in the bedroom.

'No one on this floor has seen her. Apparently, she keeps herself to herself rarely has visitors and doesn't spend a great deal of time here,' Elizabeth said to Robert, closing her pocket notebook and returning it to her suit jacket pocket.

'You couldn't have known Elizabeth,' Robert said.

'What's that Guv?'

'I said you couldn't have known you were in the company of a killer. How could you? They don't walk around with 'murderer' tattooed on their foreheads; that would make our job a bit too easy don't you think?'

'I know what you're saying Guv, but I just feel that I should have had some indication, some notion of what she was when I met her.'

Elizabeth sighed, and leant back against the work surface too, her arms across her chest, mirroring her boss's stance.

'You never really know anyone Elizabeth. You can only go on what they tell you and their observable actions. You weren't to know. And besides, you did have doubts about her. You researched her on the internet and found her on your spreadsheet, so don't be so hard on yourself. A part of you knew exactly what she was,' Robert said reassuringly.

'Thanks,' Elizabeth smiled.

'You know, I think I met her – Louise. I think I saw her leave the club with the third victim, Dan Taylor,' Robert confessed.

'Seriously? What makes you say that?' Elizabeth was stunned. She couldn't imagine that Robert would have missed an opportunity to apprehend the killer.

'Just a feeling – a bit like yours. I didn't react on it at the time because I doubted myself and because there was absolutely no evidence. And to be honest at the time I was more interested in her looks than I was in interpreting my hunch. It was only afterwards that I became more convinced.'

'The mind does most of its great work at a subconscious level,' Elizabeth stated, wisely.

'Indeed. But I can't help but feel guilty. If I had acted then, the third and fourth murders would probably never have happened.'

'You don't know that. You don't know that the woman you saw was Mina.'

'Well, either way, I feel responsible for the deaths of those two men and that is something I shall have to live with for the rest of my life,' Robert confided.

'There were four of us in the club that night Guv, so we all missed her. We all failed the victims, not just you,' Elizabeth said. 'At least now we can seek some retribution for them by capturing the fucking bitch.'

Robert smiled at her and she placed a gentle, comforting hand on her boss's shoulder and gave it a squeeze. They both felt as if they had failed; it would take them a long time to get over their self-condemnation.

They moved out of the kitchen and headed into the bedroom to see how the searching officers were getting on. There wasn't enough room for all of them in the room so Robert and Elizabeth stood just outside watching the officers. Tony was helping and was searching inside the wardrobe.

The smell they had noticed upon entering the flat appeared to be stronger in this room and the odour was causing the officers to breathe through their mouths.

'We should be wearing fucking face masks,' one of the OSU team said before noticing Robert standing in the doorway. 'Sorry guv.'

'You don't need to apologise, I agree it fucking reeks. I'm guessing the smell is her trophies – rotting.'

This statement made everyone in the room feel queasy, especially the men. The thought of rotting flesh was abhorrent enough but to think the stench was being caused by rotting male genitalia brought bile into the throat of those with even the sturdiest of dispositions.

'Can't bloody find where it's coming from though. And we haven't found any of the bondage gear,' another OSU officer said.

'Maybe it's not kept here?' Elizabeth suggested.

The officers tore the bedroom apart, they searched under the bed, in the bedside cabinets, in the bags stored on top of the wardrobe, they pulled back the carpet, they searched through all Louise's clothes and still nothing.

Tony sighed disappointedly as his search of the wardrobe also drew a blank. Then he spotted it. There was a discrepancy between the depth of the wardrobe on the outside and the depth of the wardrobe on the inside; the inner wardrobe was at least twenty centimeters deeper. Tony tapped the back of the wardrobe with his knuckles.

'Guys, I think this wardrobe has a false back. Give me something I can get the back off with,' Tony said, excitedly.

'Can we pull the wardrobe forward?' one of the OSU team suggested. Tony looked at the inside of the wardrobe, paying more attention to the furniture itself this time as opposed to its contents.

'No, unless you've got a screw driver. It's fastened to the wall.'

'If there's something behind it, I'm sure she would have an easier way of getting to it. She wouldn't want to be unscrewing it every time,' Elizabeth proposed. 'No hinges or anything Tone? Does it slide?'

Tony looked again, scanning the back panel for clues of an opening mechanism. At the bottom of the back panel he noticed a small aperture just big enough for a couple of fingers to be inserted.

Gingerly, not knowing what to expect, Tony slid his forefinger and index fingers into the opening and pulled forwards, he then pushed backwards and then he pulled to the left; this time he felt the panel give a little, so he pulled to the left again, this time a bit harder. He could see now that the back of the wardrobe was on runners and as he pulled it to the left, the panel slid smoothly into the bedroom wall, revealing a further closet space, built into the wall.

As the panel opened up to reveal the secret cavity space, Tony brought his forearm across his nose, the stench from within causing him to recoil momentarily. Various expletives and groans of disgust were muttered by those in the room as the smell permeated, some of the officers covering their noses with their sleeves, others resorting to pinching their nostrils shut.

The wall cavity was dark and Tony couldn't see what was lurking within. He carefully and gently ran his hand around the edges of the cavity, feeling for a light switch or pull, his hand finally resting on something that felt like it was designed for that purpose.

He flicked the switch, a dim, yellow light bulb burst into life, and the wall cavity was bathed in a dirty, yellow glow. Tony took a step back, momentarily startled by a number of people standing in the light with their backs to him, and let out a grunt of surprise. It took him a second to realize that he wasn't looking at human beings but in fact, a collection of wigs. He moved further into the wardrobe to get a better look.

'Holy mother of God,' he whispered, as his eyes took in the contents of the concealed wall space. He shook his head in disbelief. He couldn't believe what he was seeing.

Chapter XXXVI

The opening behind the back wardrobe panel was just tall enough for a person under six feet tall to stand in and just wide enough to allow that same person to turn fully to their left or right. At six-foot-three, Tony was too tall to stand inside the space and so he surveyed the area from just outside it, standing hunched within the closet like an over-sized bogeyman.

He put a hand across his nose and mouth, trying not to breathe in the odour emanating from within; it was so over-powering Tony had to try very hard not to be sick.

The inside of the space was raw brick work, rough to the touch and rudimentarily built, and after some initial confusion as to how Louise had even been able to construct the cavity without intruding into somebody else's property, Greg had worked out that it was actually built into the space underneath the stairs to the first floor.

No one had access to this space from the communal corridor because the under stair area had been sealed up many years before by the building management company, tired of people using the space to store bicycles, suitcases and other such belongings, creating a potential fire and vermin hazard. Louise had been able to erect this space freely, knowing that it would not be discovered from outside the flat.

The wall behind which Louise had chosen to build her secret place was an internal wall and therefore only made of plaster board; it would not have been difficult for her to make a hole through it. Then she had simply built an extra mini-room within the space under the stairs, bought a wardrobe to place in front of it, wedging the piece of furniture several inches into the gap, and then fastened the wardrobe to the wall.

She had needed to adapt the wardrobe by bringing the existing back panel forward in order to create a runner system and to allow enough room for the wardrobe to actually be pushed into the cavity. It was a simple, yet ingenious, design.

The wigs that had startled Tony hung on several hooks at eye level at the back of the bricked space, a variety of different colours, hair styles and lengths. They were good quality wigs and would appear natural when worn, which was why Tony had momentarily thought the wigs were actually real hair on actual human heads.

Below the wigs on another set of hooks hung an array of whips, ranging from small, single-stranded leather ones, to large, multi-stranded, rubber ones. There was also an assortment of thin canes, some of which could be folded for easy transport.

Underneath the whips, ran three horizontal metal rails, each one supporting a number of shoes, which dangled from the rails by their high heels. Two pairs of thigh-high PVC boots were propped up against the back wall, their shiny surfaces glinting in the light.

Tony turned his head to the left and saw two wooden shelves. The top shelf contained a variety of makeup and contact lenses, and a circular mirror was placed in the centre of the ledge. Tony could almost visualize Mina standing in front of the mirror, checking her reflection and deciding what eye colour she was going to sport that night.

The second shelf held an assortment of implements, the purpose of which Tony didn't recognize. They looked like medical instruments that may have been used by surgeons in the early 1900s; not that Tony knew really what those looked like, it was just the impression they gave him. Some looked like pincers and forceps, another was circular with sharp pins around the circumference.

Next to them lay two four-inch, hand-crafted stakes, fashioned out of metal and honed to an evil looking point. They were solid and weighty, their tips burred and rough. As Tony looked at them, he knew he was looking at the implements Mina used to plunge into her victims' eyes.

On the floor beneath the two shelves, was an old-fashioned, wooden trunk, the type one might associate with pirates and hidden treasure. Tony lifted the lid with a gloved hand; inside a quantity of neatly-folded leather, PVC and rubber garments were collected, arranged according to the material they were made from; a couple of corsets lay on top of them. There were a large number of outfits in the chest, enough for many nights of killing.

Tony turned his head to the right. Again there were two wooden shelves on the right-hand wall but the top shelf was empty. The second shelf contained four small brown cardboard boxes, fourteen by twelve centimeters in length and depth respectively, which were stained at the bottom, dark patches creeping across their surfaces. The boxes also appeared a little wet in places, their sides slightly bowed where moisture had seeped into the cardboard, weakening the structure.

'I think I've found the trophies. Can I have another set of gloves please?' Tony asked, removing his hand briefly from his face so he could speak. He grimaced at the smell anew; it reeked within the cavity.

A hand promptly appeared over his shoulder handing him a clean set of gloves; Tony removed the gloves he had used to touch the trunk and put on the new ones, placing the dirty ones into the anonymous hand that was still hovering over his shoulder.

Tony tentatively picked up one of the boxes, carefully handling it so that it didn't disintegrate with his touch, slowly pulling open the lid. He was finding it hard to breathe in the enclosed space, the stench permeating from the box in his hand overwhelming and obnoxious.

He looked inside the box and saw a shriveled piece of meat, black and red in colour, with a greenish hue where a mould-type substance had started to sprout. The process of decay had caused the flesh to cave in on itself in places making it look like a partially-emptied, lumpy sausage skin. Tony could see an abundance of skin at the base of the lump of flesh and was appalled to see dark curly hairs.

He quickly closed the lid on the box and put it back where he had found it. He'd seen enough. He was relieved to step out of the cavity into the bedroom; the air tasted so much sweeter after the pungent odours of that confined space. He bent over at the waist, placing his hands on his knees and breathed, sickened by what he had seen in the box.

'You alright?' Robert asked.

'Yeah, I'll get over it.'

Tony detailed what he had found, and then said: 'Think I just need to step outside though and get some air. I can't get the smell out of my nostrils.' Robert patted him on the back as he passed, and signalled to the search team to begin collecting the evidence, requesting that they photograph the items in situ first.

'Well, we've got the evidence, now we just need the suspect,' Robert said matter-of-factly to Elizabeth and Greg. 'We need to try and establish her movements, where was she last seen?'

'She was last seen with me on Friday night getting drunk,' Elizabeth said, despondently.

'Ok, so Friday night, we know she was definitely in London and she was drunk, so she probably stayed in this flat or with someone else in town that night.'

'She doesn't have a boyfriend so she probably stayed here,' Elizabeth deduced.

'Ok, so we're looking at Saturday morning or afternoon. That's the earliest she probably left this place. Or she left in the wee hours of this morning, which I doubt. That bed does not look slept in.'

They all looked at the bed; the covers were neatly tucked under the mattress and the pillows were plump.

'She didn't know we were coming, she doesn't know she's a suspect, so she may well come back here. Elizabeth, can you call the control room and get them to send a couple of officers to sit in front of the block. Make sure they turn up in plain clothes and use one of the unmarked cars, we don't want to spook her if she does come back. I'll authorize the surveillance for now, but we'll need to get Meadows to approve it once we're out of here.'

The search team officers were making slow progress, delicately removing items and carefully packaging them in separate bags and containers, the exhibits stacking up in the corner of the room. They would be there for at least the entire morning and probably into the afternoon as they diligently seized, packaged and itemized each piece of evidence.

Robert couldn't wait for them to finish; they had a killer to catch. He ushered Greg and Elizabeth into the living room and tapped on the window to catch Tony's attention, summonsing him to come back in. Tony still looked pale when he rejoined them in the flat.

'The OSU guys are going to be here for hours sorting this shit out,' Robert said, 'so I want you to get out of here, go back to the station and partner up. I want everybody out there shaking the trees to see if anything falls out. Visit all of the people she is associated with: friends, family... any address that she is linked to, places she is known to visit. It's time for some good old-fashioned leg work. Tony could you revisit the boss please? He hasn't been entirely honest with us and I want to know why. Bring him in for formal questioning if you have to.'

Tony nodded, pleased to have been tasked with a job that would get him out of the flat.

'I'm going to stay here and oversee the search. Check in with me as you go and I'll see you all back at the nick later,' Robert concluded.

Greg, Elizabeth and Tony left the flat, relieved to be out of the stagnant air and away from the rotting pieces of human flesh.

'I can't believe she just keeps the trophies in cardboard boxes, without any form of preservative. And how could she live with that fucking smell?' Greg asked of no one in particular.

'It's like she's living two lives,' Elizabeth said. 'She's got to have some sort of split personality disorder.'

'Well you would know,' Greg teased, cracking the first joke of the day and lightening the mood considerably.

'Funny, Greg, seriously. You're a comedy genius,' Elizabeth retorted, inflecting a bored tone into her voice. Greg simply grinned.

'Penises in boxes,' Tony said, out of the blue. 'You couldn't make it up. If I told you I'd been to a crime scene and found four penises in boxes you would never believe me, would you?'

Despite Tony's deadpan face and serious tone, Greg and Elizabeth couldn't help but chuckle, partly because what Tony said sounded so funny and partly because they needed to, just to remind themselves they were human and to temporarily push the awfulness of the discovery from their minds.

'Come on, let's get you out of here and get you a nice cup of tea, hmm? You're clearly traumatized, Tony,' Greg said only half-joking, taking Tony by the arm and steering him towards the front gate.

'I've seen much worse than that in my time, but that is just... sick. Penises in boxes, complete with pubes.' Tony looked at them and shook his head. 'I'm going to take the tube back. I need a few minutes.'

'Sure you don't want a lift in the car?'

Elizabeth asked, worried about him.

'Nah, you're alright. See you guys in a bit.'

Tony wandered off in the direction of the tube.

'You reckon he's alright?' Elizabeth asked Greg.

'Yeah. He just needs a bit of space. So, where shall we start?'

'Well, I reckon that we should go to her old home address, the one listed on my spreadsheet. It's as good a place to start as any.'

'What makes you think she would go there?' Greg asked, unconvinced. 'Surely we should start with places we know she's visited recently.'

'If you were a schizophrenic, split-personality, psychopathic killer and you wanted to hide out, where would you go?'

'Dunno.'

'Maybe you'd go back to where it all began?' Elizabeth suggested.

'Maybe, but why does she need to hide out? She doesn't know we're on to her yet.'

'That we know of. She could have remembered about her faux pas with the car in the car park, or she could have remembered her Freudian slip with me on Friday night. One thing we do know about her is she is smart and calculating. I wouldn't be surprised if she knew we were on her trail. Besides, she's not here is she? She must know something is up.'

'Fair point I guess. You got the address with you?'

'No I need to nip to the office to get it. We can brief the others whilst we're there and then head off to the address. What do you reckon?'

'I reckon… that's a plan.'

****

The house looked pretty much as Mina remembered it; it still had the same depressing, uninviting air about it. The only real difference she could see was that it now presented signs of dereliction - peeling paint, broken guttering and a couple of broken windows. It was clear that the house had remained unloved and unoccupied for the past twenty-three years.

Mina guessed that her mother's name would have been on the deeds and as such the house couldn't be sold without her permission. She probably hadn't wanted anything to do with the place whilst she was in prison. What would happen to it now she was dead? Would Louise and Michelle inherit the place? What a wonderful thought.

Mina drove the car up the driveway and parked it in front of the old, dilapidated garage. Sections of the roof had caved in and Mina was pleasantly surprised that the garage door opened when she tugged it skyward.

The garage was empty except for a few roofing tiles and portions of rotten timber so there was still sufficient room for her to park the car. She drove in and parked up, leaving the keys in the ignition and the car doors unlocked. It was not like there was anyone around who was going to steal it.

Mina left the garage and pulled the door shut behind her. Although the property was partially hidden from the main road and only visible up the driveway if you slowed down and craned to look up it, Mina didn't want any of the neighbours noticing the vehicle. After years of abandonment, a vehicle on the driveway would be out of place and she didn't want anybody asking questions, or worse still, coming to investigate.

It wasn't hard to gain access to the house. The back door, which led into the kitchen, was barely hanging on its hinges where it had been forced open by squatters or kids looking for a place to hang out.

It was an unusual quirk of the house that the driveway actually led to what would be considered the back door; the front door was on the opposite side of the house and was only accessible by foot.

The kitchen was filthy, as was to be expected, years of dust and grime settled on the floors and work surfaces, and the windows were thick with dirt. Graffiti had been scrawled on some of the walls and there were old food wrappers and beer cans strewn across the floor.

In front of her was the kitchen sink and Mina briefly saw herself standing there, scarlet, washing blood from her body at her mother's behest. She felt a reaction within her, but couldn't determine what the emotion was. Sadness? Anger? Fear?

To her right Mina saw the door to the basement and it made her shudder involuntarily. The door was closed, which Mina was grateful for. She was not yet ready to face the demons she knew she would find in that place.

Instead, Mina moved slowly through the ground floor, stepping over broken bits of furniture, more rubbish and human feces. Anything of value that may have been in the house had long since been removed, although who might have removed it was anyone's guess. After satisfying herself that there was nothing of interest on the ground floor, and more importantly no vagrants or squatters lurking in the shadows, Mina made her way up the stairs towards the bedrooms.

As she ascended the stairs she could hear her mother's voice behind her, telling her to be quick. She looked down at her hands and saw they were covered in blood, his blood from all those years ago. She wiped her hands on her jeans and looked at them again – they were clean. She was imagining things. Maybe it hadn't been such a good idea to come back here, but Mina wanted closure and Louise wanted to try and understand.

The master bedroom, which had been shared by her mother and that monster, appeared relatively clean compared to the downstairs; it was dusty and the curtains were falling off the rails but the furniture was still present and intact. Mina didn't enter this room, content to simply look at it from the threshold. Maybe the reticence she felt had been shared by whoever had been squatting in the house; no one had wanted to go in and ransack that room because it oozed evil.

Mina walked across the landing and past the bathroom. The toilet was still in place but the sink had been ripped off of the wall; the bath was full of debris and rubbish. She wondered why her mother had wanted her to wash in the kitchen sink instead of in the bath on that fateful day. Perhaps she had panicked, or perhaps she hadn't wanted Louise to spread the blood through the house? Mina would never know the answer to that question; she didn't reflect upon it for long as she was keen to move on to the next room.

She pushed open her old bedroom door and for a moment saw the room as it used to be with its pink walls, bright sunshine bursting through the windows and her and her sister's beds made up with pink and yellow bedspreads. Then she saw it as it was now, the walls grey with dust, dingy from the dirt on the windows and the bed that Michelle used to sleep in upended. The way it looked now reflected how it used to make her feel; sad, uncared for and unloved.

Mina moved over to her old bed and sat on the edge, oblivious to the dust cloud her movement had instigated. She sat with her head bowed, unpleasant memories and dark thoughts running through her mind. As she sat there, her hand gently running over the bedspread, forming swirls of dust, Mina's facial expression changed, becoming softer. Tears formed in her eyes as she recollected what had happened in this house, the pain, the misery, the fear and ultimately the death. Louise remerged and the agony of what had occurred tore through her soul.

'Why?' Louise asked the room. 'Why did this have to happen to me?'

Because you were weak Louise,' Mina replied.

'I wasn't weak. I was just a little girl.'

That's what made you weak to him.'

'No!' Louise screeched, her voice echoing through the house. 'No!'

Her body shook as she tried to regain control of her emotions. The expression on her face changed repeatedly from one of sadness to one of hate, then from one of fear to one of determination; she was battling with herself, her inner emotional turmoil creating a further internal conflict within her mind. Was she Mina or was she Louise? How could she regain control of her personality when she didn't know which one she was or which one she wanted to be?

'I was not weak! I was just – powerless.'

'Until I came along. I protected you. I killed him for you. You owe me.'

'You did save me. But now you're going too far. Why are you killing those men? Why can't you just let go now?'

'Because they need to pay! They can't get away with it. Men are the scourge of the earth Louise. And besides, I didn't kill them. You did,' Mina said belligerently.

'No, no, no, no!'

'Yes, yes, yes, yes! You made me., I was born to help you cope, to help you survive what those fuckers did to you. I saved you so it's only right you do what I need every now and then.'

Louis balled her hands into fists and slammed them against her forehead, rocking backwards and forwards on the bed.

'I can't take this! It's too much. It's all too much. I can't deal with all of this!' she screamed.

'Louise, you don't have to deal with it. That's why I'm here,' Mina said comfortingly. *'Just let me handle it, hey? Stop fighting me.'*

'I don't know what to do. I don't know who I am.'

'You're Mina.'

'I'm Louise.'

You're Mina!

'I'm Louise!'

'No, you're Mina!'

Louise stood up and repeatedly hit herself with her fists, she punched herself in the face, the head, the chest, the legs.

'Leave me alone!' she cried, distressed. 'I can't deal with you in my head and all these memories, all this pain.'

Louise dropped to the floor on her hands and knees and sobbed into the dirt.

'Louise? Louise? Come on. Pull yourself together. You're of no use to anyone if you break down.'

Louise ignored the voice in her head and continued to cry, years of pent up anger, pain, resentment and hate gushing out of her, each emotion fighting to be dealt with.

'I didn't deserve any of this. He made me this way, didn't he? How could anyone do that to a child?'

'Only a man could do that to a child. Only a man could break you so completely Louise. You see why we have to kill them? They need to pay.'

Louise leant back on her knees and sat up, looking around the room. Her face and clothes were covered in dust, just as she had been covered in blood twenty-three years earlier. She stopped crying and stood up. She'd heard something. She listened intently, head slightly cocked to one side.

Then she heard it, car tyres on gravel as a vehicle approached the house. Once again she was briefly transported back to the day she had killed her father, the sound reminding her of her mother's car retuning home.

She moved over to the window, carefully wiped a small, circular hole in the dirt covering the glass pane and peered out; a car was slowly inching its way up the drive. She couldn't see who was driving the vehicle or how many occupants there were, but Louise was convinced it was the police.

'Fuck, what now? Why are they here?'

'Because you're a stupid fucking idiot!' Mina screeched at Louise as she pushed herself forward as the dominant personality, allowing Louise to once again retreat into the safety of her own mind.

Chapter XXXVII

'Jesus, this place wouldn't look amiss in a horror movie,' Greg said to Elizabeth, leaning forward so he could get a good look at the house through the top of the windscreen as he slowly drove the car up the driveway.

'Yeah, it's a bit grim,' Elizabeth agreed from the passenger seat. 'You can almost imagine phantasms drifting around the place, their only purpose to ward off human life forms.'

She wiggled her fingers in front of her face as if they were nefarious, clutching spirit hands. Greg looked at her from the corner of his eye.

'You watch way too many creepy movies.'

'You'd have thought they would have knocked this place down. It clearly hasn't been lived in for a long time,' Elizabeth commented, ignoring Greg and noting the house's ramshackle appearance.

'There must be a reason why they can't. I wonder how long it's been unoccupied. I guess no one wanted to live here after what happened,' Greg observed.

Before heading to the address, Greg and Elizabeth had performed the requisite intelligence checks on the property to ensure that there were no known officer safety issues at the house, such as mad, axe-wielding police-haters, which would require them to attend the premises with backup. They also ran the checks to see if they could establish the owner of the property and to see if there were any intelligence reports of note on the system that they should be aware of.

They had been unsuccessful in trying to establish who the property belonged to as the records were old and had not been fully updated, and there were no registered voters at the premises. They had, however, found some interesting intelligence reports, one in particular that related to a murder that had occurred at the house over two decades ago.

The report stated that a woman, Mrs Nicola Adams, had killed her husband in the basement of the house by stabbing him repeatedly in the face and body with a sharp metal object. The face of the body was so badly battered that it was unrecognizable. Two young girls, aged eight and eleven, had been removed from the house by the police and handed over to social services.

It went on to say that the motive for the murder was unknown but there were suspicions the mother may have been protecting her youngest child, who it was believed my have been subjected to sustained sexual abuse.

Mrs Adams never spoke to police about what had happened and the children were too young and too traumatized to question at the time the intelligence report was created. The report ended with the inputting officer's name, rank and number.

One of the other intelligence reports of interest to Elizabeth pertained to a domestic violence incident where Mrs Adams had taken herself to hospital for a suspected broken arm and hand, and claimed she had been assaulted by her husband. She had been treated at the hospital, police had been called but Mrs Adams had not wanted to press any charges.

Elizabeth had been incredulous that no action had been taken against the husband until Greg reminded her that in those days, police weren't able to prosecute domestic violence cases unless the victim pressed charges, unlike today where perpetrators of domestic violence could be prosecuted without the victim's consent.

'What a way to begin your life eh? Your mother is beaten by your father, he sexually assaults you, she kills your father and then you get put into care,' Elizabeth had said morosely, feeling for the little girl that Louise once was. 'It's little wonder she developed a violent and murderous alter-ego.'

Now as they drove up the driveway towards the house, Elizabeth was even more saddened by the early life Louise must have experienced in this dismal place. Greg parked the car half way up the drive and the two detectives got out, stretching their legs and arms as they did so. The drive should have only taken an hour but it had taken closer to two due to the ubiquitous London traffic, and now their limbs were stiff.

As they walked towards the house, Greg spotted the garage and noticed that the grass in front of it had been recently flattened.

'Elizabeth, look.'

He pointed at the squashed grass and then looked up at the house; he had a feeling that they were being watched. Elizabeth followed his gaze up to the first floor window.

'Do you think she's here?' Elizabeth asked, sensing the presence too.

Together the detectives made their way to

the garage door, their nerves tingling in anticipation, their bodies preparing for fight or flight. They looked at each other and Elizabeth nodded to indicate she was ready. Greg gently raised the garage door just enough so that Elizabeth, who had dropped to her knees, could see inside.

'There's a car, it's clean unlike the garage. It hasn't been here long.'

She quickly scribbled down the vehicle registration mark in her notebook and then signaled to Greg to lower the garage door back down. Elizabeth moved away from the garage and stood next to their police car so she could watch the front of the house whilst she called the control room to ask them to run a check on the number plate.

Greg stayed next to the garage so he could watch the side of the house and also keep Elizabeth in his sight. He saw Elizabeth nod as the operator provided her with the information she needed. After hanging up the phone, Elizabeth joined Greg by the garage.

'Registered keeper is Louise Jackson. Fucking hell, Greg. She's here.'

****

At first the officers had been completely oblivious to her presence, casually strolling up the driveway and over to the garage. They hadn't seen her, but she was watching them. They'd quickly worked out that there was a car in the garage and had promptly opened the garage door and found her vehicle. They'd both then suddenly looked up at the window, causing Mina to jump back, startled, afraid they would see her. Somehow they knew she'd been watching them, their sixth sense on high alert.

After a few minutes, Mina had dared to look out the window again, keeping her body next to the wall and her face in the shadows. The female pig was on the phone and the male pig was stood by the garage. Mina was au fait enough with police practices to know that they would be running her number plate right at that moment. So, now they knew she was here – with or without their sixth sense.

Mina didn't recognize the male pig; he was big, muscular, with broad shoulders and a shaved head. Mina briefly imagined how he would look after she had worked on him for a while, strapped to a bed, unable to defend himself, his face and legs covered in blood. She closed her eyes relishing the image. Not that she would get that chance. She didn't have her ropes, or tools with her and he didn't exactly look like the type of man she could easily overpower. It was one thing to tie up a man who thought it was part of a sexual game, quite another to try and tie one up when he didn't want it.

It had taken her a moment to work out where she recognized the female pig from; she knew she'd seen her before but she couldn't immediately recollect where. Then it had come to her. She was a friend of that stupid bitch Louise. She was the one that Louise had been drinking with, the one Louise had blabbed to, the one who had seen a glimpse of Mina. Her presence made Mina distinctly uncomfortable.

Louise's unfortunate phrasing about the 'bondage killer' had been a worry to Mina from the moment Louise had uttered it; for a split second their personalities had been too close and Louise had almost seen all of Mina's memories. She'd quickly withdrawn hoping that the female pig hadn't picked up on the word Louise had used. She hadn't and Mina was pretty sure they'd gotten away with it.

Then Mina had almost taken over again and revealed her dark side. This, the copper had noticed, but Mina was confident she had put it down to the alcohol and Louise's recent break up with that fuckwit, Steve. She certainly hadn't said anything to make Mina think she had any cause to suspect that Louise possessed two personalities.

Even if the copper had pegged Louise for a killer from those two things alone, it was all circumstantial, Mina knew, so there had to be some other reason that these pigs were here now, sniffing around, trying to track her down like fucking bloodhounds sniffing out a rabbit. They wouldn't have come all this way on a hunch. How had they even found the place? There had to be something else. Then it dawned on her – Derek fucking Cooper.

Fuck, fuck, fuck!

Mina was furious. She paced the bedroom thinking back to that night, the night when she had killed out of context, hadn't followed her killing ritual. How could she have been so stupid? She had been so busy trying to protect Louise that she had failed to protect herself. She'd made a grave mistake and now the police were here.

Mina had taken it upon herself to kill Derek because Louise hated him and his threats against Ben were causing Louise a great deal of distress. Louise's pain was Mina's pain and as such she had wanted to remedy the situation, make Louise's life a little easier. It would have been fine if she had just killed him and then left, but that wasn't how she operated. Mina had a message; she wanted men to feel afraid and to realize that the only thing that set them apart from women was their genitalia – without that they were emasculated and weak, in the same way they thought women were weak.

The mistake she had made was not putting her glove back on after she had cut off Derek's dick. She remembered that she had stumbled whilst fleeing the car park and had fallen against a car near the fire exit. She had touched it with her ungloved hand, leaving a lovely little clue for the Old Bill. Mina was so angry, she wanted to hurt herself. Or some police officers.

Ordinarily, the police having her prints wouldn't have been a problem, but that stupid bitch Louise had gone and got herself arrested for punching that other stupid bitch Melissa. The police had her DNA and fingerprints on record and a speculative search of the prints recovered from the car would have identified Louise Jackson as the killer. Ultimately, Steve was to blame for all of this because if he hadn't cheated on Louise, she wouldn't have punched Melissa and she wouldn't have been arrested; once again Mina's problems stemmed from the actions of a man.

Mina sighed and shook her head. What was done was done and she couldn't undo it. Time to stop beating herself up over it and deal with the present; the police were here and she was running out of time. She needed to prepare, to be ready for them when they came through the door. A quick glance out the window satisfied her that the pigs were still outside; they were now stood together next to the garage.

She dashed out of the bedroom and down

the stairs, heading for the kitchen. She needed to find a weapon of some kind and she had seen a kitchen knife lying on the kitchen floor beneath the dirt and rubbish on her earlier scout around the house. The blade would be blunt but that didn't bother Mina. She grabbed the knife off the floor, yanked open the basement door and ran back out into the corridor, pressing herself against the wall. She calmed her breathing and composed herself; she was in charge. She knew where they were and they hadn't seen her yet, so she was in the strongest position.

In a few moments the pigs would be coming through the back door into the kitchen. But that was ok. Mina was ready for them.

****

'We need to call the DI, let him know what we've found,' Greg said. Elizabeth nodded, not really listening. She thought she had heard movement inside the house, someone running down the stairs.

Greg took out his mobile and phoned Robert. After a short conversation Greg hung up the phone and said: 'He doesn't want us to go inside. He wants us to wait for back up because if she's in there she could be dangerous.'

'No shit she's dangerous!' Elizabeth scoffed. 'But we can't just wait here. What if she has another victim in there? What if she's holding someone captive?'

'I know what you're saying, but if we go in there now, just the two of us, one of two things may happen. One, she may attack us and do us serious harm – not being funny but my can of pepper spray does not make me feel entirely safe. And two, she sees us and legs it out of the house and we lose her for good,' Greg argued.

'Or three, we go in, stick together and arrest her like we're supposed to,' Elizabeth added, looking at Greg, hopefully.

'Come one Greg! There are two of us and one of her.'

'That's debatable!'

'But we can't just sit here and wait. We need to do something,' Elizabeth beseeched.

'You watch plenty of horror movies. You must know that it's always a bad idea to disobey orders.'

'Yes, but the bad guy always gets caught in the end.'

'After one of the two heroes dies,' Greg countered.

'Greg, I want to catch this woman. I went to school with her, I was out drinking with her for Christ's sake. I have to do this, I have to put right that missed opportunity.'

Greg looked at Elizabeth's earnest face; she reminded him of himself when he was younger. He'd been so keen, so up for it. He understood how she felt and truth be told he didn't want to stand there waiting for backup when there was a murder suspect loose in the house anymore than she did.

'Ok, we go in. But we stick together. No heroics. Batons ready,' Greg said.

'Of course.'

Together the two detectives walked towards the back door, their hearts pounding in their chests, adrenaline pumping through their veins. Elizabeth took the lead, Greg following close behind. When she arrived at the back door, Elizabeth noticed it was ajar, and there were fresh footprints in the dust around it. Elizabeth looked over her shoulder at Greg and pointed the footprints out to him. He nodded in acknowledgement and motioned to Elizabeth to continue.

The back door didn't need much persuasion, a gentle push was sufficient to open it wide enough to allow ample room for Elizabeth and Greg to pass through.

With a deep breath, Elizabeth stepped across the threshold, gripping her baton tightly, her senses heightened.

It took Elizabeth's eyes a moment to adjust to the comparative gloom of the kitchen and she waited just inside the door until her vision returned to normal.

She moved further into the room, Greg just behind her, and listened carefully for any noises elsewhere in the house. Cautiously, Elizabeth moved further into the room, carefully stepping over the detritus and debris that littered the floor. Elizabeth moved towards the kitchen sink, when she noticed a door to her right; it appeared to lead down to a basement area and the door was open.

She moved towards the open door and poked her head inside. Beyond a set of wooden stairs leading down to the basement, Elizabeth couldn't make out any of the features of the room. It was pitch black down there and she would need a flashlight. This must have been the basement where Mrs Adams had murdered her husband. The thought brought chills to her skin and caused the hair on the back of her neck to rise.

Just as she was about to turn to mention this

to Greg, Elizabeth was pushed roughly in the back, the force of the blow catching her off balance and sending her tumbling down the stairs into the impenetrable darkness. She rolled over and over, falling for what felt like forever, the wooden steps hard against her body.

Finally, she came to rest at the foot of the stairs, dazed and in pain. Her right wrist was broken and she was pretty sure she'd felt a rib crack as she'd smashed against the stairs during her plummet. The only source of light available to Elizabeth was coming through the open basement door and she looked up towards it to see if anyone was coming down the stairs after her.

Then she heard Greg shout out and heard feet moving rapidly about the kitchen above her. She tried to get up, wanting to run to the aid of her partner, but she was too dazed. Her head was spinning and the dizziness was affecting her vision. She managed to pull herself up onto her knees, but promptly fell backwards again as her body struggled to regain balance, the lack of light adding to her disorientation.

The struggle above her continued for a few seconds longer then stopped suddenly and Greg fell silent.

'Greg!' Elizabeth shouted up from the basement, wincing in pain at her broken rib. The absence of noise was worse than hearing the scuffle because she had no indication, no clue whatsoever, as to what was going on above her head. The silence was eerie.

Then, the basement door slammed shut and Elizabeth was alone in the dark.

Chapter XXXVIII

Robert was worried. Neither Greg nor Elizabeth was answering their mobile phone; Greg's just rang out and Elizabeth's went straight to voicemail. Robert had been in the game long enough to know that this meant trouble.

When he had spoken to Greg, Robert's instructions had been explicit – do not enter the house, wait for back up, keep an eye on the place and we'll be with you soon. Although, he hoped they had listened to his orders and were still standing outside, calmly waiting for back up to arrive, Robert suspected his words had fallen on deaf ears. Elizabeth definitely would not have wanted to hang about, Robert was sure, but he was hopeful that Greg had been able to convince her to do as she was asked for once in her bloody obstinate life. He could but hope. He knew they were both competent detectives with good unarmed combat skills, but Mina was a vicious murderer who undoubtedly had a few skills of her own.

The unmarked car was travelling as fast as it could in the rush hour traffic, its sirens blaring, the blue and white lights in its grill flashing as JB negotiated the roads and swore profusely at the drivers that did not immediately get out of his way. Tony, who was in the back, echoed JB's sentiments and joined him in his insults like a vociferous parrot with Tourette's Syndrome. Because the car was unmarked, other road users didn't always realize that it was a police car and that the sirens were in fact coming from that vehicle, and as such they didn't always move out of the way, costing valuable time, and frustrating the hell out of JB.

A marked police vehicle was also en route at Robert's request. He didn't know how many officers they would need to apprehend the suspect and to ensure Greg and Elizabeth were alright, but there were now seven on their way in total.

Robert pressed redial on his phone and tried to call Greg again for the umpteenth time to no avail.

'For fuck's sake!' Robert threw the phone onto the dash board in temper, the device skittering across its surface before dropping to the floor as JB made a tight turn.

'Anything from Elizabeth, Tony?' Robert asked.

'No, I can't raise her. Her phone is still off or out of range. I'll try sending her a message again. It may get through if she moves location.'

Tony was beside himself with worry; he needed to know Elizabeth was alright. He couldn't bear the thought of her getting hurt, or worse. She had only just come into his life and he did not want to lose her. He typed out a quick text simply asking her to let him know she was alright and pressed send. He sat staring at the phone for a few minutes then returned the device to his pocket. Wherever she was, she was out of reach.

'Get out of the fucking way you fucking reject!' JB shouted at a silver Honda Civic that was failing to move over. He gesticulated angrily with his hand, eventually catching the driver's eye. The car finally moved over and JB stuck his middle finger up at the driver as he screeched past.

'Sorry Guv. But seriously, these fucking people!'

Robert didn't say anything. He didn't care how many people JB offended on the drive to the house, he didn't care how many complaints they generated from the general public. All he cared about was getting to his officers as fast as possible. He just hoped they weren't already too late.

****

Mina's mood had greatly improved now that she was back in charge. She'd even impressed herself by how easily she had managed to take care of the two pigs. The female pig was now trapped in the basement, and Mina had just finished strapping the male pig to the circular kitchen table, each of his dangling limbs fastened to a table leg, his head hanging over the edge. Despite her earlier reservations, the male pig hadn't proved that difficult to take down after all, the element of surprise working in her favour.

She'd heard them creeping into the kitchen and had waited in the corridor, perfectly still, perfectly silent, poised and ready for the perfect moment to launch her attack. That moment had come when they had both had their backs to her; the female pig had been at the top of the basement stairs, and the male pig had been stood just behind her. Mina had come barreling into the room as fast as she could, the male pig had only had time to turn his head halfway before she had shoulder barged him in the back, her momentum carrying him forward and causing him to ram into his colleague, sending her flying down the basement stairs.

He'd only just managed to save himself from sharing his colleague's fate by spreading his arms out and catching hold of the door frame, his defenseless position allowing Mina to attack him with impunity. She had struck him around the base of the neck repeatedly with the knife handle, aiming for the vagus nerve, knowing that if she hit him there enough times and hard enough he would eventually experience vasovagal syncope and become temporarily unconscious.

After a brief struggle with him as he fought to push himself away from the door frame and Mina's incessant onslaught, he had finally fainted, falling backwards onto the kitchen floor, catching the back of his head on the kitchen table as he fell.

Once he was incapacitated Mina slammed the basement door shut and pushed a rickety kitchen chair under the handle so that the female pig couldn't escape. She knew she didn't have long before the male pig woke up and so needed to act expeditiously.

It was not going to be easy to get the man onto the table; he was big and he was heavy and Mina suspected that knocking him out was going to prove the easy part of this endeavour. However, Mina was nothing if not resourceful.

She lay the kitchen table on its side and rolled the male pig over, rubbing him in the dirt like a breadstick in flour, until his back was firmly pressed against the table top. Then she ripped off the pull from the blind in the kitchen and promptly fastened his right arm to a table leg. Mina ran into the living room and ripped down the curtains, and with the aid of her blunt knife shredded them into strips she could use as restraints.

Back in the kitchen, she tied Greg's right leg to another table leg, giving him the appearance of a broken marionette, two limbs up in the air, two limbs on the floor under his body.

All she had to do now was stand the table upright. Mina placed her hands on the two raised table legs, gripping them near the bottom for extra leverage, and then leant forward onto her arms, effectively pushing her entire body weight onto the table legs. She grunted with exertion.

For a brief moment nothing happened and Mina thought the table legs would actually break under her, but then the table rocked towards her, raising off the ground a couple of inches.

Encouraged by this, Mina tried again and after a few failed attempts eventually managed to tip the table upright. Her father had liked expensive furniture and the sturdiness of this table was testament to the old adage: you get what you pay for. The legs of a lesser quality table would most likely not have withstood her weight.

As the table tipped upright, Greg's body flopped to the side so that he was hanging half on and half off the table. There was a pop as his arm was pulled out of its socket and his shoulder dislocated, the force of his body falling off the table too much for his restrained arm to take. Now that two of his limbs were fastened to the table legs, supporting half his weight, it wasn't hard for Mina to maneuver the rest of his body onto the table top.

She quickly fastened his free arm and leg to the remaining two table legs and shoved a dirty piece of fabric into his mouth, securing it in place with more of her improvised curtain restraints by tying it tightly around his jaw and across his mouth. Satisfied that he would not be able to break free or spit the cloth out, Mina stood back to admire her handy work and mentally applauded herself for her ingenuity.

She was breathing heavily, tired from the push-pulling and lifting of the table and the body, but she still had lots to do – there was no time to catch her breath. She considered killing the male pig there and then but decided she wanted him to wake up before she began her ritual. It was no fun if she couldn't see the fear in their eyes. She needed her victims to know that she was the one in charge, she had the power to kill them or let them live, and she liked to hear them beg for mercy.

The sun was setting fast, shadows were beginning to shroud the house, and the growing darkness was rapidly reducing visibility. Mina knew the approaching dusk was going to make it very difficult for her to carry out the rest of her tasks. She searched for a flashlight under the sink to no avail. She didn't bother heading out to the garage to look in there because she'd already noted that the garage was pretty much empty except for the timber and roof tiles from the sections of collapsed roof.

She looked around the kitchen trying to think of a solution to her problem when she noticed a light switch on the wall leading out to the corridor. Surely the house wasn't still connected to the national grid? Confident she already knew the answer, Mina tried the light switch anyway.

To her amazement and delight the kitchen light came one. She shook her head in wonderment a broad smile spreading across her face, a cackle of glee escaping her. Someone was looking out for her. One of the previous squatters must have tapped into the neighbouring power supply, effectively abstracting electricity. The neighbours would probably never know their electricity source had been compromised because the squatters wouldn't have used a lot of power, just enough to illuminate a few light bulbs, maybe an electric kettle. The increase in their electricity consumption would have been minimal and probably not even shown up on their bills. And it wasn't like there was someone here all the time. Mina briefly wondered why the squatters had left?

The house was surrounded by trees and as such was relatively private, the lights shouldn't attract the attention of the neighbouring houses, but Mina wasn't taking any chances. Now that she had artificial light she no longer needed the natural light coming through the windows and so could now cover these up to keep out of sight of prying eyes. She dashed upstairs and pulled down more curtains so that she could use them to cover the kitchen windows. Once this was done, Mina nipped outside the house to see what the view was like from the driveway. The house still appeared unoccupied.

Bloody marvelous. You are awesome!

About ten minutes had passed since she had knocked out the male pig so he should be waking any moment now, although with his head hanging lower than his body the waking process would most likely be delayed somewhat.

She skipped back into the kitchen and stood next to Greg's head, looking down at his face, the kitchen knife in her right hand held above his left eye. Mina used her left hand to rub his body, running her hand across his chest, across his stomach, across his penis which she could feel through the soft fabric of his trousers. She felt an overwhelming urge to sit astride him but was doubtful the table would take both their weights.

She unfastened his belt and unbuttoned his trousers; ideally he should be naked because that was how she liked them before she killed them. Naked, exposed and vulnerable. Derek had been fully clothed, but that kill had been exceptional. This one would be different.

She lay the knife between Greg's legs and using both hands, ripped open his shirt, sending buttons flying in all directions. She admired his muscular body for a moment, running her finger nails down his torso, and then pulled his trousers down his thighs. She couldn't pull them any further because Greg's legs were spread apart by the restraints she had fashioned from the curtains.

She picked up the knife and put her hand inside Greg's pants grabbing hold of his penis; she was prepared to change the order of her ritual for this male pig. She would begin with the mutilation, the pain from the jagged blunt blade might help wake him up.

Mina's peace was then shattered. The basement door was being struck from the other side as the female pig tried to break her way out.

Oh no you fucking don't!

Mina ran to the basement door and shouted through it.

'You do that again you fucking whore I'll tear your fucking eyes out!'

There was silence on the other side. Mina found the light switch for the basement and turned it

432

on. She heard feet running down the basement stairs and saw a sliver of light beneath the door, clearly the lights were working down there too. Mina looked at the male pig, sprawled out on the table. He wasn't going anywhere. She wanted to be able to take her time killing him, to enjoy it, and she wasn't going to be able to do that with the female pig interrupting her every few minutes.

It was time to deal with the demons in the basement.

****

Elizabeth had never been so frightened in her life. The darkness in the basement was impenetrable and the air was dank and cold. She was worried she was going into shock as she was experiencing tachycardia, was sweating profusely and was totally disoriented. Her body was shivering violently, making her teeth chatter.

She told herself to calm down, repeating soothing phrases in her head, and eventually managed to slow her breathing; she needed to stay focused if she was going to get out of here.

After a few minutes, Elizabeth managed to calm her mind sufficiently to allow her to take stock of her situation; there was nothing she could do, however, to calm the pain.

She pulled her mobile phone out of her pocket to try and call for help; her heart sank when she realized that she didn't have a signal. The phone did, however, provide a dim light source. She heard movement overhead, the sound of furniture being dragged around. She wondered what had happened to Greg. She hoped he was still alive.

Using her phone as a pitiful flashlight Elizabeth slowly managed to crawl to the foot of the stairs where she sat for a few more minutes until she felt ready to try and stand up. Using the wall for support, Elizabeth stood, her legs slightly wobbly, pain searing through her side and wrist. Now she just had to get up the stairs.

The ascent was slow and painful but eventually, Elizabeth made it to the top. She pushed against the door and was not surprised to find it was barricaded shut. There was no key in the lock, so Mina must have placed something in front of the door to secure it shut. Elizabeth started banging on the door with her left forearm, putting as much force behind it as she could, hoping to either dislodge whatever was barricading the door or to alert someone to her presence.

She heard Mina scream at her and then suddenly the basement lights flashed on. Elizabeth ran down the stairs, a fresh jolt of adrenaline energizing her and making her forget the pain in her ribs and wrist. Mina would be coming after her soon.

Now that she could see, Elizabeth took in her surroundings from the foot of the stairs. The room had been made into a small bedroom. There was an old, dirty double bed in the middle of the room and a sofa and two chairs to the left of it, pressed up against the back wall. In places, beige foam was protruding out of the sofa cushions where the fabric had become worn with age, and one of the chairs was broken, laying on its side, two of its legs snapped off. Anyone sitting on those seats would have been looking straight at the bed.

On the other side of the room was a large child's play mat with a couple of broken children's toys abandoned upon it. She couldn't imagine any child wanting to come down here to play. The whole place was covered in dirt, dust and grime, years of neglect taking their toll. Vegetation was beginning to sprout in the corners of the room where the damp proofing had eroded away and mould was setting in, contributing to the dank odour. Girl's clothing was also strewn about the place, littering most of the floor.

There was nowhere for Elizabeth to hide and nothing she could use as a weapon. She had dropped her baton during her tumble and didn't know where it had rolled to.

She heard the basement door open slowly behind her so she moved quickly away from the stairs, pressing herself against the back wall instead, putting as much distance as she could between herself and whoever was coming down the stairs.

Mina's first steps into the basement were tentative, as if she didn't really want to come down. She held a kitchen knife down by her right side, the forefinger on her right hand nervously tapping the handle, her eyes wide with fear and excitement.

Elizabeth watched her as she descended; it was clear that Mina wasn't interested in her at that moment, she was revisiting a time and place in her own mind. Elizabeth was temporarily forgotten.

'This is the place, this is the place...' Mina spoke quietly, and continued to descend.

When she reached the bottom step, Mina slowly surveyed the basement; her eyes passed over Elizabeth but she didn't see her standing there, she was so immersed in her own world. Suddenly, Mina screamed, an ear piercing, blood-curdling sound, which made Elizabeth jump.

'Don't hurt me daddy, no! I'll do what you want.'

'Stupid fucking creature. Get on you knees.'

'No, I'll be good. Please don't hurt me.'

'I said quiet bitch. Open wide.'

'No!' Mina shouted, striking herself in the face with her left hand. 'No!' she hit herself again.

Elizabeth froze, she didn't know what to do, how to react. She tried to make sense of what she was witnessing and understood that Mina's personality was also split. The voice Mina was speaking in was now that of a child, the second voice was deeper and more masculine as she replicated the voice of a man.

'I don't want to ride anymore. Those men hurt me. Can't I just go and play? Please daddy?'

'You'll do as you're fucking told cunt! Stop wriggling! You'll only make it hurt more.'

'It hurts! Stop! Please stop!' Mina began to cry as she moved further into the basement, heading towards the bed.

The closer Mina moved to the bed, the more space she opened up behind her. Elizabeth wondered if she could sprint past her and dash up the stairs before Mina realized what was happening.

Mina was now standing at the foot of the bed, her head bowed as she looked at the floor, so Elizabeth seized her chance.

She didn't get very far, her movement catching Mina's eye. Mina turned on her almost immediately and pointed the knife at her throat.

'Fucking stop right there pig. I haven't forgotten about you,' Mina's voice had returned to normal, the child was gone. Elizabeth took several steps back and raised her hands to show she wasn't armed and wasn't going to fight.

'Where's my partner? Is he ok?' Elizabeth asked, her voice crackling from the dryness of her mouth and throat.

Mina looked at her, eyes full of menace and madness.

'This is where I was born you know,' Mina said, ignoring the question. 'Down here in this very room. Louise couldn't take the pain anymore so she conjured me up. I'm stronger than her you see. I protect her from people that want to harm her. People like you!' Mina spat.

'I don't want to harm her. I want to protect her too. I want to get her the help she needs,' Elizabeth said, her tone conciliatory.

'You want to arrest her, put her in prison! How will she survive in a place like that?'

'Louise needs professional help, psychiatric help.'

'I am not letting her go into a mental institute! That would be the end of her and it would be the end of me. I will not let you do that to her, you hear me?'

Mina was moving closer to Elizabeth, her eye blazing with rage, the knife still raised at Elizabeth's throat. Elizabeth slowly moved to Mina's right hoping to eventually circle round her.

'Do you know what they did to her? Those filthy fucking animals? They abused her for fun. He pimped her out like a fucking whore, her own father. How could anyone do that to another person, let alone their own child?' Mina was crying, tears of hate staining her dusty cheeks.

'I don't know, Mina. I don't know how someone can do that to a child. It's despicable. Let me help you.' Elizabeth reached out towards the knife.

For a moment Elizabeth saw something else in Mina's eyes, a flicker of hope that she could be saved, a yearning for human compassion and love. Then it was replaced with something malign.

'No! Keep away from me!' Mina slashed at Elizabeth's hand.

Elizabeth circled round Mina a little bit more and Mina followed her movement unconsciously. There was now a clear route between Elizabeth and the basement stairs.

'She didn't kill him you know. Our mother, she didn't do it. On no. That was me. I fucking did it. I stabbed him in the eye over and over and over. I loved every second of it because he fucking deserved it. That's why I killed those other men and that's why I'm going to kill your partner, upstairs. Men are evil – look at the pain they cause.'

Elizabeth didn't say anything, she just wanted to get a little closer to the stairs before she made another run for it. There wasn't that much space between her and Mina and she didn't want to give Mina an opportunity to stab her with the blunt, rusty knife she was holding menacingly in her hand.

'I'm not going to stop. I love to kill – I need to kill. You'll be the first woman I've had the pleasure of murdering.'

Mina lunged forward but Elizabeth was ready. She dashed past Mina and started to run up the stairs. She was about half way up when Mina grabbed her ankle and brought her crashing down onto the stairs. Elizabeth was winded and felt another rib crack on impact, followed by a searing pain in her right shoulder as Mina stabbed her in the back, causing her to cry out in agony.

She felt Mina withdraw the blade, its jagged, rusty edges, ripping through her flesh. Elizabeth managed to roll onto her back so she could face her assailant, who was coming at her again, the knife raised. Elizabeth kicked out, her booted foot connecting with Mina's jaw, her raised position on the stairs giving her the extra height she needed.

Mina recoiled and screamed in pain and anger. She reached forward and managed to grab hold of one of Elizabeth's ankles, successfully avoiding her flailing legs. She dragged Elizabeth down the stairs, the back of Elizabeth's head connecting with every step. White stars flashed before Elizabeth's eyes and she struggled to focus; she squinted her eyes to try and narrow her field of vision.

Dust was whirling around them as they wrestled on the floor, filling up Elizabeth's nostrils and caking her throat, making it hard to breathe. Mina seemed oblivious to the dirt as she sat astride Elizabeth, one hand around her throat, the other holding the knife inches from Elizabeth's left eye.

Using all her strength, Elizabeth grabbed Mina's wrist with both hands, oblivious to the pain in her own broken wrist as she fought to stay alive, and locked her arms by pushing her elbows out so that Mina couldn't get any closer to her with the blade. She was more concerned about being stabbed in the eye than being choked out by the hand on her throat.

Elizabeth wriggled beneath Mina, twisting her body from side to side in an attempt to unbalance her, all the while keeping a firm grip on the arm that was controlling the knife. Elizabeth could feel her strength ebbing away as she bled from the stab wound in her shoulder, she wouldn't be able to hold Mina off her for much longer.

Mustering all her energy, Elizabeth dug her heels into the floor and raised her hips, twisting her body as she did so, relieved to feel that she had unbalanced Mina enough to cause her to fall onto the ground beside her. The momentum carried Elizabeth over so that she was now straddling Mina in a complete reversal of positions.

'Elizabeth, what are you doing to me?' Louise's voice spoke to her. 'Why are you attacking me?'

Elizabeth paused for a second, momentarily confused. Her moment's inattention gave Mina the opportunity she needed.

She thrust the knife up towards Elizabeth's face, aiming for her eyes. Elizabeth slammed her hands downwards defensively, clamping Mina's hands against her own body. The knife pierced Elizabeth's left hand, the blade passing all the way through from her palm to the back of the hand. She screamed in pain as blood exploded from the wound onto Mina, who was still struggling beneath her.

Mina tried to pull the blade from the wound but it was stuck; it wasn't sharp enough to cut sideways through Elizabeth's hand and she was in the wrong position to pull it out from underneath. Elizabeth had Mina's arms effectively pinned against her breast.

Elizabeth leant forward, her hands and arms crushing Mina's, and head butted Mina hard in the face, breaking her nose. Mina didn't appear to notice the pain, she didn't make a sound. Elizabeth head butted her again, this time dazing Mina, who released her grip on the knife. Elizabeth let go of Mina's arms and raised her own, the knife still wedged through her hand.

She slammed her right fist into Mina's face as hard as she could, before Mina had an opportunity to react, still reeling from the head butts. Then Mina's arms shot upwards and clasped around Elizabeth's throat, squeezing the breath out of her.

Elizabeth struck Mina's arms on the elbow joints to try and collapse her arms; on the third strike Mina relinquished her grip and Elizabeth was able to take hold of Mina's arms by the wrists, the knife pushing painfully further through her hand. Elizabeth then fell forward so that her body was lying on Mina's, preventing her from moving, and pinioning Mina's arms above her head.

'That all you got officer?' Mina teased, spitting a globule of phlegm into Elizabeth's face.

'That's all I need, bitch.'

Elizabeth head butted Mina again and this time, Mina passed out.

Elizabeth rolled off of her adversary's body and lay on her back in the dirt, her breath coming to her in ragged gasps, the pain in her body becoming more and more severe as the adrenaline subsided. She could hear sirens approaching so she knew help was on its way. She looked over at Mina; she was out cold, it was over. Elizabeth closed her eyes, she was exhausted and losing blood, she needed a rest. She closed her eyes.

She heard feet running down the stairs towards her just before she slipped away.

Chapter XXXIX

Two weeks had passed since Louise Jackson had been arrested, two weeks since she'd been hauled off in the back of a police van and taken straight to a secure mental hospital where she was currently under heavy sedation and constant watch. The doctors at the hospital didn't think Louise would ever be fit enough to stand trial and as such she was destined to spend the rest of her days locked up in the one place she had never wanted her to be.

The prosecution for the case had told the court that there was little point conducting a trial as the woman had been declared mentally unstable; she was not fit to give evidence and a court appearance might well put back her recovery, that is, if she was ever to recover. She was a huge risk to the public, in particular to males, and as such the Crown would offer no evidence for a criminal trial but recommended that the judge order her to be sectioned.

The defence supported this suggestion as the only defence they could offer for their client was on the grounds of poor mental health. The court was advised that Louise had been diagnosed as a dangerous paranoid schizophrenic with dissociative identity disorder by the doctors treating her. There was very little prospect of her ever being fit enough for reintegration into the general public.

The judge had ruled that Ms Louise Jackson

would be remanded indefinitely in a high-security mental health unit where she would come under the care of trained professionals. The judge had wound up proceedings, stating that he was saddened by Ms Jackson's unfortunate story and that she was very much a product of her early environment. He was sorry for the victims' families and hoped that they would find some peace knowing their loved ones' killer would never be released.

Robert, who had been sitting at the back of the court throughout the proceedings, left the court building not entirely a happy man, but a satisfied one.

Louise Jackson would never again experience freedom. In many ways being remanded to a mental institute was worse than prison because she would have less rights and absolutely no say over what happened to her. She was in the hands of the medical staff and from now on, they would be the ones to tell her what she could and couldn't do. She had no control over her own life.

The Crown Prosecution Service had also decided not to prosecute Ben Matthews for lying to the investigating officers and perverting the course of justice. It was decided that since the murder suspect wasn't going to have to face trial, it was unfair and disproportionate to prosecute her boss for lying. When arrested, Ben had said that it was all a mistake, an error, he hadn't done it on purpose, and since nobody could prove or disprove his account, it was decided that there wasn't a realistic prospect of conviction and so the matter was dropped.

Two weeks had passed since Greg had been found by the uniformed officers, sprawled on the kitchen table, barely conscious. Greg had woken up shortly after Louise had descended into the basement and he had tried in vain to free himself from his bindings. He had periodically raised his head up, even though it hurt his neck and his dislocated shoulder felt as if it was on fire, to ensure that he didn't pass out again from too much blood to the brain.

It had felt like forever as he lay there on that kitchen table, expecting Louise to return at any moment to finish the job. When the uniformed officers had arrived, closely flanked by Robert, Greg had cried with relief.

Whilst a couple of officers had tended to Greg, the others had run down into the basement, where they found both Mina and Elizabeth unconscious. Mina had started to come round as the officers handcuffed her behind her back. She had sworn at them and tried to bite their hands and faces as they lifted her up the stairs and placed her into the back of the police van.

Tony had rushed over to Elizabeth and held her head in his arms until the ambulance arrived. She'd been rushed to hospital, her loss of blood causing concern. She had not regained full consciousness for almost three hours after the incident.

When she had opened her eyes, Tony had been there and she had burst into tears at the sight of him, her relief at being alive overwhelming her. Once her tears had subsided she asked after Greg; upon hearing he was ok, she fell asleep.

Elizabeth had spent several days in hospital recovering from her stab wounds, broken wrist, cracked ribs and severe concussion. The doctors had

444

told her she was lucky to still have use of her left hand; the knife had only just missed shredding several of her nerves.

Tony had visited her every day, filling her in on what was going on in the world beyond the four walls of her ward and their romance blossomed as the pair became closer and closer. Other members of the team including Robert, JB and Greg, had also popped in to visit her whilst she was convalescing.

The reunion with Greg had been emotional. Elizabeth blamed herself for almost getting them both killed, the guilt eating her up inside.

Greg had told her to stop being so stupid, pull herself together and get over herself. She wasn't that persuasive and if he hadn't wanted to go into the house, he wouldn't have. He'd then kissed her on the forehead, told her she was a fucking nightmare and stated he wanted a new partner when she got out. Elizabeth had wanted to punch him but her right arm was in plaster, her left hand was in bandages and her shoulder was in a sling. They'd laughed at her futile attempts.

Greg had also said his retirement plans were on hold - for now at least. He wasn't quite ready to trade in his badge, wasn't quite ready for a life beyond the job. And besides, he wasn't ready to leave Elizabeth; he felt like her protector, even though he knew she didn't really need his protection.

Today was Elizabeth's first day back at work. She was on restricted duties and so would be office bound until she was fully healed, but she was pleased to be both out of the hospital and out of her flat. She'd been going stir crazy and Tony had been making things worse, waiting on her hand and foot and smothering her with TLC. She wasn't really complaining because it was nice that he cared so much. She had just missed her independence.

As Elizabeth walked toward the office, several uniformed officers that she didn't know told her it was great to see her back, patting her on the back as if she was some kind of hero. She walked into the office bemused by this extra attention and was stunned to see the whole team standing in front of her grinning beneath a welcome back banner. Several poppers were pulled showering her in coloured strands of tissue and glitter.

'You guys. What have you done?' she laughed, flattered by their welcome.

'We just wanted to make you feel welcome after your long break,' JB said, emphasizing the word 'long'.

'Jeez, can't even get time off the job after being stabbed and beaten by a lunatic without getting abuse from you,' she retorted.

JB stepped over to her and said: 'Only joking Elizabeth, it is great to have you back with us. Even if you can't do much.' He moved in for a hug and Elizabeth reciprocated.

'So, DC Lane, what have you learnt?' Robert asked, his tone teasing.

'I have learnt that JB is a shit driver – seriously man, what took you so long?' JB feigned indignation, then smiled.

'And I have learnt that you guys are actually a big bunch of softies.'

'Yes, and maybe you've learnt a little something about doing as you're told occasionally, or is that too much to hope for?' Robert asked, one eyebrow arched, optimistically.

'Guv, I was stabbed not lobotomized.'

'Thought it might have been a bit too much of a stretch to expect anything else from you,' Robert chuckled. 'Come here you bloody stubborn woman.'

He gave her a quick hug and then said: 'I'm very proud of you Elizabeth, you and Greg. Although neither of you listened to me, I wouldn't have expected anything less from such diligent and conscientious officers as yourselves.'

Elizabeth blushed from her boss's praise. 'Thank you,' she said, humbled.

Tony sidled in next to Elizabeth and took hold of her right hand.

'Would *madame* care for a slice of cake?' He led her over to her desk and opened the cake box that was resting on it. Elizabeth couldn't stop laughing.

'You clowns!' The box contained a chocolate cake decorated with a Superman S and the words 'Super Cop.'

'Who's for cake?' she asked, addressing the whole room and cutting the first slice. One thing coppers couldn't resist was a sweet treat.

As the officers tucked into their slices of cake and chatted together, they put the bondage killer to the back of their minds. The investigation was complete, the killer had been apprehended, the public were safe and Meadows was happy. They couldn't ask for more than that.

Epilogue

From the outside the hospital didn't look that bad with its landscaped garden and rows of colourful flowers lining the pathway to the front door. It was only once you went inside that you realized what it was – a prison for the criminally insane.

The corridors were painted in a pale green which was supposed to be calming and wire mesh covered each and every window. Every door was operated by either a swipe card or a key, or both, and every inch of the place was covered with CCTV, which was monitored twenty-four hours a day by security guards.

Patients were allowed to have visitors but these visits were closely monitored and there were strict rules about how visitors should comport themselves once inside the hospital. It wasn't dissimilar to the procedure visitors undertook when visiting inmates in prison.

As he followed the friendly nurse through a labyrinth of corridors, Ben asked himself why he had come. Louise was a murderer, she had killed four men and she had mutilated their bodies to satisfy her sick needs. She had tied up a police officer, lining him up as her next victim, and she had badly injured another one. She had an inner darkness that she had kept hidden from the world and from him, so why did he want to see her? Because that was not the

Louise he knew. The Louise Ben had fallen in love with was funny, intelligent, considerate and kind, and more importantly, incapable of murder. He wanted to believe that woman was still there, that she hadn't been consumed by her hatred, that Louise Jackson still existed. He needed closure.

The nurse stopped in front of Louise's room and motioned for Ben to go in. Ben hesitated, feeling uneasy. The woman in front of him didn't look like Louise. She was gaunt and thin, she must have lost a stone from her already slender frame, her eyes were underlined by dark blue circles, and her hair was limp and greasy. She was sitting in an armchair that was nailed to the floor, staring vacantly ahead, wearing a pale green hospital gown. Ben didn't recognize her.

'You can go in Mr Matthews, but don't expect her to say a lot. She is currently heavily sedated.'

'Why is she sedated?' Ben asked, upset by what he was seeing.

'Without the medication she is violent and hostile. Her mind is struggling to cope with the things that happened to her in her childhood, and she's also fighting to curb the violent urges she feels as an adult. She doesn't have the emotional or cognitive ability to process all of that in one go. By keeping her sedated, we can keep her calm enough to hopefully begin the recovery process, letting her deal with things in her own time,' the nurse explained.

'She can hear me?' Ben asked, uncertain. Louise hadn't moved or looked at him since he'd arrived.

'Yes she can hear you. I'll be waiting just down the corridor when you're finished here, ok?' The nurse gently patted Ben's arm reassuringly.

'Thank you.' Ben managed a half-hearted smile.

Once the nurse had left, Ben entered Louise's room and sat on the edge of the bed next to her. Louise still failed to look at him or acknowledge his presence.

'I had to come and see you Louise. I haven't been able to stop thinking about you since – well since everything came out.'

Louise didn't respond, she just continued staring vacantly ahead.

'I don't know if you can hear me, the nurse said you can. I wanted to see how you are. I was hoping you'd look well, like your old self. It must be hard for you in here.'

Ben paused and ran a hand over his face, pressing his fingers against his eyes, stifling the tears he could feel welling up.

'I'm so sorry Louise. So sorry you've ended up like this. I know how scared you were about ending up in a mental hospital. But from what they tell me this is the best place for you right now. You can get help in here and maybe one day you'll be well enough to be released.'

'I wanted to bring you flowers, but they're against the rules apparently. Not even allowed to bring chocolates.'

Ben eased himself off the bed and knelt in front of Louise, looking up at her face. She was still beautiful, he decided, in spite of everything. He raised a hand to her cheek and rubbed it gently.

'I love you Louise. Even though you've done those terrible things, I still love you. I'm just sorry I never had a chance to tell you before. Maybe I could have helped you.'

Ben was crying now, unable to hold the tears back any longer. He lowered his head and his tears fell on Louise's hands which were clasped in her lap. This was useless, his words were meaningless; Louise was just a shell now, the woman he loved was lost. Ben was saddened by this realization.

'Good bye Louise.'

Ben stood up and left the room, he didn't look back for if he had he would have noticed the single tear that trickled down Louise's cheek.

A few minutes after Ben had left Louise stood up and closed the door to her room. She knew now what she had to do; there was nothing else for her, no reason for her to continue this miserable existence. Mina had left her or was ignoring her and Louise didn't know how to cope without her. And now Ben, a man who loved her despite everything, had also washed his hands of her.

She quickly took off her hospital gown and folded it into one long strip. She knotted a makeshift noose at one end and tied the other end to the door handle. She knelt down, her back to the door and placed the noose around her neck.

She felt nothing as she fell forwards, the fabric becoming taut and squeezing her airway shut. Images flashed before her eyes, places she'd been, people she knew, people she'd killed, people she'd loved. The pain was over, the fear was gone. As her life force drained away, Louise felt at peace.

Her body spasmed and jerked violently as death's icy fingers crept over her heart. And then finally...

Sweet oblivion.